Suffer the Children

A Christopher Worthy/Father Fortis Mystery

A Novel by
David Carlson

coffeetownpress

Kenmore, WA

coffeetownpress

A Coffee Town Press book published by Epicenter Press

Epicenter Press
6524 NE 181st St.
Suite 2
Kenmore, WA 98028

For more information go to:
www.Camelpress.com
www.Coffeetownpress.com
www.Epicenterpress.com

Author's website: www.davidccarlson.net

Suffer the Children
2023 © David Carlson

ISBN: 9781684921270 (trade paper)
ISBN: 9781684921287 (ebook)
LOC: 2023936028

Printed in the United States of America

Suffer little children, and forbid them not, to come unto me;
for of such is the kingdom of heaven.
Matthew 19:14 King James Version

Dedication

Suffer the Children is dedicated to the refugees
of the world who desire their lives to be
defined by their gifts and potential rather
than the accident of where they were born.

Acknowledgments

I am grateful to so many who have supported my writing efforts. I remember fondly Mrs. Black, my eighth-grade Language Arts and Social Studies teacher, and Mrs. East, my high school Latin teacher, who were always encouraging and demanding.

Contrary to what some readers might assume, writing believable fiction is based on hours and hours of research. Writing Suffer the Children required that I research the Indigenous communities of the Northwest Territories of Canada, the plight of Bosnian refugees in Italy, and contemporary mystical theology.

That I loved every minute of the research for this mystery is a debt that I owe to Dr. David Wallace, Dr. Robert Campbell, and Professor Robin Barbour, grad school professors who taught me how to conduct proper research and how to persevere until I uncovered something promising.

I am also indebted to my wife, Kathy, for her daily encouragement, her incredible editing skills, and for the beautiful covers that she paints for the series. I also want to thank my agent, Sara Camilli, who has been with me all along the way and my editor at Coffeetown Press, Jennifer McCord, who is a wonderful critic and friend.

CHAPTER ONE

Rome—Christopher Worthy's New Life

The shiny brass plaque outside the second-floor office read:

Christopher Worthy
Private Investigations and Discreet Inquiries, Ltd.
English-speaking Clients Welcome
Santa Chiara 733
Roma, Italia
Tel. 39-8237-09

"What do you think of my gift?" Lena Fabriano asked.

Christopher Worthy had a hard time believing what he was looking at. "I guess it's official. I live and work in Rome—at least part of the year."

"I thought about having the plaque read 'Christopher Worthy, Consulting Detective,' you know, like Sherlock Holmes, but I thought that was a bit much, even for Rome."

Ever since taking Latin in high school, Christopher Worthy had dreamt of visiting Rome, but he could never have dreamt of living in the Eternal City, standing next to a beautiful woman who was his fiancé, soon to be his wife, and turning the key to an office in his name. But then two years before, the Vatican had invited him, along with his friend and colleague in crime, Father Nicholas Fortis, to work on a series of chilling murders spanning Rome, Constantinople/Istanbul, and Jerusalem.

On that case, he'd met stunningly beautiful Dr. Lena Fabriano, a specialist in the psychology of religious mystics—genuine and fraudulent—and their relationship had evolved from sparring to respecting and finally to loving. For the past two years, they'd carried on a long-distance relationship, Lena remaining as a university professor in Rome while Worthy returned to his job as a homicide detective in Detroit. Lena had visited Worthy three times in Detroit—once joining him on the case of a missing priest—and Worthy had returned to Rome four times.

The last of those four visits had been just three months before, again at the invitation of the Vatican. This time Worthy was hired to investigate a scandal within the Roman Curia. It was on the morning after he'd solved the case, in late September, that Worthy had awakened Lena to say, "I just had a crazy idea. What if I worked part of the year here in Rome as an investigator for English-speaking clients? I'm thinking mainly during the tourist season, maybe from April to October." Before Lena could clear her head and respond, he added, "Oh, and I think we should get married."

As Lena rolled over in bed, her first response was a groggy, "You must be dreaming, Chris." But then she rolled back over and kissed Worthy. "Did you just ask me to marry you, or was I dreaming?"

"A bit of both," Worthy said, kissing her in return. "Is that a yes?"

Lena lay back and smiled. "I need to be fully awake before I answer something so serious as a marriage proposal. But are you serious about . . . about moving to Rome?"

"Think about it, Lena. The Vatican has invited me to investigate two cases, and you know they've paid well. But I'm not just referring to the Vatican. Think of all the binds that American, Canadian, and British visitors get themselves into here in Rome. We're easy targets for scam artists and pickpockets. Or, we rent a car and end up hitting a pensioner in a crosswalk. Then there are the hotel rooms that are broken into. It was just the other day that Capitano Sesto complained to me about the problems he has dealing with English-speaking residents, pilgrims, and tourists. Apparently, English speakers tend to be demanding."

Lena was fully awake by that point. "You're serious, aren't you?"

"More importantly, I'm serious about us getting married. I'd never ask you to move to Detroit, and you know that I've loved Rome since I was a teenager. Look, it doesn't mean that I won't work cases in the States. But once I retire from the force, I can exploit my reputation in Detroit and out in New Mexico where, as I've told you before, I solved two widely-publicized cases."

"You'll be an international detective, is that what you're saying?" Lena asked.

"But we'll live here. I'll even get serious about learning Italian."

For the next two days before Worthy's return flight to Detroit, they talked about little else. Of the two proposals, getting married was the easiest to agree upon. They'd managed their long-distance relationship over the last two years, but both admitted that the times when separated were becoming increasingly painful.

When they considered the other proposal, Worthy working at least half of the year in Rome, their moods and conversations ranged from excitement to skepticism. Did English-speakers really fall victim to enough crimes in Rome and elsewhere in Italy to support such a business?

As they said goodbye to one another at the airport, Lena said, "While we're apart, let's both think seriously about all this. You know I love you, but it's because I love you that I can't bear to think that you will regret later what you're proposing—the business, I mean. I'd rather settle for what we have now, as hard as it is, than to lose you."

"Of course I'll think about it. It's all I am thinking about. But I'm not naïve. Living in Rome for six or seven months will be an adjustment. But we both know we're not talking about living in some isolated hill town where no one speaks English. There must be thousands of English speakers in Rome, and I've met few Romans who don't speak some English."

Lena had closed her eyes and nodded. "Just promise me one thing. When you're back in Detroit, contact everyone you've worked with in Rome—the Vatican's security, the police, the Carabinieri, and the Guardia de Financa. You'll need their endorsement when you apply for a license to work in Italy. And ask them to be totally honest about hiring you when cases involving English-speakers come up."

"Look, Lena, I don't intend living off of you."

"That's not my worry. I love you, and that means I want you to be happy. You and I both know that you won't be happy if you aren't working cases. Am I right?"

Worthy kissed her again. "You're right. But here's something else that's right. This is the first time I've left you and not hated having to leave. Brace yourself, Lena. This could be the last time we say goodbye to each other."

"Hmm, what a wonderful thought," she said.

As Worthy entered one of the security lines, he turned back and called Lena's name. Holding up his passport, he said, "Think about all the Brits and Americans who lose their passports and credit cards!

And don't forget the crazy Canadians and Australians. I'm going to be so busy!"

Worthy wasn't back in Detroit more than two weeks, taken up with signing all the retirement papers with the Detroit Police Department, before Capitano Stefano Sesto called and asked for his help. An American college student was found dead, bound and gagged, in one of Rome's more remote catacombs. Fear reverberated through the thousands of American students who were studying in Rome.

Worthy would always remember the case as both one of the saddest he'd worked on and yet the one that confirmed his dream of working part of the year in Rome. Early on in the case, he dismissed the rumors in the media that the motive for the woman's killing was religious or anti-religious. The breakthrough came when he interviewed students from the same American university and Worthy noticed a strong physical similarity between the victim and another student. That was when Worthy began to think the murdered student was the victim of mistaken identity. Working with Capitano Sesto, Worthy made sure that the lookalike student was kept under surveillance. By the second week after the murder, the young woman with the strong resemblance to the victim unwittingly led police to where her Italian boyfriend, fearful for his life, was hiding.

Further interrogations of the two led to the full story coming out. The student had been recruited by her Italian boyfriend to sell pot and hash at clubs that were popular with American students. One evening three weeks before, the American and her boyfriend had branched out beyond their normal territory and sold drugs at a different club.

Unbeknownst to the American and her boyfriend, the drug ring that controlled that club followed the student home. The next morning when the lookalike American left the dorm and walked to the bus stop, she was grabbed, forced into a van, and not seen until her decomposing body was found ten days later in the catacomb.

Because of Worthy's assistance, the police were able to arrest the killers and shut down the drug trade in four of Rome's sketchiest nightclubs. Throughout the investigation, Worthy stayed at Lena's apartment, giving her another opportunity to observe close up how he approached a homicide. The first had been the year before, when, on one of her visits to Detroit, Lena had worked with Worthy and Father Fortis, Nick to her, on the disappearance of a young priest in Michigan.

From the beginning of the investigation involving the American student found in the catacomb, Worthy had concentrated on not withdrawing into himself as he was prone to do on cases. "Why do you shut me out like this?" was the question that his wife, Susan, had asked for years before she asked for a divorce. His new commitment was to share with Lena every night how the case was progressing. If at first he feared that Lena would prefer to know nothing about the pain and sorrow that were constant parts of homicide cases, he soon realized Lena thought otherwise. As she expressed it, "I want to know all of you, love all of you, and that means everything that you're facing."

Then, as that case was wrapping up, Worthy's license came through just has he was offered another case, this from an unusual source, Lena herself. She had been hired by one of the monastic communities in Rome, the Order of the Sacred Wounds, to evaluate the possibility that one of the order's recent abbots, Father Boniface, had experienced mystical experiences, messages from Jesus. As Lena had investigated a similar case two years before, she jumped at the opportunity.

Nothing in Lena's research concerned Worthy until she came home early on what was Thanksgiving Day back in the States, poured two glasses of Prosecco, and sat down next to him on the couch.

After toasting the holiday, Lena put her head on Worthy's shoulder. "Do you mind if I give you an early Christmas gift?" she asked.

"I thought we agreed that we'd wait a year for the Ferrari," Worthy joked.

"No, not a Ferrari, but maybe something better, Chris," she replied. "How about a high-profile murder case?"

"Really? Here in Rome? Did I miss something in the newspapers?"

"I guess we both did. I learned about it at the motherhouse."

"The motherhouse? Do you mean the monastery you're working with?" Worthy asked.

Lena nodded. "Until earlier this month, a Canadian priest in the order, Father Robert, was the director of an orphanage in northwest Canada. But three weeks ago, there was an explosion in one of the orphanage's cottages. Three boys, all indigenous, died in the fire. That would have been tragedy enough, but when the local firefighters looked for Father Robert, they found him in an alcoholic stupor, barely conscious."

"Ow," Worthy said, wincing. "And he's been murdered?"

"Patience, patience. I'm coming to that. The fire investigator determined that there was nothing Father Robert could have done to save the boys. But the fire and then the authorities finding Father Robert too drunk to give the boys last rites, well, that caused Father Robert to be recalled to Rome. That was a little over two weeks ago. His case was being reviewed by a committee at the monastery, and it seemed possible that he'd be defrocked."

"Did you ever meet him?" Worthy asked.

Lena shook her head. "I saw him a few times in the library and I was told why he was at the monastery, but no, I never talked with him. In the days before he was killed—yes, I'm getting to that—I remembered seeing him on one of the library computers. Not just for a few minutes, but for hours. Now, about his murder. Yesterday morning, Father Robert's body was found propped up on a bench in Piazza del Popolo. He'd been stabbed from behind."

Worthy got up, went into the kitchen, and retrieved the bottle of Prosecco. "Piazza del Popolo. We've been there, right?" he asked as he sat back down.

"Very good, Chris. Yes, we walked through it when we went to the gardens on the Pincio. The piazza is usually crowded, except in the middle of the night."

"And they're saying that's when he was killed," Worthy surmised. "I suppose the police are looking into the pedophilia angle. What makes you think the police would let me in on the case?"

"Do you remember meeting Abbot Lorenzo a couple of weeks ago at the motherhouse?" Lena asked.

"Sure. It'd be hard to forget his booming voice, and my hand is still sore from shaking his."

"He hasn't forgotten you either, Chris. The order's main work and support is in North America, so, most of the monks at the motherhouse are Americans and Canadians. In other words, they're English speakers whose Italian is limited at best. Abbot Lorenzo has already spoken to the police and made his request known."

"And he's requesting me?"

Lena nodded. "He remembers your work with the Vatican two years ago."

Worthy took another sip of the Prosecco and didn't say anything for a moment. In one way, the case could help cement his usefulness to the various law enforcement agencies in Rome. But he also had to weigh the possibility, even with the license, that the police might resent his involvement.

"I'll need to tread carefully with the police and the Carabinieri," he said.

"Of course, Chris. But it isn't as if you haven't just finished that case with Capitano Sesto. He's in your corner."

Worthy nodded. "That's true. You know who'd be a big help on this case?"

Lena smiled. "I've already thought of that. Nick will already be here for the wedding in a couple of weeks. We could invite him to come over early."

"How hospitable do you think Abbot Lorenzo would be to a Greek Orthodox monk staying at the monastery?" he asked.

"They welcome retreatants, so I don't see a problem unless you're expecting Nick to go under cover."

Worthy shook his head. "No, Nick wouldn't go for that. Anyway, he's not good at lying. Nick's best cover is his chatty nature—as long as Capitano Sesto is comfortable with a second American looking into the case."

Lena let Worthy fill her glass to the half-way level. "Anything you'd like to do right away?" Lena asked.

Worthy nodded. "I wouldn't mind taking a look at the scene of the crime."

"Now? This late? It's a good walk."

Worthy rose from the sofa, returning with Lena's coat and his own. "We'll take a taxi. Oh, and by the way, Happy Thanksgiving."

CHAPTER TWO

Rome—Piazza del Popolo

Because Lena's apartment was near the Pantheon, one of Rome's most ancient monuments and a main tourist attraction, Worthy and Lena found a taxi without any trouble. Traffic at that time of night was light, so twenty minutes later, they were walking into Piazza del Popolo. Despite the late hour, the site was filled with locals and tourists milling about. Christmas lights were already in place, fanning out from the top of the obelisk in the piazza's center to create the look of a massive Christmas tree.

As Worthy and Lena strolled the perimeter of the square, Worthy noticed several pairs of police and asked Lena if their presence was normal.

"Normal? Well, wherever there's a crowd in Rome there are bound to be pickpockets. The Trevi, the Colosseum, the Pantheon, even outside St. Peter's. And there are also outdoor Christmas markets that attract families."

"But how many police are usually in the piazza after midnight?"

"Ah, you could be right if you're thinking they're here because it's only been days since Father Robert was killed. I don't know if anyone knows exactly when he died, but the body was discovered propped up on that bench," she said, pointing off to a corner of the square, "at about one-thirty in the morning."

"Discovered by the police?" Worthy asked.

Lena shook her head. "No, by sanitation workers who work late nights collecting garbage."

"Do the police know if he was robbed?"

"I'm sure somebody does, but I don't know. What I do know is that you wanted to come here tonight, and you're pumping me with questions about his death. It sounds like you're going to take the case. I know it would mean a lot to Abbot Lorenzo if you—and Nick—looked into it."

Worthy slowed and motioned for them to sit on a near bench. "So far, there's nothing that makes me want to pass on the case. And it would be good to work with Nick again. It's been over a year. But this piazza is huge. If the police permit it, the first step I'd take would be to look at CCTV footage."

Lena pointed in the direction of the Pincio Hill, rising to the east of the piazza. "You might remember from the last time we were here that we can see the whole piazza as well as the city lights from up there."

Others, locals and tourists, obviously had the same goal, because the overlook was crowded with couples. Finding a vacant spot at the low stone wall, Lena and Worthy contemplated the scene, not saying anything at first.

Finally, Worthy said, "It's like we're looking down on the whole city. I think I can see the dome of the Pantheon and St. Peter's, of course, but I bet I don't recognize a tenth of what you do."

Lena nodded. "Or we just notice different things. You see the monuments; I see the different neighborhoods of Rome." Pointing off to her right, she said, "For example, can you see that rise over there with the lights on top?"

Worthy nodded. "The hill with the lit churches on it?"

"Yes, that's Aventino, the Aventine Hill. That might mean nothing to you until I remind you that that's where we had our first real conversation two years ago. Remember?"

Worthy laughed. "How can I forget? Wasn't the day before that when you treated me as a typical American male?"

Lena put her arm around Worthy's waist and drew closer. He felt a shiver pass through him, still in awe that this tall, beautiful woman had chosen him.

"I thought you were posturing, trying to prove you were the expert in the room," she said. "It took me until the next day, when we met up there on the Aventine, to realize you were just curious."

"And I remember exactly how I felt. Here I was, in Rome at the request of the Vatican and the Ecumenical Patriarch of the Orthodox Church, charged with finding an assassin whose motive was unclear. I was so confused, and I felt like an imposter. Maybe I was still dealing with jetlag, but I felt useless, like I should turn around and go back to Detroit. But then, up there on that hill, you offered me a ride back to my hotel."

"And that led to coffee and then dinner. As you Americans say, 'The rest is history.'"

With his free arm, Worthy swept the panorama in front of them. "No, this is 'the rest is history.' Everyone who lives in Rome is living in a history textbook."

"Except most of us are so used to the monuments, the ancient churches, and the ruins that we only curse them for causing traffic jams. I guess we're spoiled."

"So tell me this. When you were studying in the States at Notre Dame, didn't you miss all of this?"

Lena nodded. "Oh, yes. Rome and South Bend, Indiana—two different worlds. I couldn't believe how flat Indiana was, like a tabletop. And every building looked so new. This might sound weird, but one of my hardest adjustments was accepting that there weren't any ruins. Everything looked so temporary."

"Whereas for me, I'd been seeing these monuments ever since I first took Latin in school. When I finally got to Rome, I felt that I'd been here before. But then you took me to Ostia. That was something I hadn't expected, and it was a shock. I remember our walking down that main street of cobblestones, and you pointed out the ruts that were left by ancient chariots and wagons. And just as I was trying to get my head around that, a jet flew over from the airport."

"Now that disorientation is something I have experienced. Do you remember the amphitheater in Ostia?"

Worthy nodded. "Of course."

"A few years ago, I saw a play there by Sophocles with the actors dressed like ancient Greeks. Just as the play ended, a huge jet flew low over us. People all around me gasped, and a man sitting right in front of me actually fainted. It was like centuries were colliding with each other," Lena said. "That's something Carl Jung understood."

"Jung, the psychologist?"

"The same. He lived in Switzerland, so coming to Rome would have been easy for him. But the truth is that he boarded the train for Rome several times, but he always got off and returned home. You see, Jung was fascinated with archetypes. So he thought all the archetypes from Rome's past would assault him, even crush him, if he came. He was literally afraid of all the centuries speaking to him at once."

"That's something Father Robert might have had in common with Jung. Not the archetypes, but the wish to turn around and go back where he came from. Rome must have felt like a prison to him."

"Or the inquisition," Lena said. "Yes, he's a Catholic priest, but he's in Rome facing the possibility of being defrocked."

"What does the Church do with priests who've been thrown out?" he asked.

"That's changed lately. For sexual abuse, ex-priests face criminal charges and prison. But as far as I know, there's nothing like that in Father Robert's case. If he were defrocked, he wouldn't be a 'Father' anymore. He might have been sent to some out-of-the-way place, someplace where he wouldn't be in charge."

"Someplace where he couldn't cause another problem?"

Lena nodded. "Exactly. It's possible if Father Robert were given the choice of dying or being defrocked, he might have chosen being stabbed in the piazza."

Ohio—St. Simeon's Monastery

As Father Nicholas Fortis opened the wedding invitation from Worthy, written in both English and Italian, ambivalent feelings rose within him. On the one hand, he considered Lena Fabriano an answer to his prayers for his friend Christopher Worthy. Ever since his divorce, Worthy had lived in what Nick had once described as "the cemetery of broken marriages." The description was accurate, but unfortunate, as Worthy had accepted the absence of love in his life as something he deserved.

In Nick's mind, God had changed all that when Lena and Worthy met two years before on one of the most highly-publicized highly publicized case in modern Italian history. He turned the invitation over to read Worthy's personal message on the back. *Nick, Lena and I are so grateful that you will offer a few words at our wedding.*

If Nick celebrated the joy that Lena brought into Worthy's life, that didn't mean that Worthy's other decision to begin a new career in Rome didn't leave a hollow feeling in his stomach. He knew that Worthy would work part of the year in Michigan , but Worthy's decision to live in Rome at least half the year meant that the two of them would work together less frequently, if at all.

Nick knew that his being confined to St. Simeon's Greek Orthodox monastery in the future would please some of his fellow monks. Monks were allowed to have "hobbies," such as keeping bees, weaving, painting of icons, and research as long as it was spiritually-centered, but Father Fortis' "hobby" of working with Worthy on homicide cases had always strained Nick's relationship with his community.

The truth was that Nick lacked any interest in bees, sitting at a loom, or painting icons. In the past, he had contributed scholarly articles on the topic of early Christian chant, but that interest had largely been replaced when he began assisting Worthy. No, he wasn't a detective in the sense that Worthy was. In his work with Worthy, he never stopped being a monk, a priest, and a confessor.

He remembered his astonishment when Worthy, against his wishes, had met with Nick's abbot and convinced him that Nick was more, not less, of a monk and priest, on homicide cases. If Worthy and he shared the same goal of stopping a killer before he or she could kill again, Nick had an additional hope—that the murderer would have the chance to unburden his conscience by confessing to him.

But now Worthy would be investigating many, if not most, of his cases in Italy—without his help. Not that Nick worried about Worthy "flying solo." Worthy was considered one of the most capable homicide detectives in Detroit, if not in the entire Midwest. Besides, over the ten years they'd worked together, only a modest percentage of Worthy's cases had been with his help. Worthy, he knew, would manage just fine.

Nick walked slowly from the chapel to his room in St. Simeon's. He knew he should be honored—and he was—that Lena and Worthy had asked him to speak at their wedding. But he couldn't deny that the wedding would also be a type of funeral, a ceremony signaling the end of his work as a sleuth.

In his room, Nick made the sign of the cross as he bowed before an icon of the Theotokos—the Mother of God—holding the Christ child. On his knees, he prayed softly that God would give him the grace to put his own sadness aside at the upcoming wedding. Opening his eyes, he saw the light flashing on his old-style answering machine.

Hitting the button, he heard Worthy's voice, asking him to return the call as soon as possible. He leapt to his feet, hoping that Worthy needed his help on a case. But then he realized that his friend was more likely calling about the wedding.

He looked at his watch and calculated that it was ten o'clock in the evening in Rome. He weighed the option of postponing the phone call until the next day, but then shook his head. Worthy had told him to call back "as soon as possible," and that he would do.

Worthy answered his call on the second ring with "Nick, thanks so much for calling me back. How the heck are you?"

"I'm fine, Christopher," Nick said. "I hope nothing is the matter on your end."

"Yes and no, Nick. Lena and I are fine, but there's been a tragedy—a murder—here in Rome. A couple of days ago, a Canadian priest's body was found in Piazza del Popolo. Maybe you remember the place."

"Good Lord, how awful," Nick said, aware that his response wasn't the complete truth. "Are you involved in the case?"

"It looks like I'm going to be. The deceased was temporarily staying at a monastery here in Rome, and Lena is researching another mysticism case at the same place. To make a long story short, the abbot has asked me to look into it. Not only is the victim Canadian, but most of the other monks in the community are from North America as well. In other words, English is their first language."

"Which puts the Italian authorities as a disadvantage," Nick said.

"Exactly, Nick. And that's why I'm calling. Actually, I guess I'm begging."

Nick felt a surge of adrenaline. "Beg away, my friend. You know I'm happy to help in any way I can."

"I was hoping you'd say that, Nick. It involves some unusual travel."

The comment confused Father Fortis, as traveling to Rome hardly seem "unusual."

"If you need me in Rome early—before the wedding, I mean—I think I can do that."

"I do need you here in Rome, but before that, Nick, I need you to fly to Yellowknife in the Canada's Northwest Territories. Father Robert was the director of an orphanage up there."

"Northwest Territories means Yellowknife is in the far north, I take it."

"Yes, but before you decide, let me tell you what I know about the case," Worthy replied, before telling about the fire at the orphanage and then Father Robert being recalled to Rome.

"What should I be looking for in Canada, Christopher? Tell me this isn't a pedophilia case."

"No, nothing like that as far as we know. If you're willing, I need you to talk to those who knew Father Robert, especially what he was like right before the fire and then afterwards. Really, anything you can find that might connect the fire with Father Robert's murder here in Rome."

Nick pondered what he was hearing. The thought of three burnt bodies of young boys brought something else to mind. "Even if the victims were orphans, there might be relatives I should interview."

"Good thinking, Nick. I can't see how Father Robert's killer could be from four thousand miles away in the north of Canada, but it's a possibility we have to rule out. So, what do you say, Nick? I've been assured that the order here in Rome will cover all expenses—yours and mine."

Nick didn't hesitate. "I'm happy to still be of service."

"What do you mean 'still?'" Worthy asked.

"Sorry, Christopher. That was a poor choice of words." Pausing, he added, "After I've finished in Canada, will I be coming to Rome?"

"Absolutely, Nick. I want you to work the case with me, and then there's the wedding, of course. Do you need me to contact your abbot there at St. Simeon's?"

"No, what you said to him last year changed everything."

"Good. I'd feel a lot better working this case with you at my side. And it's been over a year since we've seen each other. In my opinion, that's much too long, Nick."

Nick felt a lump form in his throat. "Amen to that, my friend."

CHAPTER THREE

Rome—Motherhouse of the Order of the Sacred Wounds

Sitting in his central chair in the monastery's refectory, Abbot Lorenzo looked around him at the monks as they ate dinner. His eyes settled on the vacant chair where Father Robert had sat. Everyone in the community knew of Father Robert's death, but the abbot had yet to tell the community about his request for Christopher Worthy's help.

Abbot Lorenzo remembered the brief conversations he'd had with Father Robert when the priest arrived. The abbot had already read what Father Robert's bishop had sent him as well as material from Canadian authorities, how Father Robert's orphanage served all First Nations people, but he hadn't realized until he met Father Robert that the priest was himself half First Nation.

For his first week in the monastery, Father Robert had seemed numb. In their initial meeting, Father Robert said that he'd accept being defrocked, if that was what the order decided. His only wish was to be allowed to return to the orphanage in some capacity and serve the families. When Abbot Lawrence asked for Father Robert's assurance that he wouldn't touch a drop of alcohol while in Rome, the priest had simply lowered his head and nodded.

Father Damian, serving as Father Robert's confessor, perhaps knew him better than anyone else. And Father Zacharias, who oversaw Father Robert's afternoon work in the library, might have gained some sense of the Canadian priest, although what passed for chatter in the outside world wasn't common in the monastery.

The abbot looked past the monks to the view from the window set in the refectory's far wall. With the Order of the Sacred Wounds perched atop a slight rise on the Aventine Hill, the view of Rome from the window was majestic. However, from the window, no one could see Piazza del Popolo, where Father Robert's body was found.

Not for the first time, the abbot wondered what had drawn Father Robert to that piazza, not just that last night, but the two nights before as well, according to the police. The piazza, nearly always filled with tourists and locals, was certainly not suitable for quiet reflection. But then again, if Father Robert wanted to be distracted from his memories of the fire, the piazza would have had an appeal. What didn't make sense to Abbot Lorenzo was why Father Robert went to the piazza at one-thirty in the morning.

The odd time and the three visits to the piazza made the abbot wonder if Father Robert had gone there for another purpose—to meet someone. But with Father Robert being in Rome for only two weeks, the abbot wondered how many people outside the community Father Robert would have known. The abbot sighed as he accepted that the priest had met at least one person that night—his killer. Making the sign of the cross, the abbot was disturbed by another thought. What if Father Robert had known no one outside the community? Did that mean his killer was one of the brothers eating at this table?

Yellowknife, Northwest Territories, Canada

Traveling to Europe was nothing new to Nick. With relatives in Greece, his family had visited the island of Santorini at least once every five years. And he'd been in Italy twice when helping Worthy on cases.

On all those transatlantic flights, he'd never been as tired as he was now after travelling from Ohio to Yellowknife, less than three hundred miles from the Arctic Circle. On a map, Yellowknife was far closer to Nick's monastery than Europe, but his journey to Yellowknife had been broken up by a flight from Toledo to Chicago, then a flight from Chicago to Edmonton, where he had to stay overnight before catching the one daily flight to Yellowknife. All together, his trip took three times as long as a flight to Rome.

If he'd arrived by car rather than by airplane, Nick might have thought Yellowknife was on the shore of the ocean. But as the plane descended from the clouds, he could see that the city nestled on the shore of the massive Great Slave Lake, already frozen over in late November and dotted with ice-fishing shacks. He wondered when the body of water had taken that name—Slave. From a guidebook he purchased in Chicago's O'Hare Airport, he'd read a list of the indigenous peoples for whom Yellowknife had been home—Cree, Chipewyan, Inuktituk, and the Yellowknives Dene or Great Slave Lake Dene —but the guidebook didn't say if the lake had been given that name before or after Europeans arrived.

As the plane circled and made its approach, Nick shivered as he looked down on the frozen landscape. He'd read about the average late-November and December temperatures for Yellowknife online, but looking down, he thought he might as well be landing at the North Pole. He'd packed the warmest coat he owned, as well as thermal underwear and two woolen sweaters, but, as he looked at the barren landscape, he knew his first task would be to purchase a warm hat, gloves, and boots.

The airport in Yellowknife was small, but it did have a shop geared toward visitors unused to the cold, where he was able to buy a fur-lined hat with earflaps, down-filled gloves, and warmer boots. He was also relieved to see that two rental car companies were available at the airport. When he'd called ahead to the local Catholic priest, Father Jacob, to set up a meeting, the priest volunteered to pick him up from the airport, but Nick declined, saying he would likely need a car for some of his interviews.

He took the advice of the rental car clerk and opted for a four-wheel drive SUV. The young clerk smiled as she said, "Every one of our vehicles is equipped with studded tires and emergency survival equipment, just in case. And we recommend that you always have a half tank of gas. Again, that's just in case something happens."

"Good to know, but I have my cellphone," Nick said.

The clerk's smile turned into a worried look as she glanced out the windows to the snow coming down. "Phone coverage around Yellowknife can be a bit tricky, sir."

"Ah. Anything else I should know?"

"Watch for bears, moose, and elk. They can make a real mess of your vehicle if you should meet one accidentally." After a pause, she said, "I don't mean to be nosy, sir, but what's the meaning of the robes you're wearing."

Nick smiled at a question that he'd been asked on almost every flight he'd taken. "I'm an Orthodox monk. I'm also a priest."

"I don't think we have any of your churches here, sir. I mean 'Father.'"

Nick thought that what she really wanted to know was why he'd landed in Yellowknife. But he sensed if he told her the real reason for his visit, the information might be all over town before dinnertime.

"I'm here for a few days to visit some folks." Thinking that was enough information, he picked up the keys to his rented vehicle and pointed to a side door. "I assume my vehicle is outside."

"Yes, Father, but you'll be warmer if you wait by the door until Norbert brings your car up to the wait area. That's where you'll return it as well. And I hope you have a good stay."

Norbert turned out to be a proud member of the Great Slave Lake Dene First Nation. He explained the car's features, particularly how to engage the four-wheel drive. As Nick lowered himself into the driver's seat, he asked Norbert, "Can you tell me the way to St. Anne's Catholic Church?"

Norbert smiled. "I should know that. I was an altar boy at St. Anne's." He took a small map out of his pocket and circled the location of the church before handing the map to Nick. "Everything in Yellowknife is no more than fifteen miles from anywhere else. But be careful on the roads outside of town."

"Yes, I heard about the bears and moose," Nick said.

"Keep an eye out especially at night, Father. With this being almost December, night begins about three in the afternoon. Too bad you weren't here in June. Then it's light all night long."

As Nick drove toward his motel, he pictured the night of the orphanage fire. The fire was first reported at three-thirty in the morning, which meant the night of the fire would have been pitch black and no doubt freezing cold. He thought of the ancient images of Hell, some cultures imagining it as unbearably cold, others as unbearably hot. Nick realized that if the three orphan victims had lived for even a few seconds after the blast, they would have felt both—first the heat of the explosion and then the frigid cold of the night. And he also knew that Father Robert, even in a drunken stupor, would have awakened to the smell of burning building materials and human flesh. *It's a wonder he didn't commit suicide*, Nick thought. *But he'd died instead by a knife wound to his back four thousand miles away. But maybe on his last night, he welcomed death.*

After leaving his luggage in the motel room, Nick drove to St. Anne's Catholic Church, a squat building that fit in with the other low buildings of the town. Wearing his new hat, gloves, and boots, Nick walked briskly to the door marked "Office," thinking that he wouldn't have been surprised if Father Robert had been killed in Yellowknife instead of Rome. The three victims might have been orphans, but that didn't mean they didn't have relatives in the area.

"You must be Father Fortis," the young man said as Nick stepped through the door. "I'm Father Jacob. Please, let's go into my office. It's the warmest room in the church."

"Thank you, Father," Nick said, "but if you don't mind, I'd like to offer a prayer in the sanctuary."

"Of course. If you'll let me join you, there's something you need to see."

Father Jacob led Nick to a side aisle in the sanctuary where a small altar was dedicated to the Blessed Virgin Mary and the Christ Child. On an easel set up to the right of the altar were photos of the three boys, photos Nick recognized from an online version of Yellowknife's neewspaper.

"Ah, yes, I see," Nick said in a whisper as he made the sign of the cross. As both priests knelt in front of the altar, Nick realized that the boys would have been members of St. Anne's—as was Father Robert.

After a few moments of silence, Father Jacob said, "The parish is having a very hard time accepting what's happened. First the fire, and now Father Bob's murder. As I'm sure you'll understand, this will be a very sorrowful Christmas."

"I wish I could say that my friend Lieutenant Worthy and I will bring comfort to your parish and to the town, but I can't promise that. In a tragedy such as this, I'm not convinced there is such a thing as 'closure;' just time passing."

Father Jacob sighed. "I agree. I'll be honest with you. There were a few in the parish who saw Father Bob being recalled to Rome as letting him off the hook. Others feel his superiors are blaming him for the fire."

"Even though the authorities never considered charging him?"

"That's true. It didn't take long for the fire investigator to determine that the fire started in one of the heating systems. The explosion beneath the cottage happened without warning with Father Bob sleeping off . . . well, being over two hundred yards away in his cottage. So, there's no logical basis for blaming him."

"But human beings want someone to blame," Nick said.

"Yes, and that's the challenge I'm facing. Some parishioners blame the directors of the orphanage, others the fire inspector, but it seems everyone wants to blame God. More than one of my parishioners asked why, if God could save Daniel and his friends in the fiery furnace, he didn't save the boys. Others demanded the bishop change the name of the orphanage."

"'Safe Haven Orphanage.' Yes, I can see why those words might be too painful to live with. Did you conduct the funerals, Father?"

Father Jacob nodded. "Three funerals, four if you count one of the boys' grandmother who had a heart attack when she heard the news. And I also administered last rites to the boys with Father Robert being in no shape to do that. And that brings me to what I've been praying for since I received your email, Father."

"Go ahead."

"When I heard Father Bob's superiors in Rome were sending someone to Yellowknife to ask questions about the fire, I reacted irrationally. I confess that I was fuming. All I could picture was a stranger asking questions about the fire; that's the last thing we need here. But then I received your email, and I thought God was merciful. A priest, even a monk, was coming. So that's what I was praying for just now, that you'd be more a priest than an investigator."

Nick put an arm on Father Jacob's shoulder. "The best guarantee that I won't infringe on the grief of the boys' relatives is for the two of us to conduct the interviews together. Will you do that with me?"

Father Jacob looked down but said nothing, leading Nick to say, "They don't know me, Father, but they know you. It would be a big help to the investigation—to me."

"The selfish part of me would like your being here to give me a break from all the sorrow in Yellowknife, but that's not the part of me that I want to make my decisions. Yes, I'm willing to come with you and smooth the way if I can."

In the office, Father Jacob gestured toward a rectangular table with chairs. After Nick sat, Father Jacob said, "I've made some fresh coffee. Can I interest you in a cup?"

"I won't say no, and please call me Nick."

Returning with two mugs, Father Jacob said, "And I'm Jake. I'll do my best to answer your questions, but let me answer the first one the media asked—'Was Father Bob a pedophile?' The answer is no, not one shred of evidence of anything like that—ever. Is that what they think in Rome?"

Nick shook his head. "Not according to what I've been told. So let's put that aside. Can you give me a sense of Father Robert, both as a priest and as the director of the orphanage? Did he ever concelebrate Mass with you here at St. Anne's?"

Father Jake nodded. "Oh, yes. I came to Yellowknife a little over a year ago. Father Bob and I quickly agreed on an arrangement. He would celebrate Mass with me one Sunday every month, and I'd return the favor one Friday a month at the orphanage. And given the distance to another Catholic parish, we served as each other's confessor."

Nick thought about that last piece of information. He took a sip of coffee before saying, "I know from hearing confessions that some people reveal a lot about themselves, maybe even too much, while others offer little that's personal. I hope you don't think I'm trying to break the privacy of the confessional if I ask which describes Father Robert."

Father Jacob nodded. "No, I don't mind. I'd put Father Bob somewhere in the middle. He could be outgoing, but I always thought he was holding something back. And of course, I respected that."

"Do you think that alcohol was what he might have been holding back?"

Father Jacob sighed heavily. "I've asked myself that a thousand times since the fire. I mean, it's not like two Catholic priests in a town the size of Yellowknife can drink together in one of the local bars. But no, I don't think Father Bob had a problem with alcohol, which is what made what he did so unexpected. I keep thinking I missed some clue."

"Don't be too hard on yourself. Why don't you tell me what you know about his past?"

"I think he'd understand my sharing what I know. His mother was indigenous and tangentially related to one of the tribes up here. She died when he was in his early teens. That's when his father rejected him. Father Bob grew up in an orphanage in British Columbia, which must have influenced his desire to work with orphans. Like many of us, he went to a Catholic high school for boys on the road to the priesthood. From British Columbia, he went to a seminary in Toronto. After that, he served as an assistant priest outside Toronto for a year or two before the assistant director position at Safe Haven opened up. He became director when his predecessor retired."

As Father Jacob talked, he looked out the window toward the mounds of plowed snow at the edge of the church's parking lot. Nick remembered the woman at the car rental agency gazing outside as she was talking with him. He could see how the snow mesmerized those who lived this far north.

"How about Father Robert as an administrator? Running an orphanage can't be an easy," Nick said.

"No, it isn't easy, though a couple of staff members worked under him. They all seemed to like him. Before the fire, I'd have said Father Bob was on top of things at Safe Haven and well liked in the community."

Nick could imagine how quickly the fire would have destroyed that reputation. "I'm sorry to return to the alcohol issue, but do you think he might have restricted his drinking to late at night when someone was less likely to intrude on his privacy?"

Father Jacob shook his head. "I doubt it. Father Bob told me more than once that the boys would knock on his door at all hours of the night."

Nick pictured a priest who was always on duty, never a minute to himself. "I guess all this is leading me to ask if Father Robert came to you for confession after the fire."

The priest shook his head. "Not immediately. The police and fire officials were questioning him, and then the press descended on Yellowknife. Our little town was national news. He didn't come for confession until the day before he flew to Rome."

"How did he seem?"

"Exhausted. But then again, I was still conducting funerals for the children, so I was pretty tired too."

"What did he say about the fire?"

"Not much, and I didn't want to be the umpteenth person to ask him about that night. He must have known that I'd been interviewed and read all the news reports. And Father Bob and the fire were all that anyone in Yellowknife was taking about. What he couldn't accept was that he'd failed the boys—not by the fire, he knew he could have done nothing to prevent that—but by being too drunk to give the boys last rites."

Nick nodded, knowing he would have felt the same in those circumstances.

"How did he feel about going to Rome?"

"He wanted to stay here, even though he know that meant he'd have to face some people who would never forgive him. He talked about going to Rome as 'facing the inquisition.' At the time, I thought that was his way of saying he thought he'd be defrocked. But now, I wonder if he meant something else, something more."

"Like what, Jake?"

Father Jacob shrugged. "This will sound strange, but could he have had a premonition that he would die in Rome?"

CHAPTER FOUR

Rome—Lena Fabriano's Apartment

The next morning as they ate breakfast together, Worthy asked Lena what she could tell him about the Order of Sacred Wounds in preparation for his meeting with Abbot Lorenzo.

"Right now, I've been mainly in the library, so, to this point, I've had conversations with only the abbot and the librarian."

"But you've attended some of their services, right?" Worthy asked.

"Twice. I suppose that gave the community a chance to see me, although I can't say I learned much from those services. Monastic orders based on the Rule of St. Benedict are quite similar."

Worthy nodded. "What about the ages of the monks?"

"Most are over fifty, which is typical these days. A few could be in their late seventies or eighties."

"Any young monks, novices, maybe?"

"I'd say there are not more than two in their thirties," Lena replied.

Worthy poured more coffee for both of them. "So Father Robert, being fifty-one, would have been somewhere in the middle?"

"If I was seeing the entire community in the services I attended, I'd say so."

"How about the order itself? Is it on the Church's conservative or liberal wing?"

Lena shook her head. "It isn't always one or the other, Chris. Most monasteries have a bit of both, but I think they'd prefer the terms 'traditionalists' and 'progressives.'"

"Good to know." After a moment, he asked, "Would the other monks have known why Father Robert was there?"

"Maybe not all of them. It's common for monks to return to the motherhouse for sabbaticals or when they're going to be reassigned. The abbot told me that the ethics committee charged with reviewing his case was composed of three senior monks, but they would have been bound by the rules of confidentiality. Of course, Father Robert's confessor at the monastery would have known about the fire."

"What about after he was killed? Does the community know the full story now?"

Lena nodded. "I'm sure Abbot Lorenzo shared about Father Robert's death. He wouldn't have wanted the community to hear about in the newspaper or on TV."

Worthy took a sip of coffee. "You mentioned that Father Robert had a confessor. I might leave him for Nick to interview. I'll wait and see."

"Because Nick would be less of an outsider?"

"Right. No one understands monks and nuns better than Nick. Plus, because people associate me with the police, they tend to clam up."

Lena smiled. "I think you're being too hard on yourself. I've seen you with people, and I think you're quite good with victims' families and witnesses."

"Okay, I'll do it, but we both know that Nick exudes something, if that makes any sense."

"I'd think the word you're looking for is 'safety,'" Lena said. "Nick isn't like a lot of extroverts. They can be egotistical, in love with hearing their own voices. We both know that Nick talks a lot, but I remember what you told me once. Even when Nick is talking, he's always listening. Whereas you . . ."

Worthy smiled. "Go on, finish your thought about me."

"It's nothing bad, Chris, and it's probably what makes you a good detective."

"Now you're just trying to ease my pain. Go on, spill it."

"What I'm trying to say is that when you listen, you listen . . . well, you listen hard."

"I listen hard? What does that mean?"

Lena laughed. "It means when you're listening to people, you look at them the way you're looking at me now. It's like you're trying to see what I'm thinking behind my words."

"Huh. I need to think about that, because if that's true, some people might assume I don't believe what they're saying."

"No, that's not what I mean, Chris. "I'm not saying you give the impression that you think people are lying. It's more that you sense when a person knows more than they realize. I wish I could give you an example."

Worthy shook his head. "It's not necessary. I admit I do what you say I do. The only way I know how to listen is, as you say, to listen hard. I think I've always been this way."

"Even as a child?" Lena asked.

"Maybe especially when I was a kid. I've told you that my father was a minister, what you probably don't know is that Baptist ministers, like my dad, don't have much security. If someone in the church didn't like my dad's sermon on Sunday or felt he should have visited Aunt Lucy in the hospital earlier than he did, my dad could be in trouble. Maybe even fired."

"Did you feel that pressure as his son?"

Worthy nodded. "Oh, yes, all the time. If my sister or I misbehaved, my father would hear about it."

"It sounds like you lived in a fishbowl. Maybe that's why you became a detective."

Worthy laughed. "Well, I have wondered what I might have become if my father had been a plumber or a car dealer."

Lena reached across the table to lay her hand on Worthy's. "If you father were alive, I'd thank him. I like the way you are."

"We'd better stop. You're starting to sound like Mr. Rogers."

Yellowknife—Safe Haven Orphanage

With Father Jacob agreeing to join Nick in his interviews, the two drove five miles outside of town to the orphanage the next morning. The buildings on the shore of Great Slave Lake shared a similar brown block construction and looked to have been built sometime in the mid-twentieth century.

As they drove onto the grounds, Nick said, "I only see two pick-up trucks. Is the orphanage closed?"

"It is temporarily," Father Jacob explained. "While the fire is being investigated, the orphans have been resettled in foster care."

As Nick pulled into a parking space in front of a building marked "Administration," Nick said, "So, the investigation isn't over yet?"

Releasing his seatbelt, Father Jacob said, "From the Province's point of view, it is, but the bishop for the diocese hasn't found a new director yet. My fear is that no one acceptable to the board will apply."

"Is that likely?" Nick asked.

Father Jacob made no move to leave the car. "I apologize. Once again, I was thinking selfishly. I don't want the bishop to appoint me, you see."

As they entered the building, Nick paused in front of four photos, all men, all priests, who'd held the position of orphanage director. "So, Father Robert was director for the past sixteen years?"

"That's right. As you can see, he was only the fourth head—all priests of the Order of the Sacred Wounds."

"Does the director have to be a priest?"

"That's been the policy so far, but the bishop and the board of directors could change the rule and hire someone, maybe someone with a social services background. Of course, there are rumors, given the tragedy, that the board is considering closing Safe Haven. As much as I'm hoping the bishop won't pick me, I hope even more that they don't do that. The need for an orphanage to serve the First Nations communities is as great now as it's always been."

Just as Nick was about to ask if the orphanage served only indigenous peoples, a short, gray-haired woman stepped out into the hallway. "Ah, it's you, Father," she said.

"I hope you don't mind us stopping by. Tula, this is Father Fortis. Father, this is Mrs. Elkhorn. Father Fortis is looking into Father Bob's death."

As Nick reached out to shake the hand of the native woman, he saw her grimace as she heard the reason for his visit. "Please, come into my office," she added in a soft voice.

After offering chairs to the two priests, Mrs. Elkhorn shut the door before she sat down behind a desk.

Sighing deeply, she said, "Does your visit mean that they haven't found who killed Father Bob?"

"Not yet, but it's still early in the case," Nick replied.

Mrs. Elkhorn looked down at her hands, not saying anything for a moment. "But he was killed in Rome, which seems like the other side of the world from here. How can we help?"

Nick thought that was a question he was likely to be asked many times. "At this point, we're trying to get a better understanding of Father Robert."

Mrs. Elkhorn sat quietly, and Nick remembered the silences of other native peoples whom he'd interviewed in New Mexico. Finally, she said, "You want to know what Father Bob was like before or after the fire?"

"Let's start with before," Nick said. "How long did you work with Father Robert?"

"I've been here for seven years. Always as a social worker."

It struck Nick that Father Jacob might be praying that the bishop would choose Mrs. Elkhorn as the next administrator. "Did you get along with Father Bob? Did you like him?" he asked.

Without hesitation now, she replied, "Oh, yes, Father Bob was easy to like. You see, he always put the children first. That is, until . . . well, you know."

"And where does Safe Haven get funds?" he asked.

"From the diocese and private donors, but our budget is set by the board of directors."

"How did Father Robert get along with the board?"

As others in Yellowknife had done when talking with him, Mrs. Elkhorn looked out the window at the falling snow. "As I said, Father Bob put the children first. That's not how everyone on the board thinks about Safe Haven."

Nick waited, hoping she would offer details. When she didn't, he asked, "Can you say a bit more?"

Mrs. Elkhorn looked at Father Jacob. "You already know what I'm going to say, Father. The bishop and Father Bob had their run-ins. Almost always about the budget."

Father Jacob cleared his throat. "Our bishop is relatively new. He's headed the diocese for only the past year. And before that, he served in Toronto."

Nick understood the coded response. The bishop was from the city, while his current diocese covered hundreds of square miles of forests, lakes, and small towns.

"Does that mean that Father Robert tended to overspend the budget?" he asked.

After another pause, she said, "Father Bob has been over-budget every year I've been at Safe Haven. But it was only when the new bishop joined the board that Father Bob's spending became an issue."

"What did he spend money on?" Nick asked.

"After food and utilities, he spent most on computers and paying for reliable internet service. The board couldn't argue with that. It was the sport equipment that they argued about."

Father Jacob sat forward. "Father Bob was a great hockey fan, and he knew the children loved the sport as well. Mid-October, every year, he'd start flooding the back parking lot here to make a rink. That didn't cost much, but skates, pads, and sticks do. The bishop wanted him to shift to a less costly sport, like soccer, but Father Bob refused. Yellowknife had seven to eight months of ice and snow, two more of cold, and only two at the most for a sport like soccer."

"But always for the children," Mrs. Elkhorn repeated. "If the budget was tight, he would use his own salary, small as it was, to buy what was needed for the children."

"The children must have liked him."

"They loved him," Mrs. Elkhorn said. "And so did the tribal leaders." Frowning, she said, "Of course, some of them changed their opinion after the fire—but not everyone."

Nick waited for a moment before asking, "Were you surprised when you heard about the drinking?"

She frowned. "At first, yes." Sighing and looking out the window again, she added, "When I leave Safe Haven at night, I go home, my husband gives me a hug, one of us makes dinner for the two of us and our children, and I can think about something else besides the sad stories that the children tell me. For my people, the Great Slave Lake Dene, balance is essential in life, and my family gives me that. But who did Father Bob have at the end of the day? I hope I don't offend you, Father," she said, looking at Father Jacob, "I know you could say he had God, but sometimes . . ."

"No, I understand," Father Jacob said, "It's the lot of a priest."

"But I never smelled liquor on him, and I know the smell of that," Mrs. Elkhorn said. "So, when the fire officials found him that way, I was shocked. I'm still surprised."

She closed her eyes as if in pain. "The younger kids called him Father Happy." She paused before adding, "The three who died called him that."

CHAPTER FIVE

Rome—McCafferty Liquors

That afternoon, while Father Jacob was making hospital calls, Nick took the priest's suggestion and drove to the strip mall that housed McCafferty Liquors. In the front window display, Santa was portrayed commanding a sleigh filled with various brands of Canadian whiskeys. The store was empty except for an older man, bald and chewing on a toothpick, who was perched on a stool behind the counter. He looked up from a crossword puzzle when he saw Nick and said, "What can I do for you, Father?"

"Could you be Mr. McCafferty?"

"In the flesh, what's left of it," the owner replied, extending his hand across the counter.

Returning the handshake, Nick, "I'm hoping you can answer a few questions."

"I'll do my best. Just call me Mac."

"Thank you, and I'd be happy if you called me Nick. I'm working with authorities looking into the death of Father Robert. I'm hoping you might help me gain a better sense of the man."

Mac McCafferty extracted the toothpick from his mouth and studied it. "Don't know if I've ever heard a sadder story. First the fire—I'm not one of those who blame Bob—and then him being murdered. It's like a movie so bad you want to turn it off."

"You liked Father Robert, then?"

The owner sighed deeply. "I've known him for fifteen, maybe sixteen, years. Never Father Robert to me; always Bob and always a pleasure to speak with. He had a wry sense of humor, the kind I like. I gave him my best discount when he came in every three months, like clockwork, to pick up communion wine. It's hard not to respect someone willing to run an orphanage. Until the damned fire, you couldn't find a person in Yellowknife who'd say a bad word against him. But now, some have decided to crap all over his memory. Ah, well, maybe not their fault. Yellowknife has a long history of grief. So when the town got the news from Italy, well . . ."

Nick paused, letting the sentence remain unfinished. He wasn't sure how Mr. McCafferty would receive his next question, but he knew he had to ask. "Father Robert was found in pretty bad shape the night of the fire. And they found empty whisky bottles in his room. Did he often buy whisky?"

Mac McCafferty's face reddened. "There are two things I do here. I sell liquor, and I don't judge people. Yes, Bob bought the whisky from me, but only that once, the day before the fire."

Nick thought about what the store owner was saying. "But Father Bob might have bought whisky from other liquor stores in town, right?"

The owner slapped his palm down on the counter. "You want to understand Bob? Well, the first thing you need to know is that Bob was never the sneaky sort. I'd swear on my mother's Bible that he wasn't a secret drinker. I've been in business thirty-four years, and I can see in my customers' eyes how they handle their liquor. Some of them even tell me. And as I told the police, Bob was never on friendly terms with the hard stuff while he was here in Yellowknife. Maybe he was before he came to Yellowknife, but not since."

Nick considered the comment. Yes, it was possible Father Robert had trouble with alcohol in the past, before Yellowknife, and Nick figured if anyone knew about that, it would be the bishop who had a file on every priest in his diocese. "So, Mac, were you here the day he bought the whisky?"

"I was."

"Did Father Robert ask your advice on what to buy, or did he seem to know what he was looking for?"

Creases formed on the owner's forehead. "Bob knew what he wanted," he said as he jammed the toothpick back into his mouth and turned away from Nick. "Now, if you don't mind, I'd like to get back to my crossword."

A Busy Street in Rome

Worthy wondered if Rome would feel different once he began living in the city instead of simply visiting Lena. But with each passing day, Rome continued to fascinate him. Every morning, he awoke amazed that he was in the city of the Colosseum, the Imperial Forum, the Baths of Caracalla, and St. Peter's Basilica.

Of all the hours of the day, morning was Worthy's favorite in the city. Given the crisp air of Rome in the last days of November, he was happy to walk the two miles from Lena's apartment to the Order of the Sacred Wounds on the Aventine Hill. The mornings were full of sounds able to wake even the sleepiest visitor—shopkeepers raising the metal guards on their shops and mopeds revving as they wove between the vendors who were pushing carts of cheeses, salamis, greens, wines, and Christmas decorations meant for the trattorias and restaurants.

Today, he let the noise of the city take him back two thousand years when other shopkeepers and vendors must have plied their wares on these same streets. The thought raised a question that he wondered about before—were there people like him in ancient Rome, those taxed with dealing with crime? If a stranger were found stabbed in the Rome of the Caesars, would that have been taken seriously, or would the body have been simply carted off to a mass grave somewhere outside the city's walls?

As Worthy waited at a busy intersection, he reviewed what he knew about Father Robert's life and death. Father Robert was in Rome because he'd failed as a priest and orphanage director in Canada's Northwest Territories. Then, two weeks after arriving in Rome, Father Robert was murdered. Was that a coincidence, or was there a connection?

Revenge was a powerful motive for murder, but Worthy had a hard time believing someone from Yellowknife had come to Rome for that reason. Besides, he knew the police would have checked passenger lists for Canadians from the Northwest Territories who had arrived in Rome after Father Robert.

Worthy knew that he couldn't dismiss another possibility, that one of monks at the monastery had, for some reason, killed Father Robert. But he couldn't help but wonder what Father Robert could have done in two weeks to provoke such a reaction.

Skirting the Trevi Fountain and its clog of tourists, he considered another possibility—that Father Robert had met someone in Rome outside the monastery, and that relationship had somehow led to his death. This seemed a more likely option to Worthy, although he knew that finding that person would be difficult, especially if the relationship were clandestine.

Fifteen minutes later, as he passed on the west side of the Circus Maximus, he thought of another possibility, one he feared the most. Father Robert could have been the victim of a random attack, perhaps a robbery that went bad. Random killings, those without a clear motive were always the most difficult to solve. The difficulty with that theory, he admitted, was that there were no signs of a struggle on Father Robert's body.

After walking up the south side of the Aventine Hill, he came to the gate of the monastery. After ringing the bell and waiting, he was greeted by an elderly monk, stooped and with eyebrows that looked as if they'd never been trimmed.

"I'm here to see Abbot Lorenzo," Worthy said as he showed him his ID.

"Follow me, please." Shuffling slowly, the monk escorted Worthy along a walkway that led around a cloister with a fountain in its middle. "Did I see on your identification that you're from Michigan?" the monk asked.

Deciding not to explain how Rome was now his home, he replied, "From Detroit, actually."

"I was brought up in Steven's Point, Wisconsin, if you know where that is," the monk said.

"I do. I drove through there on my way to do some fishing in northern Minnesota a few years back."

The old monk stopped to smile at Worthy. "My father worked at the brewery there. Do they still make Point Beer?"

"According to the billboards, yes, they still make beer." After a minute, Worthy added, "Steven's Point is pretty far from Rome. How long have you been here?"

Starting to shuffle again, the monk said "I'm one of the old monks of the order—been here going on fifty-three years. Though it doesn't seem more than ten."

Worthy thought about asking if the monk knew Father Robert, but decided he should postpone that until he met with the abbot.

After a soft knock on a heavy wooden door, the elderly monk escorted Worthy into the abbot's office. A tall and burly man, sporting a crewcut of gray hair, came around the desk to shake Worthy's hand. "We met at a reception about a week ago. It's good to see you again, Lieutenant Worthy."

"Please call me Chris."

"For Christopher, I presume?" Abbot Lorenzo asked, motioning for

Worthy to take a chair facing the desk. "A very auspicious name." After sitting behind a desk, the abbot said, "First things first," the abbot said. "I want to thank you for agreeing to help us." Clasping his hands together, he added, "We are in unfamiliar territory, Christopher. Of course, monks do die and quite a few have died lately, given the ages of those in the community. But no one from the community has ever been murdered. To make matters worse, I confess that we didn't know Father Robert very well. As far as I know, no one in the community knows why he was in Piazza del Popolo that time of night."

Worthy nodded. "I understand. The police now know that Father Robert was in the piazza his last three nights, not just the one."

The abbot ran his fingers through his hair, short as it was. "Yes, the police told me that as well. As I said, it's clear that we didn't really know Father Robert." After a pause, he added, "Despite that, I hope we can be of help to you. Can I ask where you're thinking of beginning?"

"I'll need to speak with Father Robert's confessor."

"I can assure you that Father Damian will cooperate. Actually, I can promise cooperation from the entire community, although, as I said, I'm not sure what we know."

Worthy nodded, even as he wondered if the abbot understood that every monk in the community was a suspect. "How many monks are in the community, Father?"

"Currently, we have twenty-eight."

"Are there others from outside the community who work here?"

"Yes, but no more than two or three. If we have a minor problem with our plumbing or electricity, we have a couple of brothers who know how to fix that. Although I'm not sure that what we do is completely legal." Shrugging, he said, "Italy is awash with regulations."

"So I've come to understand," Worthy said, remembering the forms that Lena and he had to fill out to put new locks on his office. "What about guests who've been here over the past two weeks?"

"Beside Father Robert, only three. They all left at least a week before Father Robert's death, but I can give you their names and addresses if you want."

"Yes, that would be helpful. Anyone else I should know about?"

The abbot thought for a moment. "We don't ask the names of those who come to the chapel for prayer during the day. Could that be important?"

Worthy shrugged. "Probably not, unless one of them was from Canada."

Creases formed on Abbot Lorenzo's forehead. "Hmm, yes, I see. As I said, we don't ask their names or where they're from."

"I understand many of your monks are from Canada. Do you know if any of them have had relatives or friends visiting the community over the past two weeks?"

"That can happen, but I'm quite sure that wasn't the case over those weeks."

"Have you had any other guests here, doing research like Lena?"

""I suppose it's possible that some of our day visitors came because they wanted to see Abbot Boniface's grave. That's who Dr. Fabriano is researching."

"Hmm. Would Father Robert have had any dealings with them?"

The abbot shook his head. "I can't see how. Two of our senior brothers meet with visitors. Pausing, he added, "And something else just dawned on me. It's about our guests. They have to reserve their visit months ahead of time. Each would have reserved a visit long before any of us knew Father Robert would be arriving."

As Worthy continued to jot notes in his notebook, Abbot Lorenzo asked, "When will your friend, Father Fortis, be arriving?"

"Father Nick coming isn't a problem, is it?" Worthy asked.

"No, absolutely not. And I should add, while the investigation is taking place, we've cancelled all retreats and day visitors."

Worthy stood and said, "That's very kind, Father. But to answer your question, Nick should arrive in a few days."

After both men rose, Abbot Lorenzo made the sign of the cross over Worthy's head. "Until then, may Our Lord bless your work, Christopher. All I ask is that you keep me abreast of what I need to know, especially if you find something that can lift this cloud that hangs over us."

Yellowknife—The Church of St. Anne

Hours later, but still morning in Yellowknife, Father Jacob called Nick's hotel room. "Nick, I hope I didn't wake you."

"No, I've just finished breakfast and was going to call you. I'm hoping we can talk with some of the boys' relatives."

"Yes, that's what I'm calling about. Nothing that happens in Yellowknife stays private. Folks have heard about why you're here. About ten minutes ago, one of the tribal leaders called and asked if she could talk with you. I offered the church and told her to come by at ten o'clock. I hope I did the right thing."

"You did, Jake. I'll come a bit early."

"I'll be here. I should warn you. Some people might have as many questions for you as you do for them."

An hour later, Nick stepped from his rental SUV in the church parking lot and shivered. The temperature was well below zero, and he was glad for his new hat, gloves, and boots. He hurried toward the door of the church, but managed to glance at another vehicle, also a SUV, parked in the lot. Instead of bearing a Northwest Territories plate, the vehicle's license plate bore the name Great Slave Lake Dene.

He entered the church and hurried down the hallway to Father Jacob's office. Opening the door, he was hit with a blast of hot air, and the skin on his arms and hands started to itch.

As quickly as he could, he shed his coat and gloves. Mrs. Elkhorn turned from a printer to offer a smile and to say that she would let Father Jacob know he'd arrived. Inside the priest's equally overheated office, he saw a couple, the young woman cradling a sleeping infant in her arms.

The man had risen to his feet, and when the woman began to follow, Nick said, "No, please don't trouble yourself."

Seeing a look of fear cross the woman's face, he fought an urge to apologize for being at almost a foot taller than the man and outweighing him by at least a hundred pounds. He would never forget the child who, when visiting St. Simeon's with her family, called him "Hagrid." As he sat in the chair offered by Father Jacob, he reminded himself to tone down his normal speaking voice.

"I want to say how sorry I am about what happened at the orphanage. I also want to thank you for talking with me," he said softly.

"No, Father, thank you for letting us talk with you," the man said.

A moment of silence followed as Nick offered the couple a chance to say or ask whatever they wished. Finally, the man said, "We are the Sabois from the Dene nation. Billy Sabois was my cousin's youngest child. He was one of the three boys who died."

Nick let that fact linger without immediately responding. "I can only imagine how much you must miss him. I remember seeing Billy's picture. Billy appeared to be about nine or ten."

"He was nine," Mrs. Sabois said. "Billy was in the orphanage, but he was loved, Father. He was at Safe Haven because he had six older brothers and sisters, and both parents have . . . well, they have some problems." Dabbing at her eyes, she added, "Billy was a sweet boy, so sweet."

In the cases that Nick had worked with Worthy, he'd seen adult victims of homicide, but never children. He would never forget his mother's words when his younger brother was killed in the first Gulf War. "Parents shouldn't have to bury their children. It's against nature," she said.

"Billy's death must be very hard for his parents."

Mr. Sabois nodded. "We're here because they asked us to come. They aren't ready, you see."

"Of course, of course. Please tell them that I am praying for them and for Billy. Did they give you any questions for me in particular?"

Mrs. Sabois looked at her husband, who was looking down at the floor. "They . . . no, none of us know what to think about Father Bob's death. Did he suffer?"

The question took Nick by surprise. *Do they want to hear that Father Robert had suffered or that he'd been spared?* he thought.

"From everything I've read, his death was sudden."

The young man didn't look up, but nodded as did his wife. "That is a mercy," she said in little more than a whisper.

Nick felt the lump in his throat and could see that Father Jacob had been similarly affected. "Did you know Father Robert well?" he asked.

"Everyone knew Father Bob," Mr. Sabois shared. "Especially the Dene people. On his mother's side, Father Bob had Dene relatives."

The room was silent again until Father Jacob said, "I know that Father Bob wanted to talk with the families of the three boys before he left. Did he meet with your cousin's family?"

"I know he tried, but my cousin's family is like some of the others. They didn't want to see Father Bob," Mr. Sabois said, looking down.

"Because they blamed him for the fire?" Nick asked.

The Sabois looked at one another. In Mrs. Sabois' arms, the baby whimpered as she woke up. "I'm sorry to say this, Father," Mr. Sabois said looking at Father Jacob, "but many don't blame Father Bob; they blame his God."

"Believe me, I understand," Father Jacob said. "I've noticed a drop in attendance here at St. Anne's since the fire."

Mr. Sabois slowly nodded.

"Does that mean that most of the victims' families don't blame Father Robert?" Nick asked.

"I can't speak for everyone, but I know that some of the families say if Father Bob hadn't been drunk, he could have called the fire department earlier. But most of us accept the government report, that the explosion was too sudden for anyone to do anything. It looks like the boys . . . well, they died in their sleep."

Mrs. Sabois lifted the baby onto her shoulder. "After Father Bob died, some people remembered that he complained before about the heating at the orphanage, that the system was old and needed to be replaced. So now a lot of people think the fire wouldn't have happened if he'd been listened to."

"Listened to by whom?" Nick asked.

"By the board of directors or whoever checked the furnaces," Mr. Sabois replied.

Turning to Father Jacob, Nick asked, "Is there documentation about that complaint?"

The priest shook his head. "Not that I've seen, but I have heard that a few families remember Father Bob saying that. But no one reported that until after Father Bob's death."

Nick took a minute to consider the new information. "So Father Robert didn't mention that at the inquest?"

Father Jacob shook his head. "No."

Nick made a mental note to ask the bishop. Determining if Father Robert had complained about the orphanage's heating system wouldn't change the fact that three boys died that night. It wouldn't change Father Robert being found that night in a stupor, and it wouldn't change his murder two weeks later. But the question deserved an answer. It would give Father Robert a final gift, the gift of the truth about that fateful night.

CHAPTER SIX

Rome—The Order of the Sacred Wounds

After reading Nick's email, informing him that some people in Yellowknife remember Father Robert complaining about the heating system at the orphanage, Worthy changed his mind and decided not to wait until Nick arrived in Rome to interview Father Damian, Father Robert's confessor.

Every homicide investigation benefitted when discrepancies are found in clues or witness statements, and Nick had already uncovered a significant discrepancy. Worthy had assumed that Father Robert's negligence the night of the fire would have left the man swamped by guilt, but, if it were true that the priest had complained about the heating system, then Father Robert's emotional state after the fire was all the more necessary to understand.

Worthy texted a reply, congratulating Nick on what he'd found out and agreeing that Father Robert's complaint was something he should ask the bishop about. Worthy also considered the question a good one to pose to Father Damian.

He heard the squeak of rubber soles in the hallway before the door opened. Entering the room was a monk in his sixties with glasses so thick that his eyes seemed nearly double size. The monk approached Worthy and offered a smile as gentle as his opening words which echoed the abbot's, "Mr. Worthy, it is good of you to help us."

After the two sat in chairs facing one another, Father Damian said, "I understand that congratulations are in order."

"Oh?"

"Sorry, on your marriage to Dr. Fabriano. We think very highly of her. I didn't see her today, though. I hope she is well."

Worthy nodded. "She's fine; she's just working from home."

Father Damian nodded in return. "I look forward to talking with her again about her research. Abbot Boniface's cause for sainthood is naturally important to our community. And Dr. Fabriano is brilliant, but then you know that."

"That I do, Father."

The two sat quietly as Father Damian looked down at his ink-stained hands. "Vanity; all is vanity."

"Pardon?"

"My hands. This is the problem with fountain pens. You see, I still use them in my work, in taking notes and then transcribing those notes for our files. But fountain pens are messy, or maybe it's me that's at fault."

"You must not be alone in your preference. I've seen several pen stores in Rome. From the prices in the window, I'd say it can be an expensive hobby," Worthy said.

The monk winced. "Which only compounds my sin of vanity. My pens are on the inexpensive side, but not nearly as cheap as ballpoint pens. And ballpoints, of course," he said, turning over his hands to reveal his palms, "don't leave these messy stains. So I have no real defense. But you don't want to talk about fountain pens, so why don't you ask your questions and, if it doesn't break the confessional seal of privacy, I'll do my best to answer them. I will say at the outset, however, that Father Robert said nothing to me that would lead me to think that his life was in danger here in Rome."

"I understand. How would you describe Father Robert's mood while he was here?"

"He was downcast, especially when he first arrived. That seemed appropriate, given the tragedy in Canada, and on top of that he was facing the possibility of being defrocked. You have to understand, Mr. Worthy, there's no greater catastrophe for a priest than to be denied his vocation. How many happy ex-priests do you know?"

Worthy understood the question was rhetorical, but he still tried to imagine how Nick would feel if he were ever thrown out of the monastery. "It sounds like you're saying that priests don't usually have a plan B," Worthy said.

"That's it exactly. The priesthood is all we know . . . and all we want to know."

"But you said Father Robert was like that at the beginning. Did he change?"

"I would never say that I saw him happy, but toward the end he seemed to be focused; maybe I should say preoccupied. You could see in his eyes that he had something on his mind. I have no doubt that he still carried the guilt, but there was something else."

"Do you know if he became close to any of the other monks?"

Father Damian thought about the question for a moment. "Not that I noticed. Of course, he was meeting almost daily with the ethics committee. Outside of that, he was treated as a fellow brother, which he was. What I mean is that he prayed the Daily Office with the community, which is six prayer times a day along with daily Mass. I know he was given a work detail, which was mainly odd jobs working on the grounds like watering the shrubs and flowers in the cloister and spraying them for pests. I heard that he also more spent a considerable amount of time in the library on one of our computers toward the end."

"While he was here, would he have been supervised or unsupervised?" Worthy asked.

Father Damian's face reddened. "I can't say that he was being watched every minute. Despite the ethics committee review of his vocation and future, we treated him as a fellow monk, a brother. He wasn't a prisoner, you see."

"But it must have been unusual for a monk to be out in the city that late at night."

"We're all wondering about that," the monk replied. "With our first prayer service being at three in the morning, we tend to go to bed after Compline, which is at eight in the evening."

"Given what you know about Father Robert, why do you think he went to the piazza?"

Father Damian looked down at his stained hands again. "Please understand that I have no proof, but I think he must have been meeting someone."

Both men sat in silence for a few moments. Finally, Worthy said, "My colleague Father Fortis is interviewing people who knew Father Robert in Canada. He's heard from one of the families of the victims that Father Robert complained about the heating system, the one that failed, before the fire. Did he ever mention that to you?"

Father Damian's jaw dropped as his eyes held Worthy's gaze. "No he didn't. Why he didn't, if that's true, mystifies me. Yes, it completely mystifies me. Please, if you're going to interview those on the ethics committee, you must bring that to their attention. We have a duty . . . yes, we have a duty to Father Robert's memory."

Worthy nodded. "Father Fortis and I feel the same." Pausing for a moment, he added, "That's all the questions I have for now, unless you know something else that might help us understand Father Robert."

Father Damian shook his head, then stopped. "There is one thing Father Robert said. It refers to something long ago, so I doubt if it's important."

Even as Worthy replied in a calm voice, he could feel his heart rate quicken. How many times had witnesses said those exact words before revealing something significant? "I would appreciate knowing anything he said."

"Perhaps you already know it. The last time Father Robert and I spoke, I asked if he was enjoying anything about being in Rome. I expected him to say 'no,' given the circumstances, but he said he'd been to Rome before, for Holy Week many years ago when he was a seminarian."

"No, we didn't know that. Do you have any idea when that might have been?"

"Given his age, I'd think that would have been twenty to twenty-five or more years ago. I think he said it was just for a week, maybe ten days, so, like I said, it's probably not important."

"Maybe not, but it's good to know." Worthy phrased his response to be as noncommittal as possible, but the new clue intrigued him. He wondered if Father Robert's killer could be someone whom he met thirty years before.

Rome—Police Station

Capitano Sesto was a short, wiry detective who could be a brother of Al Pacino. Initially, Worthy had learned to be wary when dealing with local law enforcement, but Capitano Sesto seemed only too happy to call on Worthy when English-speaking tourists and residents of Rome were victims of muggers and pick-pocket artists. He'd also called Worthy in on the case of the murdered American college student. And every time he had asked for Worthy's help, Worthy had delivered.

After welcoming Worthy into his office and offering him one of the chairs, the captain said in passable English, "Signore Worthy, I realize something this morning. It is your name 'Worthy.' I hear it before. Then I remember. I meet another Worthy last year. Allyson Worthy. From internet, I see you have daughter by that name, yes?"

"Yes, Allyson's my older daughter. You worked on that case at the refugee camp?"

"I exaggerate nothing when I say she save many lives. But then she must have told you. I remember because she was FBI but worked with CIA."

Worthy felt a combination of pride and regret when he heard Sesto's compliment of Allyson. "She's still with the Bureau, but don't ask me where she's stationed." Allyson had made it clear that she wasn't always allowed to tell him where she was assigned, but Worthy suspected that this was also her way of keeping him at a distance. He accepted the blame for that. Allyson had suffered more from his divorce than his younger daughter, Amy, and Allyson was the one who'd blamed him for the family falling apart.

Thanks as much to Nick as to time passing, his relationship with Allyson had improved. Six years before, when she had an internship with the Venetian police, they'd even been thrown together on a case. *Yes, our relationship is better, but not completely healed,* he admitted to himself. With his ex-wife, Susan, offering little justification for the divorce, Allyson had been the one who'd listed his many mistakes as a career-centered husband and father. As she had so eloquently put it at the time, "You care more about the dead than the living."

"Have you seen the piazza where the padre died?" Sesto asked, breaking into Worthy's memories.

"I have, though my visit only brought up more questions," Worthy replied.

Sesto nodded. "Certo, of course. CCTV show padre enter piazza three nights, but we no see him sit on bench. The bench, it is in a blind spot."

"So we don't know if he went there to meet someone."

Sesto shrugged. "One of many questions." He handed a folder across his desk. "Please, these are photos from the morgue. You can see, there are two stab wounds in his back, one hit the right lung and the other pierce the heart."

Worthy focused on the photos of Father Robert's face. He'd seen enough photos of homicides to know that not all victims looked peaceful in death. Father Robert, however, looked almost relieved.

"And no defense wounds," he said.

Sesto shook his head.

"Three nights in the same piazza and very late. What did you think originally?" Worthy asked.

The captain leaned back and looked up at the ceiling. "Was he there for sex, sex with a minor, maybe?" Shaking his head, he added, "But no word of that from Canada. Not from monastery either."

"I agree. There's not a shred of evidence of that," he said. "But I've just learned from my colleague, Father Fortis, that Father Robert had been in Rome once before. That was over twenty years ago, when he was in seminary. I'm going to ask Father Fortis to get a list of others who were on that trip. That might yield something—or nothing."

"But this time, padre not in Rome for pleasure, yes?"

"No, he was here, I guess you could say, against his will. He was in Rome because of the fire in Canada. The monastery here was deciding if he should be defrocked—being removed from the priesthood. There's something else we know. In the days before he died, he was in the monastery's library for hours on one of their computers. But that's about it."

"Yes, it is not much, but still early."

Worthy nodded. "I do have a question about the CCTV on the night he was killed."

"Of course."

"When did he arrive in the piazza?"

"A little after midnight."

"And his body was found at one-thirty?"

"Si, si."

"Do you know how he got to the piazza? It's a long walk from the monastery, so what—a bus or a taxi?" Worthy asked.

"Ah, I think he take the Metro, our subway. And if he did, we have CCTV of that."

"The subway runs that late at night?"

Sesto opened his computer. "Si, all through the night. That late, there are fewer people. And more good news," he said with a smile as he turned the screen so Worthy could see. "See? We have facial recognition. That's how we see he was in same piazza three nights."

On the screen, an image of a tunnel appeared with people spilling out. "This doesn't look like a subway," Worthy said.

"It is the Metro exit near Piazza del Popolo. Computer scans face, and voila, we work backwards, and find his face on other two nights."

Worthy studied the images of Father Robert on all three nights. Each night, Father Robert walked out of the tunnel and turned in the direction of the piazza. In addition to gloves, Father Robert wore a hat and a puffy coat, but Worthy noticed that the clerical collar was visible. The expression on Father Robert's face changed, however. His face on the second of the three nights looked particularly grim, his eyes glanced neither right nor left, and Worthy was left with the impression that Father Robert was on a mission.

"All because we have face recognition program," Sesto said, ready to turn off his computer.

"Before you do that, let the footage from the second night run a bit." After a moment, Worthy said, "There. See them? Could those three teenagers be following him?"

"Ah, yes, maybe. Gangs target tourists in Piazza del Popolo. I do face recognition on them too."

Worthy had no proof that the youths were following Father Robert, but he thought a robbery gone wrong was a possibility. *But if that's what happened,* Worthy thought, *why weren't there any defensive wounds on the body?*

Yellowknife—St. Anne Parish

"You want to talk with Bishop Bruno?" Father Jacob replied to Nick's request. "The diocesan office is down in Edmonton, but I know the bishop left for Toronto right after the funeral for the boys." He reached for his desk phone and dialed a number. "Give me a minute, and I'll find out when he's expected back."

Nick listened while Father Jacob made small talk with the diocesan secretary before asking about the bishop's schedule. After pausing, the priest said, "Yes, I'll get back to you."

"Bishop Bruno is in Toronto for an indeterminate stay. I'm not surprised. He wasn't exactly welcomed with open arms by the families at the funeral. And he's originally from Toronto, so my guess is that he went there to lick his wounds."

"What's your sense of the bishop?" Nick asked.

"I hadn't many dealings with him before the funeral. But I'd say he spoke more as the chairman of the orphanage's board of directors than these people's shepherd. He was defensive, I guess you could say."

"Did he meet with Father Robert when he was here?"

"I assume he did, but maybe not. As I said, he left soon after the funeral."

"Well, I guess it's a case of the mountain coming to Muhammad, then. I have some questions only he can answer, so it looks like I'll stop in Toronto on my way to Rome. But before I leave, are there other relatives of the boys I should talk . . . or listen to?"

"Yes, there's a grandmother of one of the boys who wants to meet with you. But Bessie Free Woman is old, so I thought we'd drive out to her home rather than ask her to come to town."

"Today, then?"

"She said she'd be at home all afternoon," Father Jacob said.

Because of the snowstorm the night before, it took over an hour for Father Jacob and Nick to pull up in front of a small government house, one identical to those around it. Nick was also not surprised to see, apart from a sadly deflated Santa on a neighbor's lawn, an absence of Christmas decorations. As Father Jacob had said, this would be a sorrowful Christmas in Yellowknife.

Father Jacob kept the car and its heater running while they sat for a moment in the car. "We'll wait a minute, to let Bessie get used to our being here."

"I learned the same lesson on a case in New Mexico. Those were Pueblo and Navaho people."

"Hmm. I'm from Winnipeg originally, so I'd have made a ton of mistakes if Mrs. Elkhorn and Father Bob hadn't given me a crash course in cultural etiquette. But the indigenous patterns I've been exposed to impress me. Take this waiting for example. I see it as offering respect," Father Jacob said.

"Not to mention teaching us a bit about patience," Nick added.

After a few moments, a front curtain was pulled back and a white-haired woman gestured toward the car. When they stepped through the door, Nick saw the same shocked look on the woman's face as he'd seen with the Sabois. *I do feel like a giant up here,* he thought, as he reminded himself to speak softly. Once seated in the tiny living room, Nick saw another woman enter the room with a tray holding a coffee urn, cups, and a plate of cookies. The women resembled each other so much that Nick wasn't surprised when the second woman was introduced as Bessie Free Woman's daughter, Tonya.

Nick joined Father Jacob in thanking the grandmother and the daughter for the coffee and cookies as he noted on a side table a lit candle in front of a picture of a smiling boy. Above the table was a crucifix, the slumped face of Jesus seeming to look down in sorrow on the boy. *May it be so, Lord,* he thought.

Father Jacob finished his cookie before saying, "Bessie, Father Nicholas is working with an American detective on Father Bob's death in Italy. Father Nicholas is in Yellowknife because he wants to know more about Father Bob—how people saw him before . . . and after the fire."

When Mrs. Free Woman turned her attention to him, Nick could see the evidence of advanced cataracts in her eyes. Raising her hand in the direction of the other woman, she said, "Father Bob, he came to see us."

"When was that?" Nick asked.

"The day before he left on the big airplane."

Nick inserted he information into his timeline. It would be good to hear what Father Robert was like and what he was thinking about so near his departure.

"Father Bob brought that candle," she said as she pointed to the small table, "and then he prayed."

"It would help me understand Father Bob if you would tell me what you talked about."

Mrs. Free Woman rested gnarled hands on her knees. "Father Bob was like one of my own sons. He came here often . . . to talk. Maybe he wanted for that last time here to be like before, but it wasn't."

"No, of course not," Nick said, then waited.

Her gaze turned toward the photo of her grandson. "He told us that he wished he'd died and not the boys. But I told him something he already knew, that our people believe people live as long as the time they are given. We live long enough to give to the world what we are meant to give; then we die."

Nick didn't say anything, letting the comment hang in the room. "You say he already knew that."

"Yes, he was one of us, part Dene, I mean. But he said my faith was stronger than his. Then he told me how much he loved Connor's smile, how much he missed that. He said Connor always made the other boys laugh. Some of the other children are so sad, you see."

Again, Nick felt that Mrs. Free Woman's comments deserved to be followed by silence. Finally, he said, "You said that Father Bob often came to see you. Did he come in the days before the fire?"

She closed her eyes before saying, "He came the morning before the fire. Sad, his eyes, his mouth, were heavy, very heavy. He said he had received bad news from far away. I asked him what the bad news was, but he just smiled and said I was not to worry."

"Do you think it was about the orphanage or something else?" Nick asked.

She shook her head. "I don't know, but I had a feeling."

"Yes?"

"I believe the bad news surprised him. It was bad news he didn't see coming . . . until it came."

Nick considered the comment before asking, "When Father Bob came that last time, the day before he left for Rome, did he say anything more about this bad news?"

Mrs. Free Woman, her eyes closed again, shook her head.

"How about Rome? Did he talk about going to Rome?"

"I asked if he was going to see the Big Father in Rome. He said, 'Yes, in a way.' He said he didn't want to go. I asked if he was afraid of the long journey, of flying in the big airplane. He said 'no,' he wasn't afraid of the journey, but what would happen there."

Nick glanced at Father Jacob, remembering that the priest's similar memory of Father Robert's feelings about going to Rome. He'd assumed that Father Robert hadn't wanted to face the real possibility of being defrocked. *And maybe that's all he meant when he said he was afraid of what would happen there,* he thought. *Or maybe he was afraid of something more, some secret he kept to his grave.*

CHAPTER SEVEN

Rome—Lena's Apartment

That evening, Lena and Worthy pored over the file that the monastery had on Father Robert. What Worthy was particularly hoping to find was information on Father Robert's visit to Rome twenty-five years before. But as so often happens when searching for a certain answer, the researcher stumbles on other even more valuable information. Father Robert's secular name was Robert Porter. He was born in British Columbia and put into a Church-sponsored orphanage in the same province at the age of thirteen. After he indicated a calling to the priesthood, he was sent to a secondary school for boys in Toronto.

From there, Robert Porter had entered St. Catherine's, Toronto's foremost Catholic university, and majored in medieval philosophy. From his transcript of grades, Worthy could tell that Father Robert had been a better than average student, but not one who merited a recommendation to post-graduate studies. Upon graduation, he declared his desire for monastic life and, on the advice of a chaplain, had entered the Order of the Sacred Wounds. After taking his solemn vows, he served as an assistant priest for two years at a Catholic boy's prep school in Toronto until he was sent to Yellowknife and Safe Haven Orphanage. He served as assistant to the director for seven years, then became the director.

"But no mention of a seminary trip to Rome," Worthy said.

"No, but maybe that was so usual for seminarians that it didn't bear mentioning."

"Hmm. I'd still like to know how he felt about the trip. Also, was it unusual for him to be a monk on his own in Yellowsknife instead of staying in a monastery?" Worthy asked.

"Not really. Monks are often assigned to missionary service. I'm sure the director of the orphanage before him was a member of the Order of the Sacred Wounds. So, the two of them would have been monks together."

After looking through the final pages in the file, Worthy stood and stretched. "Nothing like hoping for answers and ending up with more questions."

Lena leaned over and kissed Worthy. "Early days, Chris."

"You're right, but you know my approach."

"I should by now. Before we can find the killer, we have to 'find' the victim."

"And I think we both have to admit that we're far from finding Father Robert."

Inflight to Toronto

Later that afternoon, Nick came back from Mrs. Free Woman's to find Worthy's last email. Worthy agreed with Nick's plan to stop over in Toronto and interview the bishop. That change of plan was made easier by Father Jacob, who was able to arrange for Nick to meet with Bishop Bruno the following afternoon.

The next morning, Nick returned the rental car by noon and checked his luggage. Two hours later, he was airborne, looking down at Yellowknife, a town that should have been getting ready for Christmas but was instead reeling from a series of overwhelming tragedies—the death of three orphans and then the death of a priest who was still beloved by many.

At the end of the coronavirus pandemic, people had talked a lot about returning to normal. Nick could imagine a day in the future when the people of Yellowknife might forget about the pandemic, but he knew the town would never forget the fire and its aftermath.

Nick was grateful that the person in the adjoining seat leaned back for a nap as soon as the plane took off, leaving him time to reflect on what he'd learned about Father Robert in his short stop in Yellowknife. From Mrs. Free Woman, he knew Father Robert had received bad news the day before the fire. Father Robert hadn't said what that was, but Mrs. Free Woman thought the bad news had come as a surprise. That was also the day when Father Robert had made an uncharacteristic purchase of whisky—two bottles. *Bad leading to bad leading to more bad. Bad news followed by a very bad decision the night of the fire, leading to a bad death in Rome,* he thought.

After the fire, Yellowknife was divided and remained so. A minority blamed Father Robert while more blamed God or the board of directors whom they now believed had ignored Father Robert's warnings about a faulty heating system. What Nick didn't understand was why Father Robert hadn't mentioned making such a complaint at the inquest—if, in fact, he had given such a warning.

CHAPTER EIGHT

Rome—Order to Sacred Wounds Monastery

The next morning, as Worthy walked back to the monastery, he thought of what Capitano Sesto had told him. CCTV covering the Piazza del Popolo was only partially helpful, as the obelisk and fountain in the center of the piazza obscured the bench on which Father Robert had sat. What no one knew was if Father Robert's being hidden from the CCTV cameras had been simply bad luck or had been intentional on Father Robert's part. Then again, Worthy reasoned, Father Robert's positioning could have been arranged by the killer.

Walking along the quiet Via San Teodoro, he came to one of Rome's most important and massive ruins, Circus Maximus.

He'd first seen this site in photos in his first-year Latin textbook. Now, as he'd done two years before on another case, he paused to take in the immense oval.

With the monastery being on the other side of Circus Maximus and halfway up the slope of the Aventine Hill, Worthy was certain that Father Robert had gazed on this same scene more than once. He wondered if Father Robert had thought of the circus as it was in ancient times, when criminals and Christians were thrown to the beasts, or had he been too preoccupied with his own problem. That was the first mystery they'd have to solve—Father Robert's state of mind at the end. He hoped his morning interview with Father Silas, a member of the ethics committee investigating Father Robert's case, would shed some light on that.

When Father Silas entered the conference room, Worthy was surprised by how young the monk was, in his early forties at most. But the greater surprise was Worthy's realization that the dark-haired monk was indigenous. *That can't be a coincidence,* Worthy thought. The orphanage in

Yellowknife had been for First Nations' children. Father Robert was Dene as well, at least on his mother's side. And now one of the monks on the ethics committee that was investigating Father Robert shared a similar heritage.

After Father Silas greeted Worthy, he said, "The abbot briefed me on why you want to speak with me, Mr. Worthy. The entire community is praying that your work will be successful." Sitting down, he added, "This is a tragedy that doesn't seem to have an end. First, the loss of the children and then the death of Father Robert. Perhaps in your work, you grow accustomed to murder, but nothing like this has ever happened to us before."

Worthy shook his head. "No, I've never gotten used to murder. I don't think I'd be much good as an investigator if I forgot that none of my victims deserved to die the way they did."

The monk was silent, and Worthy could see that Father Silas was studying his face. "Is that usual for a homicide detective?"

Worthy shrugged. "There are other approaches, some not so focused on the victim."

After another silence, Father Silas nodded. "I think I understand, but I know you want to talk about Father Robert. What would you like to know?"

"To start, maybe what he was like when he first met with your committee."

"I'd describe him as depressed, but he was less so in our last sessions. I think we were all surprised when he didn't defend himself. He had one focus, one goal, and that was to return to the orphanage. He said he could accept not being kept on as the director, or even a priest, if he could return in some capacity. He even said he'd be willing to go back as a janitor. Everything was secondary to going back. He reminded me of the prodigal son in the parable, begging to be allowed to be a servant in his father's house."

"I understand that he didn't defend himself at all. But did he explain his behavior on the night of the fire?"

Father Silas shook his head. "He disputed nothing in the charges. But he was clearly pained that he was prohibited from attending the funerals. As he told us, he'd been the priest who baptized the three boys, and he's also known the family circumstances that brought the boys to the orphanage."

Worthy remembered what Nick had put in his last email. "My colleague has been in Yellowknife interviewing the orphanage staff and some of the families. Before coming to Rome, Father Robert visited or tried to visit the families of the three boys. I wonder if that was against the bishop's orders."

Father Silas nodded. "He did speak about that, and, yes, it was against the bishop's order. We got the impression that there'd been longstanding tension between Father Robert and the bishop."

"Can I ask what your committee was most likely to recommend?"

Father Silas sighed heavily. "Assuming you're asking if he would be defrocked, I honestly don't know. You see, he never explained what you asked about—his drunken state—the night of the fire. All he would say was that he'd been sober for twenty-three years before that night. If that was the truth, that would be commendable, given that a priest, unless he has an assistant, must consume whatever is left of the communion wine after the Mass."

"But was he admitting that he had a problem with alcohol in his past?"

"That was the impression he gave me."

Worthy thought about what Nick had emailed him, that Father Robert getting drunk the night of the fire coincided with him telling a relative of one of the victims that he'd received unexpected bad news.

"The toxicology results in the police file here in Rome indicated there was no alcohol in his bloodstream the night he died in the piazza," Worthy said.

The two men sat in silence until Father Silas said, "I'm relieved to know that, but not surprised. You should know that our committee was scheduled to meet with Father Robert the morning after he was killed. We intended to tell him that our recommendation would depend on his explaining the circumstances of his lapse on the night of the fire. But we never had the chance to tell him that."

Worthy nodded. "That's one of the questions we still need to answer."

Father Silas held Worthy's gaze. "Do you really believe that his drinking the night of the fire has something to do with his being murdered here?"

"It's too early to tell. With the fire and his death here being more than four thousand miles apart, it seems unlikely. But my instincts tell me that there is a connection. What we know is this: One, something drove Father Robert, apparently after twenty-three years of sobriety, to drink until he was nearly unconscious the night of the fire. Two, some family members of the victims blame him for the fire, despite the fire investigator's report. And three, just weeks after the fire, Father Robert is murdered here in

Rome. So you see, the facts are clear. It's the connections that are missing. And that's where I hope you can help."

"I don't think I know anything else."

"Maybe not, but in your meetings with Father Robert, did he ever mention that he had previously complained about the orphanage's heating system?"

Father Silas' eyes widened. "Is that true?"

"We don't know. Some of the families in Yellowknife say they remember him telling them that he complained to the board of directors. And I should mention that the bishop serves on that board."

"And the board members deny this?"

Worthy shook his head. "I don't know. My colleague is meeting with the bishop later today. We'll know more after that conversation. But if it's true, why wouldn't he have brought that up in his defense?"

Shrugging, Father Silas said, "It makes no sense. All I can think is that he was totally focused on the future, on getting back to the orphanage. Of course, we'll never know if he intended to mention a complaint about the heating system in our next meeting. And even if he did complain about the heating system, that doesn't explain his drinking the night of the fire ."

"No, you're right, but if it's the truth, then there are others who bear more responsibility than Father Robert for what happened that night."

A Luxury Hotel in Toronto

Nick took a taxi from the monastery outside Toronto where Father Robert had stayed after seminary. The temperature in Yellowknife had been below zero when he left, but Toronto was in the mid-fifties and felt even warmer. Despite the warmth, the city's center was already dressed for the season, with decorated Christmas trees on nearly every corner.

Arriving an hour early for his appointment with the bishop, Nick retreated to the hotel's luxurious lobby to consider what he'd learned at the monastery. Father Robert had been an unexceptional novice, but, when assisting in the parish, he'd shown a gift for working with street youth.

The puzzle piece that Nick uncovered was that Father Robert's trip twenty-three years earlier to Rome had come as part of a seminary trip.

The abbot whom Nick had talked with agreed to send a list of the names and addresses of the others who were on that trip.

With still forty-five minutes before his meeting with the bishop, Nick decided on a walk outside in the sunshine. From looking into shop windows displaying jewelry and designer fashions, he soon realized that he was in one of Toronto's more affluent neighborhoods.

Nick felt like a visitor from another planet as he wondered what kind of person needed a watch costing thirty-six thousand dollars. He looked down at his own twenty-nine dollar watch and thought of the similarly cheap watch that Pope Francis wore. Nick stopped himself from prejudging the bishop based on the hotel he chose to stay in, but he knew that he'd look to see what kind of watch the bishop wore.

At the end of the block, he came to a faux-gothic building with a doorman guarding the entrance. He read the stone-carved sign over the doors—"The Britannia Club"—and then stopped to read the smaller sign in one of the door panes—"For Members Only." The doorman frowned at Nick, as if a monk in the long flowing robes had violated the rule just by stopping.

He crossed the street and started back toward the hotel when he noticed a group of men leaving The Britannia Club. In the middle of the group and clearly the center of attention was a Catholic priest, trim with silver hair. On closer inspection, Father Fortis recognized the crimson sash of a Catholic bishop.

I can't believe there'd be two bishops on the same block, Nick thought. His guess was confirmed when the group walked in the direction of the hotel, said goodbye to the bishop, and watched him enter the hotel.

Not wanting to keep the bishop waiting, Nick crossed the street and entered the lobby just as the bishop looked around before glancing at his gold watch.

"Sorry, your Eminence, I just stepped out for a bit of fresh air."

Bishop Bruno turned and flashed the kind of smile that Nick thought went over well in The Britannia Club but not so well at a funeral in Yellowknife.

"Father Fortis, I assume. Please," he said, gesturing toward a pair of leather chairs on opposite sides of a coffee table. "Can I get you anything? Coffee, tea, something stronger? They have a full bar here."

Nick wondered if the offer of alcohol were a test, given Father Robert's fall from grace. "Coffee for me, please."

As if by prearranged signal, a waiter approached as soon as the two were seated. "What can I serve you, Your Eminence."

"Two coffees, Caleb," the bishop said.

Smooth, smooth, Nick thought. *Without you saying so directly, I now know that this is home base when you're in Toronto.*

"Now, if I remember correctly, you've flown in from Yellowknife," the bishop said. "The edge of world, I've said. Was your visit there helpful?"

"A bit helpful, a bit confusing, and on the whole, sorrowful."

Bishop Bruno frowned as he sighed. "Such a tragedy, one that won't be quickly forgotten. And now the death of Father Robert." He paused before adding, "I understand you're working with a homicide detective from Detroit."

"Lieutenant Worthy has retired and now works part of the year in Rome."

"Indeed? What a nice arrangement . . . or 'gig' as the young folks would say. Has your homicide detective friend found out anything definitive about Father Robert's death?"

Nick's instinct was to share little with the bishop. "I can't tell you much. I'm flying to Rome tomorrow, and that's when we'll have a chance to compare notes. The case is still in the early stages."

"Yes, of course, of course. But isn't it strange that Father Robert was in that public square so late at night? I've asked myself what possessed him, and, frankly, I've drawn a blank. Please don't misunderstand my concern, but did the autopsy reveal alcohol in his bloodstream?"

Nick let the question hang in the air before shaking his head. "No, not a drop. No drugs either," he added, then returned to silence.

After an awkward moment, Bishop Bruno looked again at his gold watch and asked, "Well, Father Fortis, if I can help you, I certainly will. Maybe I can save us both some time by saying that there is absolutely no evidence of sexual abuse."

Nick nodded. "I heard nothing along those lines in Yellowknife, either. But I'm hoping you can tell me what kind of priest was Father Robert— before that horrible night, I mean."

"Hmm, well, what do I say? As much as I'd like to protect his reputation, especially now that he's dead, I must be honest. Father Robert could be prickly, even argumentative. I'm not saying I'm always right, but Father Robert seemed to find it necessary to challenge whatever I suggested."

Nick thought for an opening salvo, the bishop's words hardly suggested a desire to protect Father Robert's reputation. "How about his devotion to the community, especially the First Nations communities?"

The bishop nodded vehemently. "Absolutely no doubt about Father Robert's commitment to the boys and their families." After pausing, he added, "But what I'm saying is that a bishop when making decisions has to consider the needs of every parish, every ministry in the diocese. And the diocese hardly has a generous budget."

And yet you stay in this hotel where waiters know your name and your favorite drink, Nick thought.

"Perhaps it's the same in the Orthodox world, but priests can easily be consumed with matters in their parish. A form of tunnel vision, I'd say. It's only the bishop who must always keep in mind the bigger picture." Shaking his head, he added, "Over the past year, Father Robert saw only the orphanage. Don't get me wrong. I'm a big supporter of Safe Haven. You might not know this, but I'm chairperson on the board of directors."

Nick nodded. "I was told in Yellowknife about the hockey issue."

The bishop tilted his head back and laughed. "Hockey. Yes, the hockey issue. Is there a more expensive sport to equip youth? Replacing hockey with soccer would have saved the orphanage thousands of dollars, no, more than ten thousand dollars, but Father Robert insisted."

"Someone told me that he funded fund the hockey out of his own pocket," Nick said, trying to make the comment sound innocent.

Bishop Bruno took a sip of coffee. "Yes and no. I thought the diocese gave him a generous sports budget, but over the past year, Father Robert continued to violate diocesan protocols by contacting parishes directly and asking for money for his hockey program. I'm sure you agree, if a diocese allowed every priest to fundraise on his own, contacting the same donors, chaos would result. When I put a stop to that, I heard he'd starting telling people that he was putting his own money into that program. I can't imagine his contribution was very much."

The bishop paused for a moment before adding, "Yes, I'm sorry to say that the hockey issue is a perfect example of Father Robert's stubbornness. It wasn't more than two months ago that I reminded him that all the indigenous peoples across the Northwest Territories were poor. What his boys needed was computer training, not hockey."

Nick nodded, hoping to give the impression that he understood the bishop's frustrations. He didn't need the bishop to feel he was on the defensive, given that he was about to ask his more critical questions.

"What did you think when you first heard about the fire?"

The bishop's hands stretched out as if he was holding a large ball. "As I said, the alcohol issue was a total surprise to me. I immediately consulted Father Robert's file and made a few phone calls. Did I find something incriminating, something I should have been warned about before?" He held up a single finger. "One issue, just one, and that was back in Father Robert's seminary days. He was arrested for disorderly conduct with alcohol apparently in the mix. But when a priest? No, nothing. And we both know what a demon alcohol can become for priests. And when you add to that the difficulty those like Father Robert with native heritage have in metabolizing alcohol, he must have known the danger it posed."

Nick would have liked to learn more about the seminary lapse, but said instead, "You suggested that matters with Father Robert seemed worse over the past year. Was there anything that he was dealing with in the days before the fire that you now recognize might have upset him?"

The bishop didn't respond for a moment, leaving Nick to wonder if he knew nothing or knew of something he didn't want to share. Leaning forward and lowering his voice, he said, "Confidentially, I was going to ask him to step down from the directorship of the orphanage. But I'd said nothing to anyone yet about that, so I don't see how he would have known that. You see, Father Robert wasn't the type to read the handwriting on the wall." Shaking his head, he said, "I think it more likely that Father Robert would have demanded that I step down. Can you imagine? Totally unreasonable, when he wanted to be, and in the last year that was how Father Robert chose to be."

Nick let that storm cloud pass before saying, "I have just one more question."

"Good, because my schedule is a bit tight," the bishop replied quickly.

"And I appreciate your willingness to meet with me, Your Eminence. Several of those I interviewed in Yellowknife remember Father Robert complaining about the orphanage's heating system being outdated, needing replacement. Given that the fire investigator identified the source of the fire in the heating . . ."

Nick noticed the slight change in the bishop's demeanor as he sat back in his chair and looked out the lobby's front window. "Rumors are very dangerous, Father Fortis, as I'm sure you know. After tragedies, people think they remember hearing things—warnings such as you're describing—when in fact what they are describing is what they wished had been the case. Now, on the issue of the heating plant, the fire investigator noted that the heating system had been regularly inspected. The investigator who dealt with the fire was the same investigator who'd conducted the last inspections and given the system his approval, so he would know. Well, if that's all?"

Nick decided to blow right through the bishop's red light. "So Father Robert hadn't made a complaint to the board of directors about the heating system?"

Bishop Bruno started to take another sip of his coffee, then set the cup down. "What I'm saying is that the heating system had passed the routine inspections, all of them. The people you interviewed in Yellowknife are probably remembering that Father Robert was complaining about one issue after another over the last several years." Rising to his feet, the bishop said, "Now I must be going. I trust I'll be informed about what you and your detective friend uncover about Father Robert's death."

Nick shook the bishop's hand. "Thank you for your time, Your Eminence." He watched as the man walked briskly toward the elevators, aware that the bishop had as much as admitted that Father Robert had complained about the heating system. But the bishop had made another slip. The official who investigated the fire had earlier inspected the system and approved it. Was his official report, one that assigned no fault to the orphanage and its directors, the truth or what was politically expedient?

CHAPTER NINE

Rome—Fumicino Airport

As Nick's flight from Toronto to Rome circled Fumicino Airport, he remembered something from two years before, when it wasn't Worthy waiting to pick him up but, instead, him picking up Worthy. So much had happened in those two years, much of it in Worthy's life. In just a few weeks, Nick would participate in Worthy's and Lena's wedding. And now Worthy had retired and would be dividing his time between cases in the States and Rome.

Nick recognized that his own life had also changed over those same two years. Thanks to a meeting Worthy had with the abbot of Nick's monastery, Nick no longer faced the threat of being grounded permanently at the monastery. A second significant change occurred on a case in Michigan and Canada the year before, when Worthy and he had disagreed sharply. Nick gave credit to the mercy of God that their relationship had survived and, if anything, had grown stronger by the ordeal.

After retrieving his luggage and passing through customs, Nick was happy to see both Worthy and Lena waiting in the arrival area. Seeing the happiness on their faces, he teared up and gave each a restrained hug—his usual hug often overpowering those on the receiving end.

"Anyone seeing the two of you could tell that you're about to be married."

"Is it that obvious, Nick?" Lena asked.

Nick patted his chest over his heart. "It's obvious in here."

"Not fair, Nick. You aren't allowed to make me cry. Plenty of time for that later," she added.

"Good tears, all good tears, Lena," he said as the three proceeded to the airport's exit. "Where should we go first?"

"I know your time is all off with jet lag, but my guess is that you're hungry," Worthy said.

"Hmm, let me think," Nick replied with a laugh. "I actually slept a bit on the plane and missed the meal service, so yes, I can be persuaded to eat something deliciously Italian. I am your willing prisoner."

"Where should we go, Lena?" Worthy asked.

"I know a good ristorante down on the beach. My grandparents took me there every Christmas season. Where we are right now is only about two miles from there."

Lena opened the car and took the driver's seat of the car, normal size by Italian standards, but small by American.

"You take the passenger seat, Nick," Worthy offered. "I'll scrunch down in the back seat, what there is of it."

"As I said, it's only two miles to the ristorante. On the way back to Rome, you two spoiled and oversized Americans can fight over who sits where. But let's agree that there'll be no talking about the case until we're back at the apartment."

Turning to see Worthy with his knees up near his chest, Nick laughed. "Sorry my friend. But yes, Lena, I promise, though I remember we made the same promise two years ago, and, if I'm not mistaken, we broke that promise within five minutes."

"Then we'll just have to do better this time," Lena said with a smile.

And they did do better, the case not coming up in conversation until they were in the car on the way back to Rome. And then it was Lena who broke the promise by glancing in the rear-view mirror to where Nick had traded places with Worthy. "I told the abbot at the monastery that you wouldn't be arriving until tomorrow, so I hope you're okay staying in my spare bedroom tonight. That will give us time to catch each other up and for you both to discuss where things stand on the case."

"That's more than all right with me, Lena, although I'm curious as to how the monks are dealing with Father Robert's death." Turning his head around, he said, "Christopher, I remember from your email that you've met with the abbot, but remind me who else you've talked with."

"I've spoken with Brother Damian, Robert's confessor, and Brother Silas, one of the monks on the ethics committee. I wouldn't say that they withheld anything, but I'm an ex-cop and you're a fellow monk. You might ask different questions, or they might share more with you."

Back at Lena's apartment, they sat together over cups of tea in the living room with the view of the Pantheon's dome out her front windows. Not feeling tired, Nick shared what he learned in Yellowknife from Father Jacob, the interviews with the Sabois, Bessie Free Woman, and the liquor store owner, McCafferty. At the end, he summed up by saying, "I left with three consistent impressions. One, despite the fire, Father Robert is remembered with affection and pity by most in Yellowknife. Two, something was bothering Father Robert on the day before the fire, something that might have led to his drinking himself into oblivion that last night. And three, as I emailed to you, more than one person in Yellowknife recalls Father Robert—Father Bob to them—telling them that he'd complained about the heating system before the fire."

After a moment of silence, Lena asked, "They remember him saying that or only wish he'd said that?"

"That's the same question, Lena, that came up in my interview with the bishop in Toronto. He's a slippery one, and he's also the chair of the orphanage's board of directors. When I asked if Father Robert ever made such a complaint, he replied that people are confusing what Father Robert had said with what they wanted to believe he said. He also told me more than once that the heating plant had passed inspection. But here's what he told me that I bet he regrets. The inspector of the orphanage's heating system is the same person who investigated the fire and declared it was an unforeseeable accident. That makes me wonder how friendly the bishop and the fire investigator are."

"Not to mention a conflict of interest," Worthy said. "How about how friendly the bishop and Father Robert were?"

"It was clear that Father Robert made the bishop's life difficult. He's the type of bishop who wants his priests to obey him as if he is always the 'vox Christi,' the voice of Christ. The problem was that Father Robert put the orphanage and the children ahead of that kind of obedience. Father Robert being dead—murdered—didn't seem to mellow the bishop much."

"If anything, it sounds like Father Robert's death solves a problem for the bishop," Worthy mused.

Lena scratched her head. "If Father Robert did warn the board about the heating system, why didn't he say something after the fire?"

"I asked the monk heading up Father Robert's review that same question," Worthy said. "The only explanation he could give was that

Father Robert's had one goal—to get back as soon as possible to the orphanage. Clearing himself didn't even seem on his radar. Lena, you're the psychologist. Does his behavior make sense?"

Lena sat forward on the couch. "It might. It depends on how guilty he felt about being drunk the night of the fire. He might have believed that he deserved to take the fall for it."

Worthy nodded. "Which would explain something he said in the ethics committee—that if he couldn't go back to the orphanage as a priest, he'd go back as anything else, even a janitor. Nick, doesn't that sound a lot like . . . I was going to say 'self-flagellation,' but maybe I mean penance?"

Nick sighed. "I don't have a clear enough sense of Father Robert yet to say. It could be a desire for penance, in which case he was silent for his own reasons. But he was a priest, and until the night of the fire, most of those I talked with in Yellowknife described him as a good priest. His desire to return to Yellowknife as soon as possible might not be about him at all, but about the orphanage and the families of the boys. Maybe I'm saying that because that's what I want to believe."

Rome—Order of the Sacred Wounds Monastery

Nick knew that every monastery was similar, but the differences were what interested him. The aspiration of every monastic community is to produce monks or nuns who mirror something of the founder, who was often a saint, or, if not the founder, then a saint who came later in the order's history. Even as saints were different, so communities that formed around those saints took on the characters of its shining examples. In the case of the Order of the Sacred Wounds, that shining example was Abbot Boniface Clement, leader of the order from 1975 to 1998, and the subject of Lena's research.

Now, at breakfast in Lena's apartment, Nick had the chance to ask Lena what she'd gleaned so far about Father Boniface and the order.

"To be honest, I'm frustrated. Abbot Boniface asked that his diaries be sealed for twenty-five years. When that date approached a month ago, the order hired me to analyze his writings for evidence of mystical experiences. Even before the diaries were unsealed, Father Boniface was considered a 'servant of God,' which is the first rank leading to sainthood. You can imagine my excitement when they trusted me with the diaries, unsealed. But all I've found so far are reflections on the struggles he fought against a rival order."

"Ah, so more political than mystical. But tell me about the conflict."

"It's one of those issues that goes back centuries. The Order of the Sacred Wounds arose when its parent order, the French Order of the Stigmata, was outlawed during the French Revolution. For seventy years, the Order of the Sacred Wounds flourished in North America, specifically in Canada. But then the older order was resurrected."

"Ah, I think I understand. The Canadian order had something the old order wanted. Am I right in guessing that something was money?" Nick asked.

"Yes, that's exactly what it was. So from 1900 to 1974, the tension between the two orders rose and fell. It didn't help that both orders have their motherhouses here in Rome."

"What happened in 1974?"

"That was when the French order installed a new abbot, Jean-Philippe. His first act was to make a formal application to the Vatican to dissolve the Order of the Sacred Wounds and take over all its assets."

Nick thought for a moment about the dates. "You said this formal step was taken in 1974 and Abbot Boniface became the abbot of the Canadian order a year later. Not a coincidence, I take it?"

"The Canadian abbot died of a heart attack, no doubt caused by the assault on the order, and then Father Boniface Clement became abbot. His diaries offer a blow by blow of the political fight between the two orders. Instead of the diaries offering me insights into Father Boniface's interior life, they have me slogging through what you said a minute ago—politics."

Father Fortis leaned across the table for another biscuit. "Do you mind if I offer a differ perspective on the diaries?"

"No, not at all, Nick."

Fingering his pectoral cross, Nick said, "It's something I think of when I see a pearl. A beautiful pearl is only formed after a grain of sand, of grit, finds its way into an oyster's shell. If an oyster has feelings, I bet the oyster finds the piece of grit irritating. But there's no pearl without the grit. That could be the case for Abbot Boniface as I think it was for Father Robert."

"Father Robert?"

"Yes. From what I know so far, whatever good Father Robert accomplished as a priest and director at the orphanage owes a lot to the setbacks and frustrations he felt in his life, including the frustration he felt toward the end with his bishop." He paused before asking, "Do you remember Christopher talking about Lieutenant Sherrod in Detroit?"

"Yes, he called Sherrod his nemesis."

"Nemesis and grit, the same thing. Lena, we both admire Christopher's patient approach to cases, the time he spends trying to understand the victim. But isn't Christopher the way he is, at least to some extent, because Sherrod never lost an opportunity to criticize his approach?"

Lena said nothing, but then nodded. "Father Jean-Philippe was Abbot Boniface's nemesis, right? Instead of racing through the diaries to find evidence of Abbot Boniface somehow becoming a pearl, a saint, I need to pay attention to all the political fighting Abbot Boniface had to deal with."

Nick smiled. "There is no pearl without the grit." His smile disappeared as he slapped his hand down on the table.

"What is it?" Lena asked.

"Something I should have thought about before. When I was in Yellowknife, I never asked if Father Robert left any writings. I'm not saying he left a diary. Father Jacob in Yellowknife would have let me know that if he had. But maybe there are letters, even notes scribbled somewhere, that will give Father Robert another chance to speak to us."

CHAPTER TEN

Rome—Order of the Sacred Wounds

Nick was welcomed to the monastery by the Guestmaster, a monk in his sixties who'd kept the tonsure of the more traditional monasteries.

"I understand you've been in Rome before, Father," Brother Callistus said as he carried Nick's suitcase to his room in the guesthouse.

"Yes, twice. Most recently two years ago."

"That was when you helped on the assassination attempts against the pope and the ecumenical patriarch, wasn't it?"

"Yes, that was the case."

Brother Callistus made the sign of the cross. "Mysterious are the ways of God, don't you agree, Father? What the assassin meant for evil, God used to bring the His Eminence and the Holy Father closer together."

"So true, so true," Nick managed to reply as he tried to keep up with the monk who, despite being older than him, seemed to be flying up the stairs to the third floor of the guesthouse. Finally, he was able to catch his breath and renew his vow to exercise when Brother Callistus opened a door to a room with a bed, a desk, and an adjoining bathroom.

"I hope you will be comfortable here," Brother Callistus said, but before leaving, he added, "I'm sure you already know this, but the death of Father Robert is a dark cloud over the community. We pray that you can help the police lift that cloud."

"Thank you for your prayers," Nick said as he put his briefcase and toiletry bag on the desk. "And you're right about the cloud. The passing of a fellow monk should be a solemn but joyous moment for the community, a time when we commend him to Our Lord and Our Lady."

Brother Callistus stood in the open doorway, his head bowed, "I'll leave you to unpack, Father. There is a schedule of services and meals on the desk. I will look for you in the refectory for supper tonight."

"That's very kind. Before you go, I have a question. I was told that Father Robert stayed here in the guesthouse, but did anyone notice him leaving late at night?"

"No. Perhaps we made a mistake, but we didn't treat Father Robert as a prisoner. He must have left when the house was asleep and returned before morning prayers. If there's nothing else . . . oh, wait, I almost forgot. You'll find a copy of Father Robert's personnel file in the desk drawer."

"Thank you. I look forward to interviewing community members who knew Father Robert while he was here."

Brother Callistus gave Nick a searching look, and Nick wondered if the monk understood that everyone in the community had to be viewed as suspects in Father Robert's death.

Alone in the room, Nick opened the personnel file and sat at the desk to look over its contents. The first entry was a personal statement, written by Father Robert when he applied to enter the order nearly twenty-five years before. Nick made the sign of the cross over the document as he realized that this was the first time he'd be reading Father Robert's own words.

"I was raised in a Catholic home by a loving mother. My father was abusive toward my mother and me. When she died, my father left me—I was thirteen—at the orphanage of St. John Bosco in Kamloops, British Columbia. The orphanage saved me from life on the streets. When I was there, the chaplain, Father Roch, encouraged me to pray to discern if I had a religious vocation. From that moment on, I have always wanted to be a priest.

"Father Roch was a member of the Order of the Sacred Wounds and suggested I consider his order. After reading the order's history, I felt that Christ was calling me to join the order."

Nick could understand how Father Robert being an orphan himself had influenced his desire to work with other orphans in Yellowknife. And Nick could also understand that if Father Robert would be barred from returning to Safe Haven Orphanage, he'd be leaving behind the only home he'd known.

Looking up from the file, Nick's gaze rested on the crucifix hanging above the desk. As he expected, given the name of the order, the wounds on Christ's body were painted in vivid red color. It made sense to him that a thirteen-year-old boy, a boy abused by his father and dropped off like a load of trash at an orphanage, should see in the image a mirror of his own scars.

Rome—Police Station

After a lunch break, Worthy sat with Capitano Sesto and the police's IT expert as she brought Father Robert's image up from the second of his three visits to the piazza, the night when Father Robert's expression changed dramatically. The first night, Father Robert had dawdled like other tourists, pausing to look at what was featured in the shop windows. On the second night, however, Father Robert's looked determined, his focus straight ahead as he hurried toward the piazza. Again, Worthy had the sense that Father Robert was on a mission.

He murmured to the screen, "We'll know why you died when we find out your mission."

"Scusi, sorry, what did you say?" the technician asked.

"I was just thinking out loud," Worthy said, "but I do have a question. We know the teenagers followed Father Robert out of the Metro exit on his second visit to the piazza. Can we tell from face recognition if they followed him on the other nights?"

It took less than ten minutes for the technician to scan the teenagers' faces and determine that the three had also followed Father Robert out of the tunnel on the first night, but not the third.

"That is no coincidence," Sesto observed.

Studying the images of the teenagers, Worthy said, "Maybe they were stalking him on the first two nights, but for some reason not the night Father Robert was killed." After a pause, he added, "How about this? What if these teenagers were waiting for him in the piazza on that last night. If that's what happened, we can't rule out the possibility that we're looking at Father Robert's killers."

The technician interrupted them and directed their attention to an attachment now visible on the computer screen. Sesto bent down and read the Italian notice below the drawing. "One of the teenagers matches a composite drawing in our system. That teenager, according to one of our informants, could be Bordy Vladic, pronounced Vladich."

"He's a petty thief?"

"Yes, a thirteen-year-old pickpocket. If this is Vladic, the other two are likely accomplices."

"So they're part of a gang?"

Sesto nodded. "A Bosnian gang."

"How do we go about finding him?" Worthy asked.

Sesto shook his head. "Bosnians are nomads. They are everywhere; they are nowhere."

"Even with face recognition?"

"We can try," the technician said. "But Rome is a big city, so searching could take a while."

Sesto grunted. "I have a question. Would a pickpocket stab a priest? If yes, Vladic is probably gone, not in the city now. He might be out of Italy."

Worthy looked at the drawing of the boy and then back at the CCTV photo. The boy was supposedly thirteen, but his face could be that of someone ten years older.

"Maybe Vladic and his buddies only robbed Father Robert," Worthy said. "But they might still have seen his killer."

"Si, si. If this is true, Vladic maybe still in city, maybe still around piazza."

Worthy agreed that it was unlikely that a petty thief would have advanced to murder, but the other possibility worried him. "Let's say the boys did see who killed Father Robert. If the killer realized that he was watched, he won't feel safe until he eliminates the boys. We need to find them before he does."

CHAPTER ELEVEN

Rome—Library of the Order of the Sacred Wounds

In the monastery's library, Nick found an older monk sitting behind a reception desk, quietly snoozing.

"Pardon me, but I'm hoping you can answer a question," he said in a quiet voice.

The monk awoke with a start and immediately apologized. "They put me here because I keep nodding off," he said. "You must be our Orthodox guest."

"That's right. I'm Father Nick, or Nick if you'd prefer."

The elderly monk stood and offered his hand, which felt like twigs inside a soft covering. "I'm Father Zacharias, but most call me Zeke. How can I help you, Nick?"

"I'm sure you've met Dr. Fabriano, who's researching Abbot Boniface."

Father Zeke nodded. "Yes, yes, a pleasant woman and, from everything I've heard, a gifted scholar."

"She is certainly that. Dr. Fabriano is the one who told me that Father Robert spent hours here in the library in the days before he died. She saw him on one of the computers and thought he was conducting research of his own. I'm wondering if you knew what he was researching, maybe what books or resources he was interested in."

The sleepy librarian shook his head. "We're an in-house library, not a lending one. Father Robert didn't check out any of the books because that's not how we operate. He could use our resources, of course, but only here in the library or in his room."

Nick thought for a moment. "Would there be a record of the sites that Father Roberts visited online?"

"Oh, I don't have the computer skills to answer that. We use an outside

IT service, and I'm not sure even they could find that out. You see, everyone here uses the same password."

"Just one more question, Father. When was the first time you saw Father Robert in the library?"

Father Zeke paused for a moment. "I didn't see him in the library until the two or three days before he died. Then he was here each day for at least three hours."

Nick paused, considering this new fact. In the days before he was stabbed in Piazza del Popolo, Father Robert spent time in the library, apparently researching something. *Is that just a coincidence, or are his research and death somehow connected?* he thought.

Rome—Trastevere

Worthy drove Lena's car from the police department to the monastery to pick up both Lena and Nick before heading to Trastevere, Lena's favorite neighborhood for dining. He'd only been driving in Rome for two weeks, but had already discovered the secret of surviving—stay in your lane, ignore the car horns, and expect mopeds to swerve in front of you. Even so, the journey from the monastery to Trastevere, a matter of less than two miles, and then finding a parking place, took nearly thirty minutes.

When they were seated in the restaurant, Nick said, "This reminds me of eating out together two years ago."

"Except for the Christmas decorations and the weather," Lena added, with a shiver. "Rome seems to have two seasons—scorching summers and cold damp winters."

"The two cases, this one and the one two years ago, couldn't be any more different," Nick said. "Two years ago, it was the pope and ecumenical patriarch whose lives were in danger."

"And then," Lena added, "the media were all over that case, while the stabbing death of a disgraced monk from Canada hasn't merited much attention after the first report."

"There's another difference," Worthy said. "Two years ago, we worried that the assassin would strike again," Worthy said. "So far on this case, Father Robert's death looks like an isolated murder."

"What have you learned from the police, Chris?" Lena asked.

After the waiter took their orders, Worthy shared what they gleaned from face-recognition technology. Father Robert had definitely gone to Piazza del Popolo on the three nights before his death, but he'd been followed by the teenagers on only the first two nights.

"The good news is that we might know the name of one of the boys, Bordy Vladic," he said. "He's known by the police as a Bosnian involved in petty thief—purse snatching and pickpocketing in places like the piazza."

Nick leaned forward and spoke in a lowered voice. "Do the police really think teenage pickpockets killed Father Robert?"

"No, but the boys might have seen the killer."

"Wouldn't that put them in danger?" Lena asked.

Nodding, Worthy said, "Another reason why we need to find them."

"If the boys are Bosnians, they won't be easy to find," Lena said.

"Capitano Sesto says the same thing. Apparently the Bosnian gangs roam around the city, targeting the places where tourists tend to congregate."

"I remembering seeing gangs of kids two years ago. I don't know if there were Bosnian, but maybe so," Nick said.

"The Bosnians pose a moral dilemma for many Italians," Lena said. "It's not as easy of sending them back to where they came from. Life in Bosnia hasn't recovered from the war back in the nineties. But if we let Bosnian kids stay in Italy, they have no choice but to survive by their wits on the streets. Unfortunately, that usually begins with petty crime, but it doesn't necessarily stop there."

Nick started to say something, but then stopped as the waiter came with their first courses. When he left, Lena said, "Go ahead, Nick."

Nick shook his head. "It can wait until after we eat," he said. "Would either of you mind if I offer grace?"

"Of course not, Nick. And then let's not discuss the case until after dessert," Worthy said.

They kept to their promise and talked about the upcoming wedding during the meal. It was only after they had coffee and biscotti that Lena asked, "Nick, do you remember what you were going to say?"

"Unfortunately, I do, Lena. You were saying that Bosnian teenagers in the city might be involved in something more than petty crime. I'm wondering if you meant that the kids are trafficked."

Lena shuddered. "I've read reports that suggest that. Imagine being ten or eleven years old, managing to sneak into Italy, but then to be sexually exploited." After a pause, she looked from Nick to Worthy and back. "And we're sure Father Robert wasn't involved in any of that?"

Worthy nodded. "Given the revelations about what went on at Indian schools in Canada, I wasn't surprised that Capitano Sesto said they looked into that first. What he found matched what you found, Nick, in your interviews in Canada."

"And Father Robert's bishop denied it as well, and he had no great love for Father Robert. What do you say, shall we put that aside and focus on what we do know?" Nick suggested.

"Fine with me," Worthy said. "Why don't you start, Nick?"

"I did find out something from one of the monks, something that might connect with what you discovered, Christopher." Nick summarized what Brother Zeke had told him, that Father Robert hadn't used the library until two or three days before he died, but then he'd spent as much as three hours each day researching something.

"So you see, what you found out from the police, Christopher, and what the librarian told me match up in terms of timing," Nick said. "The same days when Father Robert was working on something in the library ended with him going at night to the piazza."

"What about his mood on those days?" Lena asked.

"One of the monks on the ethics committee said Father Robert did seem different at the end. When he was first there, he seemed numb, but in those last days, he was focused, like he had a new mission. Maybe what I'm saying is that he was thinking about the future, not the past."

Worthy put down his coffee. "Something in the future, something that brought him to the piazza. And it drew the attention of the Bosnian kids, at least on the first two nights. Wouldn't we like to know what they made of Father Robert?"

"I assumed they took him for another tourist, someone that they could steal from," Nick said. "Except it was after one in the morning," Lena said. "That's late for the tourist crowd."

"Well, Capitano Sesto said they only found some change on him. That could mean he was robbed, or it could mean he just wasn't carrying much money."

"Let's assume he was robbed. Why didn't he offer some resistance?" Nick asked.

"Hmm, I wonder if he decided not to when he saw that they were just kids. Maybe they reminded him of his orphans back in Canada. Maybe he even handed his money over to them."

"Finally, something that makes some sense, Lena," Nick said. "He'd have had a soft spot for the Bosnian kids. But I can't see how it helps us understand why he was killed."

They didn't say anything more about the case until they were driving back in Lena's car.

"I think we know what we have to do next," Worthy said. "Nick, I'm hoping you can interview other monks at the monastery who interacted with Father Robert. Lena, given that you're better known at the motherhouse than Nick, maybe you should interview any of the outside staff. It's possible they might have gotten to know Father Robert. That leaves me to work with the police to find Bordy Vladic."

CHAPTER TWELVE

Rome—Order of the Sacred Wounds—Cloister

The next morning, Lena took a break from her research to find Rosaria, the more energetic of the two-person cleaning and gardening crew at the monastery. Lena had run into Rosaria several times before and knew, from their brief conversations, that Rosaria had worked at the motherhouse for more than fifteen years. Equally important to Lena was that Rosaria, as a woman in an all-male community, would have a different and potentially valuable perspective.

As Lena entered the cloister, Rosario was bending over the hedges and flowering plants that encircled the fountain. Easily in her sixties, Rosario was still strong enough to attack the ground with a trowel as if it were an enemy.

Lena sat down on a nearby bench. "Morning, Rosaria. I hope you don't mind me resting a bit here while you work."

Rosaria turned her head and smiled at Lena. "Just so long as you don't mind hearing some not-so-holy language, Senora."

"I'll pretend you're praying, Rosaria."

"Which is what I should be doing instead of swearing. I should ask the abbot sometime why God allowed weeds and these pesty . . . well, pests. Look at this," she said, handing Lena the discarded shell of a grub.

"Good heavens, what is it?"

"The shell of something that doesn't belong in Italy, but now that they're here, they're almost impossible to get rid of. I'm hoping to find the nest, and when I do, they'll wish they'd picked on someone else."

Lena didn't say anything while Rosaria continued to dig into the soil with a trowel. Finally, Rosaria stopped, leaned back, and then poured a white powder in the hole.

"I just realized, Rosaria, that you and I are the only women in the motherhouse," Lena said.

Rising from the ground, Rosaria stretched before sitting next to Lena on the bench. "I think they should call it a 'fatherhouse,' not motherhouse."

Lena laughed as she opened her bag and brought out a thermos and two plastic cups. "Would you like some tea?"

"I won't say no if you have enough."

They sat in silence as they sipped their tea. "It must be lonely for you sometimes," Lena said.

"It was at the beginning, but after I leave work, I go home to my grandchildren. So I enjoy my eight hours of peace here. And some of the monks are dears. The younger ones call me 'nonna,' grandmother, and I don't mind."

"I'm sure not much gets past you, Rosaria."

Rosaria laughed. "Oh, I don't say much, but I do see a lot."

Lena paused for a moment before saying, "I guess everyone now knows why Father Robert was here. Did you get to know him?"

Nodding, Rosaria said, "Si, si. Roberto would walk around this cloister, head down, sometimes for hours. It was like something or someone was chasing him. Finally, I couldn't stand it anymore. I asked him to help me with something—moving the wheelbarrow or digging out a particularly stubborn root. I don't think he'd noticed me until that moment."

"And did he help?"

"Oh, yes. After a few days, he even volunteered. I didn't intrude; I just let him talk about whatever was on his mind. Most of the time, he talked about Canada and how much he missed the children."

"He could speak Italian?"

Rosaria brushed dirt off the knees of her work pants. "Poco, a little, but after working all these years with these monks, I know enough English so the two of us could communicate."

Lena took a sip of her tea and waited, hoping that Rosaria, who worked in a community that favored silence, would relish the opportunity to chat.

As Lena had hoped, Rosaria didn't seem in a hurry to get back to the gardening. She sat back on the bench and said, "Toward the end, Padre Roberto asked me how to say certain things in Italian, and not the typical things."

Lena did her best not to seem overly interested. "Oh?"

"Si, I think he was trying to write a note or a letter to someone."

"Someone here in Rome?"

Rosaria raised both hands, the Roman equivalent of a shrug. "Someone in Italy, at least, maybe Rome. He asked me how to spell In Italian 'I'm not what you think.' And there was something else . . . what was it? Oh, yes, I remember. He asked how to spell 'Let me help you.'"

Rome—Order of the Sacred Wounds Monastery

From the abbot's list of monks, Nick knew that Brother Ethelbert was a second monk on the ethics committee investigating Father Robert. An exchange of notes had led to Nick going to the monk's room that morning.

Knocking at the door, Nick heard a shaky voice say, "Come in." He entered the room having a bed, a prie deux, and a monk in dark sunglasses sitting behind the desk with a white cane in his hand.

"You'll excuse my not answering the door in person, but as you can see, I'm blind," Father Ethelbert explained. "I've memorized every inch of my room, of course, but it still takes me a bit to make my way. Please have a seat. It's Father Fortis, isn't it?"

"Please call me Nick."

"Ah, nothing I like more than a monk who doesn't stand on ceremony. I'm Bert." With a smile on his face, he asked, "How do you like the view from my window, Nick?"

Nick glanced out the window at a sprawling orchard before he realized Bert was playing a joke on him.

"You might think a blind monk can't enjoy the scenery," Bert said, "but when spring comes, I smell the flowering apple trees before anyone else. Please sit, so we can talk about that poor soul—Father Robert."

Nick took Brother Bert's comment as a sign he was eager to talk.

"I appreciate your offer, Bert. Father Robert is a bit of a puzzle. I'm hoping you can answer a few questions."

"Of course. I should say that there's a third member of the ethics committee, Brother Onesimus. He might give you a different angle on Father Robert. He would have seen the expressions on his face, although I believe that I can feel a person's expression. You, for example, have an open face, one that isn't afraid to look at another person square on."

"I can say the same about you, Bert. The only lines I see on your face are smile lines."

"Ah, they give me away. People sometimes don't believe a blind person can have a blessed life. But it is true. There are worse forms of blindness than physical. Now, back to Father Robert."

"Again, thank you, Bert. How often did Father Robert meet with the committee?"

"After he got settled in, we met nearly every day."

"Others have told me that there was something on Father Robert's mind or heart in his last days. Did you sense that he was troubled about something?"

"Troubled? No, he was excited. I remember our last meeting when he said God wasn't through with him yet. What surprised me was the way he said it. I asked him what he meant, but he said he'd tell me in a day or two. Unfortunately, that night he was killed."

Nick had heard that Father Robert seemed to be on a mission. Now he added "excitement" to what they knew. "Bert, do you think Father Robert was thinking about something here in Rome or something back in Canada?"

Bert drummed his fingers on the desk. "I suppose it could be both." After a pause, he added, "It was as if he'd received good news or had resolved some problem."

Resolving some problem, Nick thought. *But which one?* He returned to a question he'd asked Brother Silas, the other member of the ethics committee. "Bert, after the fire at the orphanage, some of the families in Yellowknife said that Father Robert had warned the directors of the orphanage about the heating system. Did he ever mention that to the committee or to you privately?"

Brother Bert turned his head from side to side, as if he was trying to hear the question from more than one angle. "Why did you keep that to yourself?" he said in little more than a whisper.

"Pardon?" Nick asked.

"I'm sorry, Nick. I was asking Father Robert why he hadn't shared that. It would have had a profound effect on our committee's decision."

"We don't know for sure if he did, in fact, warn the orphanage authorities."

"Yes, yes, but I'm not sure why I say this, but I feel it is the truth. Was his silence about that because he wanted to be punished? Very strange."

"As I said, Bert, Father Robert remains a puzzle. There's one more puzzle piece that I don't understand. It's about Father Robert drinking heavily the night of the fire. From everyone I've talked to back in Canada, that was totally out of character. Did Father Robert talk about that with the committee?"

Father Bert said nothing for a moment, then sighed. "Nick, you should know that I'm a recovered alcoholic. A lot of people assume someone who's blind wouldn't have that kind of problem, but that just shows how little they know about blindness. Put me in a room where there's a glass of wine and I'll sniff it out in seconds. I can tell you if it's white wine, red, or somewhere in between before you even see the glass. I tell you that because I asked Robert if we shared the same addiction." Again, Father Bert paused. "He said he drank too much once when he was younger, and it had gotten him in trouble. I think he said he stopped drinking after that episode. That was long before the tragedy in Canada."

"So he didn't explain what brought on that sudden change the night of the fire?" Nick asked.

"No, he didn't, and because we met with him daily, I can guarantee that he wasn't drinking here. There aren't enough mints or mouthwashes in the world that would fool my nose."

As Nick walked back to his room in the guesthouse, he considered what he'd learned. So much about Father Robert remained a mystery, but several things were coming into focus. Something had troubled Father Robert on the day of the fire, troubled him so much that he'd drunk himself into a stupor. When he first arrived at the motherhouse in Rome, he'd was obsessed with returning to Yellowknife, if not as director of the orphanage, then in some other capacity. Then, three days before his murder, his demeanor changed. He was excited about something, and whatever it was had brought him to Piazza del Popolo not once, but three times.

Nick flirted with the idea that Father Robert was bi-polar. That would explain such abrupt changes in both Yellowknife and Rome, but there was no record of mental illness in Father Robert's personnel file. The only explanation that Nick could think of was that something or someone had not once, but twice disturbed his equilibrium and forced him to act out of character. The question was, what had been those triggers?

CHAPTER THIRTEEN

Rome—Order of the Sacred Wounds Monastery

Father Onesimus answered the knock on his door, opened it, and immediately stepped back. "Father Fortis, is it?" he asked.

"Please call me Nick, or Father Nick, if you're more comfortable."

Taking a step back had been Father Onesimus' unconscious reaction to his visitor's height, girth, and long beard. As the Orthodox monk maneuvered past him to sit in one of the room's two chairs, Father Onesimus imagined he'd just let a grizzly bear into his room.

Gazing around the room, his visitor said, "You have a beautiful room. Not just the view of the city, but also those icons."

Onesimus took a moment to survey his room, wondering how long it had been since he really noticed it. "I've lived here for the past seventeen years, so, I suppose, I take it for granted."

Nodding, his visitor said, "A friend of mine in Rome says the same thing about the city. That's very hard to believe for someone who lives in rural Ohio." After pausing, he added, "I appreciate you seeing me. I'm trying to gain some sense of Father Robert when he was here in the monastery, and so speaking with members of the ethics committee seemed a good place to start. I would appreciate any insights you can provide into his state of mind."

Father Onesimus gazed out the window, wondering how much to share with his visitor. Finally he said, "I'm quite certain I was put on the committee because Father Robert and I are both indigenous. We're from different tribal communities, but both from western Canada. I'm sure the thought was that I'd have an easier time understanding him, but, oddly, I felt a gulf between us almost immediately."

Father Onesimus' visitor nodded but didn't say anything.

Clearing his throat, Father Onesimus said, "If Father Robert were alive, he might blame me for that gulf, but in all of his meetings with the committee, I sensed he was avoiding something."

"Avoiding telling you something or avoiding facing something himself?"

"Ah, well, that's an important distinction, isn't it?" Father Onesimus asked, feeling again the frustration he'd experienced with Father Robert. "I was candid with him toward the end and encouraged him to take the opportunity that our committee was giving him to share whatever he was holding back."

"Did you think it was more than the fire at the orphanage?"

"I did, but my candor seemed to backfire. He withdrew further."

"Could I ask what the committee's final decision would have been?"

Even though Brother Onesimus had anticipated the question, he still found it difficult to answer it. "First of all, I can't speak for the other members of the committee. You see, we don't discuss recommendations with one another until the investigation is closed. The second thing is that there isn't anything worse for a priest than to be defrocked. Perhaps you would agree that being defrocked is worse than death."

"I do agree, but do you think Father Robert felt that way?"

"I was never sure. The only time he seemed open with us was when he said—and he told us this more than once—that he needed to return to the orphanage. I don't know if he believed this, but he said it didn't matter what capacity he might be in, just so long as he could go back to Yellowknife. "I guess . . . I guess what I'm saying, Father, is he didn't present a very strong argument for remaining a priest."

Guesthouse, Order of the Sacred Wounds Monastery

Back in his room in the guesthouse and feeling a wave of jetlag, Nick lay down in the bed and starred at the ceiling. What Father Onesimus had said about Father Robert leaving something unspoken seemed to be on the mark. And Nick couldn't help but think that whatever Father Robert was hiding was the reason he turned to alcohol the fateful night of the fire.

Nick closed his eyes and remembered Worthy's dictum about

investigations, that it is always tempting to believe that the breakthrough on a case will come with the next clue or the next witness statement. Worthy had told him that breakthroughs in tough cases often came when the investigator looked at something already in his possession from a different angle.

Picturing those whom he'd interviewed both in Yellowknife and in Rome, Nick wasn't surprised that the first face that came to mind was Bishop Bruno's. Clearly, the bishop hadn't shared all he knew about Father Robert, the orphanage, and the fire. But Nick was surprised when that face faded and another replaced it. It was the face of the first person he'd interviewed on the case—Father Jacob. His logical mind told him to dismiss the image, for hadn't Father Jacob been completely open with him, hadn't he agreed immediately to assist with interviews in Yellowknife, and didn't he clearly want Father Robert's murder to be solved?

Then, the truth struck Nick. The young priest hadn't hidden anything about Father Robert, but neither had Nick remembered another piece of Christopher Worthy wisdom—witnesses know less than they think they know but also more than they remember. Even as he'd failed to ask Jacob if Father Robert left any writings, Nick had missed the opportunity to ask the young priest questions that might have helped him remember seemingly unimportant clues about Father Robert.

As Nick acknowledged his mistake, the face of Father Jacob seemed to come alive. He heard the young priest ask, *Why don't you ask me those questions now?*

Rome—Worthy's Office

In his new office on Via Santa Caterina da Siena, Worthy greeted Capitano Stefano Sesto. Not counting Lena, Sesto was the first person to enter his office. Even Nick had yet to see it.

Looking around at the bare walls, Sesto said, "You need pictures, Signore Worthy."

Worthy shook his head. "Really? Look at my view outside my windows. There's the sculpture by Bernini, the back side of the Pantheon, and the piazza in front of the church."

Sesto did look. "You are right. The church, it is very famous. It is the Church of St. Maria sopra Minerva."

"I think I know what 'sopra' means and I remember who Minerva was, so is the church built over a Roman temple?"

"Si, si, but pilgrims come to this church, because St. Catherine of Siena body, it is there."

"Why isn't she buried in Siena?"

"Ah, yes, I can tell you. Her head, it is in Siena, but her body is here. She died in this neighborhood, maybe near to your office. Romans, they wanted her body here. Siena, she must settle for the head."

"Then if she is my neighbor, I suppose I owe her a visit," Worthy said. "So, Capitano, anything new on Bordy Vladic? Do we even know where the Bosnians live in Rome? Any chance we can find him in a refugee camp?"

"No, Bosnians live worse than in a camp. Do you know the road from airport to the city?"

"Of course. We were just on it to pick up Father Nick."

"Good. In the grassy part between the lanes—what do you call that in English?"

"I think you mean the median," Worthy offered.

"Si, the median. Did you see tents and shacks in medians?"

"That's where the Bosnians live?"

"Bosnians and others undocumented sleep there. But Vladic, he moves around, sleeps where he can."

Taking a sip of the coffee that Worthy had offered him, Sesto added, "Did Allyson, your daughter, tell you what some Romans call Bosnians? No? 'Termites.' They—what you say?—they bore into city's foundation. But we are in Rome, not New York City or Chicago. This is city where popes wash feet of refugees during Holy Week."

Sesto shrugged, as if the situation had no solution. "Yes, refugees, they take advantage of our kind hearts. If you are Italiano, you hope God will have mercy on us in next life."

Worthy thought back on what Allyson had shared about her work in one of Rome's refugee camps. "Allyson told me the children in the camps seemed years older."

"Someone like Bordy Vladic, he is teenager but not so. He see more horror already than most adults in a lifetime."

"It's that bad in Bosnia?" Worthy asked.

"Si, si. Corruption, poverty, they hungry. Few jobs and they be bad. Fear of war—again. Serbs hate them."

"But these boys, do they come to Italy on their own, or are they with their families?"

"For Bordy Vladic, I do not know. My guess? He come alone."

Worthy glanced out the window as a group of grade-school children in school uniforms walked past, all talking and laughing loudly. These children lived in apartments and houses, in the Rome that exists above ground. Bordy Vladic and Bosnian kids like him came out at night and knew better than to make a ruckus. Worthy wondered how long it had been since kids like Bordy had anything to laugh about.

"Those three teenagers following Father Robert. You say they are involved in petty crime. Do they work for someone?"

Sesto leaned back, his arms clasped behind his head. "Maybe yes, maybe no. When we catch one, we give them phone and tell them to call someone to come for them. Maybe we get a boss. You know what they do? They pretend they don't understand no Italian. That is a lie. They know enough. In a couple of hours, some old Bosnian woman show up, she claims to be nonna, grandmother. We learn nothing."

"So showing Bordy Vladic CCTV photo around the tents and shacks on the medians will be a waste of time?"

Sesto shook his head. "Best hope? We check for him on CCTV at St. Peter's, Colosseum, Trevi Fountain, Piazza Navona. If Bordy still in Rome, he cannot hide for long. He must eat."

Rome—Guesthouse of Order of Sacred Wounds Monastery

Late at night Rome time, Nick tried calling Father Jacob back in Yellowknife only to reach the parish secretary.

"I'm sorry, Father, but he has a funeral mass. He should be back in the office in an hour or so."

"Would you have him call me when he gets back? Here's my number in Rome."

"Isn't it the middle of the night there, Father?"

"Really, whenever he calls is okay."

While Nick waited for the call, he thought about the best way to approach Father Jacob. He knew if he started in on questions right away, the young priest would blame himself for not being forthcoming when Nick was in Yellowknife. Nick knew that nothing could be further from the truth. By the time Father Jacob called him back, Nick thought he'd found a way to ease into the questions.

"Thank for getting back to me, Jake."

"I'm just sorry it's so late Rome time. How's the case progressing?"

"Well, some answers, but more questions. That's par for the course, but it's also why I wanted to talk with you."

"Just let me know how I can help, Nick."

"That's great. Am I right in thinking that Father Robert didn't leave anything like a diary?"

"As far as what Mrs. Elkhorn told me, that's right," Father Jacob said.

"And I'm sure the authorities in Yellowknife must have looked through his emails, the ones he sent and received in that last week. But here's what I'm wondering. Do you think someone collected the mail that came for Father Robert after he left for Rome?"

"Hmm, well, in terms of mail sent to him after he died, I'm pretty sure our postal service would forward any mail to his next of kin, but from what Father Bob told me, the only family he ever felt close to was a mother, and she died when he was a teenager. If he knew where his father and brother were, he never mentioned that to me."

"So, with no kin, where do you think that mail is?"

"Well, I could be wrong, but my guess is that the postal service would stamp it 'addressee deceased' and return it to the sender. It's a cruel way for someone to find out about the death of a friend, but at least whoever sent something to Father Bob would know that he died."

Neither man spoke until Nick asked, "Would you be willing to do me a favor? On the off-chance that his mail hasn't been returned, would you see if you could get hold of it? I can't say we'll learn something from whatever he received, but we won't know until we know, Jake."

CHAPTER FOURTEEN

Rome—Police Headquarters

Capitano Sesto received authorization to place ten officers in key tourist centers of the city for the next week. They all had the CCTV photo of Bordy Vladic, but they were also on the lookout for other Bosnian teenagers.

Unfortunately, the week of surveillance produced nothing, neither sightings nor arrests, though that didn't mean that the Bosnians weren't active. On the morning of the eighth day, Sesto looked across his desk at Worthy and Nick and said, "Want to know how clever the Bosnians are? Three tourists robbed in places where my people were there."

"And no hint of Bordy Vladic?"

Sesto shook his head. "Spotting him was what you Americans call a 'long shot.' If he is still in city, he's lying low. And my boss, she won't authorize more surveillance."

Nick nodded as he stroked his beard. "I do have one idea, and I can't guarantee that it will be any more successful than what you tried. But I can't see as how it could hurt."

"Let's hear it, Nick," Worthy said.

"What if a priest took the Metro at those same late hours to those tourist spots, sat on a bench, and waited to see what happened?"

"You suggest we set a trap?" Sesto asked.

"Exactly. Priests must look like soft targets."

Capitano Sesto shook his head. "To dress up my men as priests? No, I have no budget."

"No, I'm saying a real priest. He could rotate through the sites you mentioned."

The policeman continued to shake his head. "Too dangerous, too risky. We can't use a priest as bait."

Nick glanced at Worthy. "Christopher, what if I volunteered?"

They all sat in silence until Worthy spoke to Sesto. "Stefano, couldn't Nick be wired? If he was in danger, you could have a backup nearby."

Sesto didn't say anything for a moment. "Yes, Father, but it would take weeks to cover the sites. So, not just dangerous; it's not practical."

"What if there were two priests, dividing the sites between them?" Worthy asked.

Sesto's eyebrows shot up. "Father, there is another priest from the monastery who would do this?"

Before Nick could answer, Worthy said, "No, not from the monastery. What if I pose as the other priest?"

Nick laughed as he clapped his hands. "Well, you look more than a North American priest than I do. Yes, I think you'll make an excellent Father Christopher."

"So here are your two volunteers, Stefano, or should I say guinea pigs?" Worthy said.

But when Worthy and Nick shared the plan with Lena over dinner that evening, she shivered. "I can't think of a more dangerous plan. Neither of you knows what Rome can be like in the middle of the night. You know my city in the daylight and maybe in the evening. You see the crowds eating peacefully in restaurants or visiting churches. At night, Rome is no different from New York or Detroit."

"Look, Lena, we'll be miked," Worthy assured her.

But Lena wasn't assured. "You do remember that Father Robert was stabbed from behind. Can you guarantee me that he'd be alive if he'd been miked?"

"That difference, Lena, is that Nick and I won't be taken by surprise tonight."

Lena raised both hands in protest. "Tonight? This is the way you thank me for getting you both into this? I can see that you've already made your decision, but this is crazy. We should be talking about the wedding, but all I can see in the future is a funeral for one of you."

Later that night, Worthy stood before the mirror in their bedroom. "So, do I look like a priest?"

Lena hugged him from behind. "Tell me again. How close will the police be?"

"Out of sight but close by."

When Lena turned him around, Worthy could see tears in her eyes. "Can I give this priest a kiss?"

Worthy smiled. "As long as no one sees us. Otherwise, you'll blow my cover."

He felt Lena shiver as she hugged him. "My worry is that you look more like a priest than Nick does."

"He's more like a pro wrestler, right?"

"Or, with his beard, like one of those Pavarotti imitators," Lena said.

"There is such a thing?"

"Pavarotti is our Elvis, Chris."

"Well, confusing Nick with Pavarotti isn't that far off, Lena. Wait till you hear Nick chant."

Lena paused. "And there's nothing I can do to change your mind?"

"This isn't the first time I've gone undercover, Lena, and if my business succeeds here in Rome, it won't be my last. Trust me, I know what I'm doing."

Lena slowly nodded. "Logically, I know that, and in a strange way, I wouldn't worry so much if you were wearing something other than that dog collar and black coat. When I look at you, I see Father Robert."

As Worthy completed the disguise by putting a silver cross around his neck, he glanced at himself again in the mirror. "Given my history, it does feel weird to see myself in this outfit."

"Have you thought about what you'll do if people think you are a priest?"

Worthy sat down on the edge of the bed. "I guess I need to ask Nick about that before tonight."

"Of course you could always pretend you were your father, the minister. Sorry, bad joke."

Worthy frowned as he looked at the silver crucifix around his neck. "My father and Nick are night and day, with Nick being day. Want to hear an example?"

"I know you're just trying to distract me, but go ahead."

"When I was a teenager, my dad took me to play a round of golf. The golf course was crowded that day, so the owner asked if we'd mind joining two others to make a foursome. The other two guys were total strangers to us. When my dad immediately introduced himself as Reverend Worthy, both men flinched as if they'd been hit. They hardly spoke a word to us the whole afternoon.

"On the ride home, I asked my dad why he didn't introduce himself simply by his first name, John. My dad turned and looked me full in the face. He said the two men weren't flinching at him, but at the thought of God's judgment. He said, 'That's what I remind them of. I could tell by their reaction that they were ashamed about something.' And then my dad said, 'That's part of my calling, son.' That was my first clue that, for my dad, God was a weapon."

Lena sat down next to Worthy before saying, "You're right. Nick would never do that."

Worthy nodded. "Sure, I've seen people pull back when they first meet this big bear of a man with his bushy beard and those monastic robes. But then they see how Nick is looking at them. He's almost always smiling, and it's like they get it. He likes them. He finds them interesting. It's like a big welcome light flashes on."

"Well, then, that's how you should act tonight."

"Unfortunately, that's not me."

"Hey, you're just playing a role. If anyone can imitate Nick, wouldn't it be you?"

"If Nick's face is a flashing welcome sign, I think mine is a 'do not intrude' sign."

Lena sat closer to Worthy on the bed. "Don't you think that's pretty common for someone who's gone through what you've gone through?"

"I assume you mean my divorce, but lately I've been wondering what kind of person I was before that. I know I was driven—people said that about me my whole life—but was that my DNA or was there something more? Sometimes when I look back, I think that I was trying to outrun what finally happened to me with the divorce."

"This is a still about your father, isn't it?"

"So your vote is my DNA is to blame?"

"You know that's not what I meant, Chris. It can't have been easy to be raised by someone who used God as a club."

"Both a weapon and a shield that he hid behind, now that I think about it. Even at the church, he was always Reverend Worthy."

"What about when he retired?"

"He died before that. He was only sixty-two. He died of lung cancer, which really made him mad because he'd never smoked a day in his life. I remember his last words—'When I see God, I'll tell him that he owed me a better death.'"

"I grew up with some priests like that," Lena said. "They talked a lot about being God's servants, but they acted like they were God's boss. Which is why, to my mother's chagrin, I left that God behind when I was barely a teenager."

"'That God,'" Worthy repeated, "yes, 'that God.' My dad died three years before my divorce, so he wasn't around to tell me that my divorce was God's way of punishing me. But I heard my dad's voice anyway."

CHAPTER FIFTEEN

After exiting the Metro, Nick found his way to the Trevi Fountain, his midnight-to-two a.m. assignment. The crowds that flocked to the site were an advantage for pickpockets but a disadvantage for Nick. Spotting Bordy Vladic or any of the Bosnian boys in a large crowd even at these late hours would be difficult. Given the Christmas season, Nick wasn't surprised to find that the seats nearest the fountain were filled, forcing him to lean against the wall of one of the businesses that encircled the fountain.

Although he'd visited the Trevi Fountain before, Nick was struck this time by the sound of the gushing water. He could see tourists yelling to one another as they stood with their backs to the fountain and tossed coins into the water, but their voices couldn't compete with the fountain. And that led him to wonder if the wall of noise dulled the other senses, such as touch, giving another advantage to pickpockets and purse snatchers.

Nick tried to picture how others in the area were seeing him. His being well over six foot all and two hundred and eighty pounds would make him stand out, and he imagined those looking his way were wondering what brought a priest to the Trevi at this time of night. He patted his wallet and passport that were stored safely inside his robes. Only the silver cross around his neck was a possible attraction to thieves.

Although the fountain was nothing like Piazza del Popolo, Nick thought that Father Robert must have stood out in the piazza as much as he did here. And by returning to the same site three nights in a row, Father Robert must have aroused the curiosity of regulars, such as the homeless and the panhandlers. But the noise, the constant tourist traffic, and the patrolling police at the Trevi would mean there'd be no homeless sleeping here.

He scanned the crowd slowly, trying to spot teenagers who might be part of a Bosnian gang. None seemed to be at the fountain that night, but then he realized that identifying Bosnian kids would be difficult, given that they were shorter than most of the tourists they would prey upon. As Capitano Sesto had explained, the kids, by scooting down even lower, often went unseen as they attacked the tourists from below and vanished into the milling crowd like wisps of wind.

His thoughts turned to Worthy, who'd chosen the area around the Pantheon for his first stakeout. Nick wondered if Worthy had selected that site because the Pantheon, by being so near Lena's apartment, would seem less threatening to her. And that also eased Nick's mind, as he took Lena's concern seriously. Lena wasn't a worrier or an alarmist, as she'd proven not only two years before in Jerusalem and also last year on a nearly-deserted island in Manitoba.

Seeing a group of tourists vacate seats to the edge of the Trevi Fountain, Nick moved quickly to sit at one end of a stone bench. Again, because of the thundering sound of the water, he didn't expect to be approached by anyone wanting to strike up a conversation or ask for a blessing, a thought that brought his mind back what Worthy, Lena, and he had talked about just an hour before.

"I think you should carry a rosary, Chris," Lena had suggested.

Nick immediately agreed. "Fingering the beads will also give your hands something to do, my friend."

"Okay, but where do I get one of those?" Worthy asked.

"I still have my mother's," Lena explained as she rose from the couch and walked to their bedroom. In a moment, she returned with a small oval box. Before she handed it to Worthy, she sniffed at the box. "It still has the smell of rose petals, my mother's favorite. She'd have said it will protect you, Chris. I hope she's right."

"I'll take good care of it," Worthy said, as he removed the string of red beads from the box and let it dangle from his hand. "But Lena pointed out something else earlier. What if people see me as a priest and ask me for something like a blessing?"

"Ah, well, I can see that happening," Nick said. "People might assume a priest out that late at night is there out of a sense of mission."

"I suppose I could pretend that I don't speak the person's language," Worthy said.

Lena frowned. "You look pretty American, Chris. Nick, what do you think? Could Chris make the sign of the cross over the person and say something?"

Nick looked at Worthy whose eyes were fixed on the rosary. "Would you be comfortable with that, Christopher?"

Worthy shrugged, not looking up or answering the question. "With my luck, someone will want me to hear their confession."

No, it won't be a question of luck, Nick thought, remembering what happened to Worthy on their last case together. "I'm sure Father Robert would have done that," he said. "And if you refused, it would blow your cover."

Lena caught Nick's eye. "You think the ones you're looking for might check Chris out?"

"They might find it suspicious that another priest is sitting alone at one of these sites in the middle of the night."

"All the more reason I have to be convincing," Worthy said.

No one said anything for a moment. Then, Nick said, "I'll try to make this as simple as possible. You're pretending to be a Catholic priest, so if someone does ask you to hear their confession, start by asking how long it has been since their last confession. After they answer that, tell them you're not there to judge, but to listen. You see, it's Christ who is hearing their confession through you. Then, it's a matter of being a good listener."

Worthy still didn't look up. "And at the end, what do I say?"

"Ah, yes, there's the big question, Christopher. You're only pretending to be a priest. You can't offer absolution, as it's not a matter of life or death. My suggestion is to do what I'm planning to do in that circumstance. I'll encourage them to go to their parish priest as soon as possible to have him hear their confession and give them the Eucharist."

Worthy nodded. "Yeah, I can do that. But what happens if they ask me to pray?"

"That's easy. Just offer the Lord's Prayer."

But as Nick glanced at the people tossing their coins into the Trevi Fountain, he realized that impersonating a clergyman would be anything but easy for his friend. Would the memory of his hellfire-and-brimstone father be troubling him? Or had what happened to Worthy the year before in Manitoba somehow erased that memory?

CHAPTER SIXTEEN

Rome—Outside the Pantheon

Sitting outside the Pantheon, Worthy looked down at the cobblestones at his feet. He remembered looking down at the site from the loggia atop Lena's apartment two years before and thinking about the millions who'd been drawn to the site over the centuries.

He glanced at one of the main entrances to the square, the one coming from the direction of St. Peter's and Piazza Navona. Citizens of Rome, bursting into the square with hardly a glance at the Pantheon, were easy to distinguish from tourists, who, at that same spot, stopped in their tracks, their jaws dropping, in awe of the magnificent site.

Worthy didn't doubt that petty thieves hung out near that same entrance to prey upon distracted tourists as they fumbled with their cameras and guide books. But on this night, there'd been very few children passing through the square, and none looked like Bosnian waifs. Two old men in rags, possibly homeless, approached him to beg for money. When he'd apologized with the Italian for "I'm sorry," both men moved on to others in the square, leading Worthy to wonder if they even noticed his priestly garb.

The agreed-upon plan was for Nick and him to remain at the sites until at least two in the morning. Looking at his watch, Worthy saw that it was already a quarter after one. The square was now quiet, except for the occasional group of drunken tourists who found it fun to hear their favorite songs echoing off the Pantheon, or delivery personnel whose carts piled high with goods rattled noisily across the cobblestones.

He looked down at the rosary in his hand, imagining what his father would say if he could see him. Holding rosary beads was certainly something he'd never done before in his life, and he wondered if anyone passing by wouldn't see a priest offering silent prayers but someone with no clue how to even hold the string of beads.

Prayer had been one of the casualties of his divorce over a decade before. The conviction that he'd grown up with, that God was present everywhere, had left him as completely as his wife Susan had. A sense of "nothing" had replaced the feeling, unless he were to count the deepening sense of emptiness that followed.

But then at the climax of a frustrating case the year before, he'd experienced something that he found hard to put into words. Whatever it was had lasted no more than two or three minutes, but in the months since, Worthy couldn't shake the feeling that whatever it was had not completely departed.

Nick had reacted by embracing him with tears, saying only that he'd always believed, even in Worthy's feeling of emptiness, that God had never given up on him. In the year since, Worthy kept asking himself if Nick was right. He heard his father's voice telling him he needed to go to Church, read the Bible, and pray, but it seemed only that, the voice of his father.

So he'd done none of those things, but as he sat with the rosary beads in his hand, he realized that he was waiting not just for the sight of Bordy Vladic, but for something he couldn't define, but something.

Rome—Lena's Apartment

Lena slept fitfully on the nights Worthy was on the stakeout. Her worry wasn't limited to what might happen to Worthy and Nick as they sat as bait waiting to be mugged or worse. She'd also felt Worthy pulling back from her.

She knew that Worthy was prone to withdraw on cases, his focus shifting inward, as he tried to enter the mind of the killer. She remembered him saying, "Before I can find the killer out here," he said as he pointed to the world around him, "I have to find him in here," he added, pointing to his head.

His tendency to tunnel in had proved a double-edged sword. Yes, it often preceded a breakthrough on a case, but the tendency had also led to him being labeled a loner and a headline-hunter by colleagues in his division. The trait had also, he'd confessed, been a major contributor to his divorce from Susan.

On a case they'd shared the year before, Lena and Worthy had confronted the danger of this trait to their relationship and had reached an agreement. Worthy couldn't alter the way he worked a case, but he'd agreed every night to "unpack his bags," referring to a time each evening when he would share what he was searching for within himself that he hoped would solve the case.

Now, with her conducting her research each day at the monastery and Worthy coming in after two in the morning from the stakeouts and then sleeping to noon, they hadn't been able to keep their commitment.

At noon on the day of the final stakeout, Lena returned to her apartment early in hopes of catching Worthy before he went to meet with Nick and Capitano Sesto. She caught him just as he was coming out of the shower.

"We need to talk," she said.

Worthy stopped rubbing his head with a towel to ask, "Is that why you're here instead at the monastery?"

"Yes, it is, Chris." Sitting down on the couch, she said, "It feels like there's something between us, and we both committed to deal with that rather than not say anything."

After sitting down next to her, Worthy said, "After tonight, things will go back to normal. It's the last stakeout."

Lena didn't say anything for a moment, but thought, *He's putting me off.*

"No, we need to talk about it now, Chris. Ever since you decided to go undercover, I feel like you've been undercover with me."

Worthy sat back in the couch. "I think we've both been withdrawing. I know you're still upset that we went ahead with the stakeouts."

"This is Rome, my city, Chris. Father Robert's murder proves it isn't safe to be out in the middle of the night."

Neither spoke for a moment. Finally, Worthy nodded. "You're right. I can tell when I get in at two in the morning that you've been up. I guess I was just hoping, once the stakeouts are over, that the silence between us will evaporate on its own."

Lena shook her head. "Then you really underestimated me. I feel burned, Chris."

Worthy sighed. "I'm sorry, Lena. You're as much a part of the team as the rest of us, and I think I guessed that you'd be opposed to the idea. That's why I insisted we be miked."

"Well, you're right; I haven't had a good night's sleep since Nick and you agreed to this. I felt like I was talking to a wall, and for the first time I wondered if I could do this—this watching you go off and risk your life and our life together. Look, if we're going to be married, and you're going to investigate crimes here and back in the States, I need to know that I won't be ignored or patronized. I won't be treated as some overly emotional and worried female. And I won't become another Susan."

Worthy paused. "I let you down. Hell, I let both of us down," Worthy said. "I should have realized what all this might have felt like. I felt the same way when Allyson was abducted a couple of years ago. I couldn't sleep. I couldn't eat. I was one piss-poor cop."

Lena reached over and took Worthy's hand. "I know that there's always going to be danger involved in what you do, Chris. I have to accept that, even if neither of us can predict what that will lead to. But if I'm going to live with that uncertainty and maybe that grief, I have to know that my worries aren't ignored."

She could feel Worthy squeezing her hand as he nodded slowly. "All I can promise is that I'll try to listen; I really will."

"And I promise to make sure that you hear me."

Rome—Worthy's New Office

As Worthy waited in his office for Capitano Sesto and Nick to arrive, he reflected on his talk with Lena and wondered if his marriage with Susan would have been saved if they'd had that talk. In the divorce proceedings, Worthy realized that his preoccupation with work—his daughter Allyson had called it an "obsession"—had pushed Susan away. Susan and he had let the distance between them grow until that was all that they had in common, the silence.

Looking back, Worthy understood that Susan had probably hoped her silence would be so uncomfortable that he'd get the message and change. But their marriage had faltered because he'd not just accepted her silences but welcomed them.

Nick arrived first, and after a few minutes of Nick praising Worthy's new office, Worthy told him about his conversation with Lena. When he was finished, Nick said, "Good heavens, I feel awful. I'm as guilty of patronizing her as you, Christopher."

"Maybe, but . . ."

"Of course, coming from you that would have hurt more. And the truth is that Lena has discovered as much about Father Robert at the monastery as I have."

Worthy nodded. "That's true. Nick, if there's one thing I know about Lena, it's that she doesn't want flowers or dinner at a special restaurant from us. She'd see that as another example of patronizing. And she'd be right. What she wants is for us not to repeat our mistake."

Nick shook his head. "I know you're right, Christopher, and I know the only way we can convince Lena that we're listening to her is by doing just that—listen to her."

"Yes, that's it," Worthy replied. "Maybe it's good that after tonight's stakeout, assuming it's as uneventful as the last couple of nights, we'll have to change our approach anyway."

Capitano Sesto walked into Worthy's office in time to hear the last part of Worthy's comment. "Ah, you're talking about changing the approach. Well, the priest stakeouts were worth a try."

"And to be fair," Nick said, "we still have one more night. Where are you going to be tonight, Christopher?"

"Well, I'm ready to cross the Colosseum off our list, given what happened to me there last night. Even at that hour, the place was packed. First, it was a group of skateboarders, but they were sent off by some of your people, Stefano. Then there was a group of Germans who'd bought plastic swords and pretended to be gladiators—drunken gladiators, I mean. They were the next to be driven away. But it was a busload of photographers who capped off my stakeout. There must have been twenty or more of them with their tripods and camera cases, all taking photos of the Colosseum lit up at night. If you're thinking they'd be perfect targets for thieves, you'd be wrong. They'd no sooner set up when six more of your police buddies showed up, Stefano, not to run them off, mind you, but to offer their protection. That's when it dawned on me that the photographers had official permission to be there."

"I didn't know anything about that," Sesto said. "Still, it's too bad. So where are you headed tonight?"

"Nick, I know you were at Piazza del Popolo last night. I'm thinking I'd take a turn there. I still think that's our best bet."

Nick stopped Worthy by raising a hand. "Actually, Christopher, if it's all the same to you, I'd like to go back there tonight. Last night, I had a feeling that I was being watched. And I don't mean by your men, Capitano."

"Just a feeling or something more?" Sesto asked.

"I'm not sure. It started when a homeless man held out his cup in front of me. As I reached in my pocket for some change, I pulled out the CCTV photos of Bordy Vladic and Father Robert. In my meager Italian, I asked the man if he recognized them. He looked from the photos to me and back again. I was sure he knew something, but then he only shrugged and moved on. He was limping a bit as I watched him move off to beg from others in the piazza. But then some teenagers ran through the square and distracted me. I thought at first they could be Bosnians, but then I heard them speaking Italian. Anyway, when I looked back, the homeless man was gone. Something didn't feel right. He was there one minute and gone the next."

"And he was limping, you said?" Worthy asked.

"That's it, Christopher. That's what was so strange. He'd been shuffling more than walking, and then a few seconds later he was nowhere in sight."

"I can think of five ways out of the piazza," Sesto said. "The shuffling might have been part of his act. If he'd begged enough change to get some cheap vino, he might have moved pretty quickly."

Nick sighed. "And I admit after the other nights of nothing happening, I could have been hoping that the poor man meant something. But, I'd still like to go back tonight."

Sesto nodded. "To be extra safe, I put a car just outside Piazza del Popolo. As soon as you enter piazza, they listen for you, yes?"

"Sounds good. What about you, Christopher? Where will you be?"

"From the data you showed us, Stefano, the train station is one of the most dangerous places for tourists."

"Si, si," Sesto said. "Tourists set a bag down and look at map of city, and the next minute their bag is gone. Yes, you look for Bosnians, but also look for men and woman who walk up to tourists who look lost. They ask the tourists where they need to go. They flash phony IDs and say they are taxi drivers."

"What happens to the gullible tourists who believe them?" Nick asked.

"Oh, nothing good. Most times, he takes tourists where the tourists asked to go. But he or she will charge, overcharge two or three times regular rate."

"I think I can guess the worst-case scenario," Worthy said. "The tourists are taken to another location where the driver's accomplices are waiting."

Sesto nodded. "Some are beaten and lose everything. As Dr. Fabriano said," Sesto said, looking at Worthy, "after midnight, Rome not safe."

CHAPTER SEVENTEEN

Rome—Guesthouse, Order of Sacred Wounds Monastery

Given that tonight's stakeout would be his third and last one, Nick took a nap in the afternoon. He was awakened by the sound of his computer dinging. Groggily, he rose from the bed and sat down heavily at the desk. Opening his computer, he found the email message from Father Jacob.

"Dear Nick,

We got lucky. Mrs. Elkhorn at the orphanage had kept all the mail that came for Father Bob after he left for Rome. I looked through it and, as you can imagine, most of it is unimportant. There are two sporting goods catalogs, a couple of charity appeals, and a credit card bill. It looks like the bishop was right about one thing—Bob has run up quite a bill for hockey gear. But I did come across a personal letter that I took the liberty of opening. The name S. Lonetree was written in the upper left-hand corner, but there was no return address. The letter was postmarked November 19th in North Vancouver, British Columbia. Given the Lonetree name, my first thought was that it was a charity appeal from another Native community. But when I opened it, I found this short message written in longhand:

'Little man, you haven't called or sent any message back. Maybe what I wrote made you wish I am dead. But I try one more time. You have my number.' It was signed, 'Me.'

"Nick, I have no idea if this is important or not. I asked Mrs. Elkhorn if she'd ever heard the name S. Lonetree, and she said she hadn't. If you want, I'll contact the post office in Vancouver to see if they can identify S. Lonetree. It's a pretty unusual name."

As Nick reread the message, his tiredness was replaced by a flood of energy and new questions. On the one hand, the message suggested that S. Lonetree had written a previous letter to Father Robert. But that would only be true if "Little Man" referred to Father Robert, not one of the orphans. If the letter was for one of the boys, then the letter had been sent "in care of" Father Robert.

The phrase "maybe you wish I am dead" made Nick pause. Something had upset Father Robert before the fire so badly that he drank himself into a drunken stupor. And everything that followed—the horrible fire, Father Robert being recalled to Rome, his odd return three nights in a row to Piazza del Popolo, and finally his murder—had flowed from that abrupt change in behavior back in Yellowknife. Had Father Robert set off on his dark path because of the previous letter from S. Lonetree?

Nick felt that he knew what Worthy would say, that he shouldn't overestimate the importance of the letter. Yet, there was something about the brief note that Nick felt, more than knew, could be important. Tomorrow, in the debriefing session with Worthy, Lena, and Capitano Sesto, he would share the note and hear how they read it. In the meantime, he hit reply and typed out a return message to Father Jacob.

"Jake, thanks for letting me know about the letter. It's certainly strange, and I think it bears our—actually your—taking it further. You might have already taken my first suggestion, to ask Mrs. Elkhorn to look through Father Robert's office and living quarters for an earlier letter from S. Lonetree. That letter might let us in on what we're missing—Father Robert's state of mind in the days before the fire. Secondly, ask Mrs. Elkhorn if the 'Little Man' could be a term of endearment or nickname for one of the boys. Thirdly, yes, please contact the postal service in North Vancouver to see if they know of an S. Lonetree. If for some reason Father Robert destroyed that first letter, S. Lonetree is the only person who knows what was in it."

Nick ended the note by writing, "If I didn't know that you want to understand Father Robert's sorry end as much as we do, I wouldn't ask this of you. I thank you for everything." Closing his computer, he thought, *Thinking about this new development will certainly liven up tonight's stakeout.*

Rome—Guesthouse, Order of Sacred Wounds

As Nick prepared to leave the monastery for Piazza del Popolo, his thoughts returned to what Worthy had shared two hours before.

Worthy had stopped by Nick's room, already dressed as a priest for his stakeout at the train station. It wasn't until Worthy had taken a seat that Nick realized that the two of them hadn't had a private talk since he'd arrived in Rome.

"It's hard to believe that it's been two years since we were last here in Rome," Worthy had said.

Nick had nodded. "I keep thinking we should be meeting someone from the Vatican. But I did wonder if being in Rome feels different for you, given that you live here now."

Worthy looked out Nick's window to the lights dotting the city below. "At least for part of the year. But I still have to pinch myself. Seeing Rome once was my childhood dream. Now, I live in an apartment and have an office."

"And you're about to be married to a Roman, my friend," Nick added.

"That's another thing that catches me up. Sometimes, I'm still afraid . . ." Worthy stopped and turned back to look at Nick.

"Yes, I know, Christopher. But I want you to know that I've never stopped thanking God for bringing the two of you together."

"But not *that* God," Worthy said in little more than a whisper.

"Pardon?"

"It's something Lena and I were talking about this afternoon. I ended up sharing how my father's God was someone to fear, someone anxious to punish. If my dad had been alive when Susan divorced me, he'd had said that God was punishing me for something."

Nick had waited for Worthy to say more. Finally, he sat down in a chair and said, "There's so much that I can't make any sense of, Nick. I mean, after what happened last year in Canada, you might think I'd start attending Church, reading the Bible, and praying. But whatever happened last year hasn't had that effect on me. But something in me is different." He'd paused before shaking his head. "No, that's not it. It isn't something in me, I mean. It's something different about life. Does any of that make any sense?"

"It sounds like what happened to you turned everything inside out."

Worthy had looked startled. "Yes, that's exactly what it feels like. There was a lot of fear of hell in my father's faith. He preached about the need to have God in my life . . . to *have* God. For him, I think going to Church, reading the Bible, and praying gave someone a 'get out of hell free' card."

Worthy had stopped, and Nick felt his friend was waiting for him to say something. "In seminary, we called that 'life insurance' religion."

Nodding, Worthy said, "Nick, I did all those things—the Bible reading, the praying, the taking my family to Church. But when my life fell apart, all that was left was this emptiness—total, total emptiness. I prayed so many times—God knows I prayed—for my marriage to be saved, for Allyson to come home, for my life to go back to being normal, but there was nothing. Absolute nothing. So much for life insurance."

"And now?" Nick asked.

"And now? All I know is that what happened last year doesn't fit with all that. I just wish I understood what that meant. I don't."

"'Don't put new wine in old wineskins.' Isn't that how the verse goes?" Nick said.

"Yeah, talk about an echo from Sunday School. But what are you saying?"

"What I'm saying that you should just let what happened to you last year be. Trust that what happened will take you to where you need to go."

Worthy hadn't said anything for a moment. Then, clearing his throat, he said, "Stefano told me that my office has a famous neighbor."

Nick understood that his friend needed to change the subject. "Who's that?"

"I guess I should say, this office used to have a famous neighbor. Sesto said a medieval saint, St. Catherine, lived near my office before she died. Her body's in the church at the end of the street. I expect you know her."

"I do know her. She's a saint of the Catholic Church, but you know my feelings about the saints. In heaven, there's no distinction between saints of the West and those of the East. St. Catherine of Siena's writings are extraordinary."

"Think I should read about her?"

"An excellent idea," Nick said, thinking to himself, *And I will pray that St. Catherine will go gently with my friend.*

Rome—On the Way to Piazza del Popolo

As he'd done the previous nights, Nick tiptoed down the hallway in the guesthouse as midnight approached. The monks slept in a separate wing, but he knew that one of the monks would be taking his turn on night duty. Opening the door at the end of the hallway as silently as possible, he thought again about Father Robert managing to leave the monastery without being noticed. Certainly, Abbot Lorenzo hadn't known of Father Robert leaving the motherhouse on those three nights, but that didn't preclude one of the monks being aware of Father Robert's ramblings. But if so, why hadn't that monk come forward?

As he passed through the monastery gate to the street beyond, he felt the hair rise on the back of his neck. Years before, on another case with Worthy, he'd had the same feeling and had been right in his suspicion that he was being followed. As he now approached an overhead street light, he darted behind a rhododendron bush and waited.

After several fruitless moments, Nick stepped back onto the sidewalk and continued toward the nearest Metro platform. The sidewalk leading to the Metro stop was well-lit, and he was relieved when he could hear the voices of people who'd exited one of the trains and were now walking toward him. *Safety in numbers,* he thought.

On the Metro platform below ground, he stood with a few other people and waited for the next train to arrive. When the train slowed to a stop, Nick did as he'd done the two nights before, walking toward one of the first cars. And as before, he found the car empty except for an elderly couple and an off-duty security guard. Nick knew that with each stop before Rome's train station, called Termini, the number of people in the car would multiply, providing even more safety in numbers. He patted the tiny transmitter under his robes and relaxed. Once he arrived at the piazza, he knew Capitano Sesto's men would be listening in and ready to react.

With that assurance, he thought that this final night would be more a prayer vigil than a stakeout. His prayers would begin with the three orphans who died in the fire, their grieving families, and the Yellowknife community. After that would come Father Jacob and the shadowy S. Lonetree, followed by all those in Rome, including Capitano Sesto, Worthy, and Lena, who were trying to solve the mystery of Father Robert's death.

But that was not all. Nick knew his prayers would return again and again to Father Robert, the center of the mystery both in Yellowknife and in Rome. Worthy, too, would haunt his prayers. Nick knew that God would not force Himself or His will on Worthy, and he prayed that his friend would be patient.

CHAPTER EIGHTEEN

Rome—Lena's Apartment

Lena woke from the first restful night's sleep she'd had in four nights. She'd dreamt that Worthy and she were on their honeymoon, staying on an island in Greece. In the dream, Nick was there, leading everyone in a Zorba-like dance on a beach.

Opening her eyes, she saw Worthy with his back to her as he sat, still dressed as a priest, by the window that looked at neighboring roofs.

"Oh, love, I just had the most wonderful dream. We were in Greece dancing with—"

The words died in her mouth when she saw Worthy's expression. "What is it?" she asked.

Worthy's voice sounded strained and exhausted. "Nick's missing. We don't know where he is."

Lena sat up so abruptly that she felt she might faint. "But he was miked."

Worthy sat down on the side of the bed. "The police were set up near the piazza, but he never showed up. And he's not at the motherhouse."

"I don't understand, Chris."

"Nobody understands. Sesto is pulling the CCTV from all the Metro subway stations between the monastery and the piazza. I wanted to let you sleep in before I . . . before I told you. Actually, I let you sleep because I hoped Sesto would call and tell me Nick was in the hospital with a sprained ankle or a minor concussion from falling off a curb. But there's nothing, and Nick's cellphone is dead. It could be either turned off or . . . it's been put out of service."

Lena put her head in her hands. *From dream to nightmare,* she thought. *I was worried about Chris, but he's trained to defend himself. I should have been worried about Nick.*

"Did Nick say anything yesterday about last night's stakeout?"

Worthy dropped his head. "That's just it. He told us about a weird feeling that he'd felt the night before, something he picked up from a homeless man."

"But wasn't he at a different site last night?"

Shaking his head, Worthy explained Nick's plan to return to Piazza del Popolo for a second night.

Lena shivered as she pulled the sheet and blanket up to her face. "Wasn't that where you were supposed to be last night?"

Closing his eyes, Worthy said, "Yes, I should have been there."

"No, no, you can't think that."

"You were right all along, Lena. You warned us . . . "

"That's not important now. Chris, if they don't find him on any of the CCTV cameras in the Metro stations or in the subway cars, what does that mean?"

Worthy let his breath out slowly. "It means that somewhere between leaving the motherhouse and the train station, something happened to him."

All kinds of questions rushed into Lena's mind. Was someone from the monastery behind Nick's disappearance? Had Nick been abducted by the same person who killed Father Robert? If so, had what she feared the most already happened—that Nick had experienced the same fate as Father Robert?

"What can I do, Chris? And don't tell me there's nothing, because I have to do something."

Worthy didn't hesitate. "You should come with me to Sesto's office."

Lena threw herself out of bed. "Give me five minutes."

Less than fifteen minutes later, Lena was looking out the side window of the police car that raced with sirens blazing in the direction of Rome's police headquarters. She thought Charles Dickens' *A Tale of Two Cities* could also describe Rome. There was the city that she was seeing from the car, the daytime Rome, a city full of life, a city of tourists, a city of millions traveling to work, school, or the shops by buses, the Metro, motor scooters, taxis, and honking cars. This was the Rome that Nick was familiar with, the city of old churches that he loved to visit. But Nick had ventured, like an innocent lamb—all right, a lamb the size of a sumo wrestler—into the Rome at night, the Rome that Lena's grandmother called "The city of ghosts, the city of predators."

She turned away from the blurry scenes passing by the police car, remembering what Nick and Worthy had hoped to achieve by being bait. The idea was that, by imitating what Father Robert had done the last three nights of his life, they could lure Bordy Vladic or other Bosnian kids into the net.

With both Nick and Worthy wired, she'd grudgingly accepted that the plan made a kind of sense. Now, she wished she'd resisted more strongly, even as she realized that blaming herself, like blaming Worthy, wasn't going to change anything. If anyone was to blame, she realized, it would be Father Robert. Nick was missing because Father Robert had made three middle-of-the-night forays and on the last night had been murdered. But how could she blame a dead man?

Rome—Capitano Sesto's Office and Lena's Apartment

Sitting next to Lena in the police car, Worthy remembered other cases when Nick had been in danger. Each time, Worthy had had the same feeling of nausea and dread as he worried that his friend would pay with his life. It was no consolation that Nick had always volunteered. Nor did it offer much relief to realize that Nick was likely, at that moment, calm and at peace.

When Lena and Worthy entered Capitano Sesto's office, the policeman looked up from his computer screen. Seeing the strain on his face and his bloodshot eyes, Worthy knew he had no good news to report.

"We're still scanning CCTV from Metro stops, but so far we have these images," he said, as he turned his monitor around so they could see. "In this one, Father Nick, he waits at the Metro stop near the monastery. The time is eleven-forty five." He touched a key and a second image appeared. "This is eight minutes later. See, he gets on the B line for Termini, the train station."

"Which is logical," Lena said. "He has to go to Termini to transfer to another line for Piazza del Popolo."

"Stefano, do you have CCTV in the subway cars or just at the station platforms?" Worthy asked.

"Both," Sesto replied, "but we still look to find what car your friend was in. Do you wait or should I call you when we have something?"

Even before he could ask what Lena wanted to do, she moved a chair to sit down.

Doing the same, Worthy said, "I don't think either of us will get anything done until we . . . until we find out more about Nick."

A long hour later, an image of Nick sitting in a nearly empty subway car appeared on screen. Worthy could see the knotted prayer cord in Nick's hand and remembered the rosary that had been part of his own disguise on the stakeout. Putting his hand in his pocket, he felt the smooth beads and silently offered the only prayer he could come up with: *Save my friend.*

With each stop, Nick's car picked up more passengers. Nick stood out, but Worthy saw no evidence of teenagers or children. And when CCTV showed the car emptying at Termini, Worthy again saw no one suspicious.

"You must have CCTV in the train station," Worthy said. "Can you run face-recognition software to track Nick?"

"Yes, but that will take much time," Sesto answered.

"I have a simpler idea," Lena said. She pointed to the top right of the computer screen. "Here's the time when Nick arrives at Termini. It would take him no more than ten minutes to transfer to the other line, the A line. Why not check the CCTV on the A line platform for the following ten to twenty minutes?"

"Si, si, good idea," Sesto acknowledged. He hit a few keys as he said, "Many more people on A line leaving Termini, but Father Fortis should be easy to see."

But after viewing and reviewing an hour of CCTV videos, they had to conclude that Nick hadn't arrived at the A line platform.

"I don't get it," Worthy said. "Where is he?"

Sesto rubbed his eyes. "Something caused your friend to change his plans at Termini."

"Or someone forced Nick to change his plans," Lena said.

"But I was at the train station," Worthy said. "How could I have missed Nick?"

Lena shook her head. "Don't blame yourself, Chris. Termini is like a small city, one level built upon another. At the lowest level are the subway lines. At the next level up are shops. And on the upper level are the regular train lines coming in from all over the country, plus more shops. And outside the station there are at least fifty bus stops as well as the taxi ranks.

That's why pickpockets love Termini. It's very confusing for tourists, and they spot that."

His head in his hands, Worthy said, "I still can't believe that Nick and I were in the same place."

"Face recognition will find your friend at Termini," Sesto said. "Let the computer do the work while we rest, yes?"

While Worthy knew that Sesto was right, he doubted if he'd be able to sleep. *The computer will take some time to find Nick, but how much time does Nick have?* he thought.

To his surprise, Worthy managed to sleep three hours at Lena's apartment, but it would be fairer to say he passed out. When he woke, he found Lena sitting at the kitchen table with a cup of coffee and a closed folder.

"Are you okay?" she asked, as he poured himself a cup and sat down.

"No, but I got some sleep. Is that our wedding folder?"

Lena nodded as she rested her hand on it. "We'll put it aside until we find Nick. And we will find him, Chris."

He focused on stirring sugar into his coffee, not wanting Lena to see that he was far from convinced that she was right. What, he wondered, would happen if Nick had been taken by the same people who killed Father Robert.

Lena rested her hand on his arm. "I thought of something while you were sleeping. I don't know if it's important or just a coincidence."

"I'm open for anything."

"I was thinking about something you said to Capitano Sesto. You were talking about your being at Termini at the same time as Nick."

Nick set the cup down. "And?" he said.

"If your stakeout had you for two hours at Termini, I assume you moved around, not staying in the same place."

"I did do that, but I still don't follow."

"It's like this. Nick had to be abducted in Termini itself. The people who did that had to be waiting for him there. With you being dressed as a priest, those same people must have seen you. Selfishly, I'm glad they didn't abduct you instead, but why did they take Nick?"

Worthy looked up, now fully awake. "I went to the bathroom more than once, which was empty both times. That would have been a perfect chance to abduct me. But whoever is behind this didn't do that. So you're saying that they were waiting specifically for Nick."

"I think so, but what does that mean?"

Neither said anything for a few moments. Finally, Worthy said, "Let's go back to what Nick said yesterday. He wanted to go back to Piazza del Popolo because he had a feeling from the night before that a beggar had recognized Father Robert's photo or Bordy Vladic's CCTV photo."

"Yes, yes, Chris. And didn't Nick say that the beggar seemed to vanish? So, isn't it possible that Nick, on the night before, spooked whoever abducted him?"

Worthy nodded slowly. "If only they'd waited until Nick arrived in the piazza, Sesto's men would have picked Nick up on his mike and would have intervened before they could have taken him. But they took him before he got there."

"Was that just luck on their part or something else?" Lena asked.

"I'm not a big believer in luck," Worthy said. "The beggar must have some part in their scheme. Maybe he works with the Bosnians. Maybe he's Bosnian himself, and maybe he's the front man. What I mean is that he goes from one tourist to another, begging, and in the process, he spots the easy marks. He gives some signal to the Bosnian kids and they move in."

"But Nick changed everything by showing him the photos of Father Robert and Vladic," Lena said.

"Right. He knew that Nick posed a danger. So what did they do next?"

"Wouldn't it make sense that they followed Nick back to the monastery?" Lena said.

Worthy shook his head as he pushed his coffee cup to the side.

"You don't think so?"

"No, Lena, I do think so. But what if they did more than follow Nick back to the monastery? What if, three weeks before, they followed Father Robert back to the same monastery? Wouldn't they put two and two together and realize that Nick is working on Father Robert's murder?"

"I agree. I bet they figured out that Nick was part of a trap. But they could avoid the trap and find out what the police know by abducting Nick."

Neither Lena nor Worthy said anything, but words weren't necessary. They both knew that Nick was in serious danger.

CHAPTER NINETEEN

Rome—Police Headquarters

Returning to police headquarters, Lena and Worthy found Capitano Sesto at his computer. "Any news?" Worthy asked.

Sesto looked up and shook his head. "Poco, a little," he replied. "Face recognition found Father Fortis on three cameras, but then 'poof,' he disappears. Here, I show you."

Lena looked down at a black-and-white image of people, some with suitcases, standing on an escalator. Despite knowing that Nick must be somewhere in the photo, her heart skipped a beat when she spotted him.

"That's the escalator that would take him up to the next level," she said, hearing her voice quake.

"Yes, the way to A line," Sesto said in agreement. "Here is next time we see him."

"Stop, stay on the first photo for a minute," Worthy said. "Can we see who's behind and in front of Nick?"

Lena leaned down to get a closer look at the photo. In front of Nick and nearly at the top of the escalator was a group of teenage boys, but by their haircuts, clothes, and laughing expressions, Lena realized they were local boys, not Bosnian refugees. To her surprise, the person directly behind Nick was a security officer. The officer looked bored, as if she were heading home after her shift. Behind the security officer was a figure in a dark hoodie. But the person was looking away from the CCTV camera, making it impossible to tell if the figure were a man or woman.

"Can you identify the woman in uniform?" Worthy asked Rossi.

Sesto zeroed in on the security officer and hit a key to take an enlarged photo. "She with Metro security. I can track her down. What about that one in the hoodie?"

Lena saw Worthy take out a small notebook and pen, writing as he said, "About a foot or more shorter than Nick, about as tall as the security. So that makes him or her about five feet, four or five. Can you make out the writing on the hoodie?"

"I can't see all of it, but I don't think it's writing," Lena said. "It looks more like the edge of some image, a circle maybe."

"Maybe logo for a football club or a band?" Sesto suggested. "Ah, the railing, it blocks most of his body. But wait. Sometime, shoe tells us something."

"I don't remember the person in the hoodie in Nick's car on the Metro," Lena said. "But I suppose he or she could have been in another car on the same train and was still following Nick."

"My people can check other cars." Looking up at Worthy, he said, "Ready for next picture?"

The second image showed people walking in opposite directions on a well-lit and wide corridor. "I can tell from the posters on the walls, the ones advertising English language classes and upcoming theater productions where Nick is. I've walked through that same corridor thousands of times," Lena said.

Again, it wasn't hard for any of them to spot Nick, who towered over almost everyone around him. "I see him," Worthy said, "but he's so massive that he obscured who's behind him."

Lena pointed at Nick's image on the screen. "His expression looks weird somehow."

"Si, si. It's like he recognize someone he just pass," Sesto offered.

Worthy took a closer look. "Or, the person behind him said something to him. But we can't see who that is."

"And look at Nick's left hand. Is that a sign?" Lena asked.

"I see that too," Sesto said. "I think he make V sign for some reason. But don't you Americans use V sign for 'victory?' I don't understand."

The question hung in the air until Lena said, "I know exactly where Nick is here in this photo. He's coming to a junction. If he turns right, that takes him to the A line platform. If he turns left, he'll come to another escalator, this one leading a level up to the shops and the trains above. Does that mean that he turned left instead of right?"

With new energy in his voice, Sesto said, "Si, si. That explains the third photo." On the screen was a scene showing the bright-lit shops on the train station's street level. Despite the early hours of the morning, there was a considerable number of people milling around.

"Here's your friend," Sesto said, pointing to the back of a figure heading in the direction of the exit to the street outside.

"Do we see the person in the hoodie?" Worthy asked.

"I don't," Lena confessed, "but the men to Nick's right and left are walking awfully close to him."

"Zoom in on the three of them," Worthy said.

In the close-up, Nick seemed to be escorted by two men. "They're leading him out," Lena said.

"That is exit on west side," Sesto said.

Again, Lena saw Worthy jotting down notes on a pad. "I estimate that the one on the right is a couple of inches shorter than Nick, so about six feet. The other one is even shorter. As you said, Lena, the arms of the guys are almost touching Nick. Now look at Nick's left hand."

Zooming in still further, Lena could see that Nick's left hand was angled backward. "It looks like his thumb and forefinger are making another sign."

"I think Nick counted on CCTV catching him. So what do the two signs mean?"

Lena looked at the police captain. "Does CCTV in Termini record images in sequence?"

Sesto nodded. "I choose this one because it is clearest. But let me . . .," Sesto left off while he hit more keys. The screen showed three smaller images side by side. Pointing his cursor to the first one, Sesto said, "Here is your friend, coming off escalator on to street level."

No one said anything for a moment until Lena pointed to someone's leg appearing just behind Nick's robe. "Who's this?"

Sesto zoomed in on the image. "He is hidden behind Father Fortis. Is that accident or on purpose?" Hitting another key, the policeman magnified the leg, showing a dirty pant leg and a ragged athletic shoe.

Worthy tapped the screen. "That's a kid's shoe, and a pretty well-used one. Look at the trailing shoelace."

"And look how short the pant leg is. The pants are much too small for him," Lena said. "If that's the person in the hoodie, he could be Bosnian."

Sesto enlarged the third image, which revealed the back of a figure in a long coat and stocking cap obscuring a complete view of Nick.

"I'm thinking that's the same man who ends up on Father Fortis' right in the final photo, the one you showed us before," Worthy said.

Sesto pointed to a figure at the edge of the photo. "Look at this guy coming into the frame. He could be man who in next photo is on left of your friend."

"I don't see the kid in the hoodie," Lena said.

"He's gone," Sesto replied after studying the image. "Bosnian kids, they are trained to melt into crowds. One minute, here; next minute, gone."

"That's what Nick said about the beggar in Piazza del Popolo. He just disappeared," Worthy said.

Lena shivered as she realized what they were looking at—Nick being handed over from the kid in the hoodie to the two men.

When nobody said anything further, Sesto hit another computer key. "This is last CCTV of your friend," he said.

In the shot, Lena could see Nick and the two men standing alongside a black car, its back door held open by the man on the right.

"It's completely dark inside the car," Worthy said. "Can you brighten the image at all?"

Sesto shook his head. "This is bright as I can make it. The windows on the car, they are tinted. It's like looking into a cave. But we have license plate number. Unfortunately, the plate is bogus."

"So, nothing more?" Worthy asked.

Sesto sat back and exhaled. "My tech guy, he got one ping off your friend's phone, then dead. I think we find phone in garbage bin or in gutter near Termini."

Lena could see on Worthy's face the effect of every bit of bad news from Sesto.

"And no help with CCTV on the streets outside the station?" Worthy asked.

"Maybe, but only on main streets. Hundreds of small streets branch off. No CCTV there."

Worthy asked no further questions as his head slumped to his chest. Lena could imagine what he was thinking. Seeing the time on the screen when Nick was shoved into that car, he'd be doing more than asking himself where he was at that same time in the train station. Despite the constant crowds and confusion in Termini, he'd be blaming himself for being in the wrong place at the wrong time.

Sesto broke the silence. "Do we tell the media now?"

Worthy shook his head. "I say we wait. I can just see the headlines. 'Second priest attacked. Serial killer of priests on the loose.'"

Grimacing, Lena added, "A serial killer of priests in the city with the largest populations of priests and nuns in the world. A headline like that would throw the city into a panic."

CHAPTER TWENTY

Rome—A Warehouse Outside the City

The pain in Nick's neck woke him, but he was far from alert. He had trouble focusing on where he was, knowing only that his left wrist was chained to the steel frame of a bed. He shook his head, but in doing so, managed only to send the pain in his neck into his brain. He realized that he'd been sedated but couldn't remember when that had happened.

The only thing the low-lit and musty-smelling room had in its favor was its warmth. He lay back and listened for human sounds, but heard none. Slowly, he remembered bits of what had happened to him. He remembered being in the back seat of a car with something covering his head. The voices in the car had spoken Italian quite rapidly, and he'd understood nothing.

He closed his eyes, trying to recall how he'd ended up in the car. Slowly, he remembered two men escorting him through the bright lights of Rome's train station toward an exit. He had looked around, hoping to see Worthy in the crowded station, but without success. The fingers on his left hand tingled, and he remembered making the sign of a V in the hope that the gesture would be recorded on Termini's CCTV cameras.

But why did I do that? he asked himself. *What was I trying to say?* Then another figure came back to him, the boy in the hoodie who'd moved up behind him on the escalator in the train station and poked him with the sharp end of a knife.

"I hear you ask for me," the voice had said. "Keep to walk, and you will be not hurt." Even before glancing back, Nick knew the voice must be Bordy Vladic's. Yes, that was how it had all begun. Bordy Vladic; then the two men, one showing a glimpse of a gun; the car ride with his head covered; and finally this room.

Yet Nick knew there was something even before all that, something that took a moment to come clear in his foggy mind. Finally, he remembered the word "vigil." Yes, his last night in Piazza del Popolo was meant to be a prayer vigil. *Well, it's still that,* Nick thought. *There's just more to pray about now.*

Nick lay back down and looked at the concrete block walls and the stained ceiling. By the size of the room—in the dim light it seemed to be about twenty by forty feet—he concluded it was part of a warehouse. *One of thousands,* he thought, *in and around Rome—if I'm still in Rome.*

Straining to look harder into the gloom, he spotted two windows at the other end of the room, both so dirty that the light they let in was faint. He closed his eyes and concentrated on listening.

That was when he first heard the sound of an airplane taking off in the distance. He waited. Was that a jet or a smaller plane? If it was the latter, that meant he was in a warehouse near a small airfield. But then he heard another jet followed by a third and then a fourth.

I'm near Rome's airport, Fumicino, he thought, the wave of hope he felt with his deduction dampened when he thought of the many warehouses that would be in the vicinity of one of the world's major airports. But it was a beginning, one piece of the puzzle.

With his eyes closed, he returned his thoughts to Bordy Vladic. He wondered if the boy was nearby, and that brought back a question Worthy had asked him just days before. "Nick, when Lena and I picked you up at the airport, do you remember seeing tents and shacks on the medians of the road leading into the city?"

"No, I was so happy to see both Lena and you that I didn't notice. Why?"

"It's something Sesto explained to me. That's where the Bosnians and other undocumented refugees live—if you can call that living." It was only then that a vague memory of the sorry dwellings had returned to him, but now the images appeared with clarity and guilt. He had barely seen them with his distracted mind, but his heart had missed them altogether. As he stared up at the ceiling, he whispered the prayer he knew best: "Lord Jesus Christ, have mercy on me, a sinner."

✝

Rome—Coffeeshop near Police Headquarters

Lena and Worthy sat in a small coffee bar near the police department. Neither needed to state the obvious, that finding Nick was all that mattered.

Lena noticed Worthy's left leg jumping underneath the table. She appreciated that Worthy wasn't hiding his worry, even as she knew that his feelings of guilt could easily paralyze him.

"Chris, do you remember what Nick told you when Allyson was abducted?"

"Sorry, what did you say?"

"I asked if you remembered what Nick told you when Allyson was kidnapped."

Worthy only shrugged.

"He told you that feeling guilty wouldn't help at all. What Allyson needed then—and what Nick needs now—is for you to be the detective that you are. Yes, he's our dear friend, but he's also a missing person. So, tell me where we should start?"

Although Worthy didn't say anything, Lena noticed that his leg had stopped jumping. He took out his notepad and opened it to a blank page. "We should start with the clues that Nick left us," he said. "The hand signals."

"Good. His first signal was when he was on the escalator, the V sign. What was he trying to tell us?"

Worthy exhaled slowly. "The sign has to be something basic, something he knew that we'd understand."

"Is it too obvious that the V sign was Nick's way of letting us know that the person standing behind him was Bordy Vladic? V for Vladic?"

After scribbling a note, Worthy said, "I can't think of what else the sign would stand for. So if Bordy Vladic forced Nick to change his plans, the kid must have had a weapon. I suppose it could be a gun, but I think it's more likely that it was a knife."

"I agree. Italy isn't like the States. It's much harder to have a gun. What about the second signal, the one when Nick was being taken out of the station by the two men?"

Worthy raised a hand with index finger and thumb raised. "It looks like a gun to me."

"Okay. Wouldn't that mean that at least one of those men had a gun on him?"

She could feel Worthy's leg jumping again. "Here's what I don't understand," he said. "If Vladic had a knife on him, why didn't Nick fight back? He was a heavyweight wrestler in his high school. A boy with a knife wouldn't intimidate him."

"Maybe he thought the boy would take him to Piazza del Popolo where he knew Sesto's men would step in."

Worthy shook her head. "But the kid took him up to the street level floor of shops. If Nick had created a scene in that crowded area, he could have scared the boy off."

Neither said anything for a moment. "It's like Nick wasn't thinking clearly. That's not like him, is it?" she asked.

Worthy slowly nodded. "You're right, or else . . . How about this? If he'd caused a scene, Vladic would have slipped into the crowd and escaped. And if that had happened, Nick knew we'd never see Vladic again. I think Nick realized that the only way we'd find out who killed Father Robert was for him to stay with Vladic."

"So the boy thought he'd caught Nick, but it was Nick who'd caught him," Lena said. "Yes, that must have been what Nick was thinking. I hope it wasn't a mistake."

CHAPTER TWENTY-ONE

Rome—In a Warehouse Outside of Rome

Without his watch and with the windows nearly opaque, Nick had lost any sense of time. But he estimated that he'd been awake for over an hour when two armed guards entered the room and shone a flashlight into his face. One of them bent down to unlock the chain that bound him to the bed frame, saying nothing as he led Nick toward a door that led into another room.

Panic rose within Nick as he wondered what the two men planned to do with him. But when one of them opened yet another door in the adjoining room, Nick saw that he was being led to a none-too-clean but well-lit bathroom. After the man pushed Nick inside, the door closed behind him. Gazing at the door handle, Nick realized it had no lock.

Even while using the meager facilities, he looked around the bathroom for any clues it might hold. The room was without a window or mirror and obviously unvented. There were two rags, neither of them clean, handing from a nail by the sink.

He reminded himself of all the reasons that he had to survive his ordeal. He'd faced death more than once on previous cases with Worthy, and his hope for rescue now had little to do with a fear of being killed. The reason he had to survive was the same reason behind his letting Bordy Vladic take him captive. The boy and the other Bosnians still seemed his best chance of finding out who killed Father Robert.

The second reason he had to survive was for Worthy's sake. Nick knew that if he didn't survive, Worthy would blame himself, and the weight of that guilt would crush his friend.

When Nick was brought back to the bed, he found a tray with a bottle of water and a plate of bread and cheese. Until he saw the food, he hadn't felt hungry, but now he wondered how long it had been since he'd eaten. After he was chained again to the bedframe, he saw the two guards watching him as he made the sign of the cross, offered a prayer for the food, and ate everything on the plate. When he was finished, one of the men took the tray and left, leaving the other armed man as guard.

Within minutes, a much different person stepped into the room carrying a folding chair. He was unmasked, and Nick recognized the tall, bearded man in the dilapidated coat as the beggar in Piazza del Popolo.

The man unfolded the chair and, to Nick's surprise, sat down close enough to the bed for Nick to strike him. The man looked intently at Nick, offering nothing until he said, "Yes, you and I, we have seen each other before."

Nick guessed the man was in his late fifties or early sixties. His tattered wool coat was open to reveal a stained white shirt beneath a thin tan vest. Despite the shabbiness of his dress, the man sat erectly, giving an impression of formality. Nick also noted that the man's English was fluid, with a suggestion of a British accent.

"You are a priest, but I think not a Catholic one," the man said.

"I'm an Orthodox priest, Greek Orthodox actually," Nick said

"Ah, I have met Serbian priests, also Orthodox, I believe."

And most Bosnians are Muslims and view Serbians as butchers, Nick thought.

As if reading Nick's mind, the man said, "Do not worry, Father. I know from our meeting the other night in the piazza that you are American, not Serbian."

Nick studied the man even as the man was studying him. When the man crossed one leg and rested his joined hands on a knee, Nick had a clear view of the man's shoes, scuffed at the toe and worn down at the heels. Yes, once again, it was the sense of the man's dignity that impressed him.

"Please tell me, Father, how you came to Italy," the man asked as casually as if the two were meeting over drinks in a bar.

The question confused Nick. He'd expected to be asked why he'd been in Piazza del Popolo, why he'd been showing the photos of Father Robert and Bordy Vladic, not how he'd come to Rome. "I'm sorry, I'm not sure what you're asking," he said.

The man looked away, taking in the bare room, before asking, "Please, it is not a trick question. Did you arrive in Italy by boat or was it by airplane?"

Although still confused, Nick replied, "I arrived by plane."

"I hope it was a pleasant flight. Did they serve you a meal? Maybe you flew first-class? Were you satisfied with the service?" Each of the questions was delivered slowly, with a pause of a few seconds between them.

"No, not first-class. My seat was in the back."

"But still comfortable, I trust?"

Nick searched the man's face, trying to detect a trace of mockery. "Perhaps you could tell me why you want to know about my flight."

The man lifted his index finger, as if asking for Nick's patience before answering. In the same matter-of-fact voice, the man continued. "I am told that travelers are sometimes frustrated in the airport when they have to wait in line for twenty or thirty minutes to have their passports stamped. I hope you did not suffer this. I hope the customs official smiled and welcomed you to Italy."

Nick didn't respond, finally sensing where the man's questions and statements were heading. He wondered how much of this conversation the two guards were comprehending. Certainly, Bordy Vladic's command of English on the escalator in the train station was minimal.

"If you travelled by car or bus from the airport into Rome, you probably passed where I live—no, where I sometimes sleep. I have many homes, a tent here and a tent there. The tents keep out the rain, at least."

Nick felt his face redden at the memory of his failure to notice the tents in the median. He wondered if a warm apartment or house in Bosnia or what had been Yugoslavia haunted the man's memory.

Neither man spoke until Nick decided to turn the tables and ask a question. "Your English is excellent, and, if I'm not mistaken, more British than American. Have you lived in England?"

Shaking his head, the man replied, "No, I have not had that privilege. But in Sarajevo, before the war, I taught modern English literature as well as classes in English."

"You were a professor."

The man bowed slightly. "I like to think that I still am. That is what my friends here call me–professor."

"But after the war?" Nick asked.

The man offered a slight smile, even as his eyes remained as blank as before. "The war was a long time ago, and yet, maybe not yet over. Bosnia is poor, and the people have little need for Shakespeare and Milton. But that is a comparatively small tragedy. As you can see, I am at least alive—as you are."

Nick wasn't sure if the man's comment was meant as a threat or merely a statement of fact.

"So, the two of us have that and something else in common," the man said. "We are both in the glorious city of Rome. May I tell you how I arrived in this beautiful city?"

"I assumed you were getting around to that."

"Ah, 'getting around to that.' An Americanism, yes? I will try not to bore you. I came to Rome from Trieste in the back of a truck. We were seventeen in the truck; at least, that was the number when we left Trieste. Do you know Trieste?"

Nick shook his head. "Only that it's an Italian city on the border with another country, Slovenia, maybe. Or, is it on the border of Bosnia?"

"No, not Bosnia. You were right the first time. Trieste is situated on the border with Slovenia. The journey from Bosnia to Slovenia, if a person takes that journey on foot, can take over a month, much of it over mountains. You see, I am a travel expert of sorts. I've made the journey from Bosnia to Trieste six times. Of course, the first five times, border officials in Slovenia or in Trieste found my group and turned me back. I didn't have the right papers, you see." The professor opened his hands to show that they were empty. "To be honest, I had no papers at all. Three times, the officials in Slovenia beat me before passing me along to the Croats. The Croats were not as kind. They beat me every time before dropping me across the border into Bosnia."

The professor took a deep breath and paused. "When I was at the university in Sarajevo, I was fond of telling my students that life is a school. I told them that life offers lessons every day if a person is alert. So each time I was deposited back in my country, I learned something for the next attempt. Usually, it was a small lesson—a better route, a farmer I could bribe so I could sleep in his barn, that sort of thing. I learned enough to end up this time, my sixth try, in Rome. So, I am one of the lucky ones, despite that fact that no one smiled at me and said 'Welcome to Italy.'"

When the professor first began talking, Nick thought he was appealing for sympathy. But the longer he listened to the man, the more he realized that there was no appeal at all. The man relayed the information as a person might in mentioning the day's weather forecast at a bus stop or commenting on the price of beef to a next-door neighbor. It was this tone, one that conveyed hopelessness, that bothered Nick the most.

"I apologize for the simple food, but it what is easiest for us to . . . what shall I say?—easiest for us to come by."

"It was fine."

The professor sat up even straighter in the chair. "We are not animals, Father, despite what you might have heard or what you might believe. Circumstances force us to live like animals here in Italy, but our situation, Inshallah, if God wills, is only temporary."

In that moment, Nick heard what was beneath the words of this highly-educated and cultured man, his captor. The professor was a man who fought every day to hold on to his dignity not just for himself, but for those whom he guided.

The professor rose, bowed, and reached into the pocket of his coat to remove several sheets of paper. "If you have never read this, I think you will find it interesting. But please know, it is a fairy tale," he said, laying the pages on the edge of Nick's bed before turning to leave the room. Nick watched the man say something to the armed guard by the door, which resulted in the guard shaking his head.

Nick unfolded the pages to find the English version of the Thirty Articles of the United Nations Charter of Human Rights written in 1948. *Interesting, but it's a fairy tale,* Nick remembered the professor saying, as he began to read.

Rome—Worthy's Office

Sitting next to Worthy in Capitano Sesto's office, Lena thought the policeman looked more hopeful.

Opening his computer, Sesto said, "I receive email last night," he said, turning the screen for Worthy and Lena to see. "It is from Canadian Embassy in Rome. It is request to them from Father Robert. He want to meet with ambassador about immigration. You can see the embassy say no, but he can meet with another official. Meeting was to take place morning after Father Robert, he was killed."

Worthy couldn't hide his frustration. "Any reason why we're finding out about this now?"

"Father Robert, he not show up for his appointment, so he crossed off as what you call a 'no-show.' Do you two want to go to embassy, or should I?"

Worthy noted that Capitano Sesto was making an effort to include Lena. "We'll do it," he said.

Sesto nodded before scribbling something on a sheet of paper. Handing it to Lena, he said, "This is embassy address. I hope you find something useful."

It took Lena and Worthy over an hour through heavy traffic to arrive at the Canadian Embassy on Via Nomentana. They used the time to speculate on why Father Robert would have sought a meeting with the embassy about immigration.

"What does fit, Chris, is that Father Robert's behavior changed dramatically in his last days," Lena said. "Before that, he just seemed to be awaiting his fate. Then, something changed. He was in the library for hours researching something, and, at night, he left the monastery to go to Piazza del Popolo."

"You're right," Worthy agreed. "Something got his attention and woke him up. His focus changed. Now all we have to do is figure out what that that was."

"Huh. I wonder . . ."

"What?" Worthy asked.

"I'm not sure, but we know something happened to give him a sudden burst of energy. It's like he had a sense of mission, a new mission?"

Worthy didn't say anything for a moment. "And something to do with immigration, a visa, it seems. What if he realized his work at the orphanage in Yellowknife was over? Maybe he'd changed his mind and was planning on remaining in Italy."

Lena shook her head. "That doesn't sound right. If he'd wanted to stay in Italy, wouldn't he have gone to the Italian authorities, not to Canadian Embassy? Let's hope someone here knows something."

At the entrance to the Canadian Embassy, a young man in military uniform met and escorted them into the building and down a hallway to a large lobby area.

"I'll let them know that you're here," he said, before exiting through heavy wooden doors.

Worthy glanced around at the lobby, empty except for them. On one wall were nostalgic posters advertising the Canadian Pacific Railroad. There were scenes of mountains and glacial lakes, as well as others showing skiers, canoeists, or hikers. On another wall were similar scenes from the Maritime Provinces showing sailboats and fishing boats nestled in quaint harbors. Worthy assumed that the scenes were placed there not only to boost tourism but also to offer the embassy staff a sense of home.

His thoughts were interrupted by Lena whispering. "I think I should talk with the librarian at the monastery again."

"About Father Robert's research?"

"Sort of. I know I said that the librarian wasn't much help, but what about the IT firm that the order uses? We do know the dates when Father Robert used one of the monastery computers."

Just then, the heavy wooden door opened. Coming toward them was a woman of medium height, seemingly middle-aged, with grey hair parted down the middle. She was dressed in a dark blue business suit and looked the part of a government official.

The woman introduced herself as Simone LaTour and invited them to follow her.

On the other side of the wooden doors was a thickly-carpeted hallway. Office doors, most of the closed, lined the hallway. The third one on the left was open, and it was into this office that the woman led them. She gestured to two leather-covered chairs before sitting down on the other side of a desk. Worthy noted the woman's full name and title "Simone LaTour, Deputy Assistant to the Ambassador" on a nameplate on the desk.

The walls in this room displayed artifacts of Canada's Indigenous Peoples—beaded headdresses, miniature replicas of sealskin kayaks, and pieces of carved whale ivory. Lena looked from the walls back to the woman on the other side of the desk and realized she was Indigenous herself.

"Those are so beautiful," Lena said, nodding toward the headdresses.

"Yes, and very old. Of course, not as old as Rome," she said in Lena's direction. "Your English is superb, but from your name I assume you're Italian."

"I am. In fact, I was born here in Rome."

"Then let me compliment you on your home. I've only been here for three months, but I'm already hoping my stay will be longer." She turned to Worthy. "And you are Mr. Worthy, the detective. From what is on the internet about you, I understand that you are a homicide detective in Detroit."

"I was that until I retired a month ago. I'm in private work, back in the States but also with an office here in Rome."

Ms. LaTour's eyebrows rose. "A private detective here?"

Worthy explained the kind of detective work he planned to do in Rome, how he specialized in serving Rome's English-speaking residents, tourists, and pilgrims.

"And now you're working on the death of Father Robert. I hope you're making progress."

Worthy frowned. "I think we are, but the case has taken a bad turn. Our colleague on the case, another priest, has been abducted, we think by the group that was either responsible for Father Robert's death or has information about who killed him."

"Oh, good heavens," Ms. LaTour said. "Did I miss that in the newspapers?"

"No, we're trying to keep that under wraps for the time being."

The Deputy Ambassador frowned. "I hope our delay in notifying the police didn't have anything to do with his abduction."

Worthy weighed how to respond. Instead of confirming the embassy's culpability, he said, "No, we don't hold anyone here to blame."

"Did this happen recently?" Ms. LaTour asked.

"Two days ago," Lena offered. "We believe our best hope of finding our colleague is to solve Father Robert's murder."

"Yes, I think I understand, and, of course, we'd do anything to help. What would you like to know?"

"Father Robert died the night before he had a scheduled meeting here at the embassy, but we're hoping you can shed some light on what he was wanting," Worthy said.

"Of course. Again, I'm sorry for the delay in notifying the police. In my capacity as one of the ambassador's assistants, I receive a monthly log of requests made to all the offices here in the embassy. That log lists the meetings that did occur but also the meetings that didn't. For example, as in this case, when the petitioner fails to show up. Unfortunately, I didn't receive last month's log until yesterday. Because of that, it wasn't until I looked through the log last night that I saw the name of Father Robert Porter and realized that I'd seen the name before. A bit of online searching led me to accounts in Toronto and Ottawa newspapers from two weeks ago about his murder here in Rome. What can I say, other than it was an oversight."

"Actually, we're grateful that you made the connection at all," Worthy said. "Would I be right in thinking that you record the phone calls you receive?"

"Yes, and I have a recording of that ready to play as well as a written transcript," she replied as she handed sheets of paper across the desk, one to Lena and the other to Worthy. "As you can see, his call to the embassy was quite short." While Ms. LaTour gave Worthy and Lena a moment to read the transcript, she opened a desk drawer and brought out a small digital recorder.

Setting it down on her desk, she pressed a button. Immediately, they heard the voice of the embassy receptionist.

"This is the Canadian Embassy. With whom am I speaking?"

"Hello, yes, this is Father Robert Porter. I'm from Yellowknife in the Northwest Territories."

This was the first time Lena had heard Father Robert's voice. His voice was high but forceful, she thought.

"One moment, sir," the receptionist said. "Did you say you are the father of a Robert Porter?"

"No, my name is Robert Porter. Father is my title. I'm a priest, you see."

"I understand. How can I assist you, Father?"

"I need to speak with the ambassador. Yes, I'd very much like to do that." His voice had changed, with the words coming more quickly.

"What is the nature of your issue or concern, Father?"

"My concern? Yes, how should I put it? I suppose it's about visas, or maybe I mean immigration."

"Do I understand that you've lost your passport, sir?"

"No, no, this isn't about me." After a pause, Father Robert continued, his voice rising even further and sounding almost panicky. "What I need is difficult to explain. I'm sure I can make myself understood if I can meet with the ambassador."

"Unfortunately, the ambassador doesn't handle this type of concern. But I can give you an appointment with another embassy office that does handle such matters."

"Well, I don't know. I was hoping . . . you see, I don't know how complicated all this is here in Italy, I mean. When could I meet with the right person?"

"There are a number of officials in that office. I've pulled up their schedules, Father, and it looks like there is an opening tomorrow at three p.m. in the afternoon. Would that suit your schedule?"

A protracted period of silence followed, leading the receptionist to ask, "Are you still there, Father?"

"Yes, sorry. I'm just trying to think. You said three in the afternoon tomorrow? There's nothing before that?"

"I'm afraid not. Will that time suit you?"

"Yes, I will make that work. But I don't know where you're located. I can't afford a taxi, so I'll be taking a bus or the Metro."

"That's no problem. Our embassy is located on Via Nomentana. Do you know that street?"

"No, I'm sorry, I don't. Can you give me directions?"

"Of course. Do you know how to get to Termini, the train station?"

"Yes, I've been there . . . well, several times. Is the embassy close to that?"

"Not very close. Once you've arrived at the train station, I suggest you go outside to the bus stops and take bus number fifty-six. Via Nomentana is on its route. Most of the bus drivers understand basic English. Tell the driver that you want to be let off near the Canadian Embassy. When you get off the bus, look for number two-forty-three on Via Salaria. Would you like me to repeat that?"

"No, no, I think I have it. You see . . . well, this is very important. That's why I wanted to speak with the ambassador."

"I can assure you that your issue will be taken seriously. Is there anything else I can help you with, Father?"

Hearing no response, Worthy assumed that Father Robert had ended the phone call.

After a moment, Lena said, "He sounds agitated. Is it common for people to ask to speak directly with the ambassador?"

Ms. LaTour nodded. "Quite common, I'm afraid. But Father Robert was a bit more insistent, which fits your observation about his agitation. Is there anything else we can help you with? You see, I can't help wondering if things would have been different if Father Robert had been able to see the ambassador. Please, please don't hesitate to contact us if there's anything else within my power."

Worthy and Lena stood, both shaking hands with the embassy assistant. "That's very kind of you, Ms. LaTour. We're grateful that you kept Father Robert's phone call," Worthy said. "When we solve his murder, we'll more likely to know what he wanted here at the embassy."

"I pray that you'll succeed. One more thing, Mr. Worthy. Do you have a business card? You see, I think it possible that we will need to use your services in the future. Some of my fellow Canadians in Rome find themselves in some sorry straights, mostly minor, I'm happy to say," nodding in Lena's direction, "but they would likely find it easier to explain what's happened to them to an English-speaker like yourself."

Removing a business card from his pocket, Worthy passed it across the desk.

"Very good. Thank you," she said. "And I hope your colleague will be found safe. He must be very frightened."

Worthy glanced at Lena and knew that they were thinking the same thing. Nick being frightened wasn't their worry. His survival was.

In the car, Lena asked, "What's your thinking now about Father Robert?"

He thought about the question for a moment before answering. "Hearing his voice changed my mind a bit. I don't think he was asking about a visa for himself. Did you hear him say 'I don't know how complicated this is in Italy'?"

"Yes, what do you think that was about?"

"As you said before, Father Robert seemed to have found a new mission toward the end. We just need to find what that mission was."

Rome—A Warehouse Outside of Rome

When Nick awoke, he assumed he was now in the third day of captivity. That he was still alive—if, in fact, those who abducted him were responsible for Father Robert's death—gave him hope that his captors believed he could be of some use.

The professor had yet to return a second time, and the guards hadn't interacted with him other than to escort him to the bathroom or bring into trays of food and water. While the guards were always armed when Nick was able to use the bathroom, his treatment had so far been respectful.

He thought back on his conversation with the professor the day before. It had seemed more like a tutorial than an interrogation. The professor hadn't asked the questions that Nick had expected—what connection did he have with Father Robert and how had he gotten a photo of Bordy Vladic? Instead, the professor had focused the conversation on life in Italy for Bosnians without papers.

Nick found himself hoping that the professor was the adult who looked after the Bosnian teenagers, as he found it difficult to imagine the professor ordering the death of Father Robert on a whim. The less desirable possibility was that others above the professor made the decisions. Nick's fate, then, would be in their hands.

Hoping for another visit from the professor, Nick thought about what he hoped to learn. Uppermost were the questions of how Father Robert had died and if Bordy Vladic and the other teenagers had been somehow involved in his death. But then he realized that to begin the conversation with those questions would cast him in the role of the impatient and demanding American. No, he decided, he would wait.

He thought back on what the professor had chosen to talk about. From what little reading he'd done about the refugee crisis, he assumed the Italian officials routinely sent undocumented refugees back to their nation of origin. He had no idea, however, that Bosnians returned home would try over and over again to reach Italy. He was reminded of the migrants at the U.S.'s southern border, coming in waves that receded only to wash onto the shore again.

What must Bosnia be like, he wondered, for men, women, and children to risk a perilous journey and then, if they're lucky enough to slip into the country, to live in tents or makeshift shacks as they eke out an equally perilous existence in petty crime. *Have I even given five minutes to imagine what such an existence would be like?* he asked himself. Coming back with shame was a memory of dropping loose change in the cups of the Bosnian mothers with infants who begged in the Metro stations.

The reality was that Italians had established ways, becoming unconscious habits over time, to avoid the Bosnians. Travel guides warned tourists of the danger the undocumented refugees posed, as did posters in the metro stations. That meant that to survive, the Bosnians had to develop countermeasures. Nick thought of a dance where each partner had grown accustomed to the moves of the other.

The image of a dance brought a new thought to Nick about Father Robert's death. Had the Canadian priest done something to disrupt the dance, the normal pattern, something that Bordy Vladic, or even the professor, had interpreted as a threat?

CHAPTER TWENTY-TWO

Rome—Worthy's New Office

That same morning, Worthy was surprised to find the light on his answering machine blinking when he entered his office. Hitting the button, he listened to two messages. The first was from an American couple, the other from an Irish couple, both stating that they'd been victimized in a scam the night before.

In both messages, Worthy heard the panic in the tourists' voices. When they'd reported what happened to the police, they'd been told there was little the police could do. When the couples had refused to accept that conclusion, a policeman named Sesto had given them Worthy's number.

Thanks for nothing, Stefano, Worthy thought as he listened to the rest of the messages left by the couples. The American's message was, "Is there any way for us to get us our money back, Mr. Worthy? Please help us." The message left by the Irish couple was similar. "We've been robbed! Our vacation is over. What can we do? What can you do?"

Given Nick's abduction, Worthy's first thought was that he had no time to spend on petty crimes such as this latest scam. But then he realized that that the trick played on the two couples was not "petty" to them. Furthermore, he was now in business, a business that relied on his taking cases like this, cases that the Rome police didn't want to handle.

He doubted that he could do little more than what the police could, but that little bit was what he would agree to try. He would meet with the couples and listen to their tales of woe. After that, he would spell out the couples' options, assuming they had options. He hoped that the meeting with the two couples would take no more than an hour or two, giving him time to return to CCTV footage of Nick's movements in the train station.

But his plans changed when the couples arrived later that morning and told their stories. It was immediately obvious to Worthy that both couples had been victims of the same scam in the same neighborhood and likely by the same perpetrators.

The scam was one that Worthy became aware of two years before on his first case in the city. The scam began with a tourist or two were stopped by a man who, in passable English, shone a flashlight on a map of the city and said he was lost. Could the couple help him find the route back to his hotel?

The second stage of the scam began when the gullible couples agreed to help the man out. Looking at the man's map, however, they quickly became confused. While the map had the word "Roma" at its top, none of the street names were familiar. The man kept the couples engaged by saying how important it was for him to be back at his hotel, as his wife and children were expecting him.

The scam's third stage began when a car screeched to a halt, followed by two men jumping out and yelling at the man. Shining their flashlights on badges, the two men claimed to be policemen who'd been tracking the man with the map. "He is a con-artist," they claimed, and said they were there to arrest him. One of the men posing as a police officer had then turned to the couples and said that the scam artist had an electronic device on him, like one had been used to access ATMs, that allowed him to access and compromise the couple's debit cards while they'd studied the phony map. The policeman said that the only way to determine if the debit cards had, indeed, been compromised was to let him call in the numbers of the tourists' debit cards to the nearest police station.

While all this was happening, the other officer and the man with the map were creating a distraction by screaming at one another. After the call had been made, the policeman handed the debit cards back to the couples and told them that he'd secured their accounts. He encouraged each couple, once back in their hotel rooms, to check their bank balances.

The scam ended with the man with the map being forced into the back of the police car. The couples thanked their lucky stars that the police had intervened, but all that changed once they were back in their hotel rooms. That's when they found out that their accounts had been emptied of every dollar. They'd been scammed by the man with the map and the two men posing as policemen who were working with him.

"I'm sorry this has happened to all of you," Worthy said at the end of their stories. "I do have a suggestion of something you can do, although I can't guarantee that it will work."

"We'll try anything," the Irish woman said. The American couple agreed.

"Okay. Banks in Ireland are already open, but banks in the US won't be open for a few hours. I'll make the initial call once I have the phone numbers. I'll explain who I am and that I work closely with police here in Rome before I explain how you've been duped. I'll emphasize that you are innocent victims of very clever thieves, which the police can substantiate, and that everyone would benefit if the banks showed good faith and reimbursed you. The banks, after all, have insurance for fraud cases like this."

"Oh, that's wonderful. And you think it could work?" the American husband asked.

Worthy shrugged. "All I can say is that it's worth a try. But Worthy also knew he could do something else that might aid the forlorn couples. From them, he could get descriptions of the three men and the location of where the scams had taken place. He could then stake out the area and possibly photograph the three men in action. Those photos handed over to Sesto would go a long way toward arresting the men, which might lead to a recovery of all or at least some of the stolen money. Such an outcome would not only aid the couples but also bolster his credibility and usefulness with the Rome police.

"Before I call the banks, I'd like you to give me a description of the three men," he said. "I think it's likely the same men are behind both scams. Let's start with how they spoke. Obviously, they knew some English, but I'm sure it didn't sound like their first language."

"I just assumed it was Italian," the American woman replied.

"I thought the same," the Irish man said. "I know a little bit of Italian, enough to get by in restaurants and shops, so when the two men were yelling at each other, I'm sure they were speaking Italian."

"Not an Eastern European language?"

The American couple looked confused by the question; the Irish couple frowned. "No, definitely not," the Irish woman said.

Worthy nodded. "Okay, let's talk about the physical description of the three men, starting with the man who approached you with a map."

"He was on the short side," the American wife said.

The Irish husband shook his head. "The one who approached us was of medium height, maybe even taller."

Worthy thought for a moment about the difference, then asked, "Would you say the man's height was five feet eight or nine?" As Worthy expected, the couples agreed on that, proving that the man with the map would look shorter to the tall Americans than to the Irish couple. The couples also agreed that the man wore glasses with black frames.

"So, let's assume it was the same man who approached you both." When Worthy asked about a watch, jewelry, or any distinguishing facial feature, both couples said it was too dark to notice.

"What about his clothes?" Worthy asked, looking particularly at the two women.

The Irish woman answered first. "He wore a short jacket, the puffy kind." The American nodded in agreement, but neither could suggest a color. "They kept shining their flashlights in our eyes," she said in explanation.

"Did you notice his shirt or slacks?"

"No, sorry," the Irish woman said. The American woman also said she hadn't noticed.

Unexpectedly, the Irish man said, "I remember his shoes. They were brown loafers. I think they looked quite new."

"Okay, let's talk about the other men. I assume they weren't wearing police uniforms," Worthy said.

Both couples agreed, but could add only that the two phony cops were maybe wearing leather jackets. "They looked like plain clothes cops on TV," the American man offered.

"Which I suspect was the plan. Tell me what you remember about this badge that they showed you."

The couples looked at each other. "They couldn't have flashed the badge for more than a second. To be honest, I didn't get a good look at it," the Irish man said sheepishly. The Americans agreed.

"Don't beat yourself up about that," Worthy said. "They didn't want you to get a good look at it. It had to be a false one." Worthy opened a map of the city. "Now, you both said you were approached after you left restaurants. Can you show me on the map where you were approached and where you ate before that?"

The two couples looked down at the map. The Irish husband spoke first. "We ate in a trattoria just off this place," he said, pointing at Piazza del Popolo.

Worthy hid his new interest. "And you were on your way back to your hotel. Can you locate that on the map?"

The Irish man had no trouble pointing out the location. "So, you must have been approached somewhere in this vicinity, between Piazza del Popolo and your hotel."

"Aye, closer to the piazza," he agreed.

The Americans were whispering between themselves. "What is it?" Worthy asked.

"Our answers are almost exactly the same. The restaurant was different, but close to the piazza. And our hotel is just one block farther."

Worthy's mind was racing. "My guess is that you all were followed after you left the piazza. And you're sure that the man with the map and the two guys in the car were Italian, not Eastern European."

Both couples continued to insist that the men were Italians.

After Worthy promised to call them after he'd communicated with their banks, they thanked him for his efforts. When he was alone in his office, he reviewed his notes. The scam was higher up the criminal ladder than picking pockets, and with the couples' shared conviction about the nationality of the men, he concluded that the scammers could not have been Bosnians. Yet, he was certain that the two gangs, the Italians and the Bosnians, had to know of each other, given that both were working out of Piazza del Popolo.

He wondered if that meant that the two groups had come to an arrangement. Or, were both gangs being run by a third party, possibly organized crime?

Worthy looked up from the words "Piazza del Popolo" that he'd underlined in his notes. Slowly, pieces, like Lego blocks, seemed to come together. On the last three nights of his life, Father Robert had gone to the piazza, the center of at least two crime operations. That meant that his returning to the piazza three nights straight had to have been noted by the gangs. *And how would those gangs have interpreted the priest's weird behavior but as a possible trap. One of the gangs, and I'm putting my money on the Italians,* Worthy thought, *decided to act.*

Of course, Worthy knew that none of that changed the fact that Bordy

Vladic was involved in Nick's abduction. But it did offer Worthy a glimmer of hope that if the Bosnians were holding Nick, they were less likely to have killed Father Robert even as they might know who did. And more importantly, if the Bosnians were Nick's captors, they might not have any plans to kill him.

Rome—Abbot Lorenzo's Office

While Worthy was listening to the two couples who'd been scammed, Lena was meeting with the monastery's librarian. As Worthy and she had agreed, she asked for the contact information for the motherhouse's IT provider. Acquiring that information was the easy part. The harder part came when she contacted the company's main office in Milan. For over an hour online, she was transferred from one employee to another until she was connected with Giancarlo Corsi, a technician who sounded as if he'd yet to celebrate his twentieth birthday. But he did think he could help.

"It's good you have the dates and times," he said, "but this could still take me a couple of hours."

Lena decided that the best use of her time waiting would be spent reading more of Abbot Boniface's papers. She'd barely begun, however, when a monk approached her and set down a note. Opening it, she read Abbot Lorenzo's request that she stop by his office when she was free. She decided that now was as good a time as any.

As she entered his office, Abbot Lorenzo rose from behind his desk, holding what looked like a letter in his hand.

"First of all, Doctor Fabriano, is there any news about Father Fortis?" he asked.

Lena felt a wave of irritation, wondering if this was why he'd requested to see her.

"Not anything concrete, but we remain hopeful," she said.

The abbot sighed and shook his head. "First, Father Robert and now, Father Fortis. Please know, Dr. Fabriano, that we are praying for Father Fortis in all of our services." After he invited her to take a chair, he handed her the letter. "I don't know if this is important, but I thought you ought to see it."

Reading quickly, Lena realized the letter was from Father Jacob, a parish priest in Yellowknife, Northwest Territories. It was addressed to Nick in care of the Order of the Sacred Wounds Monastery. At the top of the page were the words "Please forward this letter to Father Nicholas Fortis." Below that, Lena read:

"Father Nick, I don't know if you're having trouble with your email account, but I've left several messages and haven't heard back. I trust that this letter finds you well and progressing on finding Father Robert's killer. On this end, I've been busy on what we discussed about S. Lonetree."

Lena paused, remembering Nick saying, the day he was abducted, that a parish priest in Yellowknife was trying to track down someone by the name of S. Lonetree who'd sent a piece of mail to Father Robert. What Lena distinctly remembered Nick saying was that S. Lonetree had written that Father Robert might wish him dead.

She read on. "As I promised, I've contacted the postal authorities in North Vancouver, asking for any information that might have on S. Lonetree. The Royal Mail is obligated to protect the privacy of citizens, but I explained that the letter from S. Lonetree might help in a murder investigation.

"My argument must have been convincing, because I just received an email from the post office in North Vancouver saying that while they have no address for a S. Lonetree, a man by that name does have a post-office box. The post office suggested that any correspondence for S. Lonetree should be sent to P.O. Box 8730, North Vancouver, British Columbia.

"Father Nick, please email me what you'd like me to do next. I am happy to send a message to S. Lonetree at the address the post office gave me if you tell me what the message should be. On another matter, the closest relatives of the three boys who died in the fire have filed a lawsuit against the orphanage's board of trustees. They claim that Father Robert alerted the board to the dangers of the aging heating system. We both know that will be difficult to prove, given that there is no written record of Father Robert ever doing that. I tell you this in case you discover something in your interviews in Rome that might bear on the question."

The letter was signed by Father Jacob with his email address following.

"I wouldn't have opened the letter, except that it was, as you can see, sent to Father Fortis through me," the abbot said.

"No, you did the right thing. Will you let me take this? I need to show it to Chris and our contact in the police."

"So you think this letter can be of some help?"

"It's too soon to tell. But I can promise you that we'll contact Father Jacob in Yellowknife." Lena rose and started to leave—then stopped. "We're all worried about Nick—Father Fortis. Please let the monks know that we appreciate your prayers. And I'm sure that Nick does too."

CHAPTER TWENTY-THREE

Rome—At a Warehouse Near the Airport

Nick had no idea what time of day it was, but when he awoke, he was surprised to find Bordy Vladic sitting next to his bed. Nick raised himself up and studied the face of the teenager. Bordy's hair was unevenly cut, and Nick thought it likely that one of the other boys had cut it with a pair of scissors none too sharp. Every visible inch of Bordy's skin, on his face, neck, and hands was darkened by ground-in dirt. He was wearing the same hoodie and oversized trainers that he'd worn in the train station. But it was the boy's teeth, so many missing, that struck Nick the most.

Bordy sat with his thin arms folded across his chest, turning his head to carry on a conversation with one of the armed guards. *So, at least one of them is Bosnian,* he thought. Although Nick didn't understand a word of it, he detected the tone of bravado in Bordy's speech. The boy could be no more than thirteen, Nick realized, but he was talking as if he were an adult.

"Are you here to talk or just look at me?" Nick asked as he sat on the side of the bed.

"You speak Bosnian?" Bordy asked with a sneer. "No, so I have speak your language. See, you in chain, but even so, you have advantage. You," he said, pointing at Nick, "think you better than me."

"What I think is that life is unfair," Nick said slowly. "Neither of us chose where we were born."

Bordy didn't say anything for a moment, leaving Nick to wonder if the boy understood what he'd said.

"How many people in America?" Bordy asked, the words sounding like a challenge.

"I'm not sure. Over three hundred million, I think."

Bordy turned and asked the man behind him a question. After they answered, he nodded.

Turning back to Nick, Bordy held up three fingers. "Bosnia, three million. When war," he said, as he lowered one of the fingers, "that many killed. How many that?"

"I think you're saying that a million Bosnians died."

Bordy sat forward, as if he were ready to pounce. "You think I too young to know. That I born after war over. War not over. People not die of bombs, but no food. No medicine. First, father die. Then brother, two sister. My mother, when Serbs came to village, she was . . . No, no, is enough. What you think, American?"

Not sure how to answer the question, Nick didn't say anything for a moment. "What I think is that I should know more about the war in Bosnia. But I don't."

Bordy continued to hold Nick's gaze. "Professor, he say Americans watch sport on TV all day and all night. Never stop. Sport, sport, sport. Bosnia dying, you watch sport."

Nick knew he could share that monks watched very little TV, but he knew that didn't change the fact that he along with most American monks knew little about conditions in Bosnia. How could Bordy understand that Americans viewed the Balkan War and its aftermath as old news? Bosnia was a story from the nineties, a story buried beneath more recent news from Syria, Haiti, Yemen, Afghanistan, Ukraine, and so many other countries.

"Can I ask how you came to Italy?" Nick asked.

Bordy's expression changed, now looking pleased with himself. "Me, I make journey one time. I smart. No catch me."

"How long have you been here?"

"Maybe two year. I here to stay. I have big plan, secret."

It was a boast, but Nick could tell that Bordy believed it.

"Does the professor have the same big plan?"

Bordy laughed. "My plan bigger. Big house. Fast car."

"It sounds like you expect to stay in Italy legally."

"What 'legally' mean?"

"It means you'd be treated as an Italian, not worried about being sent back to Bosnia."

"I not go back. Yes, I be Italian. Is plan."

"Don't you worry that the police will catch you and send you back to Bosnia?"

Bordy held up both hands, at first clenched, then suddenly open. "Poof. I am shadow. I here now, then not here. I walk same street as you. You big, no hide good. I know all places for hide."

Nick didn't doubt that Bordy and the other Bosnian kids knew the streets of Rome better than most Italians, maybe even better than the police did.

"It would be harder for the professor to hide. Do you worry he could be caught?"

Bordy stood and pointed a finger at his chest. "Me worry for Bordy. Professor he worry too many."

With that, the boy rose from the chair and swaggered as he moved to the door. Nick wondered why the boy had come in the first place. The visit from the professor had seemed a kind of test. Perhaps, he thought, Bordy's visit was another test. But if so, why did the boy's visit leave him with the feeling that its purpose was far darker?

Rome—At a Trattoria near Worthy's Office

Over lunch, Lena and Worthy shared their findings, Worthy relating what he'd learned from the two couples after Lena showed him the letter from the priest in Yellowknife. Nick, Worthy knew, would have understood the message from the Canadian priest, but Worthy's first thought was to dismiss Father Jacob's letter as a distraction. Worthy couldn't see how a letter received by Father Robert in the days before the orphanage fire could help them rescue Nick.

But after a moment's reflection, Worthy knew why they wouldn't ignore Father Jacob's letter. . For one reason, Worthy thought that what troubled Father Robert on the night of the fire could be connected to his murder in Rome, and his murder in Rome was certainly connected to Nick's abduction. But Worthy knew that the main reason Lena and he would follow up on Father Jacob's letter was that Nick would have done that. In some way, their following up on the letter brought Nick closer.

"Lena, email Father Jacob and let him know what happened to Nick and ask him to track down this S. Lonetree if he can," Worthy said.

"I'm fine with that. What do you have planned?"

"I'm seeing Sesto about the debit card scam. Then I'm going to go through the CCTV footage from Piazza del Popolo over a ten-day period."

"Do you mean before Nick was abducted?"

"And also after. What I learned from the couples is that the Bosnians aren't the only sharks preying on tourists in and around the piazza."

Lena's cellphone buzzed and when she saw who'd called, she looked surprised. "It's the IT techie from Milan. He's getting back to me sooner than I thought. Cross your fingers. Maybe he's found something."

When she punched the speakerphone button, Worthy heard "Dr. Fabriano, this is Giancarlo. I've managed to isolate the websites that users from the monastery viewed within the time parameters you gave me."

"That's terrific. I thought you said it would take a lot longer," she said.

"I did say that. But on the days and hours you gave me, only seven websites were viewed. I don't know if that's normal for a monastery, but that's much less traffic than we have with businesses and schools."

Lena remembered what the librarian had told her, that when he left for afternoon prayers and then returned to the library afterwards, Father Robert was still online. Lena now thought Father Robert had planned it that way, so that he wouldn't be observed.

Opening her purse, Lena took out a pad of paper and a pen. "You said seven sites, Giancarlo?"

"Yes. Somebody at the monastery checked for rugby scores on two websites."

Lena shook her head at Worthy. "Next, please."

"Somebody at the monastery went to the site for the Canadian Embassy in Rome. Whoever did that was only on that site for a few minutes."

Lena made a note as she said, "That fits. What else?"

"Someone opened two Vatican websites. Both are about the process of sainthood."

Lena stopped writing. "That was me. It has to do with my research. You said there are two more?"

"Yes. Someone looked at two sites, one about orphanages in and around Rome and another about adoption procedures in Italy. Is that helpful?"

The look of surprise on Lena's face changed after a few seconds to a broad smile. "That's more helpful than you know, Giancarlo. Email me the name of your supervisor, and I'll send her or him a message bragging about you."

Giancarlo laughed. "Thanks, but I am the supervisor."

"What? How old are you, Giancarlo?"

"Almost twenty-one. But I oversee several techs here who are younger than me. I hope that doesn't make you feel old."

"Oh, it makes me feel very old, but given what you just told me, I can live with that."

After the call ended, Lena asked, "Adoption and orphanages around Rome. Could the sites Father Robert was looking at explain his mission?"

Worthy nodded. "Maybe the ice is finally thawing."

"Ice?"

"Just an expression. That's what we'd say in Detroit when a stubborn case started to break open. So here's the first crack: in the days before he died, Father Robert was looking on the internet for orphanages near Rome."

Lena put down her glass. "And he also looked up the Canadian Embassy website."

Worthy smiled, the first smile Lena had seen on his face since Nick had been abducted. "It's like we're finally getting Father Robert's final days in focus," he said. "During those days, he was researching Italian orphanages, visas, and passports. And on all three nights, he was in Piazza del Popolo. And what would he have noticed? The Bosnian kids and what they were up to."

"Oh, my God, Chris. The Bosnians must have reminded him of his orphans. He was looking for a way to rescue the boys."

Worthy exhaled slowly. "I feel like I can finally breathe. Father Robert's mind wasn't focused on the fire back in Yellowknife anymore. He was thinking about the future, some way that the Bosnian kids could shelter in an orphanage."

"First websites about orphanages near Rome; then, information about visas," Lena said. "What makes sense to me is that Father Robert was looking for orphanages that would be willing to take the Bosnian boys. What if he found on those sites that what he hoped for was impossible? I can see his hope changing. Maybe the visit he'd set up to the Canadian Embassy was about getting the boys Canadian visas that would allow them to stay legally in Italy. That's what Father Robert reminds me of—a guardian angel. I can see him thinking he could take care of them."

"You mean, he'd start his own orphanage here for the Bosnian boys?" Worthy asked.

"Exactly. And he called the Canadian Embassy to see if they could help him navigate my government's bureaucracy, the legal red tape, I mean. He sounded agitated on the phone call, but maybe he was excited and obsessed with the idea. No wonder he wanted to speak directly with the ambassador. He was hoping the ambassador could pick up his phone and make it magically happen."

"Well, you're the psychologist, Lena, not me. But everything you said makes a kind of sense, although if Father Robert hoped to set up an orphanage in Italy, he was a dreamer."

"I don't dispute that. From the night he got roaring drunk before the fire to the three days here before he was killed in the piazza, he was depressed. He must have felt he was alone in a deep hole with no way out. Such a person doesn't feel like giving up; they've already given up. Then, out of the blue a whole new possibility hits you. It must have felt like a gift from God to him as a priest. He'd been given a new mission, an orphanage for the Bosnian boys."

"Like God was giving him a second chance after what happened in Yellowknife," Worthy said in a barely audible voice.

CHAPTER TWENTY-FOUR

Rome—Capitano Sesto's Office

After lunch with Lena, Worthy drove to the police station where he found Sesto eating a sandwich at his desk.

"Please, Chris, sit. I receive a call from one of my sergeants. He showed photos of scammers in our files to the two couples. No luck. They say, too dark, flashlights in their eyes. Sorry."

"That might not matter, Stefano" Worthy said. "I've thought of another way we might identify the scammers."

"Oh?"

"We know the general area where they approached the two couples. I propose that Lena and I stake out that area for a few nights. Maybe we can catch the perps on camera."

Capitano Sesto initially shook his head, then stopped. "You not think to pose as tourists?"

"No, we'd only be able to walk through the area once before raising suspicion. We're going to take photos, that's all, but we can use night-vision lenses."

"Ah. Sure, yes, we have night-vision cameras. I see no problem."

"There is something else that I hope you can help me with. I'd like to scan through more of the CCTV footage from the piazza."

"Again?"

"Not the footage we've already looked at but footage from four or five nights before Nick went there and also four or five nights after he was abducted."

Sesto looked puzzled. "What you hope to find?"

Worthy thought carefully about his answer, as he didn't want to cast any blame on police efforts to curb crime in the piazza. From the very beginning, the captain had been nothing but helpful. Worthy couldn't say that about everyone he worked with in Detroit.

"We now know that the piazza is the staging area for at least two criminal enterprises—the Bosnians kids working the pickpocketing and purse-snatching scheme and Italians working the debit card scam. They're able to do this despite your officers stationed in the area, which tells me that the Italians involved are well-trained. What I'm hoping is that with facial recognition and our two sets of eyes, we can identify other 'regulars' in the piazza."

Capitano Sesto nodded. "Even if we have a week, there's too much footage. But we have something better. It is new. I call one of our tech officers. She is absolute wizard. With new software, she search footage, spot anyone who appears more than once in piazza. She find answers in maybe five, six hours."

Any hope that Lena's simple Italian lessons would help him grow more comfortable with the language evaporated as Worthy listened to Sesto's phone call with his tech colleague. Worthy understood an occasional word, but he doubted that he'd ever be able to make sense of the back-and-forth of native-born Italians.

Sesto ended the phone call. "She will do it. It is like we do her a favor. This is first time she have chance to try out new program."

"And you said this could be done in a matter of hours?"

The captain shrugged, both hands raised to the ceiling. "So maybe I exaggerate a bit. She tell me she have results by tomorrow morning. Okay?"

"Certo, certainly," Worthy said.

"Bravo, you speak Italian, Chris!"

"No, I spoke one word of Italian. That's very different from your English, which is excellent."

"But not good like Dr. Fabriano."

"Remember, she studied in the States. She had to learn it to survive."

"Like the Bosnians, yes?" Frowning, Sesto added, "I say before that some Italians hate Bosnians, the Romani, and other refugees. But, really, we pity. We see they have a hard life. And if life is hard here, what could it be where they come from?"

"That's something that Nick likes to say—nobody chooses where they're born."

"Your friend, he is wise," Sesto said.

Worthy felt the lump in his throat. *You are right, Capitano, Nick is wise. But will that be enough to save you, my friend?* Worthy thought.

Rome—In a Warehouse Somewhere Outside the City

Nick sensed that his confinement had fallen into a regular pattern—being watched by a guard, sometimes two; given three basic meals a day; escorted to the bathroom; visited by the professor; and left alone for hours which he filled with prayer.

With each passing day, Nick also noticed a gradual shift in his thoughts. He'd allowed himself to be taken captive in the hope that he'd learn who had killed Father Robert and why. His conversations with the professor, hardly interrogations, had convinced him that the Bosnians had nothing to do with Father Robert's death.

From their conversations, Nick also realized that his abduction had been a poorly-thought-out decision, one made in a panic because, by showing photos of Father Robert and Bordy Vladic in the piazza, he'd been circulating the idea that the Bosnians were responsible for the priest's death. The solution, to abduct Nick, was no solution at all. In fact, his abduction had surely drawn even more attention to the Bosnians by the police.

Understanding that his abduction had only compounded the Bosnians' problem, Nick could see that his captors would have to decide what options they had to resolve their mistake. He was convinced that the professor had no intention of having him experience the same fate as Father Robert, but those above him might have other plans.

Nick had faced death before, and it wasn't the fear of dying that now preoccupied his attention. He didn't blame God for his abduction—that had been his own choice—but he did ask himself more each day what he was supposed to be learning while chained to this bed.

The first lesson came from an observation he made at the following mealtimes. The meals were mainly cheese, bread, and watery soup, with slices of sausages occasionally. The two guards in the room ate when he did, and he saw that their plates featured the same food as his.

Usually, the guards passed the time by talking with one another. With the guards rotating, sometimes he heard them speaking Italian, at other times, Bosnian. That changed when the food arrived while Bosnian guards were on duty. All talk stopped as they ate hurriedly, without looking up even to keep an eye on Nick. But what Nick gradually noticed was that as the Bosnian guards ate, they would frequently moan. At first, Nick thought he was hearing the sounds of pleasure, but the more he heard it, the more he realized he was hearing the sound of grief.

Nick thought back to restaurants in Rome where he'd shared meals with Lena and Worthy. He remembered their easy conversation, the chatter from other tables, and the jocular quips of the waiters with female diners, including Lena. What a contrast, he thought, to this room. Lena, Worthy, and he had eaten leisurely, pausing to talk or just look out at passersby. No one in those restaurants moaned.

The mournful sound reminded Nick of the professor's shabby clothes, but dignified manner, which seemed to tell a story of their own. *What stories,* he asked himself, *do these moans contain? And why has it taken me so long to hear those moans?*

He remembered the professor telling him, in their first visit, that he'd walked from Bosnia to Trieste five times before he finally succeeded in staying in Italy. What hunger had these guards endured on their own journeys? What hunger had they left behind in Bosnia? Were their moans the sounds of guilt for having survived while others perished?

Nick had never stopped praying for his captors, but now he prayed for himself. Jesus' words, "He who has ears to hear let him hear" haunted him. In shame, he asked that God would use his confinement to sure his disease—the disease of deafness.

Rome-A Warehouse Outside the City

That evening, Nick heard yelling from outside his room in a mix of Italian and Bosnian. He recognized none of the voices until the end, when he was sure he heard the calm voice of the professor saying something.

His guess was validated when the professor entered the room minutes later. As he did so, the professor said something to the two guards, and then both left the room. The professor brought a chair near Nick's bed and sat down.

For a moment, neither the professor nor Nick said anything. Finally, the professor said, "We do what we have to do to survive." It sounded like an apology to Nick, and he waited for the professor to say more.

"Teaching was not just my career; it was my calling. In a perfect world, I would be preparing for tomorrow's class. I would be grading essays before I went to bed. Not every professor enjoys grading, but I did. The essays showed me what my students were thinking about, but most of all what they were hoping for. That was how I understood my vocation. I wanted to give my students hope—hope for the future, hope for a better life—I'm not talking about money—than their parents had."

Gesturing to the empty room, the professor said, "This is hardly a perfect world, but I know there are worse worlds. I see the children here, even the two men who just left the room, as my students. I am to guide and protect them. I tell them that hope is always possible, but hope comes with certain demands. Do you understand?"

Nick nodded. "I think I do. I suppose what you're describing is the difference between false hope and true hope."

The professor's eyebrows rose. "And what is the difference?"

Nick sensed that the professor was treating him as one of his students. Instead of lecturing, the professor preferred to ask questions.

"False hope is an illusion. That kind of hope believes in something that doesn't demand a sacrifice."

The professor nodded. "An interesting answer if you mean that true hope demands a sacrifice."

"Yes, I do mean that."

"Hmm. This is an interesting philosophical point, but my students here in Rome grow weary of abstractions. They would demand that we make the issue of hope personal. So I must ask what you, as someone chained to a bed, hope for. Then we can discuss if your hope is false or true."

Nick lifted his chained left arm. "It's natural for me to hope that you'll release me, but I don't see any sacrifice on my part in that hope."

The professor rose and began to pace in the room. "I agree. That is a perfectly natural hope, but not, by your definition, true hope. I'm sure that we both will accept that a body can be chained, but the mind can remain free. It is what I remind my students here, that they must never forget that their minds can be free, no matter what the circumstances," he said as he looked around the dark room. "In the essential realm of the mind, you can be as free as I am, Father. Perhaps, you are even freer. Let us agree that both of us want the same thing—to live in true, not false, hope. What might that be for you?"

"And you will tell me what it is for you?" Nick asked.

The professor offered a small smile. "I accept, but let us not rush to our answers. A few moments of silence is called for, would you not agree?"

Nick shook his head. Outside, he heard a truck backing up, its beeping sound like a steady pulse. His mind drifted, and he wondered if their conversation about hope had something to do with the argument he'd heard outside the room moments before. That would give their conversation some urgency and call for Nick to ask the questions he'd held back on before.

"As you can see, I'm a pretty big man," Nick began. "A lot of the muscle I used to have has gone to fat, but what I'm saying is that I could have overpowered Bordy Vladic in the train station. I don't say this to brag, but I chose not to save myself. I knew from the night I showed you the CCTV photo of Bordy Vladic and the photo of Father Robert, the murdered priest, that you recognized at least one of the photos. My hope was that by letting myself be captured I'd find out how and why Father Robert was killed. I suppose what I'm saying is that I hoped I'd be able talk with someone like you and get some answers."

The professor nodded. "Yes, I believe you. You sacrificed something precious, your own safety, in hopes of knowing the truth. The question is, was that sacrifice foolish, noble, or both?"

"Only you know the answer to that."

Neither man spoke for a moment, but then the professor said, "I remember the difficulty my students in Bosnia had in understanding the concept of irony. Sarcasm was a literary word that they could recognize, but irony proved to be more subtle. In the end, I asked them to simply listen to what I would say next. I told them that irony was something that life itself, given time, would teach them. I was quite young myself at the time, so I didn't know then how right I was."

Perhaps, Nick thought, it was the memory of standing in front of a class that caused the professor to pace the room slowly.

"How I would wish I could stand in front of a full lecture hall and explain how this moment offers a perfect example of irony." He stopped for a moment and looked at Nick. "If you and I had met at a conference or had by chance sat next to one another on a plane, we might as two educated persons have engaged in a discussion concerning the complex nature of hope. There would be no irony in that. But instead, we are those same two educated men pondering the complex nature of hope in this room where I, in my own circumstance, am as much a prisoner as you. There is irony in that, do you not agree?"

Nick took the question as rhetorical and waited.

The professor sat down again. "But there may be a further irony. Having agreed to share our true hopes, you stated that you sacrificed your safety in the hope of finding out how another priest died. Now it is my turn, and I believe what I will tell you will be both my truthful response and perhaps the answer to what you are looking for.

"So, I begin. I told you before about the difficult journey that Bosnians must make in coming to Italy. You might think that this as my sacrifice, but it isn't the most important one. For that, I ask that you allow me a slight digression. First, my hope. My hope has remained the same from the first time I tried to come into the country, that the Italian government would one day allow Bosnians a place of safety and a way of life in this country that is not criminal. Now, to the sacrifice that I and the children in my care have made. I believe, and have asked those in my care to accept that there is a line that we will never cross if we are to have any chance of living a decent life in Italy. Yes, to survive we are forced to prey on tourists. I wish this were not our reality, our means of survival, but it is. Because of that, I teach the boys how to identify the vulnerable among the tourists, how to pick their pockets or snatch their purses, and, most importantly, how to escape being caught."

The professor sat up straight. "But nothing, nothing beyond that! We will not kill or torture another human being. Yes, you are in chains, but you are fed. You are able to use a bathroom. You have a blanket and a bed. What we have endured in the war and afterwards in our country we will not repeat on others. If we ever resort to killing or torturing, the Italians will never accept us. That is the sacrifice we make, the line we must never cross. Do you understand? What we are forced to do to survive here is not a real life. It is a temporary measure. No one will be happier than I when we can step out of the shadows and live like human beings again."

Nick nodded. "You're saying you and the boys like Bordy had nothing to do with Father Robert's death in Piazza del Popolo."

The professor pounded one fist in his other hand. "Yes, yes, yes. We did not kill him, and we will not kill you. That I promise."

Nick wanted to believe the professor. "I can see how the photos that I was showing you in the piazza created a problem."

"Your showing the two photos around in the piazza was the same as saying one of us killed the priest. If the Italian people believe that, the authorities would have no other choice but to hunt us down as killers. What you were doing was guaranteeing that we would never be accepted here."

"So, I was abducted to put a stop to my showing the photos. Yes, I see that," Nick said. "I'm sorry that my abduction only makes your group seem more dangerous. The authorities and my friends must be thinking that you not only killed Father Robert, but are also planning on killing me."

"Of course I see that now, but what choice did you leave us? You must understand that our existence here—I won't call it a life—is fragile. We are unable to defend ourselves when we're accused of something. If we went to the newspapers, would they believe us when we told them that we had nothing to do with the death of the priest? Would they put themselves in our situation and realize that the priest's death in the piazza was the worst thing that could happen to us? The piazza is where we operate. What we do there helps us survive. Would they understand the line that we have vowed never to cross? No. Our only hope is that the police will find the real killer. Only that will take the focus off of us."

Nick groaned. "Instead, by showing those pictures in the piazza, I was shining the spotlight on you."

The professor nodded. "I had to stop you, if only to give ourselves time to think of what to do next. We saw no other course. But we are not killers. I hope you will believe that."

Yes, there is irony here, Nick thought. *This man has me chained to a bed, yet all I'm thinking about is how I might help him.*

CHAPTER TWENTY-FIVE

Rome—A Stakeout near Piazza del Popolo

Most police officers found all-night stakeouts numbing, and Worthy was no exception. The hours passed slowly, and peering into the dark for the slightest movement had the body begging for sleep.

But Worthy's stakeout with Lena was turning out to better than he'd feared. She had made sandwiches and brought two thermoses, one of coffee and the other of hot chocolate, his favored drink. Lena was also intrigued with the night-vision camera that Sesto had lent them, as Worthy could clearly see by her frequently scanning the area included in the stakeout.

From previous stakeouts, Worthy knew that as his mind tired, so did his sense of proportion. Worries tended to mushroom in the wee hours of the night and early morning. Perhaps, Worthy thought, Lena had the same experience, which would explain why she preferred talking to silence.

After her last visual scan of the area, she asked, "How many of these stakeouts have you been on, Chris?"

"If you mean stakeouts this late at night, the answer is too many to count."

"And if nothing happens tonight, will we be back here tomorrow night?"

Worthy sighed. "That's the plan. But maybe we'll get lucky tonight."

They stopped talking when they saw a couple, arm in arm, approach from the direction of the piazza. Worthy watched as Lena took repeated photos of the couple, but they passed through the area without being approached.

"Nothing doing," Worthy said.

"They still got my heart beating fast."

"Yeah, it does that. Don't erase those photos. For all we know, that couple is part of the scam."

"I don't understand."

Worthy took a sip of the hot chocolate. "Maybe the scammers send a test couple through the area to see if the police are watching."

"Ah, I hadn't thought of that. I suppose that's something they teach you in police school or whatever you call it. Not to underestimate criminals, I mean."

"I certainly wouldn't underestimate this crew," Worthy said. "This is one intricate and sophisticated operation."

"Which means that the police can't lag behind. I guess that explains the night-vision camera."

"It does, but we don't know who had the technology for this camera first—the police or the criminals."

Lena gasped. "Does that mean someone could be watching us?"

Putting his hand on Lena's arm, Worthy replied, "It's a possibility, but take what I said with a grain of salt. Even though I've worked two cases before this one in your country, I don't really know that much about Italy's crime scene. I'm mean, every American knows about the mafia, but that's just what we see in movies. I'm hoping the Bosnian kids are near the bottom of the criminal food chain because I'm convinced that they're the ones who have Nick. In contrast, I have no idea how high up that food chain these scammers are."

Worthy glanced over and saw that Lena had leaned back on the headrest and closed her eyes. He knew that no matter how tired she was, she wouldn't be sleeping. And her next words proved him right.

"Ever since Nick was taken, my mind has been split in half. Part of me is focused on what's in front of me, like sitting here tonight hoping we see the scammers. But the other half of me? That's the part of me that can't stop thinking about what Nick is going through at that moment."

"I'm the same, but what you said earlier about following up with the priest in Canada is true for what we're doing tonight. Nick would want us—and needs us—to work the case in front of us, just like we're doing. And look, here's another couple coming," he said.

Coming into view was a couple who looked older than the first, maybe in their early fifties. Both were overweight and walking slowly.

Worthy whispered, "If I were working this scam, this's the couple I'd target. They're out too late for their own good."

"Why are they out so late? They look exhausted."

"And look at the way they keep stopping to study their map. I'm betting they had a late dinner that set them back more than they budgeted, and instead of being smart and taking a taxi back to their hotel, they decided to save money by walking. And now they're lost."

"I have an urge to offer them a ride before it's too late," Lena said.

"Too late. Here's our map guy."

Lena and Worthy sat in silence, the only sound being the click of the camera as Lena shot one photo after another. The couple had dutifully stopped and seemed to be trying to understand what the man was saying as he pointed as his map.

"And second now, and the other two guys should be showing up," Worthy said.

As if on cue, a speeding car screeched to a halt, with the man in the passenger seat jumping out.

While Lena continued to take photos, she whispered, "Chris, I've got what we need. Can't we rescue the poor couple?"

"No, that would let whoever is behind the scam know we're on to them. We have to let it play—"

"Chris, look! There's someone back behind that tree. I think he's watching what's going on."

"Let me take a look through the camera."

Lena handed it to him. "He's behind that tree on the left. Can you see him?"

"Whoever he is, he talking on a phone." Worthy turned the camera back on the vehicle. "And so is the driver. That can't be a coincidence." Aiming the camera back at the figure behind the tree, Worthy inhaled sharply. "You're not going to believe this."

"What?"

"I think I recognize him, but it doesn't make any sense. This isn't his gig."

"Who is he, Chris?"

"The guy behind the tree is a dead ringer for Bordy Vladic."

Yellowknife—Father Jacob's Office

In Yellowknife, Father Jacob spent the morning catching up on the phone messages and emails he'd missed when a bad cold had forced him to bed over the past twenty-four hours. He listened to the messages in reverse order, so it wasn't until he'd listened to a dozen others that he heard a woman's voice.

"Hello, Father Jacob, my name is Dr. Lena Fabriano. I'm calling from Rome, and I need to update you on what's happened here with Father Fortis. The reason Father Fortis hasn't returned your messages is that he's been abducted. I'm sure that's a shock to you, as it has been for us. He was taken five days ago, and while we can't be sure, we think his abductors know something about Father Robert's death."

Father Jacob felt his stomach tighten. He made the sign of the cross and uttered a prayer for Nick's safety, even as he felt a pang of guilt. He thought back over the chain of events that began with the fire at the orphanage and wondered if he could have done something more, not that anything came to mind, to prevent Nick being taken.

The message continued. "Of course, finding and rescuing Father Nick is our top priority, but we know that he wouldn't want us to stop looking into Father Robert's death. So, please call me at the following number."

Father Jacob jotted the number down and looked at his watch. As it was eight-thirty in the morning inn Yellowknife, he figured it would be mid to late afternoon in Rome. He set aside the other messages and called the number Dr. Fabriano had sent.

"Father Jacob?" the voice said on the other end of the line.

In a rush, he replied, "Yes, I'm here. I'm sorry that I didn't hear your message until now. I was out of the office and not taking calls yesterday. Is there any news about Nick?"

"No, but we believe we're getting closer to his abductors. Father Jacob, I should also tell you that Christopher Worthy is here. I'm going to put him on."

"This is Christopher Worthy, Father. Perhaps Nick mentioned me."

Father Jacob felt hope creeping back into his thoughts. Nick had described Worthy and his formidable detective skills. "Yes, he talked about you a lot. What can I do to help?"

"We got your letter, so we know that you were trying to find out who

S. Lonetree is, the one who wrote to Father Robert," Lena said. "Have you had any luck on your end?"

"Not yet, but I'm still hopeful. When I didn't hear back from Nick, I wasn't sure what to do. If I had an assistant, I'd have travelled down to British Columbia myself and tried to track S. Lonetree . But I'm the only priest for my parish, so I've done what I can from Yellowknife. Sorry to say, the local police aren't that interested in helping. I have the feeling that they're tired of everything to do with Father Robert. I did better when I contacted the tribal police near the orphanage. They have contacts with other tribal police departments in Canada and, given that the Lonetree name might be native, they promised to talk with their counterparts in British Columbia. Like I said, I wish I could do more."

"I can't think of anything you haven't done, Father," Worthy said. "But I do have a question. Nick met with the bishop in Toronto before he flew here. The impression he got was that there was bad blood between Father Robert and the bishop. Is that your take on their relationship as well?"

Father Jacob didn't respond immediately. Then he said, "Let me close my door." In a minute, he was back on the line. "I have to be careful. The bishop is my boss as well, and ever since the fire, he's been pretty cold with me. After I found out that several of the families are suing the orphanage's board of directors, I called him to ask what his plans were. But he didn't return my call. Instead, I received a letter saying that he's decided to make a pastoral visit to Yellowknife and the orphanage. It wasn't a request, but a command. The visit is next week."

"Which suggests the bishop is afraid of the lawsuit," Lena said.

Father Jacob didn't say anything for a moment. "I was about to say that lawsuits aren't as common in Canada as they are in the States. But, given the discovery of burials of native children at parochial schools, the courts are taking complaints from tribal communities more seriously. So, yes, I think the bishop's visit is his attempt at damage control."

"Father, I'm sure Nick would want you to sit in on the bishop's visit, especially if he meets with relatives of the victims. Nick was convinced that the bishop is hiding something," Worthy said. "I suggest we talk after the bishop's visit or if you receive any more information about S. Lonetree. I hope Nick will be with us on that call."

"That's what I'm praying for. Please know that I'm also praying for both of you."

CHAPTER TWENTY-SIX

Rome—In a Warehouse Outside the City

After Nick finished a plate of boiled potatoes and broccoli, he found the document that the professor had left with him, the one the professor had described as "a fairy tale." But he'd hardly begun reading the document when the door opened and the professor entered the room. He looked years older than he had just two days before. He sat down heavily in the chair even as Nick sensed a new tension in the room, as the two guards failed to acknowledge the professor when he entered. And when the professor signaled to the guards that they should withdraw from the room, the guards looked at one another before complying. Only after a pause did they obey.

The professor rose from the chair and with a key released Nick from the chains. "I should have done this before," he said. "I am sorry."

Rubbing his wrist, Nick replied, "I appreciate this, and I'm grateful for the Bible."

Nodding, the professor said, "I thought of bringing another book, but then I thought you might have already read it. Hemingway's *The Old Man and the Sea*."

"I have read it, but that was a long time ago," Nick said.

The professor exhaled slowly. "The book is not Hemingway's best work, but the story and its theme came back to my mind today. You know the story. A fisherman long past his prime catches a fish too big to bring into his small boat. That leaves the fisherman with a decision, a choice. Should he cut the line and let the fish go or should he hold onto the fish, even as it takes his little boat farther and farther out into the ocean?"

"If I remember correctly," Nick said, "he decides to hang on to the fish. And don't the fisherman and the fish both die?"

"Yes, they do. Of course, Hemingway's obsession with death is found throughout his writings. If the bull in the ring is death, then it is Hemingway who is the matador who pokes at death, rouses it, tests it, inflames it. And in this book, Hemingway is the old man in the boat. But Hemingway would be harder for me to teach in Bosnia today. In his novels, Hemingway is in control of death in his novels. And in his own life, was not his suicide a final controlling of death?"

"Yes, I think it is," Nick said.

"For refugees, death is always out of our control. If we stay where we come from or if we flee to another country, it doesn't matter. Death for us is like the word 'tomorrow.' It will come . . . it will come." The professor no longer sat erect as before, but now leaned forward, his arms limp, his eyes focused on the floor.

After a long pause, Nick said, "I thought you were suggesting that I'm that fish, and you're the fisherman deciding what to do with me."

The professor waited so long to answer that Nick wondered if he'd fallen asleep. But then, he raised his head and caught Nick's eye. "I am a professor. I try to guide those in my care here. But students? Well . . ." The professor let the thought hang in the air.

"Students don't always obey the teacher's instructions, do they?" Nick asked. "And I wonder if the student we're talking about is Bordy Vladic."

Shaking his head slowly, the professor said, "I wish I knew who to blame for all the horror that that boy has witnessed in his short life. He comes from a family of seven, all called IDP—internally detained persons. Now, there is only a brother and sister left in Bosnia, still detained in a camp. If you could hear Bordy's story, Father, I think you would see him in a different light."

Nick realized that the professor for only the second time had called him "Father." That, along with the professor releasing him from the chain, gave him the impression that the professor wanted to confide something with him but was hesitating.

"I'd like to share something with you," Nick said. "Two colleagues of mine are assisting the police in investigating the death of Father Robert. Even with my being held here, I know they haven't stopped working on that case. I tell you this because I've thought more about what you said the last time we talked."

"What was that?" the professor asked, and Nick thought he heard hope in the question.

"You said that the best thing that could happen for you and the kids in your care would be for the police to find out who really did kill Father Robert. That would take the pressure off your group. The way I see it, that's the same thing my friends and I want. We want to find out who killed Father Robert. I'd like to tell you everything that my friends and I know, and maybe you would then tell me what you know."

The professor glanced over his shoulder at the door to the room, before speaking in little more than a whisper, "You would do this for us, even though I can't guarantee you will be released?"

Nick didn't say anything, realizing the professor's wish to release him might not decide his fate. And that, Nick reasoned, meant that the argument that he'd heard outside the door was a battle over leadership within the Bosnian camp.

"Perhaps we could start by you telling me your name. I assume you have a Ph.D., so I suppose I could call you doctor, but—"

Shaking his head, the professor said, "No, there is no need for that. My name is Yuri."

"And my name is Nick."

The professor smiled. "Nick? Is that the truth?"

"Yes, it's Nick."

"How fitting. Nick is the name Hemingway chose for his alter ego in his early stories. Yes, I am glad that you are Nick."

Rome—Lena's Apartment

Although Worthy experienced some joy when Lena and he had gained some clarity about Father Robert's last days and nights, he continued to find falling asleep difficult. In the darkness and the quiet, his mind found that place within him where all his fears for Nick were waiting for him. Finding out that Bordy Vladic was connected with the Italian scammers had only increased his concern.

Part of his sleeplessness, he knew, was caused by the decision he'd made that night when he recognized Bordy Vladic in the shadows. Lena had immediately squeezed his arm as she asked, "Shouldn't we try to grab him?" He'd had his hand on the car's door handle when he realized that

Bordy Vladic knew the neighborhood better than he did, and if the boy eluded capture, the scam artists Bordy was working with would know they'd been discovered. Letting the boy go had been the right decision, but it didn't feel like it.

After an hour of tossing and turning and not wanting to wake Lena, he found some blankets in a linen cupboard and retreated to the loggia on the roof of Lena's apartment. If he couldn't sleep, he could at least watch Rome, normally noisy, as she slept.

Despite the blankets, the cold seeped into him, starting at his feet and eventually reaching his ears. But he stayed on the lounge chair, feeling that he deserved the pain. With no word from Nick's captors, it was easy for him to imagine his closest friend being tortured or worse. Icy waves of guilt washed over him as he lamented involving Nick in this case. Shivering, he thought, *if Nick had remained in his monastery in Ohio, he'd be safe right now.*

But he knew that whatever Nick was facing at that moment, he wouldn't have wanted a safer life. As Nick had told him repeatedly, he was called to be both a monk *and* a detective.

Somehow, knowing that Nick, even as a captive, was doing what he felt called to do brought Worthy an unexpected feeling of calm. *This is Nick's peace and calm. This is Nick's faith, his trust in God,* Worthy thought. *I have to believe he's alive.*

As the sun rose behind him and warmed his head, his shoulders, and then the rest of his body, Worthy felt Nick somehow close by. The only words that came to him were "I know you're alive, Nick, and we will find you." In that inexplicable certainty, he fell asleep.

CHAPTER TWENTY-SEVEN

Rome—In a Shack Outside the City

Bordy Vladic's jaw throbbed, the result of the professor pulling a rotten molar with a pair of pliers. Ice, stolen by a few of the boys from a restaurant's outdoor display of seafood, and used teabags found in garbage cans, had been the only painkillers available, but Bordy had gutted out the extraction without even a moan.

Tomorrow, he reasoned, his mouth would feel better, and by the third or fourth day, he'd be able to chew on that side. Lucky for him, he'd always been a quick healer, unlike one of his brothers and one of his sisters, who'd died from different infections.

From the way that the professor had looked at him while pulling the tooth, Bordy knew that the professor sensed that the gulf between them was widening. By his count, Bordy knew that the majority of the boys in their group would side with him, not the professor, when the takeover occurred. But he was patient, knowing that that time hadn't yet come. He still had to finalize arrangements with the Italians who controlled the bigger operations in and around Piazza del Popolo.

It was six weeks before when he'd first noticed the man dressed in slim jeans and fancy loafers loitering at the edge of the piazza. Following him for several nights, Bordy had stumbled on the man's debit card scam. With his English being poor, Bordy wasn't able to follow what the three men involved said to the tourists, but he didn't need the language to figure out how the game was played.

That was when Bordy knew he would have to break from the professor. Perhaps even before observing the scam, he'd known that the professor's dream—that Bosnians would one day be accepted in Italy if they limited themselves to petty crimes—was an illusion. No one respected petty criminals; they were hardly feared. The only Italians who stopped the boys and offered help were nuns and priests, and that was just words.

In watching the debit card scam night after night, Bordy understood that the only future he and the other boys would have in Italy was to cross the professor's line in the sand. The only path to respect, wealth, and protection in Italy was to move into more serious crime. His devotion to the professor evaporated when he saw that the old man was the only obstacle to his possible future. And that meant that he had no other choice, when the time came, than to remove that obstacle.

After a week of observing the Italians, Bordy decided it was time to make contact with the Italians. But that initial encounter had been easier than he'd hoped. As he hung around for yet another night at the scammers' favorite place to snare tourists, Bordy was grabbed by someone who stepped out from the shadows.

As the man pressed a knife to Bordy's neck, he whispered something in Italian. Bordy had faced death too many times to tense even a muscle. Instead, he smiled as he whispered back, "No speak Italian. English?"

Within a matter of seconds, a car pulled up and Bordy was shoved into the back seat next to another man he recognized. He remembered that night with clarity. He'd sat back in the back seat, folded his arms across his chest, and, looking up to the front seat, noticed the Mercedes Benz logo on the steering wheel. If the men holding him had expected him to beg for his life, they must have been puzzled by his laughter as the car sped away. And when the person who put a sack over his head gut-punched him, he wasn't afraid, but impressed. *This is what pros do,* he'd thought.

They'd taken him to a basement room, removed the sack, and shoved him into a hard chair. Bordy had looked around at the men circling him, as if he were meeting his new family.

Not waiting for one of them to speak, Bordy used two English words he knew well. "Thank you."

The men looked at each other, and then the man whom Bordy had observed in the piazza drew up another chair and removed his coat. Bordy studied his face. The man was bearded like the professor, but in this man's case, the beard was trimmed neatly and even looked oiled like his black hair. The man also wore tinted glasses that made it hard to see his eyes. Tattoos of geometric shapes ran up both forearms, arms that showed that the man would hold his own in a fight. But what impressed Bordy the most about the man, as well as the other men standing behind him, was that he looked so well-fed.

"You *pazzo*, you crazy?" the man asked.

"No, me happy. I see you in piazza. You see me?"

Bordy remembered that the man didn't respond at first, letting silence fill the room. Every gesture by the man, the way he stared at Bordy, the way he tapped his foot, the way he twirled a gold bracelet around his wrist, Bordy accepted as the man's style, a style he wanted. It was like he was looking at himself in the future—well-fed, well-dressed, with gold jewelry, and so, so cool.

Finally, the man had spoken. "You Bosnian. Pickpocket, purse-snatcher. You piece of shit."

Bordy had understood every word. "Me piece of shit, but not for long. Me work for you."

One of the men in the back laughed, but the man in charge held up a hand. "You piece of shit, but got corraggio, guts. What you do for me?"

Expecting the question, Bordy had been ready with his answer. "Me and my friends like flies on food. We pests. But we pests in your food too."

The man had shaken his head. "No, you nothing."

That was when Bordy had shaken his head back at the man. "I pick pockets. I take tourist money. Now tourists no money. Go back to hotel. You stop them, but no money. You get nothing."

One of the men standing behind let loose with a string of words in Italian. Bordy didn't understood a word of it, but Bordy knew the man had confirmed what he'd just told them.

The man in charge waited until the other man ended his tirade. "What? You stop robbing tourists? You lie," he said.

"You right. We rob to eat. But me, I tell my boys, you rob this man. Other tourist, you no rob. See?"

"I say you lie. Why you not rob rich Americans, British, Germans?"

"I say already. I want work with you." Bordo smiled as he held up his arms. "I want be rich, want gold on my hand."

That was the beginning, his first meeting with Luca, the man who had called him a "piece of shit" but who'd let him go that night, telling him to come back the next night to the place where he'd caught Bordy. Even though Bordy knew that Luca might decide he was too great a risk and finish him off with the same knife, Bordy returned to the spot and waited for his second ride in a Mercedes.

Over subsequent meetings, staggered so as not to arouse the professor's suspicions, Bordy had to prove his loyalty to Luca's gang. At first, he had to give a percentage of what the other Bosnian boys turned over to him. That was painless, as Bordy had always kept a bit back.

Then, just a little over a month ago, he told Luca about a priest who stopped him and told him he knew what the boys were doing in the piazza. "He say he no go to polizia. He say he help."

Luca had frowned. "This priest, he want sex?"

Bordy didn't say anything for a moment. He remembered the priest had said nothing about sex. Instead, he talked about the boys not needing to do what they were doing. But Bordy knew he couldn't trust the priest once he knew that Brody and the other boys had no intention of stopping targeting tourists. So he said, "Yes, maybe he mean sex."

Luca had nodded and, after speaking rapidly with one of his men, gave Bordy instructions. The next night, if the priest returned, Bordy was to lure him to the bench closest to the restaurant "La Trattoria Antica." Bordy was impressed, as he knew from working the piazza that CCTV cameras missed that spot. At the time, he'd started to ask what Luca planned to do about the priest, but he closed his mouth when he saw the look on Luca's face.

Two days later, the professor assembled all the boys together to tell them that a priest had been killed in the piazza. The professor had said, "This is the worst thing that could happen to us. The police will be swarming the piazza, and we'll be under suspicion." His face had been grave as he looked from one boy to another. "I told you all to avoid this priest, but now I need to know. Do any of you know anything about how he died?"

None of the boys said a word, and Bordy remembered feeling temporarily weak in his legs.

"Bordy, did you know anything?" the professor had asked.

He managed not to flinch as he held the professor's gaze. He felt strength returning to his legs as his mind had a kind of white clarity. In that moment, he didn't see the professor as a leader but an old and timid man.

"You know where I was last night. I was with you over at St. Peter's. I know nothing about this."

The professor seemed to accept his denial, and Bordy barely listened as the professor explained how they'd have to stay clear of Piazza del Popolo for the next nights and maybe weeks. In the days that followed, Bordy tried to remember what exactly the priest had said to him in the piazza. Hadn't he said something about an orphanage? After the priest was killed, Luca had taken Bordy aside and said that the priest wouldn't be bothering him again.

Bordy thought little about the dead priest now. Luca had praised him for helping rid the city of one more pedophile and had rewarded him with a chain for his wrist that, if not gold, was shiny. From that day forward, Luca never again called Bordy a "piece of shit." Instead, he gave Bordy an assignment to watch for the police as Luca and his crew waited for tourists walking back to their hotels.

And now, Bordy thought, as he massaged his sore jaw and pulled a dirty blanket over him, he thought, *we have another meddling priest. And I know exactly who and what this priest is. He is my big chance.*

Rome—Worthy's Office

Shortly after breakfast the next day, Lena and Worthy showed Capitano Sesto the photos from the stakeout the night before.

"I know it's not clear from the pics, but you can just make out a figure hiding behind this tree," Worthy said. "Lena spotted him and when I used the night-vision camera, I zoomed in and was sure I was looking at Bordy Vladic."

Sesto looked confused. "What he do there?"

"He was talking on a phone, and we're pretty sure he was communicating with the third guy, the one in the car," Lena said.

"This is no good news. Bosnians work with local gangs, now maybe work with organized crime."

The captain had put into words what Lena had worried about since the stakeout, that Nick and no doubt Father Robert were caught up in something bigger than any of them had thought. A gang of teenagers, kids involved in petty crime, wouldn't think of killing a priest, but organized crime had proven over and over again that priests, especially those who spoke out against them, were fair game. It had only been a year before, that a priest in Sicily who'd refused to allow a suspected Mafia figure serve as a godparent at a baptism had had his throat slashed.

"I know Lena is worried about the same thing I am, that this could mean that Nick is being held by Italians who are involved in more major crimes than the Bosnians. But even if that's the case, maybe these photos can do some good," Worthy said.

"I don't see this," Sesto said.

"I'm talking about the photos of the scam Lena caught last night. I'm hoping the scammers are in your system. If so, we have their names and maybe you know where your men can pick them up."

Sesto slowly nodded. "Leave photos here, with me. I let you know if you hook a big fish last night. But there is problem."

"What's that?" Worthy could tell that Sesto was avoiding looking at him or Lena.

"Your friend now missing nearly a week. So far, media, they do not know. But with more my men . . . a leak is certain. Newspapers, TV, they come for me, and they come for you."

"How much longer can you keep a lid on Nick's abduction?"

"Two days, maybe three."

No one said anything until Worthy pointed to the photos. "Then as soon as you ID the scammers, we act."

CHAPTER TWENTY-EIGHT

Rome—In a Warehouse Outside the City

Seeing Bordy Vladic in the doorway talking with the two guards, Nick reflected on what the professor, Yuri, and he had shared with each other.

Nick had gone first, sharing what they knew about Father Robert: first, his role in the orphanage in Canada, then the fire, and finally what had brought him to Rome. When Yuri was confused by monastic terms, he was quick to ask for clarification. Nick's last point was that his colleagues and he were still trying to figure out why Father Robert returned to Piazza del Popolo on the nights before his murder.

With a deep sigh, Yuri had said, "I will tell you the truth, Nick. One of my boys, one of the youngest ones, told me that he'd tried to rob this priest on the Metro. This was against my rules. We leave priests and nuns alone. The priest had caught him in the act, but the boy broke free and ran from the Metro stop into the piazza. He knew all the ways to escape from there, and did. The boy described the priest to me, so it was easy for me to spot him when he came back to the piazza the next night. That's when I knew we had a problem. I swear we had no intention of harming him, but he was, what should I say, bad for business. So that second night, I sat down, as a beggar, next to him. He didn't draw back, as many people do, and I could tell he wanted to talk, especially when he realized that I understood English."

"What did you talk about?" Nick asked.

"I asked why he was in the piazza so late at night. He told me about the attempted robbery and his desire to find the boy. I played dumb and asked him what he meant. He said he was looking into ways to get the boys off the streets and into an orphanage. He was very emotional, saying it was something he needed to do, something he had to do."

"Good Lord, so that was his mission," Nick said. "Of course, it makes sense."

"Mission? I don't understand."

"Father Robert changed over his last three days. He had been depressed about the fire and about maybe being defrocked, but then he became focused, energized by something. Until this minute, I didn't—we didn't—know what that was. But everything now makes so much sense. Given the death of the boys in Canada, he would see your boys as a chance to atone."

The professor shook his head. "The priest was dangerous to us because he was naïve. His plan was impossible. He would bring the police and the immigration authorities down on us, and so, yes, I knew that I had to stop him. I talked to the boys about the problem that the English-speaking priest posed to us, but we never talked about harming him. My plan was to avoid the piazza until the priest gave up and stopped coming. That is the truth. So you see, the night the priest was killed, none of my boys were in the piazza. My boys didn't kill him, and they weren't there to see who did. But that's not what the police and the newspapers believe."

Rubbing his face, Yuri had added, "Staying away from the piazza after the priest was killed was a great hardship for us. Piazza del Popolo is our best source of income. There are hundreds of tourists, even late at night, and the piazza has many escape routes. But we had no choice, even though what we took in was cut in half."

"But you were back in the piazza the night I showed you the photos."

"Another irony. That was our first night back. When I saw you sitting where the other priest had sat and then when you showed me the pictures, it was like a nightmare that wouldn't end."

"And you don't know who would have killed Father Robert?"

The professor had shaken his head slowly. "Once, when Bordy chafed at one of my orders, he bragged about knowing some people, some bad people, I'm sure, outside our group. I wanted to believe he was showing off to the other boys, but then . . ."

"Then you had to take Bordy at his word. I never thought the men who forced me into the car outside the train station were Bosnians," Nick said.

"No, I am what you see, a professor who is trying to protect my boys. I have no car, no men with guns."

"And the two men guarding me here?"

The professor shrugged. "The younger one is Bosnian, the other is someone who Bordy knows."

"And you're sure Bordy had nothing to do with Father Robert's death?"

"He was with me in St. Peter's Square, as I told you. And when I told the boys that a priest had been killed in Piazza del Popolo, no one seemed more shocked than Bordy."

Now, as Bordy walked toward Nick's bed, Nick remembered Yuri's certainty that the boy had nothing to do with Father Robert's death. Nick also remembered Yuri saying that Nick could never imagine what Bordy had experienced in his young life in Bosnia and in Italy. *He's just a kid who should be playing soccer or video games,* Nick thought.

When Bordy drew closer, Nick saw that the boy's face looked swollen on one side, leading him to wonder if the boy had been in a fight.

Sitting down, Bordy looked at the chain on the floor before saying, "So, professor, he release you. You think you now escape?"

"No, not escape. What the professor did was an act of kindness, but then I think we both know he is a kind man. Perhaps you think that makes him weak."

For a moment, Bordy looked stunned. Then he said, "You think you know me?"

Nick replied, "I think I know a little bit about you. In my country, you would be called a child, a teenager."

"What this mean, 'teenager'?"

"It is someone who is not a child, but not an adult yet."

Nick saw the color rise in Bordy's face. "Me, a child?" Leaning forward, he opened his mouth. "See hole? Professor pull tooth. Do I cry? No." To underscore his words, he spat blood onto the floor.

"No, I wasn't calling you a child. From what the professor said, you've had to grow up fast."

Bordy pointed at his chest. "I grow up fastest. Now a man. I say what I do, what I not do."

"It seems to me that you also say what some of the other boys do and don't do."

"Sometimes, me. Sometimes, professor," Bordy said as he studied the spot of blood on the floor.

The question "Who is going to decide what to do with me—you or the professor?" seemed to be hanging in the air, and Nick wondered if

Bordy sensed that as well. But to ask it now could be taken by Bordy as a challenge, and so Nick said instead, "The professor said I should get to know you. So, I'm wondering if you'd answer some questions."

Bordy sat back abruptly. "No, I question you! You, not me, prisoner."

Nick held up both hands in surrender. "Okay, okay. Ask me anything."

Looking over his shoulder at the two guards by the door, Bordy didn't answer for a moment. Finally, he said, "Ask me question. Speak quiet."

"Do you miss your country, do you miss Bosnia?"

Bordy rubbed his jaw. "Bosnia is graveyard. I not go back."

Keeping his voice low, Nick asked, "You don't have family back there?"

Spitting more blood on the floor, Bordy said, "Some family there. They live dead. Most so peaceful, all under ground. They dead dead."

Nick had to remind himself that he was listening to a child. Bordy's voice sounded hard, flinty, reminding him of a novice at his monastery in Ohio, a young man who'd been a boy soldier in the Democratic Republic of Congo before being rescued. As the young man's novice master, Nick had learned how killing without feeling had become normal for the young man. "When I was rescued," the novice had told him, "it took me two years before I could cry. Even if you put a burning cigarette to my face, I wouldn't cry. I couldn't."

As Nick studied the flat expression on Bordy Vladic's face, he realized two things. One, he understood what had prompted Father Robert to dream of rescuing the Bosnian boys. And two, he understood why the professor wanted him to talk to Bordy. Yuri had trained the boys to know the lines they should never cross. This was so that the boys didn't lose their humanity, Nick now saw.

Yuri had lived for decades before the war when life in Bosnia, though undoubtedly difficult, had at least been civil. He had walked or taken a bus to the university every day to open his students' minds to Shakespeare, Milton, and Donne.

But the boys under Yuri's care now had grown up in what was left of Bosnia after the war. Yuri had mentioned corruption, hunger, and, in Bordy's case, life in a displaced persons' camp. Like the child soldiers in Africa, Bordy and the other boys had never known a real childhood. Jesus' words—"Suffer the children to come unto me"—came back to Nick. Who, he wondered, had ever welcomed Bordy anywhere.

"What do you remember about school?" Nick asked.

Bordy frowned. "School? Two year, then teacher leave. No school."

"What did you like about school?"

For the first time, Nick saw a light come on in Bordy's face. "Basketball. Michael Jordan. Shaq." He made a gesture of shooting a basketball. "Three point."

A lump came to Nick's throat at the crack in Bordy's mask, that crack offering a glimpse of the boy he once was. In that moment, it was easy to picture the man-boy sitting in front of him playing games, watching cartoons on a television, and brushing his teeth at night before lying down in a warm bed. But Nick doubted that Bordy had experienced even one of those moments.

"That only question?" Bordy asked, breaking into Nick's thoughts. In that moment, Nick realized that Bordy, like other thirteen-year-olds, was enjoying being the center of attention.

"I do have another question. I'm wondering where you see yourself in five or ten years."

"What you mean 'where I see me?' I in Rome."

"What do you see yourself doing when you're older . . . if you see yourself being safe, I mean, without the police looking for you."

Bordy's eager face turned into a smirk. "What? You worry for me?"

Nick held Bordy's gaze. "Yes, I do."

Bordy launched himself out of the chair and stood over Nick. "No, I worry for me. You worry for you."

The two guards, reacting to Bordy's raised voice, came to stand behind Bordy, their guns raised.

Nick sat quietly for a few seconds before responding in a whisper, "You don't believe that Yuri worries about you, Bordy?"

Bordy stood frozen for a moment, not moving or saying anything, before reaching down and raising the chain from the floor. He put the cuff around Nick's wrist and snapped the padlock shut. Without saying another word, he turned and walked out of the room.

CHAPTER TWENTY-NINE

Rome—Police Headquarters

Capitano Sesto looked up from his computer screen when Worthy knocked on his office door. "Prego, please," he said, gesturing for Worthy to take one of chairs on the other side of his desk.

"Where is Doctoressa Lena?" he asked.

"At the monastery, doing more research," Worthy lied.

"Ah, too bad. We have good news about photos she took the other night."

"Oh? News about the scam artists or the boy in the shadows?"

"Both. The man who jumps out of car, he is Luca Piemonte. He is a hood from Napoli, Naples, but is in Rome for four years. This first time we catch him in the act, so now we find him. But he's elusive."

"Is he be capable of murder?"

"Could he kill your priest? Yes, possible. Maybe he think he impress his boss."

"And the boy in the photos? Is it Bordy Vladic?"

"Si, si, but a surprise to see him working with Piemonte."

Worthy nodded. "Seeing the two together did answer a question I had. Do you remember the images from CCTV in the train station the night Nick was abducted? Bordy handed Nick over to the two taller men, the guys that walked Nick to the car outside."

"Yes, I remember," Sesto said.

"It never made sense to me that Bosnians could have a Mercedes, much less a car. So, what I'm thinking is that Bordy handed Nick over to this guy Luca."

"Ah, si. This makes sense, but not good news for your friend."

Worthy nodded. He knew that Sesto was right. Nick's fate was in the hands of the men who'd already killed one priest.

Rome—Luca Piemonte's Apartment

In a roomy apartment in Rome's outskirts, Luca Piemonte felt a mix of confidence and irritation as he thought about his next meeting with his boss, Fausto Como. In their last meeting a few weeks before, Como had made it clear that Luca needed to increase the revenue from his patch, Piazza del Popolo and its neighboring streets. Como had a way of making everyone under him feel that he was always on probation. Of late, Luca had resented this treatment more keenly. Luca was no longer some minor player in Rome's criminal scene. Not only had he brought in consistent revenue from his activities around the piazza, but he had loyal men—and now a boy with a gang—under him.

Luca pictured a ladder, the top of which faded into an impenetrable fog. Above him, he could see only Como, but he knew there were others above him. And from that perspective, Como was the one blocking his advance. Whatever Luca accomplished, Como was quick to take credit. He'd thought about failing deliberately in order to make Como look bad, but as credit went up the ladder, so blame went down. If he failed, Como wouldn't hesitate to kick him off his precarious rung on the ladder.

The only option he could see was to somehow work around Como and deal with those still higher up in organized crime in Rome. The risk involved would be greater than any risk that he'd taken before. Como had given him the impression that he was related to his bosses—was that the truth or a lie?—but if it was the truth, Luca knew he would pay for his rebellion with his life.

But now something had changed; a new factor had come into the mix— the Bosnian kid, Bordy Vladic. The kid reminded him of his younger self, tired of living off the crumbs of petty crime and hungry to sit at the big table. The kid had already proved useful and resourceful. After the kid had presented the problem of the priest meddling in the Bosnians' work in the piazza, the kid hadn't panicked when Luca ordered one of his men to eliminate the priest. That had been a test, and Bordy had passed the test. The kid seemed to want only more.

The question for Luca was how to play this new card in his hand.

The most obvious play, in his next report to Como, would be to say he'd recruited the top Bosnian kid and through him gained control over other Bosnians. Nobody but Luca and his underlings needed to know that Bordy Vladic had approached him, not the other way round.

Luca had decided to forego the safe path and not tell Como, for the time being, about Bordy Vladic. And Luca would admit that the Bosnian boy's boldness had been a contributing factor to his new confidence. When he was next summoned by Como, he would keep his boss in the dark about Bordy and the Bosnians until the right moment—the right moment being when he would offer the Bosnians as proof to the bigger bosses that it was time for Luca to skip some rungs on the ladder.

Yellowknife—Father Jacob's Office

Hours later, when morning dawned in Yellowknife, Father Jacob was running late for morning Mass when his phone at St. Anne's rang. Not immediately recognizing the area code, he was willing to let the call go to voicemail when he realized, on the fifth ring, that the call was from North Vancouver, British Columbia.

"Sorry, hello?" he said.

Hearing only silence on the other end, Father Jacob repeated his "Hello" and added, "This is Father Jacob speaking."

He heard a man cough and then clear his throat before he said, "This is Simon, Simon Lonetree. They tell me you've been trying to reach me."

Father Jacob looked up to see the parish secretary waving to him from the doorway and mouthing that he needed to start the service. He wanted to tell her that morning Mass to the same seven older parishioners could wait, but he knew he couldn't justify that to anyone, including himself.

"Mr. Lonetree, I have to offer Mass now. Can you give me your number? I promise to call you back in an hour, maybe even less." When he heard no response, he repeated, "I promise. I really do. It's important that we talk."

He heard "604-950-6902" before line went dead.

Writing down the number, Father Jacob jogged down the hallway and entered the sanctuary. Nodding to the regulars, he approached the altar, bowed before it, and sat down behind the pulpit, trying to catch his breath.

Silently, he offered his prayer intention for the Mass, that Simon Lonetree would answer the phone when he called and would tell him something that would help resolve the mystery of Father Robert's death. Then he added an intention for Nick's safety.

Forty-five minutes later, after one of his shortest homilies ever, Father Jacob returned to his office and called the number that Simon Lonetree had given him. With each ring, he offered a prayer that the man would answer, but after thirty rings, he put the phone down. Sitting back, he felt totally discouraged and asked himself again if he should have delayed the Mass for the phone call.

He tried to imagine Simon Longtree from the voice he'd heard so briefly. The voice sounded like it belonged to an older man, but then again, he realized, it could have been the voice of someone whose voice had been damaged by alcohol, tobacco, or drugs. What Father Jacob remembered was the breathiness in the voice, as if it had cost the man something to call him.

In desperation, Father redialed as he offered a prayer. On the fifth ring, Simon Lonetree answered.

"Sorry, I was in the can taking a leak," he said.

"Oh, that's great," Father Jacob said.

There was no response until Simon said, "You think it's great that I was taking a leak?"

"No, no, sorry, Mr. Lonetree. It's great that we can talk."

"First of all, my friends call me Si, so you can drop the Mr. Lonetree business. And what do I call you?"

Father Jacob thought for a moment before answering, "You can call me Jake. I was a friend of Father Bob."

In the long silence that followed, Father Jacob could hear a jukebox playing the Righteous Brothers' "You've Lost that Lovin' Feeling" in the background.

"You said you 'was' a friend of Bobby. What, you're not friends any longer?"

Bobby? Who called him Bobby? Father Jacob thought.

"Si, can you tell me your relationship with Father Bob. . . with Bobby?"

"I asked you first. What do you mean 'was'?"

Father Jacob took a deep breath before saying, "I'm sorry to say that Bobby is dead, Si."

Simon's voice was so loud that Father Jacob had to hold the phone away from his ear. "What'd you say? You said he's dead? How long has Bobby been gone?"

"He died nearly four weeks ago. He died in Rome. I'm sorry, Si."

"I wrote him must be five weeks ago. But if he was in Rome, he wouldn't have gotten my letters, then."

"No, Si, four weeks ago, Father Bob was still here in Yellowknife. But you're right; he was in Rome when your second letter arrived."

The jukebox was now playing Roy Orbison's "Only the Lonely." "Well, I don't blame Bobby for not writing me back."

"Why's that, Si?"

Father Jacob waited for the man to answer, but he said nothing. "You still there, Si?"

"Yeah, I'm here. If you're a priest like Bobby was, you need to know some things about me. There's not more than two or three things I've done in my life that I'm proud of. When I was young, I signed up for the Marines. Not many Indians do that, but I wanted to get away. In the Marines, I saw the world, but I saw a lot of it from jail cells. It's the old story, Father, an Injun who can't handle the booze. Anyways, when I'd done my stint in the Marines, I ended up in Vancouver on the streets. That is until the winter, when I'd stay in a shelter. I did that so many years that they put my name on one of the beds. Off and on, I've been sober, but God knows I'm telling you the truth when I say that when I'm not drinkin', I'm thinking about drinkin'. You've probably heard a version of my story many times."

"Sorry to say, I have," Father Jacob said, hoping that Si would speak more about Bobby.

"At this moment, I'm sober. Have been for more than two months now, but I make no promises. But when I dried out this last time, I thought about Bobby. You see, Bobby is my son."

Father Jacob sat forward in his chair. What Si was saying made no sense. He remembered Father Robert showing him his one picture of his family. The older of two boys, Bobby was dark-haired and dark-skinned like his mother, while the other brother had red hair and freckles like the father. That was the man who, when Father Robert's mother died, had dropped him at an orphanage and driven away with his other son. Father Robert told Father Jacob that his one enduring memory of childhood was trying to please his father and always failing. It was a memory that had never stopped haunting Father Robert in his dreams.

Father Jacob started to say that Si had to be mistaken, that he couldn't be Bobby's father, when he stopped. When he next spoke, it was his thoughts that poured out. "That's what you wrote Bobby in your first letter, wasn't it, Si? That you were his real father."

Simon gave a long sigh. "When I got Millie pregnant, I couldn't think of what to do. I'd already had a taste for the booze, so I bolted, ran and signed up for the Marines. The chaplain at the shelter where I'm still staying is the one who tracked Millie down, using a computer. He said she'd died back in the eighties, but that she was survived by a husband and two sons, Bobby and Alan. By their ages, I knew Bobby was my son, so I begged the chaplain to find Bobby. That's when I found out Bobby is . . . was a priest. I wrote because I thought he, being a priest, might find it in his heart to forgive me. But when he didn't answer me, well . . . I figured I was dead to him." Then in a voice that strained with hope, Si added, "That is unless you know something different, Padre."

Father Jacob was aware that Simon Lonetree had just provided the answer to the mystery of Father Robert's nights of drunkenness. He pictured his friend on the day before the fire receiving a letter that told him Simon Lonetree was his real father. The letter had opened a hole in the ground that Father Robert—Bobby—fell into. He must have pictured the face of the man who he'd always thought was his father but who'd never once said a kind word to him, never looked at him in love. But the most painful memory would have been of his mother, the one parent he'd always believed and needed to believe had loved him. Instead, she'd chosen to conceal the truth from him and watched as her husband slowly and daily scarred her firstborn.

As all this fell into place for Father Jacob, he could feel his friend's pain. It wasn't Father Robert who'd retreated into an alcoholic haze, but Bobby Lonetree, the boy who'd been betrayed and orphaned three times, first by a man whom he never met, then by his mother, and finally by the man he always thought was his father. Father Jacob closed his eyes for a moment and saw a boy flailing in the middle of an ocean, absolutely alone, held up by nothing and no one.

"Jake, are you still there?" Si asked.

"Yes, Si, I'm still here."

"So I was wondering, Jake. It's been a whole lot of years since I went to confession, but this feels like it to me. And now that I know that Bobby is dead, it would mean more than I can say if you would forgive me or maybe say the words to absolve me, if those are the words. I know this is asking a lot given what I've done in my life, but I'm begging, I really am. I'll do anything you tell me to do as penance."

Eyes still closed, Father Jacob saw the boy Bobby, still alone in the ocean, look at him and nod. "I can do that, Si. Your penance is to stay off the alcohol, this time for good. That's what Bobby would want. Will you do that?"

He heard a sob on the other end of the line. "I'll try, Jake. I swear I'll try."

CHAPTER THIRTY

Rome—The Library at the Order of the Sacred Wounds Monastery

Lena sat in the monastery's library and tried to rekindle her interest in Abbot Boniface. It felt like months, not a week, since she'd thought about her research. What helped was keeping in mind Nick's insight about the role of grit in forming a pearl, the grit being Father Jean Philippe's attacks on the Order of the Sacred Wounds and on Abbot Boniface.

Before Nick was abducted, Lena had come to the part in Abbot Boniface's papers when Father Jean Philippe's name was no longer mentioned and when the future of the Order of the Sacred Wounds seemed ensured. From other sources, she discovered that this abrupt change in the fortunes of the order, and consequently in Abbot Boniface's life, had coincided with the sudden death of Father Jean Philippe. The first batch of papers ended there.

Opening a second folder, dated two years after the first, she read the words "My Final Confession" handwritten on the first page. She knew that if she had discovered this second folder earlier, she wouldn't have been able to resist the urge to ignore the earlier papers, those dealing with Abbot Boniface's exterior world, and plunge immediately into these pages which promised to reveal his interior world.

Nick, you kept me from making that mistake, she thought. *I pray that I'll have a chance to thank you soon.*

Turning over the first page, she began to read.

"This is a confession that has taken me much too long to make. I pray for God's mercy on me, a sinner. When I came into the order as a novice, our novice master's first words were that our life goal, should we stay in the order, would be to embrace the sacred wounds of Christ. He did not say we were to *think* about Christ's wounds, or even *meditate* on them, but to *embrace* them. I was not alone among the novices in having no idea what he was asking of us.

"After our first readings from the lives of St. Francis and St. Catherine of Siena, two saints who'd both experienced the stigmata, the wounds of Jesus on their bodies, our novice master looked at us soberly and said, 'In case you're thinking that you are here to receive the stigmata, get that thought out of your head right now.'

"He went on to say that St. Francis and St. Catherine had been embraced by the sacred wounds of Christ. Our goal might be considered as the opposite. We were to embrace those wounds. At night in the novice's dormitory, we would stay up for hours trying to make sense of the assignment, but, if anything, we only became more confused.

"Those of us novices who progressed through our first vows and then perpetual vows to the order had grasped at least part of our novice master's point. Embracing the sacred wounds of Christ would be a work of God's mercy but also the work of a lifetime. As we got to know the other monks in the order, we also understood that we would not all embrace those wounds in the same way.

"It wasn't until decades later, when I was chosen abbot, that I began to hear the voice of the wounded Christ internally. From my other papers, it should be clear that the first years of my abbacy were trying ones. One night as I prayed beneath the crucifix in our chapel, I heard Christ's voice asking, 'Boniface, do you come alone?' Thinking that this was what Our Lord wanted, I answered, 'Yes.' But as the months ahead brought more troubles for the order—and more prayers on my knees in the chapel—I continued to hear the question, 'Boniface, do you come alone?'

"I slowly began to understand that my 'yes' answer wasn't the right one. In my prayers, I asked Our Lord if I was to bring others with me in my meditations. Over the next weeks, I saw the faces of the monks under my care. When I heard Christ again ask me the same question, I answered, 'I have brought the sheep you have given me.' For many years after that, Christ's voice was silent.

"Four years later, when our order's detractors mounted an even more aggressive attack, I was again in the chapel, praying before the crucifix. Once again I heard Christ's voice saying, 'Boniface, do you come alone?' I remembered Our Lord asking Peter three times if he loved Him and thought I was to respond as I had before—'Lord, you know I come to You with the sheep you have given me.' To my surprise, Christ asked, 'Is there not someone else?' My mind was empty. I asked, 'Is there, Lord?' But I received no answer, not then and not for another five years.

"When I was told that my illness was terminal, I pleaded with Christ. 'Will you not tell me who I'm to include among my sheep?' As my body weakened to where I was confined to bed, my mind was drawn further and further to the image of Our Lord's bleeding side. And as I meditated on that image, the wound took on the features of a door. My heart understood before my mind comprehended that my dying was leading me to that door. And on the other side of the door, I perceived the shadowy outlines of a face.

"My first thought was that I was seeing the face of St. Faustina, who'd witnessed the rays of Divine Mercy flowing from Jesus' side. But the thought gave me no peace. As the shadowy image returned in my meditations, I realized it was not the face of St. Faustina, St. Francis, or another saint, but the face of Father Jean-Philippe, my nemesis. He had died more than a decade before, but over those years, I had felt no grief in my heart.

"Then it was that I understood what my novice master had said so many years before. Death was offering me a final chance to embrace the wounds of Christ. By the mercies of God, I know that if I am to enter eternity, I must embrace Christ's wounds by making peace with Father Jean-Phillippe. This, by God's grace, I have tried to do, and now, by God's mercy, I am ready.

"As my hand is too weak to write, I have dictated this confession to dear Father Crecencio, on this day, June 29, 2012."

Lena felt a lump in her throat. Nick had been right. If Abbot Boniface was a saint, he'd become a saint because God had used Father Jean-Phillippe to transform Boniface into a pearl.

She felt a tap on her shoulder and jumped.

"Sorry," Father Ambrose, the librarian, said. "The abbot would like to have a word with you before you leave."

For a moment, Lena was disoriented. It took her a moment to realize that the librarian was referring to Abbot Lorenzo, not Abbot Boniface.

As she entered Abbot Lorenzo's office, the abbot was barely visible behind the stacks of paper.

Looking up, he said, "Ah, Dr. Fabriano. Please give me a minute. I know it's here somewhere." He shifted one stack of papers and began leafing through another until he said, "Here it is. It's a letter addressed to

Father Fortis with our address, so I thought you should have it. But first of all, is there any word about Father Nicholas?"

Lena shook her head as she accepted the envelope and saw that it was postmarked from Toronto. Opening it, she found a single sheet of paper with words "Participants in St. Bernard's Seminary Trip to Rome: June 3-24, 1992." Again, she felt confused until she remembered that Nick, Worthy, and she had wondered if something had happened on Father Robert's first visit that would shed light on his death thirty years later in the piazza. But now, given Nick's abduction, she wondered if the list was important at all.

Of the sixteen names on the list, seven were followed by the word "deceased' after them, leaving nine. Of the remaining nine, eight had mailing addresses in various parts of Canada and the US. Her eyes stopped when she saw that the last name on the list, "Father Linus," was followed by the address of a Carmelite monastery outside Rome.

"There's a monk here in Rome who knew Father Robert back in 1992," she said, as much to herself as to Abbot Lorenzo.

"Could that be important?" the abbot asked. Lena could hear the unmistakable note of hope in his voice.

"I'm not sure, Father, but it's worth finding out."

Luca Piemonte's Apartment

Bordy saw Luca look up from trimming his fingernails when he'd been escorted into boss's living room. "What's wrong with your face?" Luca asked.

"I lose tooth." Ever since he'd met Luca, Bordy had wanted to see where he lived. Now, he barely noticed the apartment because of the throbbing pain in his jaw.

"In a fight?" Luca asked, returning to his nails.

"No, Someone . . . I pulled it. It okay."

Shrugging, Luca said, "You need to decide about other priest and the professor," Luca said.

Bordy Vladic wasn't surprised by his boss's words. He'd sensed in their last meeting that Luca's patience was wearing thin. And until the day before, Bordy had been prepared to let Luca's men deal with the second priest while he pushed the professor aside and took over the role of leader.

But that had been the day before. Since then, he'd hardly slept a wink. The quick healing he'd expected after the professor had pulled the tooth hadn't happened, and Bordy found it hard to concentrate. Instead of sleeping the night before, he kept replaying in his mind the conversation he'd had with the American priest. His face and arms felt hot, while his feet felt cold.

He wished now that he hadn't gone to the warehouse to see the priest, hadn't listened to him when he talked about the professor caring for him. The priest had played a trick on him, but now, with the entire right side of his head tight with pain, he couldn't figure out what the trick had been.

"Are you listening, Bordy?" Luca asked in a louder voice. "You tell me, leave it to you, and I do. Was that mistake?"

Luca's words rang in Bordy's ears, adding to the pain. *I have to think, but how can I think with my head on fire?*

"This priest, he different," he said. "He no sex. Maybe we sell him?"

Luca stopped filing his nails. "You mean, send a ransom note?"

"Yes, sure. Why not?"

Luca rose and, standing over Bordy, grabbed him around the neck. "I'll tell you why not. Because you tell me this priest know too much what goes on in the piazza. You say this priest is more dangerous than other one. If you back to being a Bosnian piece of shit, I know what I do with you. One call from me and you be back in your shithole of a country by tomorrow."

Bordy's knees weakened as the pain radiated from his jaw to his neck. But he wouldn't give in to that, not in front of Luca. He focused on a spot on the wall behind Luca as he remembered the iron-hard look on his father's face as he risked venturing through a Serb neighborhood in hopes of finding food. His father had never returned.

Bordy tensed his muscles and stood as straight as he could. "Three day, four. You get priest."

Luca released his grip. "You have two days. Don't try any trick."

Keeping his eye on that same spot on the wall, Bordy said, "No trick."

CHAPTER THIRTY-ONE

Outside Rome—A Carmelite Monastery

That afternoon, Lena and Worthy chose to take a walk that led them away from her apartment near the Pantheon and the crowds that seemed to be always there.

"The longer this case drags on, the worse Nick's situation is likely to be, not that you didn't know that already," Worthy said. "But now, the likelihood that the press will find out about Nick's abduction ups the ante."

Lena nodded. "Before I left my meeting with the abbot yesterday, he told me that there was a reporter at the monastery. And this morning, another article appeared in the newspaper about Father Robert's murder."

"Rehashing what we already know?"

"More a criticism of the police for not making more progress."

Worthy slowed his pace. "Great, just what Sesto needs. I can't help wondering if there's something we've missed."

"About Nick or about Father Robert?"

"I could say both, but I was thinking about Nick."

"I'm guilty of the same, Chris. I forgot to show you this," she said, pulling from her jacket pocket the list of seminarians who had visited Rome in 1992.

"Where did you get this?"

"From the abbot. It came in a letter addressed to Nick at the monastery, and he gave it to me. As you can see, I've circled one name—the only priest from that list who is still alive and in Rome. He's in a Carmelite monastery outside the city. Should we interview him together?"

Worthy stopped walking and turned around. "Anything's better than doing nothing."

"You mean you want to do it now?"

"As I said, anything is better than doing nothing."

It took two hours for them to clear Rome by car and arrive at the Carmelite monastery's remote setting. On their way, Lena briefed Worthy on the peculiarities of a Carmelite house.

"The Carmelites are a cloistered order, Chris."

"I thought most monasteries had cloisters."

"No, that's not what 'cloistered' means in this case. Carmelite monks and nuns are secluded. Assuming this is the monk who was with Father Robert back in the nineties, he'll speak with us through a grille."

"Do they hate the world so much?" Worthy asked.

"That's not fair, Chris. Seclusion is their way of loving the world. They pray for all of us in solitude."

Worthy didn't say anything for a moment. "I suppose all that depends on whether you think prayer is important or a waste of time. I know what Nick would say, but it still surprises me that a group like this has survived over the years."

"The one thing I've learned by working with monasteries and convents is that they're full of surprises. There's a Carmelite monastery in your country, out west, where the average age is twenty-eight and their work involves herding cattle like cowboys. They even wear those leather pants."

"You mean 'chaps?' Well, the idea of cowboy monks does surprise me. What do the monks at this monastery do?"

"They make wooden caskets, beautiful but also affordable."

"*Memento mori*," Worthy said.

"Indeed. Making a casket is a clear reminder of death."

"Not exactly a place with a lot of laughter."

Lena couldn't help but laugh herself. "That's another misconception. From my experience, monks and nuns often see more of life with humor than the rest of us."

"Then the safest thing for me to do is follow your lead, Lena. I'm likely to put my foot in my mouth in a place like this."

Around a final bend in a long dirt road, they came to a limestone gothic-looking church and a wall. Rising above the wall were peaks of tiny roofs set next to one another.

"Each monk lives alone in one of those cells," Lena said. "But they eat their meals together and pray together, of course, in the church."

Stepping out of the car, Worthy heard the distinct sounds of a power saw. "Sounds like someone's making caskets."

They walked through a pointed gothic arch and came to heavy iron-clad wooden doors. Instead of a doorbell, there was a bell with a long rope attached. Lena pulled on it, producing a sound loud enough to be heard over the machinery, and waited.

A voice came from behind the door. "Dr. Fabriano?"

"Yes, I'm Dr. Fabriano," Lena said, happy to realize that someone had in fact heard her voicemail message. "And I'm here with Christopher Worthy, a detective."

"And you want to speak to Brother Elias?"

"Yes, please."

There was a pause before they heard a voice from the other side of the door. "I will unlock the door but would ask you to wait a minute or two before entering. When you do, you will see a room off to the right. Enter that room and sit by the grill in the wall. I will let Brother Elias know you are here."

Lena and Chris did as instructed and, in a matter of minutes, were sitting in a room that looked like a small chapel. Instead of a crucifix over the altar, Lena noted the statue of the Virgin Mary holding the Christ child.

"The monks take their way of life from her," she whispered, gesturing toward the statue. "They strive for her solitude and humility."

"I can't see Nick doing very well here. Yes, he's humble, but I think he'd struggle with the solitude and the silence."

They heard the small door on the other side of the grill slide back. Even so, they couldn't make out the person on the other side. Then they heard a man clear his throat.

"I understand you want to ask me some questions." The monk spoke English in a raspy voice, and Lena wondered when he'd last spoken to someone outside the enclosure.

Seeing Worthy nod her way, Lena explained that they were looking into the death of Father Robert Porter.

Brother Elias didn't say anything for a moment. Then, he asked, "I didn't even know Bob was in Rome. How did he die?"

"He was murdered in Piazza del Popolo," Worthy replied.

Another pause followed before "I thought he was serving in Canada."

"He was until just a few weeks ago. He was running an orphanage. But he was staying in the motherhouse of the Order of the Sacred Wounds in

Rome before he died," Lena offered, deciding she wouldn't mention the fire unless it was necessary.

After another pause, Brother Elias said, "The community will pray for him."

Lena waited, in case Brother Elias asked other questions. But he asked nothing.

"Brother Elias, we're hoping you can tell us what Father Robert was like on the seminary trip to Rome in 1992."

"It's a long time ago. What do you mean?"

"For example, was he talkative?"

"Bob and I were more on the quiet side. But I remember that he liked to go out at night, to walk around the city."

Lena glanced over at Worthy. "Did you ever go with him?" she asked.

"A few times. My interest was the older churches of Rome, the churches commemorating the early martyrs. Bob preferred the places where a lot of people congregated."

"Did you know if he ever went to Piazza del Popolo?"

After a long pause, Brother Elias asked, "Is that the piazza with a large obelisk in the middle?"

Lena was surprised that someone living near Rome would be unfamiliar with one of the city's most popular sites, but then she understood that a cloistered Carmelite monk would be familiar with little in the city. "Yes, that's the one," she said. "Did you go there with Father Robert?"

"Once. But I could tell he'd been there before."

"You mean during the seminary trip?"

"Yes. As I said, he enjoyed crowds." After a moment, Brother Elias asked, "Did you say he worked at an orphanage in Canada?"

"Yes, why do you ask?"

"The night I went there with him, he'd brought a lot of change with him. He gave a few coins to the children who were begging in the piazza. Perhaps it's no surprise that he worked at an orphanage."

"No, it's not a surprise at all," Worthy said. "Father Bob was an orphan himself."

"Ah, I'd forgotten that."

Lena saw Worthy give her a nod, and she knew what he wanted her to ask Brother Elias. "This is a more awkward question, but do you remember Father Robert getting drunk on that trip?"

After a long pause, Brother Elias asked, "Is it necessary that I answer that?"

"It could be," Lena said.

"I'm ashamed of the memory. Several of the others on the trip went out every night for a beer or maybe more than one beer. Bob and I weren't interested in that. But a couple of nights before our trip was to end, the rest of the guys begged us to join them. Even after one beer, Bob's words sounded slurry. Unfortunately, some of the more regular drinkers found that funny and they kept buying him more drinks. Bob got louder and louder, until we were asked to leave the bar. I remember Bob vomiting twice on the way back to the motherhouse, and I think the police stopped us and gave Bob some kind of a citation. Of course, those leading our group found out about it. From then on, bars were off-limit until we flew back to Canada."

Brother Elias' voice had grown raspier and raspier, and now he coughed. "The priests from the seminary who were leading our group blamed Bob, but I didn't. I blamed the others."

"Did he say anything about the incident afterwards?" Lena asked.

"He apologized, of course, saying he wasn't used to alcohol. I believed him, and maybe that's why he told me later that he knew he had to stay clear of alcohol. I think he knew he'd have trouble metabolizing it, I mean. He swore to me he'd never get drunk again."

Rome—A Warehouse Outside the City

Yuri's mouth dropped as he saw Nick chained again to the bed. "When did this happen?" he asked.

"Yesterday," Nick said. "Bordy stopped by."

His face red, the professor swung around and, with his one hand, gestured turning a key in a lock. "Key," he said to the two guards.

The older of the two guards shook his head.

"I said key now!" Yuri yelled.

"Bordy, he say 'no,'" the younger guard said with smirk.

"Listen to me. Bordy is sick. He doesn't know what he's saying."

With a laugh, the younger guard said, "No English. Parla Italiano."

Dejected, the professor sat down by Nick's bed.

"I'm sorry. I never gave Bordy permission to do this."

"I assumed that was the case," Nick said. "You said Bordy is sick. Is it his tooth or something else?"

Yuri nodded. "His mouth is infected. He has a fever. I've tried to keep him in bed, but he is in pain. We will try to buy medicine, an antibiotic, off the street."

"An infection like that can be serious, can even lead to blood poisoning. Can't you take him to a hospital?"

The professor shook his head. "Remember, the police have a photo of Bordy. The doctors will see that he's Bosnian and will have to alert the police. Bordy will be sent back."

Yuri thought back to that morning when one of the boys came to tell him that Bordy was getting worse. He'd followed the boy to one of the shacks inside one of the medians of a highway leading in and out of Rome. Inside the shack, he found Bordy shivering on a soiled mattress. One side of his face was swollen to half again the size of the other half. The swelling had even closed one eye.

Looking around and seeing no blankets, he'd taken off his coat and laid it over the boy as he said, "Let me look in your mouth, Bordy."

Bordy's one good eye darted from one side of the shack to the other as he mumbled words in Bosnian.

Finally, the professor saw the boy look at him. "Can you open your mouth, Bordy?"

Bordy moaned as he slowly parted his lips. Looking into Bordy's mouth, Yuri saw pus coming from the hole left by the extracted molar. Even as he did so, he could feel Bordy trying to raise himself.

"No, you have to stay in bed."

Bordy had shaken his head violently, setting off another cry of pain. "No, no."

"You don't have a choice, Bordy. It's important that you rest until we can get you medicine. Do you understand?"

Bordy had remained seated for a moment before falling back onto the mattress. It took a moment for Yuri to realized that the boy had fainted.

Nick shook Yuri's arm, bringing him back to the present. "The boy could die before you get the right medicine on the street."

He looked at Nick and nodded. "I can't let the boy die."

"Neither can I," Nick said.

Yuri stared at him. "What do you mean?"

"I can get Bordy the help he needs, if you trust me."

Yuri shook his head as he glanced at the guards behind him. "I can't release you even if I wanted to—which I do."

Holding up his one cuffed hand, Nick replied, "I know. But I can write a note to my friends. They can arrange for a doctor to see Bordy."

For the first time Yuri wondered if Nick was trying to take advantage of him. "You forget what you already told me, that your friends work with the police."

Nick looked startled. "No, no, you misunderstand me, Yuri. If I wrote them a note, explaining that it's essential for Bordy get help without the police knowing, they will do that."

Yuri considered the offer. If he trusted Nick to write that note, Nick's friends would know he was alive. *Is that what this American is counting on?* Yuri asked himself. *If so, would that be so bad?*

"I will have to think about this," he said. But even as he said that, he realized what would happen. In turning Bordy over to Nick's friends, the boy could become a hostage. And then wouldn't Nick's friends insist on a trade, Nick for Bordy?

"I must ask you something, Nick. If you were freed, the police would certainly question you. What would you say to them? I want to believe that you would not betray us, but could you stand up to the pressure to tell them what you know about us?"

Yuri studied Nick's face as he looked down at the chain on his wrist. Finally, he said, "Yuri, these past days have given me a great deal of time to think—and to pray. Just this morning, I realized that if I am ever to be a man of God, I have to accept that I am here for a reason. I think that reason is for me to understand that I'm not the prisoner. You, Bordy, and the other boys are the prisoners."

Neither man said anything, even as Yuri saw tears form in Nick's eyes.

"If I turned you over to the police, Yuri," Nick said, "it would be the same as me sending you back to Bosnia. I can't have that on my conscience, so no, I won't turn you over to the police. But there is more. I can't pretend that you and I never met, Yuri, that we've never talked honestly with one another, or that we've never shared our hopes, and yes, our sacrifices. I can't pretend that I didn't read the UN Charter of Human Rights that you left for me. Yuri, I have to do something for you."

Yuri shook his head. "You have a good heart, Nick, but don't make promises you can't keep. I understand that you want to help us, but there is nothing you can do to save my boys or me."

Now it was Nick who shook his head. "I can't . . . I won't accept that. If I am freed, I won't abandon you, Yuri." Pausing, he wiped the tears from his cheek and reached to clasp the professor's hand. "You see, Yuri, being chained here has led me to finally understand Father Robert. In your boys, he saw his orphans back in Canada. That's what he cared about—children. You're right, I can't promise that I will finish what he set out to do, but I have to try."

Rome—Lena's Apartment

After yet another night of disturbed sleep, Worthy rose before dawn, made coffee, and sat in Lena's kitchen. The email Lena had received from Father Jacob in Yellowknife the night before provided the last pieces of the Father Robert puzzle. The priest's drunken stupor on the night of the orphanage fire had almost certainly been caused by the letter from Simon Lonetree, his biological father. As Father Jacob in Yellowknife had written in his email, Father Robert—Bobby—had been betrayed not just by the man he'd always been told was his father, but by his mother as well, the one person he always thought had loved him. And she probably had loved him, Worthy reasoned, but she hadn't protected him or told him the truth.

And after talking with Brother Elias at the Carmelite monastery, they also knew what had drawn Father Robert to Piazza del Popolo on the nights before he was killed. He'd returned to the place where, thirty years before, he'd handed over his spare change to the children begging there. Worthy thought it likely that this was the night when Robert, the young seminarian, saw himself in those children and understood his calling to work with other orphans.

Thirty years later, in Rome to very likely be defrocked, Father Robert had returned to Piazza del Popolo, the site of his first sense of vocation. Depressed and numb, what he'd seen in the piazza was a repetition of what he'd observed thirty years before—children once again moving from tourist to tourist begging, but this time also picking pockets.

That night had provided the shock that had awakened Father Robert and given him a new sense of mission. He would remain in Rome, even if he were defrocked, saving as many Bosnian kids from a life of crime as he could. That renewed sense of a life mission had cost Father Robert his life, but Worthy knew what Nick would say. Father Robert had died in peace.

Yes, the mystery of Father Robert now seemed solved, but Worthy's anxiety remained high. There was nothing now to distract him from worrying about Nick. He rose from the kitchen table, scribbled a note for Lena, and headed out for a walk.

Perhaps by habit, he walked in the direction of his office. On the way, he passed again the church, this time remembering that the church contained the relics of a famous saint. He stopped and, seeing candles burning in the dark interior, stepped inside.

At a table set up near the entrance, he found an English guide to the church, Santa Maria sopra Minerva. He sat in one of the pews and just managed in the light to read the name of the saint—St. Catherine of Siena, whose relics were housed under the altar of the church.

Returning to his mind was a memory from his childhood, that of an elderly neighbor across the street who still, in the eighties, had a statue of St. Christopher on the dashboard of his car. He knew his father had tried to talk the Catholic neighbor out of what his father called "worshipping saints instead of Christ."

Then, just six years before, Worthy had come face to face with relics— bones, teeth, bits of hair, nail filings, and instruments of torture on a case in Venice. The relics had repulsed and nauseated him.

Even more recently, Worthy had encountered relics again, when two years before he'd been on a case with Nick that made headlines all over the world. The blood of two monks, murdered in Rome, had been collected at the murder site and became instant relics. That was when he realized that the concept of relics wasn't foreign to police work, especially homicide cases. Hadn't he witnessed how, for families, keys, pens, watches, and clothing of victims had become relics, items too sacred to be discarded?

He looked up at the marble statue of St. Catherine, reclining under the altar, after reading that pilgrims came from all over the world to pray in this church. He paused, aware that as recently as a year before, he'd have dismissed such a practice with the thought, *They're just bones, just bones.*

But then something that he'd yet to understand had happened to him last year in Canada. In a moment of crisis, in a moment of life and death, he'd felt a presence surrounding him. Now, as he sat in the dark church, he wondered if that same sense of presence—of something or someone—was what drew people to this church.

He had a sudden urge to kneel, but just as quickly he vetoed the idea. *You're tired. You're worried about Nick. The case isn't going well. Whatever this feeling is, it's a trick of the room's atmosphere—the darkness and the candles—and, do I need to repeat?—your lack of sleep.*

Pushing against those objections, however, was the wish to feel again that sense of presence that he'd felt the year before. "If you're here," he whispered, "forget about me. Help Nick. Just that—help Nick."

CHAPTER THIRTY-TWO

Rome—Lena Fabriano's Apartment

Lena awoke to find Worthy's note on the kitchen table, asking her to meet him at his office after she'd had breakfast. Worthy's tossing and turning had awakened her several times during the night, and she was sure that she knew the cause. She'd even contemplated turning on a light to ask if he wanted to talk, but she knew such talk would only make matters worse.

Sitting with a cup of expresso, she looked at the wedding planning book that sat closed on her kitchen table and felt an urge to tear it up. Nothing mattered other than freeing Nick, but with no word of him since he was abducted, she knew without saying anything that both Worthy and she were struggling to retain hope.

She was roused by a muffled sound from the front of her apartment. Expecting to see Worthy come into the kitchen, she listened for his step but then heard nothing.

"Chris?"

A shiver passed through her body as she tried to recollect the sound she'd heard. Had her fears for Nick led her to imagine the muffled sound? Was it her elderly neighbor who sometimes mistakenly passed his own door and knocked on her own?

Still in bare feet, she tiptoed from the kitchen into the living room and peered at her front door. She was relieved to see that the door was tightly closed. It was then that she saw the envelope lying just inside her apartment. As she approached slowly, she dismissed the thought that the regular postal worker had slipped it under the door. The carrier would come to Lena's door only if there were a package, and this was no package.

Moving as silently as possible, she approached the envelope and knelt to look at it more closely. On it were the words in English "For Christopher's and Lena's eyes only."

She stepped backwards as if struck, before reaching down to pick up the envelope. Her hands shook uncontrollably as read again the words "For Christopher's and Lena's eyes only." There was only one person whom she knew who called Worthy by his full first name, and that person was Nick.

✝

Rome—Lena's Apartment

As Worthy used his key to enter Lena's apartment, his whole body tightened when he heard Lena sobbing in the living room. His first thought was that his prayer had been wasted and there was bad news about Nick. He let his coat drop to the floor as he rushed into the room, where Lena looked up at him with red eyes as she waved a sheet of paper.

"What is it?" he asked.

Lena, still weeping, shook her head, handing the sheet of paper to him. His eyes wouldn't focus, as if they didn't want to read what was written there.

"No, it's good news, Chris. Read it."

Worthy sat down, the piece of paper shaking in his hand. He read, "My dearest friends, Christopher and Lena. This note will assure you that I am alive and being treated fairly. Please believe me when I write that the Bosnians had nothing to do with Father Robert's death. I am allowed to write because one of the Bosnian boys has a medical emergency. If the Bosnians take him to a hospital, the authorities will learn of his presence, and the boy will be deported. But if a doctor doesn't see the boy soon, I fear he will die.

"What I am asking of you both is immense. I am asking you, Lena, to call a doctor who will treat the boy without informing the authorities. I know that I am asking you to break the law, but because the boy's condition is so serious, I beg you to do what I ask. You will find the boy resting in a shack directly across from the Bretoni Mercato at Via Ostiense number 7683.

"God-willing, and I pray it is God's will, I will see you both soon. I am in good health and, though it might sound strange, I am better for having had this experience.

The peace of Christ be with you both,

Your friend, Nick

P.S. You will know this note is truly from me because I gave the messenger the key to your building, Lena, as well as the number of your apartment."

As Worthy read the note a second time, he felt Lena's arms around his neck and her tears on his cheek. His own eyes filled with tears as he whispered, "I can hardly believe it. Nick's alive."

"I know, I know," Lena whispered. "I think we were both . . . hanging on, hoping, but it was so hard."

Worthy drew Lena closer to him. "It's like the clouds finally parted, and the sun peeked through—just a bit, but enough."

"Yes, it's enough. Chris, I want to do what Nick asks."

"I do too," Worthy said, even as he saw his new career in Rome ending before it had barely begun. That's what would happen if Capitano Sesto, others in the police, or one of Rome's journalists ever found out what Lena and he were prepared to do.

"Do you know of a doctor who'd do this, Lena?"

Lena's finger traced with her finger the words, "Your friend, Nick" at the end of the note. Inhaling deeply, she said, "Maria, my cousin. We're a year apart and have always been close. Maria will know what she is risking, but if I ask her, I know she will at least consider it."

Worthy drew Lena closer to him. "Then she must be a lot like you."

Luca never liked it when his boss, Fausto Como, asked to meet outside their scheduled bi-weekly face-to-face. And the location for this meeting was new, atop the Janiculum Hill that overlooked much of Ancient Rome. The meeting time was also unusual, ten o'clock in the morning replacing the usual late night. All Luca could grasp was that Fausto wanted to meet with him when and where they'd be surrounded by tourists.

In his poor sleep the night before, Luca kept searching for what might have provoked the meeting. The faces of those who worked for him shuffled through his brain, one at a time, with no one's situation having changed except for Bordy Vladic's. But why and how Fausto would have heard about the change in a Bosnian boy's health eluded him. For a moment, he toyed with the idea that the Bosnian they called "the Professor" had somehow contacted Fausto and lodged a complaint against him for intruding on the professor's territory, but he dismissed the notion. The only way the professor could have known about Luca's boss was through Bordy, and Luca had never divulged to Bordy or any of the boys the names of any of his bosses.

But as he ran through his morning routine of showering, shaving, and polishing his shoes, he felt something that he hadn't for years—fear. He told himself that if Fausto intended to punish him, the meeting would have occurred in an isolated place as well as in the middle of the night.

Luca parked in a lot that was half-filled with tourist buses and walked the hundred yards to the overlook near the Church of San Pietro in Montano. He crossed himself out of superstition, willing to take whatever help he could find for the meeting ahead.

He sat on a bench and waited. Floating around him was a mix of languages, of which he identified Chinese, German, and French. He waved away the men, probably Pilipino, who were hawking cheap postcards and telescopic wands to hold smartphones for selfies.

The wait didn't surprise Luca. One of Fausto's habits was to observe a meeting site from a safe distance. Luca understood that for those minutes he was bait. If someone had tipped off the police to the meeting, Luca would be picked up, not Fausto. Not for the first time, Luca understood that the higher up the ladder he climbed—was allowed to climb—the less trust he'd have.

Trust. Yes, he thought, trust was the Bosnian professor's currency and, because of that, would be his downfall. The professor might preach the importance of trust, but he'd been blind to what the other boys must know, that Bordy Vladic had already betrayed that trust.

As he waited, Luca thought also about the American priest held in the warehouse south of the city. The Americans he'd encountered in his various scam operations trusted that they were too smart to be fooled. Had any of those Americans been chained to a bed frame in a foreign country, they'd have been begging for their lives within days.

But not this American. For one thing, the guards told him that the priest looked them in the eye. As the guards studied him, the priest seemed to be studying them—not belligerently, but calmly. Luca had seen men known to be stoic dissolve in tears when they realized they would die, but he doubted this priest would behave in that way.

He'd delegated the stabbing of the Canadian priest to his most trusted man, Sabatini, who now oversaw the guards in the warehouse. When he'd asked Sabatini for the details of the Canadian priest's death, Sabatini had said little at first. "He's a man; he died" was all Sabatini said, though he looked at the floor as he said this. When he pressed for more, Sabatini said that the priest had never stirred on the bench. "He didn't even look over his shoulder to . . . you know, see me," Sabatini had confessed. "You said he was a pedophile, so I thought maybe he expected it."

Luca had been the one to cast the Canadian priest as a pedophile, knowing it would be easier for Sabatini to feel that he wasn't murdering a priest as much as dispensing justice. And he'd done that also for Bordy, who pointed out the priest to Sabatini. He wondered now if he'd also labeled the priest as a pedophile partially for himself. He'd seen plenty of men die before but was superstitious enough to believe that killing a priest could bring with it a curse.

Luca heard footsteps behind him, but didn't turn around until Fausto sat down next to him. His boss was dressed in a nondescript brown puffy coat and tan flat cap, making him look older than Luca knew he was.

"Don't look at me or say anything. When I think it's safe, I'll do the talking."

Not exactly words to make me relax, Luca thought.

Fausto aimed his smartphone at the panorama of Rome in front of them and took several pictures. "We are just two tourists admiring the view," Fausto said in a low voice.

If only that were true, Luca thought.

Fausto reached into a coat pocket and took out a guide to the city. Opening it, he said in a louder voice, "I'm wondering if you could help me, sir," as he showed the page to Luca.

Luca looked down and read the script at the top of the page. "A source tells me the police are on to you. They have photos of you and your crew scamming tourists outside Piazza del Popolo."

"Turn the page," Fausto whispered.

On the next page, Luca read, "They also want to interview you about the death of a priest."

Under his breath, Fausto said, "Don't say anything. Just point with your finger toward the Vatican as if you're giving me directions."

After Luca did so, his boss said in a louder voice, "Grazie mille" before standing. Doffing his cap, he said in a soft voice, "Before you leave, make sure you take a few pictures with your phone. Remember, you're another tourist. Don't try to contact me. Just lie low."

CHAPTER THIRTY-THREE

Rome—A Shack on Via Ostiense

Bordy's entire body was on fire. With one eye shut, he could make out only shapes in the darkened room in which he rested. His fevered thoughts featured an ever-twisting kaleidoscope of faces—his mother's, Luca's, the professor's, his younger brother's and sister's, and finally the face of the priest chained in the warehouse. The faces of the dead did not trouble him as much as the faces of the professor and the priest.

He had seen death close up in Bosnia, remembering the shallow graves still left from the Balkan War. *That's what will be left of me*, he thought, almost curious as to how much longer he had to live. He knew the professor wouldn't throw his body into a ditch, but would leave it at the door of one of Rome's hospitals in the dead of night with the word "Musulmano" pinned to his body. Within twenty-four hours, he would be buried according to Muslim tradition, a local imam reciting the short service before his body would be covered by earth.

He had witnessed too much misery to be afraid of death. In his worst days growing up in Bosnia, he'd sometimes envied the dead, not having to eat out of the garbage dump or search rubbish piles for anything to sell. In Italy, however, his envy of the dead had been replaced by a growing sense of intention or purpose. Yes, he'd eaten out of garbage bins in Italy and had slept under viaducts in the cold, but he could also see something he'd never see in Bosnia—the chance for a better life. In Italy, he'd allowed himself something that had been taboo in Bosnia. He allowed himself to dream.

He tried to remember what the professor had said when he'd last come to the shack. That could have been an hour ago, yesterday, or maybe just in his imagination. The words he remembered—that some strangers would come and take him to see a doctor—certainly seemed like a dream. Why would strangers care whether he lived or died?

"Care." He wondered if that word rather than his missing tooth was what was causing his fever. That was the word the priest had used to describe how the professor felt about him. And then the priest had gone on to say that he also cared about Bordy. *All lies*, he told himself. He wasn't even sure what the word "care" meant, but if it was something the professor and the priest felt, it must be something weak.

An image of his mother floated through his brain. It was a scene from his early childhood, when he still had a childhood. He was sitting in a broken chair within the tiny room his family shared in the IDP camp. His mother had managed to bake a loaf of bread, and, after taking it from the tiny oven, had cut off a piece and given it to him along with a small glass of milk. He remembered that they'd sat in a shared silence, a warm silence.

As he shivered, he remembered that the priest had asked about his childhood and what he liked in school. The priest had no right to do that. That was his past, a past he'd buried along with his father, mother, brother, and sister.

Racked with fever and the cold of the shack, he found it difficult to focus with his one good eye on the others who were talking in the room. But then the sound faded into the darkness. Some time later—was it minutes or hours?—he felt himself being lifted and carried. *I'm dead*, he thought, *being carried like my brother and sister were carried to the town's graveyard.*

Rome—A Warehouse Outside the City

Nick had no way of knowing what Worthy and Lena had decided. He wasn't even sure that what he asked was possible, particularly the request that a doctor treat Bordy without informing the authorities. Remembering how feverish Bordy had looked when Nick saw him last and then Yuri's description of Bordy's condition, Nick wondered what would happen if the boy, in the end, needed hospitalization to save him. How could his identity be hidden from the police?

While praying for patience and guidance, Nick could hear the two armed guards whispering. Their subtle glances in his direction told him that they were talking about him. More and more, Nick sensed that the professor was the only person standing in the way of the guards, and whoever was behind them, deciding his fate.

He thought back on Yuri's pessimism that, once he was released, he could do anything to change the lot of the Bosnians in Rome. Politics in Europe increasingly favored candidates who took a hard line against migrants. Any government official who raised the possibility of citizenship for the Bosnians would soon be out of office.

Nick imagined the millions of Bordys around the world who dreamt of safety and security. He thought back to the UN Charter of Human Rights that Yuri had given him to read just days before. Thirty articles in the charter written in 1948, almost every one of the articles offering hope and dignity to the professor and the Bosnian boys, were now ignored by the affluent nations of the world. *Yes, just as Yuri said, those promises are fairy tales*, he thought.

Nick wondered if it would have been better if the UN's promises had never been put down on paper. He could imagine Yuri carrying the charter around with him, a condemnation of everything he and his boys were experiencing.

That was when Nick realized that he knew not one world leader, not one international organization, that offered a solution to the refugee crisis facing the world. Refugees were like flood waters rising as nations responded with feeble stopgap measures—tent cities with filth and danger, walls built at borders, overcrowded rafts of refugees sent back to countries that hadn't the slightest concern for human rights. But the waters kept rising.

Nick thought of the lawyer in the New Testament who asked Jesus, "Who is my neighbor?" Two millennia later, Nick realized, humanity was siding with the lawyer, who wanted to take the question narrowly, tribally, and nationalistically. How was it that Jesus' own answer, that the neighbor was anyone in need, had been as ignored over the centuries as the UN Charter?

The crime of the millions of refugees, Nick saw, was what it had always been. They hoped.

CHAPTER THIRTY-FOUR

Rome—Driving to a Warehouse Outside the City

Luca Piemonte sat in the backseat of his Mercedes, watching Rome's afternoon traffic whiz by as he pondered what his driver and bodyguard had told him. Bordy was nowhere to be found, with rumors that he'd been picked up just hours before.

"Picked up by police?" Luca asked.

"No," the bodyguard said.

"And no one knows where he is?"

"No, but one of the boys said the professor might know."

"Well, that's something," Luca said. He knew of two locations where he might find the professor. One was the warehouse where he knew the second priest was being kept. The other would be at night in Piazza del Popolo.

"Drive to the warehouse," he ordered, remembering his last meeting with Bordy. The boy hadn't looked well, and he'd had to remind him that he needed to make a decision about the second priest. That was especially the case after Fausto, his boss, had led him know that the police were on to him. With Bordy now in the wind, Luca toyed with the idea of deciding the priest's fate himself.

To do that, Luca knew the professor would stand in his way. He'd met the professor only three times and remembered the unspoken disgust he'd felt from the man. The professor acted as the boys' father, an old man who didn't realize that he'd never be able to give the boys the security they wanted in Italy. What the professor didn't understand was that he was the Bosnian boys' past, while he, Luca, was their future.

Luca had considered getting rid of the professor just as he'd removed the Canadian priest in the piazza. What kept Luca from doing that wasn't squeamishness, but rather practical considerations. There was a place in Luca's plans for boys of Bordy's age, intelligence, and desperation, but not for the younger ones. It didn't matter to Luca that the professor looked down on him, even saw him as an enemy, as long as the professor babysat, fed, clothed, and trained the younger boys in basic pickpocketing techniques. They, like Bordy, would become his possession when they ripened.

Luca was disappointed at the warehouse, his bodyguard returning to the car to tell him that the professor wasn't there. He would have to wait until nightfall to search for the professor in the piazza. He accepted the change of plan, but exited the car and entered the warehouse. The men sitting in the first room playing cards rose when they saw Luca.

"Show me where you're holding the priest," he ordered.

Rome—Maria Fabriano's Private Surgery

Worthy and Lena watched as Maria, Lena's cousin and a doctor, stood over the shivering figure on the examination table. The left side of the boy's face was so swollen and contorted that Lena couldn't imagine what he really looked like.

Speaking in Italian, Lena told her cousin what they knew and didn't know about the boy. They didn't know his name, only that he was Bosnian, in the country illegally, and having an infection from have a tooth extracted unprofessionally.

Lena saw the surprise on Worthy's face when Maria hadn't hesitated to help. She knew Worthy was right when he said that few if any licensed physicians in the States would take such a risk. *And that's why I love being Italian,* she thought. Maria hadn't agreed just because her cousin had asked her. Maria, along with many other Italian doctors and nurses, had served on Mercy Ships, floating hospitals that brought life-saving surgeries and treatments to African nations. Lena knew Maria wouldn't balk at treating a Bosnian boy just because he was undocumented.

Maria spoke soothingly to the boy as she inserted a tongue depressor into the good side of the boy's mouth and, gently applying pressure, opened his lips and examined the infection site. When the boy's reaction was only to continue shivering, Maria told Lena that the boy was only semi-conscious.

After the examination, Maria gave the boy an injection before removing her mask and coming to sit by Lena and Worthy. "The infection is quite advanced. We won't know for maybe twenty-four hours if he's contracted blood poisoning. If that's the case, we won't have any choice but to take him to a hospital. I've given him a strong antibiotic which also contains a sedative."

When Lena translated for Worthy, he said, "Please tell your cousin how grateful we are. I don't even want to think what could happen to Nick if the boy dies."

Maria smiled at Worthy. "I understand a little English. I be . . . I am happy to help. I will keep him here until we know for certain."

"How will you know if he's going to make it?" Worthy asked.

"If his swelling and fever go down, you can take him where you think he'll be safe. But he will need to rest."

Lena clutched Worthy's hand. "If he recovers, will they release Nick?"

"I don't know, but we can hope. What I do know is that Nick wants us to help the boy regardless of what happens to him."

Rome—A Warehouse Outside the City

For two days, Nick saw nothing of the professor and assumed that Yuri, without being seen, was staying near Bordy. The two guards seemed restless, and Nick had the feeling something was being decided. He spent the hours praying—for the boy, the professor, and all the Bosnians in Rome.

While he was praying, it dawned on Nick that his situation, except for being chained to the bedframe and the two armed guards, was similar to what he'd imagined monastic life would be like—solitude, prayer, and more solitude. The reality of his life as a monk had turned out to be little like that, especially once he began working with Worthy on homicides.

But now, I have been brought back to the roots of the faith, he thought, to the saints of the Church in Rome who in the early centuries had been imprisoned. They too had faced an uncertain future, one that ended in death more often than release. They too had faced hours, days, and weeks of imprisonment with little more than prayer to break up the numbing boredom. He made the sign of the cross and asked those saints to pray that he'd be patient in waiting for God's will to be done.

On the third morning, the first major change in Nick's situation happened. Opening his eyes, he saw a stranger standing at the foot of his bed. His olive complexion and dark hair suggested he was Italian, not Bosnian, and his attire—leather jacket, black turtleneck, and expensive slacks—hinted that he was someone with clout. His eyes were lidded, his body looking completely relaxed as he said something that brought a laugh from one of the guards.

"I say to him, you look like you eat a lot," the man said in English.

"Too much," Nick replied.

"But not so much now, no?"

"I'm not complaining."

The man took a carton of cigarettes from his shirt pocket. "Want one?"

Nick shook his head. "No."

The man seemed to be moving in slow motion as he took a cigarette out and flipped open a golden lighter. "These men, they say you no complain. Why is that? The bed looks not so comfortable."

"Maybe I realized complaining wouldn't do me any good."

"Da vero, that is true," the man said, sending cigarette smoke toward the ceiling. "Another of my men, he say you don't fight when they take you in Termini, train station. You big man. You could . . . what you say? . . . why you no make big problem in train station? You no fight because you priest?"

Nick sensed that the man was more than curious. His questions were the man's way of sizing him up, his way of discovering what Nick knew and didn't know.

"I think you know that I was asking around in the piazza about Father Robert, the murdered priest."

"Si, si. Yes, I heard about that priest. A tragedy. Why you think he die?"

A shiver ran through Nick's body. There was something about the hard look in the man's eyes as he posed the question that gave Nick the feeling that he was looking at Father Robert's killer. Nick thought about responding with "You would know that better than me," but knew that such a response would reveal too much.

"I didn't resist in the train station because I thought one of the Bosnian boys might have seen who killed Father Robert. I hoped by cooperating that I'd learn what they know."

The man didn't say anything for a moment, but then shrugged. "Maybe robbery is so. Or maybe the priest, he likes boys. Many men come to piazza late at night for sex, even priests. Maybe you such a man."

"No, and I don't believe Father Robert was one either."

"You friend of the dead priest?"

Nick thought back to the night he was abducted. Bordy had likely followed him from the monastery. Because of that, he replied, "No, I never met Father Robert. I'm staying at the same monastery Father Robert stayed at. They asked a friend of mine and me to see what we could find out."

The man's eyes narrowed. "This friend is police here in Rome?"

Nick shook his head. "No, he's another American."

"Another American? You say he friend. Is this friend looking for you?"

"I'm sure he is."

"But no police?"

Nick weighed how to respond. If this man already knew the answer to that question, he was probably testing him. "I told you my friend and I were asked by the monastery to find out what we could. Naturally, one of the first things we did was meet with the police."

The man had gone back to the end of the bed. "The police, they no mind you Americans asking questions?"

Nick thought it was his turn to test how much the man knew. "Of course they minded. We're outsiders. The police gave us no help. That's why I went back to the piazza. You see, my friend and I were looking into the murder on our own."

The man dropped the cigarette to the floor and put it out with his shoe. "But now police must look for you."

Nick was about to agree when he remembered what Yuri had told him, that there'd been no mention of his abduction in the media. He would now see if this man was also aware of that.

"Maybe they're looking for me, but they might not be looking too hard. I think the police would be happy to be rid of me."

The man's gaze remained on Nick's face for an uncomfortable moment. *Pilate might have looked at Jesus this way,* Nick thought, and for a moment he understood that the man at the end of his bed did, in fact, hold his life in his hands.

CHAPTER THIRTY-FIVE

Rome—Lena's Apartment

As was true of most Italians, Lena felt compassion for refugees, especially children like this Bosnian boy and those clinging to rafts as they braved the Mediterranean Sea from North Africa to Sicily and various Greek islands. Yet, also like many Italians, Lena understood that Italy could accept only a certain number of refugees. And she knew that the Bosnians were near the bottom of immigration lists across Europe.

She had felt a pang of guilt as she reread an op ed from several weeks ago in *Il Messaggero*, Rome's main newspaper. Written by a child psychologist, the column titled "A Child Has No Nationality, Only Need" argued that the developed world needed to change the way it viewed migrant children. The psychologist's argument was brief and pointed. Fact number one: no child chooses where she or he is born. Fact number two: millions of children experience impoverished and diminished lives based on the accident of where they were born. Fact number three: An Italian, German, British, or American child has no more intrinsic value than a Haitian, Congolese, or Bosnian child. Conclusion: the situation facing millions of children in the world is immoral and can no longer be tolerated. Recommendation: In what she labelled the "My Other Child" initiative, the psychologist proposed that every parent in the developed nations accept responsibility for a child in one of the developing countries—for food, health care, safe housing, and education.

Lena remembered the flood of letters that had followed the op ed. For a few weeks, the psychologist had been a guest on local TV talk shows, often facing critics who accused her of political naïveté, impractical utopianism, meaningless first-world guilt, and neo-colonialism. Only one person, someone from the Vatican, had sent a letter to the newspaper, asking those who criticized the psychologist's position to suggest a better plan. Lena could only think how much Father Robert would have agreed with the psychologist.

As Lena looked in on the sleeping boy, he turned and moaned. Was it just her guilty conscience or did the boy, the swelling on his face now noticeably reduced, look familiar?

Rome—Lena's Apartment

With the boy recovering in Lena's spare room, Worthy knew that he wouldn't be able to leave the apartment in order to meet with Sesto. That meant that they had to think up a plausible excuse for his absence that wouldn't rouse the captain's suspicions.

When he shared his concern, Lena said, "You're right. I can't carry the boy to the bathroom, and we both need to be here if his health takes a turn for the worse." After a moment, she added, "I can think of one excuse that might convince Sesto and keep him from stopping by. Why don't the two of us come down with the flu that's going around?"

Worthy smiled. "You are devious, aren't you?"

"No, just inventive," she said, returning the smile.

Fifteen minutes later, Worthy had Sesto on the phone. "So, Lena and I aren't flat on our backs, but I did want you to know we've caught the flu. I hope you don't get it, Stefano."

He waited for a long twenty seconds for Sesto to reply. "I guess there's nothing to do. I wish you a quick recovery. What are your symptoms?"

"A killer headache and joint pain. Lena feels the same. But please, call me if there's anything I can do to help with the case while I'm stuck here. The virus couldn't have hit Lena and me at a worse time. Every day that passes without us getting closer to finding Nick . . . well, you know as well as I do what that could mean."

Hanging up, Worthy turned toward Lena. "How'd I do?"

She leaned over and kissed him. "And you call me devious."

Yellowknife—St. Anne's Catholic Church

It was one of those northern Canadian days when Father Jacob could almost believe that global warming was a myth. The temperature at its highest point of the day wouldn't hit minus twenty degrees. It seemed almost too cold to snow.

Bishop Bruno had twice cancelled the promised meeting with concerned members of the Yellowknife community, perhaps, Father Jacob thought, because the bishop hoped to discourage attendance. If that had been his intention, it had backfired. Despite the cold, the sanctuary was packed with relatives of the dead boys as well as townspeople.

The bishop arrived at St. Anne's in an ankle-length wool coat with a fur collar. His hands too were covered with fur-lined mittens. The coat and mittens made the bishop's decision to wear nothing on his head except his symbol of office, the skull cap or zucchetto, all the more incongruous, until he took off the outer garments and revealed that he'd come in full regalia.

The display of authority seemed old-fashioned to Father Jacob, something the higher clergy used to do before Vatican II when the miter and the silk zucchetto reminded the people of the distance between the laity and the Church's hierarchy. In looking around, Father Jacob was confident that the older indigenous members attending understood that once again the Church was putting them in their place.

The first reaction of the bishop when he entered the sanctuary and saw nearly every pew filled was to glare at Father Jacob, as if the overflow crowd were his fault. His second reaction was to joke about the weather and road conditions. The pat phrase "I don't understand how you can stand the cold" seemed to be an admission by the bishop that he didn't understand a lot of things about life in Yellowknife.

Rubbing his hands together, the bishop shifted next to praising the work and sacrifice of Father Robert. "We've lost a wonderful man, but even more so, we've all lost a great priest. I, for one, am struggling because I no longer have his wise counsel. But his spirit is with us today, and I'm sure he would want us not to dwell on the painful past but to press toward the goal set before us, as St. Paul wrote. I'm hoping after I share some information with you about the future of Safe Haven that we can move to consider how best to commemorate Father Robert's long relationship—I would even say his long love affair—with Safe Haven Orphanage."

Father Jacob understood the folly of the bishop's approach. The bishop was typical of so many in Canada, especially white men with power, whose gaze was always on the horizon, the future. The past was just that—past, over. Father Jacob had been like that himself when he arrived in Yellowknife and first encountered the indigenous community. He'd been frustrated with their preoccupation with past betrayals, with treaties made and broken. It had taken him months of listening to understand that for the indigenous community, the key to understanding the present lay in the past. In looking around the sanctuary of St. Anne that morning, Father Jacob knew that the only person looking beyond the fire at the orphanage was the bishop.

Bishop Bruno spoke for nearly fifteen minutes, reporting what everyone in Yellowknife knew, that the orphanage was interviewing candidates to replace Father Robert. He said nothing about the lawsuit that families of the fire victims were contemplating. Ending with a big smile, the bishop announced that he'd decided to increase the orphanage's budget in honor of Father Robert. "Safe Haven will be even a better home for the orphans of this community."

Father Jacob would always remember that moment and what followed. Obviously feeling confident that he'd handled the meeting well and his audience was with him, the bishop offered to respond to questions. When no one raised a hand, the bishop jokingly said, "Come now, good people, I won't bite."

That was when Mrs. Bessie Free Woman rose from the pew. For a moment she didn't say anything, then said in a clear voice, "When can we see the fire marshal's certification of Safe Haven's heating system? Shouldn't that be in the public domain?"

The smile froze on the bishop's face, though Father Jacob thought he should have expected the question. Perhaps the bishop was surprised to hear legal language—"certification" and "public domain"—while at same time failing to address him with his proper title. But he recovered quickly. "It's Mrs. Free Woman, isn't it? I remember your sugar cookies from my visit last year." Not pausing for a response, he plowed on. "As you know, I'm not a lawyer, but I can assure you, as a member of the board of directors of Safe Haven, that there were no irregularities on that score. What happened at the orphanage was a tragedy that no one could have foreseen."

One of the younger men from the Dene community rose. "Does that mean we will or won't be allowed to see those documents?" Again, the failure to address the bishop formally seemed to reverberate throughout the room. Bishop Bruno shot Father Jacob another angry look as if to say, "Is this your doing?" He then turned to the young priest who'd accompanied him from Edmonton and said, "Father Meinrad, jot that request down. These good people obviously desire to look at those . . . those papers." In a voice that now quavered, he turned to ask, "Are there any more questions?"

A long silence followed. Just as the bishop said, "Well, then," one of the older children who Father Jacob recognized was from the orphanage rose. "Your Eminence, my name is Morris Bowstrong. Father Robert told me before the fire that there was something wrong with the heat."

If the boy intended to say more, he was cut off by the bishop who took a step toward the boy as he said, "Morris, I know this is a concern you good people have. So, let me be clear and let us all be careful. "Many times, after a tragedy, we think we remember more than what is the truth, the facts. But let's assume Father Robert did complain about the heating system." The bishop paused, and Father Jacob wondered if he sensed that the silence in the room had taken on a sharp edge.

"The fact of the matter, my dear people, is that Father Robert, God rest his soul, complained about many things at Safe Haven. In fact," here the bishop frowned, "I can't think of much about Safe Haven that Father Robert didn't complain about. I will confess that I was at the point of asking Father Robert if he'd be happier elsewhere when the tragedy. . . the fire occurred."

That was when Mrs. Free Woman stood, left her pew, and walked slowly toward the back of the sanctuary and the exit. Father Jacob knew that her act, which was followed by others in the room doing the same, was louder than anything that could have been said.

The bishop held up his hand and in a louder voice, said, "Listen, my dear people. Now is the time to look forward. But as your bishop and shepherd, I pledge to take your questions and concerns to the meeting of Safe Haven's board of directors at the end of the month. And I promise to return with their decision."

Father Jacob thought that the promise was a lie. It seemed more likely that it would be years before Bishop Bruno stood in front of these people again.

On the Road from Yellowknife to Edmonton

Bishop Bruno sat silently in the back seat of the black Mercedes as Father Meinrad drove back to Edmonton. As he looked out at the endless miles of snow and forest, he asked himself, *What just happened?* Waves of anger rose within him. He'd travelled the ten hours to Yellowknife to quell the concerns of the people, but all his words had done was further alienate the community.

He searched for whom to blame. *I am a bishop of the Church, and this is how they treat me?* he thought. He recalled other bishops in North America and Europe complaining of lack of respect that even devout Catholics were showing their bishops, and now he had experienced it for himself. He saw the face of Father Robert. *His disrespect for his bishop, his constant challenging of the board's decisions—wasn't this the same way the people of Yellowknife had treated me? Will that man never stop thwarting me?*

Another face came to mind. Father Jacob had never openly opposed him, but what struck the bishop was that the young priest hadn't come to his defense in the meeting. If Father Robert's attitude constituted a sin of commission, Father Jacob's silence was a sin of omission.

Then a third face came to mind, that of the Orthodox monk, Father Fortis. Just a week before, he'd been in Yellowknife poking into things that didn't concern him. Father Robert's death had occurred in Rome, not Yellowknife. *I wouldn't be surprised if the monk, being Orthodox, hadn't enjoyed riling the community up, setting them at odds with their bishop,* he thought.

His ruminations were interrupted by Father Meinrad. "Those folks are in a heap of pain, aren't they, Your Eminence?" The bishop swiveled in his seat, ready to say, "What about my pain?" when he remembered Mrs. Free Woman's face as she turned and walked out while he was still speaking. At the time, he'd thought she left to show her disrespect. *But that look . . . the look she gave me just before she walked out—that wasn't disrespect,* he admitted, *but sorrow.* Then, even as he wanted to tell her that he too felt sorrow, he understood that her sorrow was more than her own. She was expressing the entire community's sorrow. *I missed that, an open wound in front of me,* he confessed.

He looked over at the bishop's staff propped next to him in the back seat of the car. The first time the archbishop had bestowed it on him, he'd felt a surge of pride and, yes, power. *This is my sword,* he'd thought at the time. And every time he entered a sanctuary or room in his official capacity, he led with the staff.

He fingered the silver head on the staff as he recalled a day from his youth, when his grade school teacher, a nun, had brought a wooden crook into the room. After she asked her students to move the desks to the sides of the room, she gathered them into the center of the room and told them that they were sheep. After she allowed them a few minutes of laughter, encouraging them to say "Baa, baa" as loudly as they could, she'd asked him, out of all the students, to stand in the far corner of the room. "This is one sheep who went his own way and got lost," she'd said.

Now, looking out the window at the snow-covered trees, he remembered that moment, the feeling of shame, certain that he must have done something wrong to deserve being singled out. He must have had tears in his eyes, because Sister Clare had comforted him and said, "It's just pretend, Bruno."

She'd returned to the rest of the class and explained that she was holding a crook, a shepherd's staff, before asking the class what a shepherd would do with it. He remembered feeling shame again as one of his classmates said the shepherd would use it to hit the lost sheep. Sister Clare didn't say anything for a moment before saying, "Now watch what the Good Shepherd does." She approached Bruno in the corner and resting the end of the staff gently on his back, she slowly drew him back to the center of the room.

He hadn't remembered what, if anything, Sister Clare had said after that, but now it was as if she were sitting next to him in the car, tapping him gently on the shoulder with the staff. He made the sign of the cross and prayed silently, *Forgive me, O Lord, and in Your Mercy give me a chance, some chance, to be a true shepherd to these wounded people, my flock. Today I failed them and You. Give me a chance, I pray, to be part of their healing.*

CHAPTER THIRTY-SIX

Rome—Lena's Apartment

"You need to see something," Lena said as Worthy came through the door of her apartment.

"What? Is there a problem with the boy?"

"I don't know," Lena replied as she led Worthy to the door of her spare bedroom.

Worthy looked in on the boy, sleeping but no longer shivering. Lena had washed the dirt off his face, a face different after the swelling had gone down. Worthy's brain was a step behind his body, as he froze.

"It's Bordy Vladic, isn't it?"

"You think so too," Lena said. "I thought it might have been my imagination."

They walked quietly back to the living room and, after sitting next to each other on the sofa, just looked at each other. Finally, Lena asked, "What does this mean?"

Worthy shrugged. "The only person who knows for certain how to answer that question is Nick. I mean, I know what Sesto would do if he knew that we had Bordy Vladic in our care. He'd charge him and deport him. And I know what I'm tempted to do with Bordy—keep Sesto in the dark and try to trade him for Nick."

"Even though that's not what Nick would want?"

"No, you're right. That's not why Nick asked us to help the boy, but it's hard to forget that the boy in there is the one who put Nick's life in danger."

Lena sighed. "He's just a boy, Chris. Here, let me tell you what happened when was washing his face. He must have been semi-conscious, because he didn't even stir. The dirt was in layers and almost ground into his skin, but I didn't want to scrub very hard. I thought his mouth might still be sore."

She reached to squeeze Worthy's hand. "The whole time I was washing him, particularly his face, I found myself wishing that I could wash away not just the dirt but his nationality. Just wipe it away. It's so crazy that because of where this boy was born, his life means less than a dog's here in Italy."

Worthy looked down at Lena's hands in his. "Who knows what he was hoping for when he left Bosnia. But I doubt if it took him more than a few days in Rome to figure out what he had to do to survive. You're right; life isn't fair, but we can't forget that the boy sleeping in there isn't a cherub. He isn't really a boy at all anymore."

Lena leaned her head on Worthy's shoulder. "Not a boy and not a man. But because he's Bosnian and a pickpocket, he's a criminal twice over. But I can't help wondering who the real criminal is, Chris."

Rome—Lena Fabriano's Spare Room

All Bordy knew in the first days he was in the strange room was that a woman washed his face and put spoonsful of soup into his mouth. While he still had a fever, he thought he was in paradise with his mother caring for him. His surprise wasn't that his mother was in paradise, but that he was. Perhaps Allah in His mercy had allowed his mother's goodness to wipe away his many sins.

In those first days, he gave in to her gentle touch, even if it meant he was dead. Death would be better than life if he could be with his mother. Her voice, like a soothing humming, encased him. And even though he couldn't yet open his eyes, he sensed a shadow at times falling on him, along with a man's voice. Was this his father? No, the voice was somehow different from his father's.

Perhaps the language of paradise is different, he thought, wondering how much time it would take for him to understand all that had happened to him. But as his fever ebbed, and as he felt strong arms helping to the bathroom and back again, he realized that he wasn't in paradise with his mother and father, but in a softly-lit room, in a bed, with clean sheets and a blanket covering him.

For a moment, he was terrified that he was in Luca's house. But then he realized that Luca, the man whose patience was running out, wouldn't treat him this well. No, this was someone like the professor, but not the professor. *So where am I?* he wondered.

Worthy's command of Italian was minimal, but he understood enough to read the headlines under Nick's photo in the following morning's paper. With Lena out shopping for groceries, Worthy was forced to use his English-Italian dictionary to laboriously translate the story that followed. Father Nicholas Fortis was described as an Orthodox monk from Ohio, USA, who'd apparently been kidnapped. The police were concerned that Father Fortis might have met with the same fate as Father Robert Porter, the Canadian priest found stabbed in Piazza del Popolo four weeks earlier.

As Worthy translated paragraph after paragraph, he was relieved that the story contained no new information. It was only in the last paragraph of the story that Worthy read the names of two individuals whom the police were interested in interviewing in connection of the case—Bordy Vladic and Luca Piemonte.

Opening his phone, Worthy started to punch in Capitano Sesto's number to ask how the story was leaked. But then he stopped. Did it really matter who'd leaked the story? What did matter was finding out all that they could about Nick's situation from Bordy Vladic, who was recovering in the next room.

Much as Worthy feared that the story might put Nick in greater danger, he decided to wait for Lena to come back for lunch before questioning the boy. Lena and he had both noticed that Bordy tensed up when Worthy carried him to the bathroom. With Lena, the boy was noticeably calmer.

As yet, Bordy had seemed only barely conscious. The night before, he'd turned his head at one point, but had made no effort to sit up. Over the days the boy had been in their care, he looked younger and younger. From Lena's patient washing, the boy's skin had turned pinker.

I wonder if he feels safe, Worthy thought. The boy must have been living day to day and hand to mouth in Rome, with life before that in Bosnia even worse. He thought about the newspaper article that Lena had shown him, the psychologist who asked a question that Worthy initially thought was naïve: why do we sentence so many children to a life of disease, crime, and even death based solely on something out of their control—where they were born?

But as each day passed and he watched Bordy slowly recuperate under their care, Worthy found himself reconsidering the psychologist's argument. For the first time, Worthy could imagine how unfair life was for refugees like Bordy. What made the boy in the next room, a boy already caught in the web of crime, Bosnian at all except for the accident of birth?

The rising tide of refugees seeking a better life elsewhere seemed to Worthy not unlike the rising tides caused by climate change. The dreams of Western and European countries to freeze the globe—its populations and temperatures where they'd been decades before—were illusions. Both tides were rising no matter what the affluent countries were presently doing. Worthy had to admit that his own goals of rescuing Nick, finding Father Robert's killer, remarrying, and setting up a detective agency in Rome had been just as narrow and selfish. *Perhaps,* he thought, *we're all versions of Nero, fiddling while the world is burning.*

Worthy looked out the window of the apartment at the pigeons circling above the piazza in front of the Pantheon. Bordy and the other boys with him were like those birds, birds that could never land, who were doomed to hover, to never settle in safety. If caught, undocumented refugees were most often sent back to where they came from, which almost always meant returning to lives of poverty, disease, imprisonment, and sometimes torture or death.

That's what Father Robert recognized when he sat in Piazza del Popolo, Worthy thought. *And that's what drove him to his death.*

CHAPTER THIRTY-SEVEN

Rome—In Luca Piemonte's Mercedes

Luca Piemonte wasn't surprised that the newspaper's lead story was on the disappearance of the American priest—Father Nicholas Fortis. In fact, what surprised him was how long it had taken the media to run the story. He'd never believed the American when he said the police would be happy to be rid of him. But when he came to the last paragraph and saw Bordy Vladic's and his names mentioned, he felt a tight band pressing in on his forehead and temples.

Before he was fully conscious of his decision, he was in his car and heading out of the city. *I have to think. I have to think,* he thought. If only his name had been listed, he'd have suspected Bordy or the professor. With Bordy's name listed along with his, however, he realized neither Bordy nor the professor had been the informant. So who, then?

Immediately, he knew that taking revenge on his informant would have to wait until later. What was critical now was protecting himself. *And not just from the police,* he thought. His boss, Fausto, would have read the article and seen the two names, and Luca knew that this meant he was in danger on three counts. One, Fausto would suspect that Luca had something to do with the disappearance and maybe the death of a second priest in Rome. Two, Fausto would see that there was some connection between Luca and this Bordy Vladic, a name the boss had never heard before. Without a doubt, Fausto would wonder what else Luca had been keeping from him. And three and most worrisome, the boss would certainly realize that the easiest solution to his problem would be to have Luca disappear permanently.

That was why Luca was alone in the car and why he hadn't communicated with any of his men. His men would understand that their new task was to prove their loyalty to Fausto, and what better way to do this but to turn on Luca and offer to kill him?

Luca thought of driving south to Naples, his home. But he knew that even there, he was only postponing the inevitable. In a matter of days, Fausto would track him down no matter where he hid.

For a moment, he played with the idea of turning himself in to the police. Even life in prison for a couple of decades would be safer than being on the run. But then he understood that his boss's reach would extend into Italy's prisons. The truth was that Luca knew too much of Fausto's activities, which meant that Luca would be killed as surely in prison as he would in Naples.

He took the backroads out of Rome, chiefly because he knew this region the least. He reasoned that they would be looking for him in his usual haunts. *I need to go where I'm a stranger,* he thought.

With every mile taking him through small towns and open countryside, Luca felt his panic lessen. Despite the danger he was in, he held on to an adage that Fausto had told him repeatedly—"Always keep a high card in your hand until you must play it."

So what high card do I have left to play? he asked himself. Immediately, he saw the face of the American priest. The American had given Luca the impression that he knew that he, rather than Bordy and the Bosnian boys, had been behind the death of the other priest. But if Luca disposed of the American as he had the Canadian priest, couldn't he point the finger at Bordy Vladic and the Bosnian boys for both murders? That would show Fausto that he knew how to clean up his messes. The death sentence hanging over his head would disappear.

Luca pulled the car over to the side of the road. Once the American was dealt with, the only obstacle to the success of his plan was Bordy Vladic. The professor didn't know how the Canadian priest had been killed, but Bordy did. Bordy knew not only that the priest had been killed on Luca's orders, but the details of that death, details that would convince the police of Luca's guilt. *But if something happens to Bordy Vladic before he gives his version to the police, aren't I in the clear?* Luca asked himself. He turned the car around and headed back toward Rome.

Rome—Riding the Metro

In a newspaper left on the Metro, Yuri saw Nick's photo and, with his basic Italian, he was able to catch the gist of the story. He had expected the media to learn of Nick's disappearance and link it to Father Robert's death, but his heart skipped a beat when he came upon Bordy Vladic's and Luca Piemonte's names in the last paragraph.

Here was yet another link between the death of Father Robert and his Bosnian boys. False claims were as dangerous as true ones if the media and police believed them.

Yuri sighed, realizing that Nick had been right. Every attempt he'd made to sever the connection between his boys and the death of Father Robert had backfired. His actions had only further convinced the police that his boys were involved in the murder.

Yuri's only comforting thought was that Bordy was safer with Nick's friends than if he were back on the streets. But as soon as he admitted this, he also realized that that the same could not be said for Nick. Luca Piemonte had undoubtedly seen the article, and that meant Luca and his bosses would view Nick as too much of a threat to be left alive. As Yuri rode the metro to the warehouse where Nick was being held, he saw that he had no other choice than to trust Nick. Nick had promised, if he were released, that he'd stand by Yuri and the boys, doing all he could to convince the police and media that the Bosnians had nothing to do with Father Robert's death.

But promises from someone chained to a bed and watched by armed guards were easy to make. Would Nick, a man he'd come to care about, keep his word if released? It was not an easy question to answer. Yuri and the boys had survived in Italy by trusting no one. Even Red Cross workers had to be avoided, once Yuri realized that the police sometimes posed as aid workers in order to trap refugees.

Yuri knew there was yet another factor he couldn't forget. Didn't this man, this priest, know more about how his Bosnian boys operated in Rome than anyone else? If Nick reneged on his promise, Yuri knew that the police would find him within hours. What would happen to the boys then? Was he absolutely sure he could trust Nick?

Yuri didn't think his boys would come across the newspaper article, but he was uneasy, thinking it possible that Bordy Vladic might. And he was certain he knew that Bordy would advise him—maybe even force him—to give Nick to Luca. Would Bordy be right?

The thought made him stop, and he saw his reflection looking back at him from a shop window. He asked himself, *Have I sunk so low that I'm even considering this? Did I lie when I told Nick that killing was a line my boys and I would never cross?*

"Allah, Most Merciful," he whispered as he turned to head to the warehouse, "guide me to do what is right."

CHAPTER THIRTY-EIGHT

Rome—In a Warehouse Outside the City

Nick thought that Yuri looked years older when he sat down next to Nick's bed.

"Did something go wrong with Bordy?" Nick asked.

"No, no, your friends seem to be taking good care of him."

"But did he see a doctor?"

"Yes. I followed your friends. They took him to a private surgery. Bordy is now in the apartment where we left the note."

Nick was moved by the thought that Bordy was recuperating in Lena's apartment. That was more than he'd imagined. But then he saw the expression on Yuri's face. "You look worried, my friend."

Yuri didn't respond immediately. Then he sighed heavily and said, "I am feeling my age. Or maybe I should say that circumstances sometimes seem . . . they seem too much." Then, looking at Nick, he added, "I understand Luca Piemonte came to see you."

"Luca, is that his name? He seemed to be a friend of one of my guards."

"He's his boss, and I think he has some hold over Bordy." After a pause, Yuri said, "What did he talk about?"

"I think he was on a fishing expedition. He wanted to know why the media hasn't run anything about my disappearing."

"When was this?" Yuri asked in a low voice.

"Several days ago."

"What did you tell him?"

"About why the media didn't seem interested in my disappearance? I said the police weren't happy about my friend and me looking into Father Robert's murder."

Yuri shook his head slowly.

"What?" Nick asked.

The professor leaned closer to Nick. "Your photo and the story of your disappearance was in the newspaper this morning."

Nick felt the blood drain from his face.

Yuri frowned. "And there was something else in the article—Bordy's and Luca's names."

"Together?"

Yuri nodded and glanced at the guard before whispering, "I'm concerned about our friend here."

Nick looked at the guard sitting by the door and reading a newspaper.

"I hope he isn't looking at today's paper," Nick whispered.

"No, I've only seen the guards reading the football news. But does he ever take a nap?"

"Sometimes after he has lunch he leans the chair against the wall, but I've never seen him sleep. Why?"

Taking a key out of his pocket, Yuri leaned over and released Nick. "I hope he didn't taste the sleeping pills I put in his coffee. I don't want you here when Luca shows up, because he will show up."

Nick was puzzled for a moment before he understood. "Ah, because of the newspaper article."

Yuri nodded. "I need to get you to a safe place."

Nick rubbed his wrist where the handcuff had been, wondering how many places in Rome Yuri and the boys knew to be safe.

"I don't want to look too much at him, Nick. Tell me when he starts yawning."

It took a long ten minutes before the guard tipped his chair against the wall and closed his eyes. In another two minutes, the newspaper in the guard's hand dropped to the floor.

"I don't know how much time we have," Yuri said. "Follow me."

Nick's knees buckled as he rose from the bed. It had been weeks since he'd done more than walk slowly with a guard to the bathroom and back. Even now, it felt like a dream. Walking past the sleeping guard and into the hallway, Yuri and Nick walked into a part of the warehouse that was new to Nick. They passed discarded auto parts until they came to two metal doors, through which light from outside could be seen.

For the past weeks, the only natural light Nick had seen had peeked through the small greasy windows at the end of the room. Now, through the crack in the doors, Rome's afternoon light was clearly visible, and Nick felt new strength in his legs.

As Nick reached out for the handle on one of the doors, Yuri grabbed his arm and whispered, "Outside, we turn left. We then pass three other warehouses and cross a field before we come to the railroad stop. If Luca or his men don't know you're gone, we'll take the train to Termini in Rome and from there to a safer place. I won't stop you if you want to leave me, Nick. What I'm saying is that you'll be free."

Rome—Lena's Apartment

That same morning, as Worthy and Lena talked quietly in the living room about the article in the newspaper, they heard a noise from the spare bedroom. The door creaked open and Bordy stood shakily in the bedroom door.

"Where am I?" he asked.

Lena could tell that Worthy was waiting for her to answer.

"You're safe here, Bordy."

The boy teetered, then slumped to his knees. "Who you?" he managed to say as he slid further to the floor.

Worthy and Lena lifted Bordy to his feet and helped him back to the bed. "It's too early for you to be up," Lena said. "Can you eat, or is your jaw still too sore?"

Bordy lay back down, opening and closing his eyes several times before raising his right hand to touch the side of his face. He uttered a moan.

"I think soup, yes?" Lena asked.

The boy didn't respond, turning toward the wall.

Back in the living room, Worthy moved to the window and peeked outside.

"What are you looking at?" Lena asked.

"It's who I'm looking for. I have to think whoever left Nick's note or another of the Bosnians is keeping an eye on this place. Or maybe I'm just hoping the person who left the note isn't Luca Piemonte, the guy in the tourist scam and who's mentioned alongside Bordy's in the paper."

Lena gasped. "I hadn't thought of that."

"Sorry; I shouldn't have said anything. Piemonte is Italian. Surely, he would have taken Bordy to some doctor he knew. No, if someone is watching, he must be Bosnian."

"This person you think is out there, do you think he'll allow himself to be seen?"

"No, but I want him to see me doing this," Worthy said, as he pulled the curtain back and waved.

"And whoever is out there will understand your message?"

"Maybe not by itself, but with the newspaper article, he's probably watching to see if police or an ambulance are coming. He has to be wondering if Bordy is still safe."

"And as long as they believe Bordy is okay, then . . ."

"Then we have to believe Nick is safe."

Returning to the sofa in the living room, Lena and Worthy didn't say anything for a moment. "The boy is getting stronger," Worthy said. "And that means . . ."

"That means things will change, one way or another," Lena said, finishing the thought. "I wish we knew what Nick's captors are thinking. I'm still hoping they'll let him go if Bordy comes back."

"Same with me, but I hate to think what will happen if Bordy leaves here and then gets picked up by the police."

CHAPTER THIRTY-NINE

Rome—Lena's Spare Room

Bordy felt that he was waking up yet still dreaming. He was in a bed unlike any he'd ever slept in. He was in a room unlike any he'd ever been in. He'd been washed by the woman in the other room and taken to a shiny bathroom by the man, and, although he'd never seen them before, they both knew his name.

He raised his hand—cleaner than he remembered seeing it—and touched a spot, still a bit sore, on his cheek. He remembered the tooth the professor pulled and the pain and the fever that followed. His next memory was of sitting next to a priest, an American, chained to a bed. The priest had said something that upset him, but he couldn't remember what it was. Then, he remembered the professor's face looking down on him as he lay in a cold room and shivered. The only conclusion he could come up with was that the professor had arranged all this—the warm room, the soft bed, and the clean hands.

He thought he knew the professor, understood him, but now he wasn't so sure. The professor was another Bosnian trying to survive in Italy, just an older version of Bordy and the other boys. He thought back to when he'd first met the professor, when another man had spotted Bordy and the boys with him who were hiding under a viaduct in Trieste, packed them all into the back of a truck, and dropped them at a warehouse outside Rome. The professor had been the one to show Bordy and the others where to sleep, how to find food left over from the outdoor markets, and how to pick the pockets of tourists.

Bordy had accepted that the professor had done all this so the boys would work for him, steal for him. That was why he kept them safe. But that hardly explained why the professor had given him over to this man and this woman, strangers who could turn him over to the police and bring down the entire Bosnian operation.

Sitting up in bed, he realized what he had to do.

Rome—At a Warehouse Outside the City

With every hour that passed, Luca realized he was in greater danger of being captured by the police or Fausto, his boss. Once again, he considered turning himself over to the police until he remembered how Fausto had often bragged of having allies in the police and prison system. His one chance of regaining control of the situation and saving his life was to rid himself of Bordy, the professor, and the American priest.

Kill or be killed, he thought, as he drove to the warehouse where the American priest was being held. Yet Luca knew he couldn't simply march into the facility. By now, the guards would have been told to look for him. Whatever plan he devised, it would have to be one that he could carry out on his own.

Luca walked in the shadows of other the other buildings until he was within thirty yards of the warehouse. He waited to see some movement, but the longer he watched the building, the more he sensed something was off. After ten minutes, he risked approaching the main door. To his surprise, he found the door unlocked.

Inside, after his eyes adjusted to the darkness, he saw the empty bed and the handcuffs on the floor. Waves of anger passed through him as he realized someone had made a decision that should have been his alone. But then he realized he was now powerless.

Returning to his car, he tried to think. He hit the steering wheel as he questioned his decision to return to the city. If he'd kept on driving, he'd be far from Rome by now. But he also knew that it was a waste of precious time and energy to question his decision. Driving away from the warehouse, he realized that he still knew where he'd likely find the professor, the one person who could deliver both the priest and Bordy to him. Looking at his gold watch, Luca saw that it was two in the afternoon, which meant he had to remain hidden ten more hours before he could head for Piazza del Popolo.

Rome—Lena Fabriano's Apartment

Opening the door to his room, Bordy could hear the woman and the man in the kitchen, and assumed they were preparing their dinner. He tiptoed down the hallway with his shoes in his hand, ready to explain, if stopped by either of them, that he was strong enough to use the bathroom on his own.

Once in the bathroom, he closed the door quietly behind him. Standing in the bathtub, he pushed aside the curtains and unlocked the window. He managed to open the window quietly and raise himself to the sill, where he paused to catch his breath before putting one leg through and then the other. He saw a deserted alley below, but also that he was too high to jump. Looking around, he spotted a drainpipe running down the wall.

He tied his shoelaces together and hung the shoes around his neck. Knowing that every second counted, he grabbed hold of the drainpipe and pulled his body over to it. At first, he felt only weakness in his arms and considered crawling back into the bathroom to wait for a better chance. But then the weakness passed, and he shinnied down the drainpipe to the ground below. Running to where the alley made a sharp turn, he knelt to put on his shoes. He closed his eyes until dizziness passed before he walked to where the alley emptied out into the large piazza in front of the Pantheon.

I know where I am, he thought, *and I know where I'm headed.*

On a Train Headed for Rome

At the same time, Nick and Yuri were heading into Rome on a train.

"Yuri, I appreciate your telling me I can leave and be free as I was before, but I'm not the same person I was then."

"That doesn't matter, Nick. You'll be safe with your friends. I made a mistake in taking you captive."

"No, not a mistake, Yuri. What I'm trying to say is that I would never have understood what your life and the lives of the boys has been like unless I was abducted. I can't simply go back to my safe life, my life of freedom, when you and so many others aren't safe or even close to being free."

Yuri shook his head. "You can't change the world, Nick."

Nick didn't say anything for a moment. "Yuri, there is more than one world. The world we're caught in looks hopeless. It's not just that this world is broken; it's that many people—I include me, I regret to say—believe that this is the way the world has to be."

"Nick, I know you mean well, but believing in utopia leads only to despair," Yuri said.

"No, not utopia, Yuri. I know you said that you aren't very religious, but you and I are both men of faith. That means we have to believe that God desires a far different world, and God wants us to do whatever we can to bring that better world into reality."

Yuri shook his head. "No, Nick, I won't let you put yourself in danger one more minute."

Nick grabbed Yuri's arm. As he did so, he realized that was the first time the two men had touched one another. "Listen to me, Yuri. In my Bible, we're told we have to become like children to enter the kingdom of God, the world as it should be. But what kind of children was Jesus talking about? Take two children, one born in Bosnia, the other in Italy or America. Neither chose to be born where he was born. And neither knows anything about nationalities or borders. As adults, we say that those two children are ignorant; they don't know the facts. But what if it's just the opposite? If these two children met one another, they would know a truth that this world would rob them of as they grew up. Every child knows when looking at another child that he is looking at someone like himself. And that is the same thing that I believe God sees when looking at those same two children.

"What I realized when chained to that bed is that you and I could be one another. Do you remember the first question you asked me, Yuri?"

The professor shook his head.

"You asked how I came to Italy. You asked if I'd had a good flight, and if I was treated well as I went through customs."

"I was bitter, Nick. That's all."

"No, you were pointing out the truth. Why are you a hunted refugee trying to find a safe place to live and not me? And why did I enjoy a pleasant flight and why was I treated with respect as I went through customs and not you? Those are questions that would certainly puzzle a child, wouldn't they? What I'm saying is that I believe those same thoughts puzzle God. If I hope to be a Christian, Yuri, I have to see the world as God does."

Yuri's eyes filled with tears. "But if you stay with me, I can't guarantee that you'll be safe from Luca and his bosses."

"No more than you can guarantee that you can keep Bordy or yourself safe," Nick replied. "We are in this together, Yuri."

CHAPTER FORTY

Rome—Piazza del Popolo

It was close to one in the morning when Worthy and Lena walked from the metro stop at the Spanish Steps to Piazza del Popolo. Because it was the Christmas weekend, Worthy wasn't surprised to see throngs of people also walking at that late hour toward the piazza. Ahead, Worthy saw fireworks arcing skyward. He understood that the holiday season and the larger crowds that would favor the Bosnian pickpockets, and he hoped Bordy had the same thought. *Like a bee returning to the hive,* he thought.

When, six hours before, Lena and he had realized that Bordy had escaped through the bathroom window, his first thought was to blame himself. "What was I thinking?" he'd asked.

But Lena had said nothing until she led him to sit with her on the sofa. "Chris, his leaving us in this way makes sense, psychologically speaking."

"How do you mean?"

"Well, imagine being so young and living on the streets. Every day you have a target on your back. If the police catch you, you'll likely be sent back to Bosnia in a day or two. But even if you avoid the police, there are other criminals, like Luca Piemonte, who might decide you're unwanted competition."

"Isn't that all the more reason to stay with us, where he was safe?" Worthy asked.

"To us, being here is safe, but maybe not for a boy who's lived in constant survival mode. You evaluate everybody on whether that person will better or lessen your odds of staying safe another day. Bordy would team up with others, but there's no true human bonding."

"It sounds like *Lord of the Flies,*" Worthy said.

"Or like the concentration camps. In grad school, I read Solzhenitsyn's *Gulag Archipelago*. He discovered that some prisoners in the Gulag held on to their humanity, but they were in the minority. What neither of us knows is how Bordy processed his time in our apartment. I won't lie. I hoped he would trust us, but this apartment, being fed and nursed, was a reality that was totally foreign to him. I think he realized he had more control back on the streets. My only worry is that we've lost our best bargaining chip in rescuing Nick."

Worthy slowly shook his head. "Maybe not, and maybe we gain something by his escaping. We know that Piazza del Popolo is where he and the other Bosnians concentrate their petty thieving. If we go there later tonight, there's a chance we'll see him."

"He's not going to be easy to catch, Chris."

"No, I'm not saying we catch him, but if we can spot him, maybe we can follow him back to where the Bosnians are hiding and where they're holding Nick."

Now, six hours later, as Lena and he approached the piazza, Lena caught Worthy's arm and forced them to stop. "We should skirt the piazza and head up to the overlook. That way we can see what's going on without being too obvious."

"I agree. Lead the way."

Once they reached the vantage point, Worthy was relieved to find other couples were standing by the railing as couples had on their previous visit. From behind them and higher up the Pincio, more fireworks were being set off. Worthy could see people in the piazza below looking up at the colorful sight.

But Worthy was searching the crowd for people who weren't looking up to the sky. Among these would be the Bosnians who would be taking advantage of the distraction provided by the fireworks display.

"There seems to be a lot of police, Chris," Lena said in a low voice.

Nodding, Worthy said, "You're right. I'm hoping we spot Bordy before they do."

"And I'm hoping Bordy doesn't see us first."

"All that is assuming Bordy is even here. He could be in the wind, maybe not even in Rome."

"Without money, I don't see how he'd do that," Lena said. "Wait a minute. Look to the right of the obelisk, Chris. Do you see those two boys hovering just behind that tourist group with red caps? Do you think those boys are working in tandem?"

"Yes, I think they are. Neither of them looks like Bordy, but they could be Bosnians. I wonder if . . ."

"What?"

"I know we were hoping to find Bordy, but let's keep an eye on those boys, especially if they leave the piazza. It's possible, just possible, that they'll lead us to Bordy."

"And, dear God, to Nick."

The watched the two boys as they meandered through the crowd, staying close to the tourist group.

"Oh no, Chris. The boys have split up. Maybe we were wrong."

"Wait a minute. There, did you see that? The boy on the left just picked that man's pocket. Now, what does he do?" After only a few seconds, the other boy passed going in the opposite direction and took the wallet in a handoff. "They're still working together, Lena. The question now is, do they go after other tourists, or do they play it safe and leave with their takings?"

They didn't have to wait long to receive the answer. The two boys were walking casually toward the southeast exit of the piazza. "Thank God they're coming this way," Lena said.

"A welcome break, that's for sure. Come on, before we lose them."

Rome—Piazza del Popolo

From a bench in Piazza del Popolo, Luca Piemonte was also watching the two boys as they wove their way through the clusters of tourists. For a moment, he'd thought one of the boys was Bordy but then realized his mistake.

Luca was wearing a false goatee, black glasses, and an LA Dodgers baseball cap that he'd kept in his car trunk. Standing every five minutes or so, he pretended to take photos with his cellphone in the hope of looking like an American tourist, an easy mark for the boys.

As the tourists began to leave the piazza, Luca wasn't surprised to see the boys walking casually toward the exit at the far end of the piazza.

He rose from the bench, pulled the bill of the cap down, and joined the throngs moving in the same direction.

He followed the boys at a safe distance, fighting off the fatigue from a day that had seemed endless. His hand found the Glock in his coat pocket as he whispered to himself, *Just take me to Bordy, and I'll do the rest.*

CHAPTER FORTY-ONE

Rome—Another Secret Location

The three rooms where Yuri took Nick were, taken together, smaller than the warehouse. Looking at the floor on the first room, Nick counted seven mattresses, all covered with blankets that were, despite being well-worn, neatly folded. In an adjacent room, he noted a washbasin and toilet. The third room contained a long table and a few chairs.

"One of your other hideouts?" Nick asked.

"We found it abandoned a week ago, and it's warmer than the usual places we've stayed. But we never know when we'll be forced to leave."

"I take it from the number of mattresses that only some of the boys are staying here."

"We rotate so that everyone gets a few warm nights."

"Does Bordy know this place?"

"Yes, but we both know he's safer with your friends," Yuri said.

"Does that mean that Luca has been here?"

Yuri shook his head. "No, but Bordy might have told him about it. I still say you'd be safer away from the boys and me."

"We've already settled that, Yuri. I'm here—or wherever you go next—until you're no longer in danger from Luca."

Rome—Police Headquarters

Sesto knew that Worthy and Lena would have seen the newspaper article and wonder why he'd betrayed their agreement and gone public with Nick's abduction. The truth was that the decision was made by his superiors. They argued that failing to let the public know about the kidnapping put Father Fortis' life in danger, but Sesto understood the real reason his superiors had overruled him. They released the account of the abduction and the names of Bordy Vladic and Luca Piemonte to protect themselves from charges of inaction if Father Fortis was already dead.

Capitano Sesto had put off calling Worthy until late that evening, and when his call was sent to voicemail, he felt something other than guilt. Why, if Worthy and Lena were recovering from the flu, would neither of them answer his phone? His call being forwarded gave him an uneasy feeling.

He thought back over his daily conversations with Worthy. Was it just his imagination, or had the American seemed more evasive with each call? He knew what he had to do. Despite it being Christmas Eve, he called the monastery. He asked the monk who answered if he'd seen Dr. Fabriano recently. After a few moments, the monk returned to say that Dr. Fabriano had been at the monastery earlier that day as she'd been almost every day over the last week.

Fearing that he already knew the answer, he asked the question anyway. "Did she say that she had flu?"

"No. She looked fine to me."

After a long pause, Sesto said, "Sorry, I must be mistaken." After he hung up, he realized he had no idea what Worthy and Lena had been up to over the last three days.

He called the number of his department IT expert. "Salvio, I need a favor, and yes, I know it's Christmas Eve. I need you to log in to our department's call list and find one of Christopher Worthy's calls to me from the past three days. Use that information to find where his phone is now."

"Capitano, I have my whole family here."

"I understand, and I know that I'll owe you, but call me back no matter what you find."

Sesto knew if Worthy's phone pinged at Lena's apartment, he would accept that he'd probably jumped to a false conclusion. But everything within him told him that his technician would find that Worthy's phone was nowhere near the apartment.

After half an hour, Salvio called back. "His phone is on the Pincio; you know, the overlook."

"You mean by Piazza del Popolo?"

"Certo, exactly. They shoot fireworks off from there over the holidays. Look, Capitano, your friend's an American. I bet he's there with the other tourists."

I only thought he was my friend, Sesto thought. His brain leapt forward. Worthy was as near as anyone could be to the piazza where Father Robert was killed. He was also at the site where Father Fortis had been headed when he was abducted. *That's no coincidence,* he thought, as he grabbed his car keys and started for the door. "Salvio, are you still there?" he asked.

"Yes, why?"

"Look, I know I'm asking a lot, but I promise I'll make it up to you. I need you to call me if there's any movement on the phone."

There was a long pause on the other end. "I want New Year's Eve and New Year's Day off."

Sesto ran down the stairs of his apartment. "Fine. You can have Easter too."

Rome—A Secret Location

"It is your Christmas Eve, Nick," Yuri said as the two men sat at the table. It had been dark for several hours, and because none of the boys was there, Nick assumed that they were out working their way through the holiday crowds.

"It's too bad we don't have something to toast with," Yuri added.

Nick closed his eyes and made the sign of the cross. "I guess I lost track of the days."

"There are special prayers that you'll say tonight?"

Nick nodded. "And tomorrow."

"The night Jesus was born, yes?"

Nick nodded again.

Looking around at the sparse room, Yuri said, "This place can't be like where you've celebrated this holy day before."

"But maybe not unlike the stable where Jesus was born. I suspect that was an abandoned structure as well."

Yuri seemed to be considering this image. After a moment, he said,

"I do not mean to offend, Nick, but the churches of this city, places where Christians worship Jesus, they do not seem like mangers."

Nick nodded. "All the gold and marble, yes, it's ironic, I grant you that. I remember a guy I was in seminary with. As I recall, he dropped out, but before he left, he asked me a question. He asked if I thought Jesus was pleased with the big and gaudy—gaudy was his word—churches that call themselves 'His house.'"

Yuri smiled. "Maybe I am wondering about the same thing. Can I ask what you replied, Nick?"

"To be honest, Yuri, I don't remember. But I've never forgotten his question."

"And your America, your Christian America. It likes big and gaudy too, does it not? Yet, if I know you at all, Father Nick—and I think I do—I doubt if the Jesus you pray to is pleased with that."

Nick felt his face redden. He doubted he was worthy of the compliment.

Yuri sighed deeply. "I had an uncle who visited America. This was before our war. He was also a professor in my country. He gave a paper at a conference in a big city. Is there a city in America called Atlanta?"

"Yes, it's in the state of Georgia."

"Do you know it?"

"I've never been there, but I imagine I know what it's like. What was your uncle's impression?"

"He asked a taxi driver to show him the city. He told me that there were churches everywhere. One on almost every block. Very big, beautiful buildings, my uncle said."

Nick waited, sensing there was more. "But?"

Another smile crossed his face. "Because there were all those churches, my uncle expected to find people acting like Jesus." After a pause, Yuri said, "You do know that Jesus is important in Islam."

"So I understand. Someone told me Jesus is mentioned in the Qur'an more than Muhammad."

"That is true. I do not say that my uncle was right."

"And I wouldn't say your uncle was wrong," Nick said. "It seems easier to build beautiful churches and monasteries than to act like Jesus."

Yuri sat forward, coming closer to Nick on the other side of the table. "I will miss these talks, Nick, but we both know that you will have to leave us, and it must be soon."

Hearing a knock on the door, both men looked to the door. "That will be the first boys coming back. When they see you, I'm sure they will be frightened. I will explain, but I ask you to be patient."

The door opened and a single boy came in. He was dressed in better clothes and was far cleaner than Nick had imagined. Only when he studied the boy's face more closely did Nick realize whom he was looking at.

"It is me, professor. It is Bordy."

CHAPTER FORTY-TWO

Rome—On a Street near Piazza del Popolo

After ten minutes of keeping the two boys in their sights, Lena and Worthy saw the boys pause at a corner. Worried that they'd be spotted, Lena and Worthy ducked into a doorway and waited to see what would happen next. Just two minutes later, four other boys dressed in similar ragged clothes approached from a side street and joined them.

"Bordy isn't one of them, either," Worthy said in a low voice. "But let's follow."

They noticed the boys exchange a few words before they walked together in pairs in the same direction. Despite the boys turning around occasionally perhaps to see if they were being followed, Worthy thought that Lena and he, walking with their arms around one another, looked like a loving couple who were walking in the same direction toward their car or hotel.

At the next corner, the group of boys split in two, three boys turning right while the other three turned left and walked in the opposite direction. Lena stopped and leaned up to kiss Worthy as she whispered, "What do we do now?"

Worthy hugged her in return and whispered, "I wish I knew, but we have to decide. I say we go left with those boys. The two we spotted in the piazza are in that group."

They paused a few seconds in front of a jewelry shop window before angling left. Worthy couldn't help but wonder if they'd made a poor choice but then reasoned that the boys might routinely split up in case they were being followed. With luck, Worthy hoped, the two groups of boys would end up at the same place.

Following at a safe distance, they noticed that shops gave way to small businesses, vacant lots, and industrial buildings. Until that moment,

Worthy hadn't realized that he'd forgotten a basic lesson that he'd taught to recruits at the police academy. "When all your faculties are keenly focused on the people you're following," he'd told them, "don't make the mistake of forgetting that someone could be following you at the same time."

He first thought that if they were being followed, it would likely be by the other boys who'd split off just moments ago. *What would be simpler,* he thought, *than for that trio to have circled around and now follow us?*

He pulled Lena closer to him. "Don't turn around."

Lena gasped. "Do you think we're being followed?"

"I don't know, but it's possible." They continued following the three boys ahead of them, with Worthy's ears trained for any unusual sounds behind them. If the other boys were following him, he expected to hear the squeaky sound of tennis shoes. Instead, he heard what sounded like leather shoes, and the gait was that of an adult.

The hair on the back of his neck stood up as he realized the man's pace was quickening, and whoever was following them was no longer worried about being heard. Instinctively, he reached into his coat for his gun before remembering that he didn't carry a weapon in Italy. When the footsteps were about ten yards behind him, he pulled Lena in front of him to shield her as he turned to face whoever was following them.

The man stopped in his tracks, then moved more slowly forward. "I think now you owe me the truth," said Capitano Sesto.

Although Luca Piemonte had never attended a police academy, he had learned from his youthful career in crime in Naples to pay attention to both the target and whoever else might be following that target. His hope of seeing Bordy in the piazza hadn't been realized, but he also thought the two Bosnian boys might lead him to where Bordy, the professor, and maybe even the American priest were hiding.

Among the many who left the piazza by the same exit as the boys, Luca noticed a couple who kept the same safe distance behind the boys, block after block. He didn't recognize either of them, although he had a suspicion that the man was northern European or North American, not Italian.

The arrival of another group of boys from a side street strengthened his conviction that he was on a trail that would lead to a Bosnian hideout and maybe to Bordy, but when the six boys split up and walked in opposite directions, he waited to see which group the couple would follow. When they chose the three boys turning left, he decided to follow the other three boys who'd turned to the right.

Maybe the couple will have made the correct decision, maybe I did, or maybe it doesn't matter, he thought. He'd heard the expression "All roads lead to Rome," and hoped that in this case all routes would lead to Bordy, the professor, and the priest. A block later, Luca looked back and thought he saw a man turning in the same direction as the other boys and the couple. "Who the hell is that?" he asked himself.

The three boys ahead of him walked side by side, looking back more and more the farther they walked. When the shops gave way to an industrial park, with some businesses identified by signs and others looking vacant, Luca felt his pulse quicken. He was certain that the boys were heading toward one of the vacant buildings, the kind of building the Bosnians were so good at finding and using as temporary lodgings.

He took the Glock from his shoulder holster and held it in his right hand. *If luck is on my side,* he thought with a smile, *all my problems will be solved in a matter of minutes. And Fausto will see that I'm not a problem, but someone worthy of respect.*

Rome—On a Dark Street

Even in the little light provided by a streetlight, Worthy could see the anger on Capitano Sesto's face. Yet, he continued to look back to the three boys who were now thirty yards ahead of them and turning right again at a corner.

"I can explain, Stefano, but you're going to have to trust us that we have to follow those boys."

"You ask for my trust? No, we go nowhere until you explain why you betray me."

Lena said, "We will explain, but Chris is right. Those boys we're following, they're Bosnians. We think they could lead us to Bordy and Nick."

As the policeman continued to stare at them, Worthy knew, with each passing second, that the chances of losing the boys were greater.

"Look, Stefano, we're leaving. If you want to hear why we kept you out of the loop, come with us."

Worthy and Lena turned and walked faster in the direction the boys had taken. After a few seconds, Worthy heard Sesto jogging to catch up. They didn't say anything until they came to the corner where the boys had turned. Peeking around the corner, Worthy was relieved to see the boys walking about a block ahead.

Worthy put his arm out to hold Lena and Sesto back until the boys were another twenty yards down the street. "Lena, you should walk ahead of us. Don't get too close to the boys, but we can't afford to lose them. I'll hang back and catch Stefano up. Okay, go," he said.

As the two men walked side by side a few yards behind Lena, Worthy explained in a whisper how Nick had contacted them by a note, informing them that he was safe while at the same time explaining Bordy's need for medical attention without informing the authorities. He ended by explaining how Bordy had escaped.

"If we'd told you, you'd have had no other choice but to take Bordy into custody. We couldn't let that happen because we hoped, by helping Bordy, that he could lead us to Nick."

"And Bordy, he is one of these boys?" Sesto said.

"No. We went back in the piazza tonight, hoping to see him. Bordy didn't show, but those boys did. That's why we're following them."

"But maybe they not lead you to Bordy and your friend."

"Consider it a gut instinct," Worthy said, even as he knew that Sesto was right. He had no idea how many Bosnian boys were in the gang in Rome or how many hiding places the Bosnians had.

As had happened to him before in a moment of stress, a Bible verse returned unbidden to his mind. "Faith is the assurance of things hoped for, the conviction of things not seen." As Worthy reflected on the verse, he realized that Lena and he had neither assurance or conviction—only hope.

Please God, don't let our hope be wrong, he thought, the words as close to a prayer as he'd given in the last ten years.

CHAPTER FORTY-THREE

Rome—A Secret Location

Yuri saw Bordy sway in the doorway as the boy looked from him to the American priest. He rushed to catch Bordy before he fell and helped him to one of the chairs.

After he gave the boy a bottle of water, he asked in Bosnian, "Bordy, why are you here?"

Bordy looked up. "You free him?"

"He is not going to betray us, Bordy. I told him it would be safer if he did leave, but he wants to stay."

Bordy put his head in his hands. "I think I faint."

Yuri motioned toward a bag leaning against the wall. "Nick, there's a protein bar in that bag. Bordy needs food."

Yuri watched as Bordy devoured the bar in three bites, the whole time the boy's eyes never leaving Nick. When the boy finished eating, he said, "I don't understand. You say he want to stay with us?"

At the same time, Nick said, "Yuri, I can't believe my friends asked Bordy to leave. Ask him what happened."

Yuri raised both hands in a plea for patience. "Bordy, so that Nick understands, I want us to speak in English. Let me know if you don't understand."

"Who is this 'Nick'?" the boy asked.

"I'm Nick, or Father Fortis," Nick said. "Why did you leave my friends?"

"Your friends?"

"Yes, the man and the woman who took care of you."

Looking now at Yuri, Bordy said, "You not have me stay with them?"

"It was Nick's idea. The infection in your mouth could have killed you."

Bordy closed his eyes and shook his head, before looking at Nick.

"Make no sense. Why you do this? Why you not go, be free with friends?"

"Yuri, I think Bordy will understand better if you explain things in his language," Nick said.

It took Yuri nearly five minutes to explain how Bordy owed his life to Nick and his friends, how the account of Nick's abduction in the morning's paper along with Bordy's name and picture had put them all in danger, and how Nick had refused to leave Yuri and the boys to the mercy of Luca Piemonte and his bosses.

At the end, Bordy didn't say anything, although Yuri wasn't sure how much Bordy had understood.

Nick broke the silence by asking, "Can I ask Bordy a few questions?"

Yuri nodded.

"Why aren't you still with my friends?"

Bordy looked down at his clean hands as if they held the answer. "I no belong there."

"Did they tell you that?"

Bordy looked up at Nick. "You think I stay forever, that it be home?" He looked around at the room. "This my home."

Nick nodded slowly, leading Yuri to conclude that Nick understood. Bordy could no more remain in Lena's apartment than Nick could change Italy's treatment of refugees.

Nick pulled up a chair next to Bordy. "I have one other question, Bordy, and I need you to tell me the truth, no matter what the truth is. What do you know about the death of Father Robert, the Canadian priest?"

Bordy slumped in the chair, but before he could say anything, they heard the door open. Turning to see who was entering the room, Yuri saw the frightened faces of three of his boys. They said nothing, standing stiffly, as if at attention. It took Yuri only seconds to make sense of the whole picture. From behind the boys, Luca Piemonte stepped into the room, his gun trained no longer on the boys but on the three of them: Bordy, Nick, and himself.

Luca couldn't believe his good fortune. In front of him were the three people—the American priest, the professor, and Bordy—whose deaths would mean he could live.

The priest and the professor looked startled but not scared. The priest made the sign of the cross much like Luca's grandmother had done before eating every meal, while the professor took a step toward Bordy, who remained seated in a chair and looked pale.

Luca's finger closed on the trigger as he paused to decide which of the three he would shoot first. He thought it logical to kill the priest first, given that it was the priest's meddling that had put him and his operation in danger. But of the three, the professor was the one who Luca resented the most, the professor shielding his boys while all the time looking down on Luca. It would feel good to see the professor fall, a bullet through his head.

Luca realized that the only one he'd feel bad about killing would be Bordy. He'd had plans for the boy, but then again, Bordy, the week before, had failed to hand the American priest over. Had the boy done so, Luca would have already handled the problem, and Fausto would have no reason to turn on him.

As he hesitated, another plan presented itself. With the gun, Luca waved the priest and the professor to one side and approached Bordy.

"I think you avoid me, Bordy, but I see you are sick. Can you stand?"

Bordy nodded slowly as he rose to his feet.

"You see what we have to do, Bordy?"

Bordy looked from the professor and to the priest before turning his confused face toward Luca. "No, what you mean?"

"Ah, you disappoint me, Bordy. Here it is—this is your big chance."

"What chance? I no understand."

Luca shook his head slowly. "Last month, you say to me, 'I want to be big time.' You follow me and say you want to join my banda, my group. Tonight, okay, you join."

Luca had hoped to see a flash of excitement in the boy's eyes, but all he saw was confusion. "You," Luca said, aiming the Glock at the professor and at Nick, "sit down. No, not close together."

Waiting until the two men had complied, he turned and offered the Glock to Bordy. "This priest, he is more dangerous than first one. Kill him and you will be boss over other boys. Do it now. You no have to shoot professor. I do that."

Seeing the professor start to rise from the chair, Luca stepped toward him and pushed him down.

Falling down into the chair, the professor began speaking to Bordy in a low voice. Luca watched Bordy as the boy's eyes moved from the gun to the professor.

"Old man, speak English," Luca ordered.

"I told Bordy that Father Nick, this priest, was the one who saved his life. He had an infection that could have killed him, and Nick saved him, not you. It was Nick's friends who got him to the doctor and then nursed him back to health." Yuri turned to Bordy. "Never forget, my son, you owe Nick your life."

Luca could see that the professor hadn't taken his eyes off of Bordy. "Look at me. Bordy, look . . . at . . . me. I say, 'Look at me! The old man, he want to control you. He afraid to die. You tell me you want to take over operation in piazza. So, this is your chance."

"Bordy, remember the vow you took," the professor said. "No killing, ever. You cross that line and you'll be lost."

"What he say, Bordy?" Luca demanded.

"Professor say we steal, yes. But we no kill."

Luca laughed. "Does professor know he too late? Who tell me about other priest? You, Bordy. Who tell me he cause trouble for boys? You, Bordy. Who want me to take care of problem? You, Bordy. He is killed because you ask me."

Now a fourth voice was heard. "Bordy, did you mean for Father Robert to be killed?" the American priest asked.

Bordy lowered his head and covered his ears with his hands. "No . . . maybe. I no know."

"Bordy, did this man tell you that he intended to kill the priest?"

Bordy shook his head violently. "I no remember."

"Think, Bordy, think," the American said.

Bordy looked up at Luca. "No, you no say that."

Luca continued to hold the gun out toward Bordy. "That change nothing. Decide now." He was about to add "Or I decide for you, and you die first" but said instead, "Bordy, you boy or man?"

CHAPTER FORTY-FOUR

Outside the Secret Location

Once Sesto and Worthy caught up with Lena, Worthy realized why she'd waited for them. The boys whom they were following had stopped outside a large building, and now one of the boys was peeking through a dirty window.

"If that's one of the Bosnian hideouts, what are they waiting for?" Worthy whispered.

The boy at the window suddenly ducked down and moved back to the other boys. Pulling them away from the building, he said something to them. Then, as if the boys were a mirage, they vanished.

"They've run off," Lena said.

Sesto nodded. "The boy, he see something through the window—something bad, I think."

Worthy's mind froze as he realized that the Bosnian boys must have come upon any number of horrible scenes. Without saying a word, Worthy crab-walked toward the same window, afraid that he'd find Nick, but Nick would already be dead.

He heard Sesto and Lena following as he closed in on the building. Gone was any concern that the boys they'd been following would see them. He crouched down below the window, taking a few seconds to catch his breath.

Raising his head, he peered into the poorly-lit room. What he saw made his heart race, first with relief when he saw Nick sitting next to an old man. Then he saw Bordy in another chair ten feet away. Last, he saw a man he recognized from the newspaper as Luca Piemonte who was standing by Bordy and pointing a gun at Nick and the old man.

Motioning Lena and Sesto forward, he gestured for them to look inside. After Sesto leaned down again, Worthy whispered, "Do you have a gun?"

Sesto shook his head. Pointing to the door, he whispered back, "Do we break in?"

Different scenarios exploded like fireworks in Worthy's mind. One had them trying the door, finding it locked. A second had them finding the door unlocked, but Luca reacting to the sound of the door by shooting Nick, the old man, and Bordy before they could overpower him. He could think of no scenario that would lead to Nick not being shot. In a moment he knew that he'd never forget, he sensed more than heard the words "trust Nick."

He looked through the window again, this time seeing something nonsensical. Luca was holding his gun out to Bordy. *Take it! Take it!* Worthy thought, realizing if the boy took the gun, then he could break into the room and neutralize Luca within seconds. But then he realized Luca's plan. Luca meant for Bordy to shoot Nick and perhaps the old man.

Worthy thought of the boy who'd slept soundly in Lena's spare room, the boy he'd carried to and from the bathroom, the boy whom Lena had nursed back to whatever health the pale boy in the chair now had. It was a bitter irony that they'd done all this only for the boy to kill Nick.

He held his breath as he saw Bordy look from Nick and the old man to the gun in Luca's hand. Slowly, as if his arm weighed a ton, Bordy took the gun and stared down at it. Although Worthy could hear nothing, he could see Luca saying something and pointing to Nick and the old man. Worthy watched helplessly as Nick made the sign of the cross. Worthy's mouth was dry as he realized that Bordy Vladic, a Bosnian boy uncared for and unwanted in both Bosnia and now Italy, would decide Nick's fate.

Bordy held the gun in his hand, barrel pointed to the ceiling. Worthy wondered if the gun felt powerful to him, if Bordy liked the feeling of the cold steel in his hand.

So many things happened in the next few seconds that even later, Worthy couldn't say for certain what happened first. He saw Bordy lower the gun and study the weapon again before he slowly turned the gun around and handed it back to Luca. At what must have been the same moment, he heard Luca scream as he took the gun back and aimed it at Bordy. As the boy cowered in obvious terror, the old man sprang from his chair and threw himself on top of the boy. Two shots rang out before Nick, in a rush, tackled Luca. The two of them rolling to the ground before another shot rang out.

"Go, go, go!" Worthy yelled as he jumped for the door and pushed it open. As he burst into the room, he heard the high-pitched screams of other boys who were huddled in a corner, before hearing Nick groan from the floor. Looking down, Worthy saw Luca's gun lying just inches from his unmoving hand.

"Nick? Nick? Where are you shot?" Lena called out as she knelt beside him.

"Lena? Is that you?" He groaned again, then said, "I don't think I'm hit. I was wrestling Luca for the gun, and then it went off."

Worthy rolled Luca over and saw the dead eyes and a bullet hole in the man's neck. Then he heard a gurgling sound to his left that he knew all too well. Looking over, he saw the old man being cradled in Bordy's lap. Two red circles on the old man's chest were growing larger with every second.

Looking up at Worthy, Bordy said something that Worthy didn't understand, but he could tell from the tears flowing down the boy's cheeks that he knew the old man was dying. Then, from the boy's lips came only one word of English. "Help."

Nick crawled to his knees and scooted over to them. "Yuri, Yuri, can you hear me?"

Blood began to pool from the old man's chest, even as the old man whispered something to Nick. Nick closed his eyes, made the sign of the cross, and said, "I won't forget, Yuri. I won't forget."

CHAPTER FORTY-FIVE

Rome—Lena's Apartment

Unable to asleep, Nick bundled himself up in a coat and blanket and climbed the stairs to the loggia atop Lena's apartment. He looked down on the streets bordering the Pantheon that would, in a couple of hours, draw tourists from all over the world.

A memory from his early school years came back to him. Maybe because his parents were immigrants, he'd been fascinated by maps. In the days before his family would travel to Greece to visit relatives, he made the mistake of telling an older cousin that he expected the land in Greece to be orange-colored. When his cousin sneered and asked him why, he'd said Greece was orange-colored on the map in his classroom. After all, wasn't America mainly green, as it appeared on that same map?

He'd been a naïve grade-school student, but now he thought that he, not his cousin, was right. People continued to see the world as it had appeared on the grade-school map, a world divided by clear and iron-clad borders, nations with different names and different languages.

Nick watched the first glimmers of light appear in the eastern sky. A new day, a day when Yuri, by Muslim custom, should be buried. Or would Yuri's refugee status follow him into death, his body rejected by the Italian authorities and sent back to Bosnia?

In the surreal hours after the previous night's shootings, Nick's concern centered on Bordy. Nick refused to answer any of Capitano Sesto's questions until Sesto assured him that the boy would be safe.

"He is witness, so no deported. He will be in safe place," the policeman had assured him.

"Not in a jail, please."

"No, Father, not in jail. A doctor will check him, then he be guarded. But I promise you can visit."

Nick did his best to explain the situation to Bordy, but he wasn't sure how much the boy understood. The boy had cried off and on until ambulance workers loaded Yuri's body on a gurney and removed him from the room. Nick thought that Bordy had never looked less like a tough teenager and more like the child he was.

As Nick walked down the stairs to Lena's apartment, he thought back on the terrible scene in the abandoned building. Luca, he realized, could have shot him instead of Yuri. But on second thought, Nick wondered if the result would have been any different. If Luca had aimed his gun at him instead of Bordy, he knew Yuri would have thrown himself in front of him.

He paused in the apartment's stairwell to pray for Yuri and Bordy. He prayed that Yuri would be in a place of light and refreshment, a place without pain or sorrow. Despite his own sorrow, Nick accepted the comfort the words of that prayer gave him. Yuri had indeed died in a kind of light, light provided by Bordy, his "son," as Yuri had called him. Yuri had died knowing that Bordy hadn't crossed the professor's line and done what Luca had demanded. Yuri had died as he'd lived, a teacher and shepherd to the very end. *Be at peace, my friend,* he thought.

Entering Lena's apartment, Nick saw Worthy sitting on the couch.

"I couldn't sleep either, Nick. Do you mind if I sit up with you?"

"Of course not, Christopher." Clearing his throat, Nick said, "I have no regrets about letting myself be taken in the train station."

Worthy nodded slowly. "I knew you could have prevented it. Did you find out what you wanted?"

"More than what I wanted. My aim was to find out who killed Father Robert. And I did find that out. As you probably know, it was Luca Piemonte who had him killed. I'm happy the media will finally know that Father Robert's death had nothing to do with Yuri and his boys. But I learned a lot more than that."

"You mean about the Bosnians."

Nick grimaced. "If you don't mind, Christopher, I can't think of them as Bosnians—not anymore. They are boys, just children really, but children who've been forced into situations no adult should have to deal with."

Lena came into the room and sat down next to Worthy. "I couldn't sleep either. It seems years, Nick, since you sat here in my apartment."

"I'd say a lifetime ago," Nick said. "Yes, at least one lifetime. So much has happened that I don't know where to begin, and I'm anxious to hear what you both found out. I suppose one place to begin would be for all of us to apologize to Capitano Sesto. I want to let him know that I forced you to go behind his back in taking care of Bordy. I don't want what I asked to damage your career in Rome."

"I think my business will be fine, Nick. Stefano understands that we kept him in the dark so that we wouldn't put him into an impossible position."

"That's a relief," Nick said, as he looked around the spacious room and wondered what Bordy had thought of his surroundings. When neither Lena nor Worthy spoke, Nick accepted that they were waiting on him. Again, he wondered where to begin. Finally, he decided to begin at the end. "Perhaps you heard me tell Yuri before he died that I wouldn't forget the promise I made."

Worthy and Lena both nodded but didn't say anything.

"Yesterday—was it really only twenty-four hours ago?—after the newspaper article about me came out, Yuri smuggled me out of where I was being held and told me I was free to leave. In fact, he wanted me to leave . . . but I couldn't. When Yuri told me that Luca's and Bordy's names were listed in the same article, I knew Luca wouldn't come only for Bordy and me but also for Yuri."

"So you stayed because you hoped you could protect them?" Lena asked.

"I guess that was partly true—safety in numbers. But I'd already made a promise to Yuri that if I was ever freed, I'd do everything I could to help the boys gain a better life in Italy. Yuri is . . . Yuri was a man of faith, a Muslim, but he was also a practical man. He told me that my heart was in the right place, but also that neither I nor any other individual could change their situation in Italy. No nation wants Bosnians, and there is no future for them back in Bosnia. The best he and his boys could do was live in the shadows in big cities and do what was necessary to survive. Everything, that is, short of causing another person's death."

"I'm not sure I follow, Nick," Worthy said. "If Yuri knew you could never keep your promise, why did he say what he did at the end?"

Nick lowered his head but didn't answer.

"I think I understand," Lena said. "When a person knows he's dying, what had once seemed impossible can look possible."

With tears in his eyes, Nick nodded. "I never knew Yuri's last name, but I knew he was an extraordinary man. Imagine, here was a man who'd been a professor of English literature and grammar in Bosnia before the war, now training children how to pick pockets." Managing a weak smile, he added, "Yuri loved Hemingway, especially *The Old Man and the Sea.* And he thought it was providential that my name, Nick, is the name of one of Hemingway's main characters." He paused, remembering Yuri's open face. "Life had been cruel to Yuri and his boys, but I never saw him give in to bitterness. He wanted to protect his boys and set an example."

Nick's hand moved to grasp the cross hanging around his neck. "The life of a monk is supposed to be a life of ongoing conversion. We're meant to change not just once or twice, but over a lifetime. It's hard for me to explain, but my conversations with Yuri were like a conversion. Our knowing one another was something God was involved in; I'm sure of that." Pausing, he shook his head. "What I'm trying to say is that it didn't take me long in talking with Yuri to realize he could have been me if he'd been born in the States, and I could have been him if I'd been born in Bosnia. No, that's still not right. If I'd lived through what Yuri had managed to survive, I doubt if I'd have cared about anyone but myself. But Yuri . . . well, he died as he lived—giving everything for his boys. So you see, I made a promise I must fulfill. Until then, I won't really be free."

Worthy sat forward on the couch. "When the shooting ended, I could see that you didn't look like a prisoner happy to be freed. And I think we now understand. If it helps at all, you should know that everything we've discovered about Father Robert suggests he felt the same as you. He died because he was trying to help those same boys."

Rome—Lena Fabriano's Apartment

Nick's first day of freedom was spent resting before Yuri's funeral. The hours before the ceremony gave him time to listen as Worthy and Lena shared their discoveries about Father Robert. Lena described how what she'd learned from the monastery's IT manager—Father Robert's interest in his final days in orphanages around Rome and the Canadian Embassy in Rome—had led them to the embassy, where they listened to a recording of a phone call from Father Robert on the day he died. In that call, he'd asked about visas.

"Why visas?" Nick asked.

"He didn't say, but I like Lena's theory," Worthy said.

"At the time, I thought he was hoping that the embassy could use its influence to obtain visas for the Bosnian boys to stay legally in Italy. He was very excited on the phone, Nick, like he had a new mission. Then I thought that Father Robert was planning to open an orphanage for them here in Rome, if the boys could get visas. But now, I'm not so sure."

"What changed your mind?" Nick asked.

"Father Robert was desperate, but he wasn't stupid. He must have realized that without having a visa to stay in Italy himself, he was hardly in a position to ask for visas for the boys. And if he did hope to stay with the boys here in Italy, why did he go to the Canadian Embassy instead of the immigration authorities here?"

"Ah, I think I understand what you're suggesting," Nick said.

"I'm still in the dark," Worthy confessed.

Lena said, "There must have been another option Father Robert was considering, one that made his call to the Canadian Embassy more reasonable. What if he was hoping to persuade the Canadian authorities to grant visas to the boys to go back with him to Canada?"

Rome—A Cemetery for Indigents

In respect for Islamic custom, Capitano Sesto was able to arrange for one of Rome's imams to conduct Yuri's funeral before sunset. The funeral was in a section of a cemetery reserved for indigents, although Worthy and Lena paid for flowers and a marker.

Surrounding the recently-dug grave were Lena, Nick, Worthy, Sesto, and Bordy. The service was brief, and as Yuri's shrouded body was lowered, Nick found himself wondering if Jesus' shrouded body had looked any different.

At one point, Bordy looked like he would faint, leading Worthy to reach out to support him. Nick's heart went out to the boy, who must have realized by now that he is truly on his own. *I promised Yuri that I'd do something to save Bordy, but what can I do?* he asked himself.

As Nick walked with Worthy and Lena from the graveside to her car, his exhaustion made his promise to Yuri seem even more impossible. In the car, he said, "I wish what Father Robert was hoping for, taking some of the boys back to the orphanage in Yellowknife, wasn't such a naïve pipedream."

Lena linked her arm in his. "You must be exhausted, Nick."

"I'm sorry. I am tired, but I'd give a lot for some way that I can keep my promise to Yuri."

"There is something we should try. I'm not saying it will work, but it's better than doing nothing."

"Anything is better than that, Lena. I promise I won't be pessimistic."

"It's something I remember from our meeting at the embassy with one of the ambassador's deputies. Early in the meeting, she admitted to feeling guilty that the embassy hadn't done more when Father Robert contacted them. Then, when we were leaving, she said she hoped the embassy could help in some way. I don't mean we should exploit her feelings. But I think we should meet with her again, explain Father Robert's plan that led to his death, and see if the Canadian government can do something to honor his wishes. Am I being too optimistic, Chris?"

Worthy looked back to the gravediggers. "Nick, let me be the pessimistic one. We won't know what the embassy will agree to do until we ask. I do know that Ms. LaTour will listen. And what was it you told me some saint said about success?"

Nick paused, his brain so sluggish that for a minute he didn't know what Worthy was referring to. But then the words came back to him. "She said, 'God doesn't ask us to succeed, but to try.'"

CHAPTER FORTY-SIX

Rome—Order of the Sacred Wounds Monastery

When Abbot Lorenzo heard the knock on his door, he looked up to see Lena enter the room. Handing a folder to him, she said, "I've submitted my report on Father Boniface to the Vatican, but I wanted to give you a copy as well."

Abbot Lorenzo looked down on the documents. "By the weight of your report, I can see that your reputation for thoroughness is well-founded. Please sit down and, if you are allowed, give me a summary of your findings."

"Of course. Well, Reverend Father, I don't need to tell you that Father Boniface was a very capable abbot who led the order through difficult times. However, the issue that I was asked to investigate was the mystical quality of his spiritual life."

Abbot Lorenzo was finding it difficult to determine from Lena Fabriano's tone if her conclusions would be disappointing or encouraging. He knew she was simply exhibiting the caution of the scholarly researcher. He told himself what he told the monks: *Be patient.*

"As I'm sure you know, Reverend Father, Father Boniface's tenure as abbot was dominated by the need to respond to the criticisms—and some might say—the attacks of Father Jean-Philippe. My judgment was that Father Boniface showed good judgment as well as a thoroughness in recording the complete exchanges among Father Jean-Philippe, the Vatican, and himself. Most of the contents of the folder concern those issues."

"I have read much of that material, Dr. Fabriano. More than once, I thought that Abbot Boniface could have been a capable lawyer. I'm referring to his ability to anticipate the other side's criticism and then answer that criticism before the opponent could even raise it. I will admit, Dr. Fabriano, that his reports left me feeling sad . . . yes, sad."

"I agree. Reading the back-and-forth between the two men left me with a headache more than once. I initially made the mistake of trying to rush through that turbulent period in his writings. But Father Fortis helped me see that this would be a mistake."

"Hmm. Well, I'm curious. I confess that I would have done the same thing. Why was that a mistake?"

"I made a false assumption, which is the bane of researchers. Because Father Jean-Philippe died years before Father Boniface, I didn't expect the strained relationship between the two men to be mentioned in the later pages of his diary. But as you will read in my report, the last diary entries reveal a great interior battle. Father Boniface had to face something he hadn't expected, the realization that he had unfinished business with Father Jean-Philippe."

Abbot Lorenzo nodded slowly. "Although I was close to Abbot Boniface, that's something I didn't know. Can you share the form that his interior work took?"

"Yes. Father Boniface described a recurring vision in which he saw the wound in Christ's side as the doorway into paradise, a door he would have to pass through. That didn't surprise me, given that Christ's wounds are the focus of your order's spirituality. And, as you know, that image is one he would have been exposed to in the writings of St. Catherine of Siena and St. Faustina."

Abbot Lorenzo had to admit that he was disappointed. "So, the image in his vision is derivative. Is there anything original in his diary?"

"Yes, I think there is. His vision of Christ's wound took a turn in the days before he died. He saw the face of Father Jean-Philippe inside Christ's wound. His nemesis was looking out at him."

Abbot Lorenzo grimaced. "I can only imagine that was painful."

"He wrote that he was in torment. He ate little, reading nothing but the Bible and a book of saints, and writing in his journal. But, here is what's interesting and, I think, significant. The crisis ended when he was meditating on the Beatitudes, particularly the one 'Blessed are the pure in heart, for they shall see God.' That was when he described a light filling the room and filling him as well. The torment was over."

Abbot Lorenzo opened his eyes. "I suppose this breakthrough could have a human cause as well. Perhaps, a guilty conscience?"

"Of course. But the next pages are all under the heading 'Pure in heart.' His penmanship, which he was always so proud of, devolved into scribblings as if he couldn't keep up with what he was understanding. He wrote that as the light flooded into his room, he saw his heart with a wall dividing it. On one side of the wall, he saw himself; on the other side, he saw the face of Father Jean-Philippe. The wall was on fire, and he realized that the fire was his anger and resentment toward his nemesis.

"In the next entry, his penmanship improved, so I assumed he wrote that sometime later. That's when he described an auditory experience. He heard Christ say, 'All who enter by my wounded side must come with an undivided heart.' As you will see, he wrote several more pages about the message. Then, in one of his last entries, he described a change, a warmth in his chest, as he shed tears of remorse and repentance for his bitter memories of Father Jean-Philippe."

Abbot Lorenzo looked to the crucifix on the wall and was overcome by shame and humility. He had hoped that Dr. Fabriano's research would support the cause of Father Boniface's sainthood and, in the process, enhance the reputation of the order. *My sin was seeing Boniface as a feather in our cap*, he thought. Now Abbot Lorenzo realized that Dr. Fabriano's findings revealed something beyond price, something even beyond the question of sainthood. Her research had revealed a message from Christ, not just to Father Boniface, but also to the whole order.

Rome: The Canadian Embassy

As the guard at the gate of the Canadian Embassy studied Lena's, Worthy's, and his passports before admitting them, Nick felt even more strongly that the three of them, like Don Quixote, were tilting at windmills. The dark wood paneling, the flags of Canadian provinces and insignias on the walls, and the deep red carpeting spoke to the world of nations, power, and officialdom. *What chance do we have of explaining Father Robert's plan to rescue the boys?* he asked himself.

Ms. LaTour, however, at least seemed courteous, just as Worthy and Lena had described her. But when Nick considered how many sad stories the woman would have listened to in her role at the embassy, he realized that the deputy ambassador knew how to say no graciously.

When Lena introduced him to Ms. LaTour, the deputy said, "I read in the paper about your release. It must have been a frightening ordeal for you."

"I won't deny that I was frightened at times, but I also learned a lot about the plight of refugees in Italy."

Ms. LaTour sighed. "Refugees are the world's greatest challenge right now, and no one has the answer. It's particularly painful when refugees are sent back when there is a chance they will be tortured or killed." With that, she seemed to wait for them to explain their mission.

"We've learned a great deal more about Father Robert since Lena and I last visited you," Worthy said. "We believe we've now solved the mystery of his last few days and his death, and that includes what he wanted to come to the embassy. But there are aspects of his story that are still unfinished," Worthy said.

"Well, as you might remember, I regret we weren't of more help to Father Robert at the time. After our meeting, I looked into Father Robert's background, especially his work with indigenous children in an orphanage in Yellowknife. I was quite moved by what I read," she said as she turned over a page of a legal pad and picked up a pen. "So, we will do whatever is in our power, but beyond that, of course, our hands are tied."

Nick thought of his hand being chained to the bed. Government regulations, he knew, would be harder to unlock.

Lena sat forward. "What we want to share is what we're convinced Father Robert wanted to ask you. In a sense, we feel a responsibility to speak for Father Robert."

"I understand."

"In your looking into Father Robert, you might have read about the fire in Yellowknife that took the life of three orphans."

"I did read about that," Ms. LaTour said.

"That was the reason Father Robert came to Rome. He was a monk of the Order of the Sacred Wounds, a monastic order whose motherhouse is here in the city. While there was nothing Father Robert could have done to prevent the fire, the police and fire personnel found him inebriated that night. He was in Rome awaiting the order's decision about his future as a priest."

"No, I didn't know that. And that had something to do with what he wanted from us?"

"Very much so," Lena said. "In the first weeks of his stay at the motherhouse, Father Robert was described as numb. For the tragedy of the fire, he didn't defend his behavior. He was prepared to be defrocked as a priest if he could return to the orphanage in some capacity, no matter how lowly. But three days before his death here in Rome, his affect changed. The cloud over his head seemed to have dissipated. The change coincided with his first visit to Piazza del Popolo. That's when he saw the Bosnian boys picking the pockets of tourists in the piazza. We think it's likely that one of the boys tried to rob him as well."

"Did he report this to the police?" Ms. LaTour asked.

"No, we think he knew that the boy would be deported. Instead, the experience gave Father Robert a new mission—to rescue as many of the boys as he could from falling deeper into crime. From examining his internet searches, we've concluded that Father Robert's first idea was to find orphanages in or near Rome that would take the boys in their care.

"Something must have convinced him that his initial plan wouldn't work," Lena said, "but he returned to the piazza a second night and tried to tell the oldest of the boys that he wanted to help them. The following morning, he called the embassy."

"Which was the recording the three of us listened to. He was asking about visas, as I remember."

Lena said, "What we now believe is that Father Robert's plan was to request visas for the Bosnian boys. His hope was that the boys could be sent to his orphanage in Canada."

Ms. LaTour raised both hands from her desk and let them drop before shaking her head. "If he'd been able to come that day for such a meeting, maybe he'd still be alive."

"I'm not sure I follow," Worthy said.

"You see, we would have told him that what he wanted was impossible. His request wouldn't have been the first that we've received from refugees in Italy who want to emigrate to Canada. We have to apply the rules consistently."

Nick gripped the cross that was hanging wore around his neck. "From everything we know about Father Robert, I don't think he would have stopped. Saving the boys, you see, wasn't just a hope; it was a mission. He would have ended up in Piazza del Popolo that night no matter what you said."

Ms. LaTour sighed. "As much as I wish we could honor Father Robert's memory in this way, I'm sorry to say the embassy's position remains the same."

As the deputy ambassador stood, with Lena and Worthy following her example, Nick remained in the chair. "I feel I can speak for Father Robert and for a man named Yuri who also gave his life for the Bosnian boys. They would say that an infant isn't born with a nationality, but rather with a need. I'm sure Father Robert and Yuri would have said that the children who steal and are trafficked in Rome aren't Bosnian, Nigerian, Somalian, or Italian. They are simply children wanting what every child wants—safety, shelter, food, and a hopeful future. From my experience being held by the Bosnians, I can only add that Father Robert was completely right. A child is only a child."

Ms. LaTour looked down at Nick before turning to Lena and Worthy. "If you'll have a seat again, I will be back soon," she said as she walked to the door. "Again, I promise nothing."

As they sat, Worthy turned to Nick. "I suppose this would be a good time to pray, Nick."

"I've already started, but feel free to add your own prayers."

After thirty minutes that seemed three times as long, Ms. LaTour reentered the room and sat down at her desk. "Some days, my job is all about saying 'no' when I wish I could say 'yes.'"

Nick feared the worst as the deputy ambassador waited to speak. "But today—well, I'll just tell you what I'm been told. It turns out the ambassador knows Father Robert's bishop back in Canada. And he put through a call. Have you met the bishop, by any chance?"

Nick's heard sank. He could picture Bishop Bruno receiving that call and, after hearing about Father Robert's request, enjoying the chance to squash him one more time.

"In a nutshell, the ambassador asked if the orphanage in Yellowknife could take in a few of the Bosnian boys that are living on the streets here in Rome, assuming he could secure the permission of the Italian authorities."

Here it comes, Nick thought.

"The bishop thinks it would honor Father Robert's memory for a modest number of Bosnian boys—he mentioned three—to be accepted at the orphanage. He went so far as to say such a gesture might help heal the wounds in Yellowknife."

Nick felt instantly dizzy. "What did you say?"

"The bishop asked the ambassador to do whatever he can to make it happen. I thought a monk might not be so surprised, Father Fortis. You are a man of prayer, I take it."

Nick struggled to gain control of his voice. "I'm a poor example, Ms. LaTour, a very poor example."

CHAPTER FORTY-SEVEN

Rome—Order of the Sacred Wounds

Seeing who was at the door, Abbot Lorenzo rose to greet Lena, Worthy, and Nick. "This is a pleasant surprise. Father Nick, thank God for your release. I hope this means you'll be joining our community again." Gesturing to chairs, he added, "Please, please have a seat."

"Thank you, Reverend Father," Nick said. "If it's convenient, I'd like to stay here for few more days. Just until the wedding."

"Oh, yes, the wedding. I nearly forgot, given what else has been going on. Congratulations again, Dr. Fabriano and Mr. Worthy."

"Reverend Father, I think it's time you called me Lena. And one of the reasons I wanted to stop by is to give you this," she said as she handed him an invitation to the wedding. "As you will see, we've postponed the wedding for a couple of days. Chris and I would be honored if you would attend."

Abbot Lorenzo smiled. "The honor is mine. But if supposed to call you Lena, then you must call me Lorenzo. Now, you said 'one of the reasons' for stopping by. Certainly, the Vatican hasn't responded already to your report."

Lena shook her head. "We both know the Vatican moves slowly. There's another reason we wanted to see you. It has to do not only with Father Robert but also Father Boniface."

Abbot Lorenzo nodded. "Once again, you have me intrigued. . . Lena."

"It was only a few days ago when I summarized my findings on Father Boniface. I'm sure you remember his vision and message about the need for a pure, undivided heart."

"Indeed I do. I've already shared that part of your report with the community, and I'm happy to tell you that the monks, all of us, have accepted Christ's words to Father Boniface as a message to our whole community."

"That doesn't surprise me, but I am pleased nonetheless," Lena said. "And it will fit in well with what Nick has to share. Nick?"

"To begin, Father Lorenzo, I must tell you that God used my time with the Bosnians to teach me a great deal. What I learned changed me—I hope for good—and I also gained some insight into Father Robert."

"I think everyone in the motherhouse would be happy to better understand our departed brother."

"Even before I was taken captive, we were convinced that Father Robert's abrupt change of mood in his last days was caused by what he observed in the piazza. He saw the Bosnian boys picking pockets, and that served to give him a new purpose, a new mission. In other words, he wanted to live, not die. After I was rescued, Lena and Christopher told me about Father Robert having made an appointment at the Canadian Embassy. He died before that meeting took place, but we are confident that we know what Father Robert wanted to ask the embassy official. His plan was to ask the embassy official to grant the boys visas so he could take them back with him to the orphanage in Yellowknife."

Abbot Lorenzo sighed. "That explains the change we all saw in Father Robert over those last days. But how does this relate to Lena's research on Father Boniface?"

"I know people might dismiss what I'm going to say next, saying I experienced a bit of Stockholm Syndrome, but while I was been held by the Bosnians, it slowly dawned on me that it was only an accident of birth that prevented Yuri, the one who watched over the Bosnian boys, from having my life and I having his. To be honest, if I had endured what Yuri had gone through, I wouldn't have remained as compassionate as he did. And if Yuri had been born into my life, I have no doubt he'd have been a better monk than me.

"That was when I began to see the boys as I now know Father Robert saw them—as children, just children, not as Bosnians. The longer I was held captive, the more I realized that seeing a child as Bosnian, Guatemalan, Haitian, Canadian, Somalian, American, or Italian is to fail to see that child as God does. From what Lena has told me, I understand that Father Boniface wrote in his diary about the ways we build walls within our hearts. Father Robert's heart didn't have those walls or the borders we see on maps."

Abbot Lorenzo didn't say anything for a moment, even as his eyes rose to the crucifix on the wall. "As you know, Father Fortis, Father Robert's death left a cloud hanging over our motherhouse. But now . . . but now, yes, I'm beginning to see. Father Robert's abrupt change was caused by his sense of a new mission, a mission he died for. May it be so that in the end, he died a blessed death."

With tears in his eyes, the abbot returned his gaze to Nick. "Is this what you came to tell me?"

"There is something more. Before we explain, it's important that you know what's developed in the last twenty-four hours. We had a meeting at the Canadian Embassy. What happened there I can only describe as a miracle. The ambassador knows Bishop Bruno, Father Robert's bishop, in Canada."

Abbot Lorenzo grimaced. "I know Bishop Bruno, but maybe that's for another time."

"To my surprise, Bishop Bruno thought that accepting three Bosnian boys at the orphanage would honor Father Robert's memory."

Abbot Lorenzo's jaw dropped. "Bishop Bruno said that? God does move in mysterious ways."

"Which brings us to what we want to ask you, Lorenzo," Lena said. "Yuri, the man who impressed Nick so much, was killed while saving one of the Bosnian boys."

"I remember something about that from the newspapers," the abbot said.

"Because Yuri, the man I told you about, is no longer there to watch over the boys, the boys need someone else who will do what Father Robert wanted to do—do what's possible to protect these boys. Without someone helping them, these boys will be forced into joining organized crime. Someone here in Rome has to remind the authorities what Father Robert came to understand—a child is simply a child. Lorenzo, could this community, Father Robert's community, continue his mission?"

Rome—A Safe House

Bordy Vladic stared blankly at the TV screen in the safe house. He had one thing on his mind—escape.

He'd escaped before. He'd escaped from Bosnia. He'd managed to escape several times when Rome's police ran after him. He'd escaped from the couple's apartment just days before. And now he reasoned that escape was the only way he could prevent being sent back to Bosnia, but what chance would he have?

I'm like an animal whose foot is caught in a trap, he thought. He looked into the kitchen where one policemen was warming up soup, and a second was sitting close to the only door that led to the world beyond. Bordy knew the door was locked. Even during the night, one of the policemen remained awake, and it was clear from the number of times they looked out the front window that they were as concerned as much about keeping someone out as keeping Bordy in.

A police captain named Sesto had invited Bordy to help his situation by telling him all that he knew about Luca's organization. Bordy had pretended that he couldn't understand the policeman's English, even as he realized that he had little to bargain with. What he knew about Luca's organization was simply Luca and the men under him, not who Luca's boss was.

As he watched highlights of football matches on the TV, he admitted to himself that escaping now would not end his problems. A little more than a week before, he'd considered Luca his ticket for a better life in Rome. But that was before Luca had tried to kill him and managed to kill the professor instead.

Now, with the professor gone, Bordy realized that there were ten other boys, all younger, who needed someone to protect and guide them. A wave of grief welled up and filled his eyes with tears. It wasn't the grief that surprised him—he'd often cried in secret back in Bosnia—but the fact that the grief wasn't directed toward him but the other boys. And with that came another realization. The boys would be better off if Luca had killed him instead of the professor.

He heard a knock on the door, causing one policeman to draw his gun as he looked through the peephole in the door. He put the gun back in his shoulder holster as he unlocked and opened the door.

Into the room came three people, the couple who'd nursed him and the American priest whom he remembered as Nick. The professor's last words to Bordy were that the American priest had saved his life by getting him to a doctor and to the safety of the couple's apartment.

After the woman spoke in Italian to the policemen, the three came into the room where Bordy was seated. He looked from one of them to another, assuming what the three wanted from him wasn't something good.

"Can I turn off the TV?" Nick asked.

Bordy didn't say anything but nodded.

Nick turned off the TV anyway before pulling up a chair. "You must be wondering what happens now, Bordy."

So that's what this is about, Bordy thought. *They've come to tell me that I'm going to be sent back to Bosnia or maybe arrested.* He said nothing, waiting to hear his fate.

"I wonder if you're aware that two people have died for you, Bordy," Nick said.

Bordy remained silent, but his mind was spinning. *Two people? What is he blaming me for?* Then it dawned on him. Now that Luca was dead, the police needed a scapegoat.

He looked up to meet Nick's eye. "I tell you before. I kill nobody."

"I remember, and I believe you, Bordy. You didn't kill them, but Father Robert, the priest who was stabbed in the piazza a month ago, and now the professor, both died to save your life."

Bordy knew he could pretend that he didn't understand what the priest was saying, but he was curious how anyone could say the other priest, this Father Robert, died for him.

"Other priest, I see him maybe two time. He talk to me, say he want to help me. That is all."

The woman spoke in a soft voice. "We now know that he wanted to give you a chance for a better life, one where you didn't have to commit crimes to survive."

Nothing he was hearing made sense. But he remembered how kind the woman had been to him when he had his fever. She'd treated him as his mother had, and he'd liked her. But maybe she was just pretending.

"Professor, he was dreamer. He say we have better life, here."

"That's the same thing that the priest in the piazza wanted for you," the woman said.

He wished they would leave. Didn't they know that this was the end no matter what the police decided? He looked down at his hands, still clean from when the woman had washed them days before. "Other priest dead. Professor dead. You go, now."

The other man, the one who'd carried him to and from the bathroom, spoke. "Bordy, my name is Chris. You need to know that Father Robert wanted to take you to Canada, to his orphanage."

Before he could make any sense of those words, Chris added, "Nick, isn't this the same thing the professor would have wanted for Bordy?"

Bordy looked at them, trying to understand why they were lying to him. He would prefer to be beaten. He glanced over to the two policemen who were looking at him with disgust, as the police always looked at him. When, he wondered, would these others admit that they were teasing him? He started to tell them again to leave, but instead he heard himself ask, "This place Canada. It is America?"

"Very near to it," the woman said.

Her face seemed so tender. He wanted to believe her and believe the other two. "What is this orphanage?"

"It's a home in Canada for boys who don't have relatives who can take care of them."

"Boys from Bosnia?"

"Not right now, it's just Indigenous boys . . . Indians," Chris said. "Do you understand?"

"Like on TV? Indians and cowboys?"

"Something like that," Chris said, with a smile. "What we've come to tell you is that you can go to that orphanage in Canada. You'll be safe there; you'll go to school; and you'll never be hungry."

Bordy shook his head. "No, I stay with other boys—here."

"Listen. Two of the other boys will be able to go with you, and if things work out as we hope, more of the boys can go to Canada."

The room was silent as Bordy thought, *If this is a dream, it's a cruel dream.* But he said, "This place. Has warm bed? Has soup?"

The woman laughed, but he could see she wasn't laughing at him. "It has both of those, and more."

For a few seconds, he saw the professor's face, and the professor was smiling. Bordy's body felt light, as if he could float away, but a painful thought brought back to the ground. "But other boys, here in city. They alone. I stay with them."

He was surprised to see tears in the monk's eyes. "There are other priests who have agreed to do what Father Robert did. They will do whatever they can to help the boys."

Bordy glanced again at the two men in the next room. "Police not send them back to Bosnia?"

"We wish we could promise that, Bordy, but these other priests will do what they can to prevent that. This orphanage in Canada, Bordy, this is the new beginning the professor wanted for you," Nick said.

Bordy felt the urge to scream that there are no such things as new beginnings, only endings. His family had barely surviving in one of the internal displaced person camps in Bosnia even before his father died. That was an ending. The death of the professor, that was the end of a good man's life. The police in the other room looking at him with hatred—they were part of the world that offered only one ending after another. Yet it was the world he knew.

But the words "new beginning" kept swirling around him, and he saw other faces. He saw his mother's face as she waved goodbye to him on his first day of school. He saw the professor's face as he talked to him about the line that could never be crossed. He saw the face of the Canadian priest in the piazza, the first person in Italy who looked at him without disgust.

He opened his eyes to see the three faces looking at him: the face of the American priest who he'd helped abduct, the face of the woman who'd washed his face and arms, and the face of the man who'd carried him to the immaculate bathroom with the soft towels.

They want me to believe that there is such a thing as a new beginning. But what is this new beginning? The feeling of lightness returned and with it the thought, *Maybe . . . maybe a new beginning is the end . . . of endings* .

CHAPTER FORTY-EIGHT

Bishop Bruno read over the letter to the Archbishop of Toronto and, after making the sign of the cross, signed it. The letter was both the hardest and the best step he had ever taken. It was a step that he doubted few would understand.

"The Most Reverend Archbishop Ignatius,

Two days ago, Father Jacob Stullmacher in Yellowknife, the Northwest Territories, sent me the full account of Father Robert Porter's last days in Yellowknife and his time in Rome where he died. As you know, Father Robert was a priest in my diocese as well as the director of the Safe Haven Orphanage in Yellowknife. My heart was pierced as I read that Father Robert was killed while trying to save some of the Bosnian children, refugees, who live by their wits on the streets of Rome.

Reverend Father, you know me well and you know that I'm not someone given to emotions. Perhaps that has made me a good administrator but not a good shepherd. Given that, I need to explain why the news of Father Robert's death has had such an effect on me. Father Robert was a hard priest for me to deal with, and, because of that, I viewed him as a thorn in my side. It was only learning more of his story that has led me to realize that I failed to treat Father Robert as I should have.

I'm sure that I don't need to remind you of the tragic fire at the orphanage in Yellowknife. Father Robert could not be blamed for the fire, but he was not in proper physical and psychological shape to function as a priest in that ordeal. Instead of reaching out and giving Father Robert a chance to confide in me, I took advantage of his vulnerability by communicating with his order's motherhouse in Rome and asking them to make an official evaluation of his suitability as a priest. Yes, it was I who caused Father Robert to be ordered back to Rome, his vocation in question. As I considered the situation, I realized that my life as a bishop would be much smoother without Father Robert criticizing my decisions regarding the orphanage.

As the Old Testament patriarch Joseph said to his brothers in Egypt, 'You meant it for evil, but God meant it for good.' Yes, in Rome, Father Robert's last days and his death led to a chain of events that will change the life of the Bosnian boys for the better, but I can take no credit for that. I forced Father Robert to defend himself in Rome, a step that might look to others as a proper concern of a bishop, but I know, and now you know, that my motives were sinful.

After Father Robert's death, I traveled to Yellowknife to meet with the families of the boys who died in the fire and with others in the community. I was treated poorly, but rather than asking how I had failed them as a bishop, I became even angrier with Father Robert. It was only in the days following that God began using events, including the letter from Father Jacob in Yellowknife, to force me to confront how poor a shepherd I have been.

Finally, in the last two days, I have experienced a measure of peace, peace that came with a decision. I am resigning as bishop of the Edmonton diocese and asking you to consider appointing me as a priest for the Safe Haven Orphanage. I ask that I not be made director, but be allowed to be a priest who works under the director.

Most Reverend Ignatius, we both know that my receiving this assignment will depend on the people of Yellowknife forgiving and accepting me. I failed them as a shepherd and failed Father Robert as well. Their acceptance of me will likely take months and maybe years, given how I failed them as their shepherd in the past.

Something else that I now realize is that the Bosnian boys who will come to the orphanage won't find it easy to adjust to a new country, a new language, and a new community. Given what they've lived through, God only knows how damaged they are. Of course, I will be there to serve all the boys, but I believe that God has entrusted these boys to me as a special mission.

Finally, I want you to know that I am asking Father Robert for his forgiveness. I know that his death will not stop his prayers for the Safe Haven Orphanage. I ask Father Robert now to include me in his prayers.

As I said, this decision has brought a measure of peace to my heart. I hope that you will accept my decision as I have, as God's will for my life and, I hope, as God's will for the boys—Bosnian and well as Indigenous—at Safe Haven.

In Christ,

Father Bruno"

Lena's Spare Room, Wedding Day

When Nick stepped out of the shower, he saw that he'd received an email from Father Jacob. Opening it, he read,

"Dear Nick,

What an answer to prayer to hear that you are safe. You were included in our Mass intentions during your ordeal and will remain so, this time thanking God for protecting you. While I know it is unlikely that you will ever be in Yellowknife again, please know that you are remembered with love for how you conducted your interviews about Father Bob.

There has been a startling development that I want to share with you. I won't say it is an answer to prayer—our prayers, at least—but maybe an answer to Bishop Bruno's prayers. Given how badly the bishop's last visit went and how he usually handles disappointment, I'm still in shock that he has asked to be relieved of his position. Yes, he wants to step down from being a bishop. Mysterious are the ways of God, indeed.

Bishop Bruno—soon, Father Bruno—wrote to me personally. And this is the even greater surprise. He has asked me to arrange a meeting with the Great Slave Lake Dene leaders where he can ask for—he used the word "beg"—their forgiveness. Reading between the lines, I discern that his last disastrous visit is what brought about this change in him. He wrote that he now realizes how he failed the people of Yellowknife as their shepherd and how he failed Father Bob.

Clearly, Father Bruno is a changed man. But the conclusion of his letter to me was even more shocking. He asked if I'd intervene to ask the tribal elders and especially Mrs. Free Woman if they'd allow him to celebrate Mass for the boys and Father Bob on the anniversaries of the fire in the orphanage. Eventually, he hopes to serve as a priest at Safe Haven.

What most moved me, Nick, was the tone of the letter. Father Bruno's letter was the letter of a humble penitent. He was asking, not demanding.

He clearly understands that the decision will be in the hands of Mrs. Free Woman and the tribal leaders.

Nick, you and I both know that I can guarantee nothing. I know just enough about Great Slave Lake Dene customs to admit that I know precious little. Yes, most in the tribal community are parishioners of St. Anne, but they also retain traditional ways. And given the strained relations between Canada's indigenous peoples and the Catholic Church because of past abuses in residential boarding schools, now might not be the right time to expect the indigenous community to forgive any priest, much less a bishop.

Pray for me, Nick, that God will give me the right words when I speak with Mrs. Free Woman and the tribal elders. All I know is that the change in Father Bruno's heart is nothing short of a miracle. Given that God brought that change about, who am I to doubt that God can change the community's hearts as well?

Your brother,
Jacob"

EPILOGUE

Lena's Apartment: Wedding Day

The winter sun added to the warmth in Lena's apartment as the small circle of guests gathered for Lena's and Worthy's wedding. Abbot Lorenzo and the caretaker Rosario attended from the motherhouse, as did Maria, Lena's cousin, and Capitano Sesto. In addition, there was a beautiful scent of fresh flowers in the room. Earlier, Worthy had told him with tears in his eyes that one bouquet had come from Allyson, his older daughter. Remembering the long journey of healing that Allyson and Worthy had been on—and were still on—Nick thought, *Yes, another reason to celebrate today.*

A judge, another of Lena's relatives, had already pronounced Lena and Worthy husband and wife, but Nick knew that the couple wouldn't feel married until he had given his blessing. He rose to speak, still feeling overwhelmed by what Father Jacob had sent him about Bishop Bruno's unexpected—no, "miraculous" was the word—change of heart. It was the latest of so many changes that had started with a tragic fire over four thousand miles away in Canada.

Nick took a moment to pray that his words would reflect all the emotions of the day, the somber events that everyone in the room had been through as well as the joy of this moment. But looking at the faces of Lena and Worthy, he knew what he wanted to say.

"Just a few days ago, Lena and Christopher, the three of us asked a young boy who'd been deeply scarred by the brokenness of this world to believe in the possibility of a new beginning. And then we saw something new on this boy's face. We saw fear. This child, who'd seen so much of what is raw and degrading in this world, allowed himself to be afraid.

"Our lives and this boy's life became entwined over the past weeks. And while there would seem to be little that you, Lena and Christopher, have in common with Bordy Vladic, there is one thing. As is true of Bordy, you are also taking a chance on a new beginning, on a future that is uncertain, risky.

"I am reminded of a story, a parable really, from the world of sailing, a pastime that I know you enjoy, Christopher. In this parable, there was a harbor filled with sailboats, a safe haven, we might say. In this harbor, the sailboat owners lived on their beautiful boats. But what was distinctive about these yachts, yachts that bore names such as 'Placid,' 'Calm Breezes,' and 'Tomorrow Will Be Another Today,' was that the beautiful craft never left the harbor.

"From one moored sailboat to another, the owners would call to one another: 'What a blessing that we live here in perfect safety. Our children will grow up and never think of leaving the harbor, protected as we are from the terrifying storms, shipwreck, and disaster out on the ocean.'

"But one day, a sailboat that no one had seen before appeared in the harbor, and on this boat were two weather-beaten sailors. The boat's hull was scarred from having been battered by rough seas, and the sails showed numerous patches, some patches even sewn on top of older ones.

"The harbor community welcomed the two sailors and offered them a mooring. 'In our harbor,' they told the newcomers as they looked at the ocean, 'we fear nothing from the storms out there.'

"To their surprise, the new arrivals declined their offer. The harbormaster stepped forward and asked, 'Why would you risk death on the ocean when you can be safe here?'

The younger of the two newcomers looked at the fear on the harbor-dwellers' faces and said, 'I'll answer your question if you answer mine.' He pointed to their beautiful and pristine boats and then to the ocean. 'If you aren't meant to risk the ocean, why do your boats have sails?'

"So today, Lena and Christopher, we celebrate the risk that you are both making. You could have chosen to remain in the safety of your separate lives and never risk love again. Instead, you have raised your sails, choosing life together on the unpredictable ocean of life. We wish you a blessed and yes, even a fearful voyage sometimes. Go with God. Go with our love."

THE END

About the Author

David Carlson is Professor Emeritus (Religious Studies) at Franklin College where he served for forty-two years. With the study of religious violence being one of his specialties, David has lectured and given radio and television interviews on ISIS, Al-Qaeda, as well as religious extremists in the US.

Now retired, David enjoys writing non-fiction related to interfaith efforts; a weekly newspaper column on religion, politics, and culture; and the Christopher Worthy and Father Fortis mystery series.

His wife, Kathy, is a retired English professor, an award-winning artist, and his best editor. Their two sons took parental advice to follow their passions. Leif is a visual artist and Marten is a screenwriter and filmmaker.